MW00861070

better
with friends

THE KALEIDOSCOPE GIRLS

better
with friends

THE KALEIDOSCOPE GIRLS

BOOK ONE

Kimberly Diede

This is a work of fiction. Names, characters, organizations, places, events, and incidents are either products of the author's imagination or are used fictitiously and any resemblance to actual persons, living or dead, business establishments, events or locales is entirely coincidental.

Copyright © 2022 by Kimberly Diede

All rights reserved.

No part of this book may be reproduced, distributed, or transmitted in any form or by any means, including photocopying, recording, or other electronic or mechanical methods, without the prior written permission of the publisher, except in the case of brief quotations embodied in reviews and certain other non-commercial uses permitted by copyright law.

Cover by Carpe Librum Book Design – www.carpelibrumbookdesign.com.

Ebook ISBN: 978-1-7351343-5-2

Print ISBN: 978-1-7351343-6-9

Large Print ISBN: 978-1-961305-03-8

In memory of my precious mom . . .

You taught me the value of friendship
and shared your amazing friends with me.
My life is better because of you.

CHAPTER ONE

J ACKIE COULD FEEL HER anxiety rise as the plane began its descent. It wasn't too late. She could still change her mind and hop a flight back to Chicago. She'd break Nikki out of the kennel first thing tomorrow morning. She hated the thought of her sweet dog, curled up on the cold concrete floor of an enclosed pen. Would the border collie think she'd been abandoned again?

When Jackie first rescued the pup, she'd promised Nikki that she'd never spend another night in a cage, and she kept that promise for almost eight years. What was it about that eight-year mark? Was seven years the maximum duration of a promise?

I wasn't the one who broke my promise, Jackie reminded herself, squeezing her eyes shut in an effort to banish the image of her ex-husband from her mind. When Todd left her and their girls, he'd left for good. She'd never do that to Nikki.

A flight attendant approached, trash bag extended, and Jackie drained the last of her rum and Coke before tossing her cup. The perks of flying first class were limited on short flights, but she'd treated herself to one cocktail. Drinking at two in the afternoon wasn't something she normally did, but visiting her childhood home and the complicated relationships within it for the first time in three years seemed ample justification for the indulgence. Facing forty-eight-year-old versions of the kids that she'd gone to high school with provided an additional excuse for the day-drinking.

She clenched her fingers in surprise when the tires bumped against the runway before she was ready. The man to her left strained to see out the half-closed window at her elbow. Jackie followed his lead, pushing the shade open all the way. A shimmer above the tarmac hinted at high summer temperatures. The house would be stifling. She'd grown up without air-conditioning but couldn't imagine living that way now.

I should have stuck with my original plan and booked a room at the Holiday Inn across town.

But her mother was upset over Jackie's suggestion of a hotel, so she'd once again abandoned the boundaries she'd tried to set for herself, agreeing instead to stay in her old bedroom for the coming week. She'd packed earplugs and a mini sound machine in the hopes she could drown out her father's snoring.

"Your father is glad you are coming home. There are things he wants to discuss with you," her mother had told her when they'd talked about Jackie's trip home for her thirty-year class reunion. "He's out of sorts these days. But we're trying to stay optimistic. I'm sorry, I shouldn't have said anything. Don't worry. Just come home, have fun with your girlfriends, and plan to give your father a little time. It must be dreadfully quiet in that big house these days, what with the girls off at school."

"Don't worry," Jackie whispered, remembering her mother's words as she scanned the trees lining the northern edge of the runway. Those two little words were a sure sign that something was going on at home.

"What was that?" the man seated next to her asked.

Jackie realized he'd mistakenly thought she'd been addressing him, even though they'd barely spoken during the flight. Her mind scrambled for a reasonable response. "I said not to worry about the weather. I hear it's hotter than blazes this week, but normally the summers are quite nice around here."

The man grinned, peering past Jackie and through the window beyond. "I know the summer weather in Minnesota can be pleasant, but I also remember some pretty wicked July thunderstorms blowing through when I was a kid."

"Are you from Minneapolis, then?" Jackie asked, thinking that he still looked like a kid to her.

He shrugged. "Minnesota, yes. Minneapolis proper, no. I've spent lots of time in a small town not far from here."

There was a commotion behind them. Jackie's seatbelt bit into her waist as the plane jerked to a stop. The flight attendant who had gathered their trash during the plane's descent rushed past.

Speakers crackled to life and the pilot's voice filled the cabin. "Please excuse the delay, folks, but it seems we may have a medical emergency. If we have any doctors on board willing to offer a hand, please press your call button or step forward. Rest assured we'll do our best to get everyone on their way as quickly as possible."

Jackie twisted in her seat to see what was happening back in coach, but seats blocked her view. "It must be serious for them to stop this close to the terminal."

Her seatmate nodded and popped off his belt as he got to his feet. "I'm afraid you're probably right."

She watched him hurry forward to speak to another flight attendant who was holding a corded phone to his ear. With a no-nonsense bob of his head, her seatmate spun and hurried back through the first-class section toward the rear of the plane. Something about the man's gait snagged her attention. He reminded her of someone.

The woman one row back caught her eye. "I might be willing to suffer a heart attack myself if it meant that handsome young man would come to my rescue," she said, winking at Jackie.

The comment and wink surprised her. When she'd first settled into her seat at the beginning of the flight, she immediately pulled out a folder of work. She hadn't even noticed the man's arrival. By the time she realized the seat next to her was taken, he'd had his nose in a book.

"It was nice of him to offer his assistance," Jackie said, disliking the woman's flirtatious attitude. Women like that made her uncomfortable.

Facing forward again, she pulled her phone out. After turning it to silent, she clicked off the airplane mode and smiled when a text from Kit popped up. She automatically slipped her readers down from the top of her head, settling them onto her nose. These days she couldn't even read a text message without them.

> On my patio enjoying a glass of pinot while I wait for you.

Still grinning, she shot off a quick response, letting her old friend know they'd landed but were stuck on the tarmac. While Jackie always tried her best to be punctual, she doubted Kit had ever been late for anything in her entire life. The one exception was the day they first met. It was a long-running joke between them.

No rush, I'm USED to waiting for you. I might even
enjoy a second glass since you're the one driving us
to Ruby Shores.

Some of the tension in Jackie's shoulders ebbed away, and she was suddenly thankful that time with her often frustrating parents wasn't the main reason she was making this trip home. She planned to spend most of the week ahead with her three besties. That would more than make up for the trials she was sure to face with her folks.

She smiled. Her besties. It would be the first time in over ten years that all four of them would be together again. How had they allowed so much time to pass? Hadn't they promised each other that they wouldn't be *that kind* of friend group? The kind that eventually drifts apart?

Jackie glanced around, her patience fraying. She heard voices behind her and thought she even caught a word or two in the deep baritone of the man she'd briefly discussed the weather with ten minutes earlier. She sighed, vowing to be patient and sending up a quick note of thanks that she wasn't the one suffering from some type of emergency on a plane full of strangers.

Kit could enjoy her wine in peace before their drive.

She suspected her friend was undoubtedly experiencing her own apprehensions about what she would find back home. The grandmother who practically raised Kit was nearly ninety now, and Jackie knew her friend worried about the woman living alone, even though her aunt checked on the elderly woman daily.

Jackie opened the photo app on her phone and scrolled through pictures she'd taken the night before.

So many memories . . .

While packing up a spare bedroom a month earlier, she'd stumbled across a pile of her old high school yearbooks. Her plan had been to bring the book from her senior class along on this trip and page through it with Kit, Lynette, and Annie. They could gossip about their old classmates over wine, sharing memories. But her suitcase was too full, and the briefcase at her feet bulged with paperwork, so she'd settled for snapping pictures of their class pages and a few other random items. She'd paged through her old album, remembering classmates she hadn't thought of in years. Annie might know what happened to some of them. She was the only one of their group that lived in Ruby Shores after college.

Had any of their classmates gone on to make a real difference in the world? How many had racked up multiple marriages or become grandparents already? She'd never been overly concerned with other people's lives, but there was just something about the people she'd grown up with that had her curious. She knew that two of their classmates had already lost their battles against cancer and one had died in a motorcycle accident. How many others from their class of over one hundred students had died? She hoped not many, but not all surprises at reunions were pleasant.

"We apologize again for the delay, folks," the pilot said. "We'll be taxiing into the gate now. We have a few passengers with tight connections, so if those of you with Minneapolis as your final destination could sit tight for a few extra moments when I flip off the seatbelt sign, we would all appreciate it."

Jackie doubted many would provide that basic courtesy. She rolled her eyes. Everyone was always in such a rush. Even if the pilot asked everyone to stay seated until the individual with the medical emergency could exit the plane, she doubted he'd get a hundred percent compliance.

She hated to be cynical, but life had taught her it was dangerous to count on the kindness of others.

By the time Jackie heaved her oversized suitcase off the conveyor belt in the lower level of the airport, her head was throbbing. At least her briefcase came with a slot on the back that she could slip over the extended handle of her suitcase. She rolled her aching shoulder; she hoped all the extra paperwork she'd lugged along to address during her vacation would be worth the effort.

She was waiting impatiently to hear something about the new job she'd applied for. It would mean an impressive promotion. She'd felt confident that she'd nailed her interview, and she knew she was the right woman for the job. But as one week turned into two and she'd heard nothing, doubts were beginning to creep in.

Had she acted prematurely by calling a listing agent about her house? The new position would mean another move, and she always liked to be prepared. She'd only intended to let the realtor know she would likely list it soon, but when the woman called back with an unexpected full-cash offer, Jackie had jumped at the chance to make a sizable profit on her home. *Bird in hand* and all, as her father was fond of saying.

The house is too big for me now that the girls are off at school, she reminded herself. *They probably won't ever come back for more than a few days here and there.*

But if this job didn't pan out, she'd have to find a new place to live in the middle of a hot housing market. Her father would be quick to point out the flaws in her approach.

She tipped her suitcase on its wheels and headed for the rental car counter. Inhaling deeply, she vowed to put her father out of her mind—at least for the next two hours. She would swing by Kit's and they'd hit the road. They had plenty of catching up to do.

Jackie slowed the rental as they reached the outskirts of Ruby Shores. The sun was still high above them. Boat traffic on the choppy waters was sparse. She rolled down her window and enjoyed the way the breeze off the lake caressed her face. Kit followed suit, and the rush of air quieted their conversation, which had flowed nonstop.

Eventually a wide grin spread across Kit's face. "Do you smell that?"

Jackie sniffed at the air. It was fresh, but she couldn't detect anything else remarkable. "Smell what?"

"Baby oil and coconuts," Kit said, holding her spiky orange bangs out of her eyes.

Jackie eased around the sharp curve in the road that hugged the lake, sighing when the beach came into view. They'd spent countless hours there as teenagers. Her eyes drank up the sight, but try as she might, she couldn't catch the scent.

Kit laughed. "Okay, maybe I'm imagining the smell of our suntan lotion, but let me have my little fantasy."

Suddenly, a blur of movement in Jackie's peripheral vision sent pinpricks of panic shooting through her veins. She yanked the wheel hard to avoid colliding head-on with a motorcycle. The passenger-side wheels crunched across loose gravel on the shoulder of the road, and the rental's backend tried to fishtail. She somehow held it steady.

The Harley shot by, unscathed, followed by a second bike, both driven by tattooed young men with girls wearing bikinis, and little else, whooping on the backs.

"That was us way back when," Kit said, expelling a sigh. "Or Lynette, at least."

Shaken by the close call, Jackie pulled off the main road into the parking lot of what had once been an old bait shop. "Where did the Mighty Minnow go?"

"Huh. I have no idea."

The two women gazed around the vehicle-filled lot. Gone was the tiny ramshackle convenience store where they used to buy cans of pop and licorice by the armload.

"This makes me sad," she said, lying her head back against the headrest and covering her eyes with her forearm. "Can't anything stay the same?"

Kit shifted to face her. "You're *sad* that smelly old shack is gone?"

Dust tickled Jackie's nose. She sneezed once, and then again, before quickly punching buttons to roll up the windows. "I'm sad that I only remember flashes of those perfect summer days out here on this lake. I'm sad that most kids nowadays will never experience how good Mr. Pibb tasted when your skin was sticky with baby oil and sand, your cheeks were sunburned, and a boombox blasted Meatloaf. Remember how we used to sing every word at the top of our lungs? Music isn't what it used to be."

"Mr. Pibb was delicious, wasn't it?" Kit faced forward again and kicked off her sandals, leaning her seat back so she could put her bare feet on the dash like they had done as teenagers. "Do they even make it anymore?"

"I'm not sure. Nice pedicure," Jackie said, nodding at Kit's bright-gold toenails. They'd already discussed her striking new hairstyle. Only Kit would be brave enough to amp up her natural auburn shades to the bright orange she'd gone with for their reunion weekend.

Kit wriggled her toes. "Thanks. It's not like I could go to the big *Class of 1988 Reunion* with ugly toes. My butt might be twice as wide as it was in high school, but my nails can still look good."

Sunshine glinted off a thin gold band supporting a smallish diamond on her left ring finger. Jackie jerked forward and grabbed for it. "You guys got *married*?! And you didn't bother to tell me? We've been talking for two hours!"

Kit shrugged. "Engaged. And it's no big deal. I was going to tell you this week. He gave it to me when we were camping this spring."

"Dean finally convinced you to marry him and you don't even bother to call me? I'm hurt. Have you set a date yet?"

Kit pulled her hand back and her smile slipped away. "Not yet."

"Because when we were kids you always wanted to get married to a great guy," Jackie reminded her. "The kind of guy you used to think your own dad was . . . before all the bad stuff went down."

"Jackie, I was *twelve* when I said things like that. When Dad turned out to be such a disappointment, I started to wonder if marriage ruins the good guys, too. Besides, most marriages don't last. Look at you and Todd."

It was Jackie's turn to shift in her seat. "Oh, no, you don't. You never liked Todd. To be honest, I didn't really like him much either, once I got to know what he was really like. But this has nothing to do with me and Todd. Kit, you are not your mother. And Dean is such a better man than your father. He's amazing. I'm so happy for the two of you!"

Jackie watched an array of emotions cross Kit's face. She visibly winced at the comparison to her mother, but her features softened at Jackie's reminder of the type of man Dean had matured into. They'd been a couple for a few years and had their share of struggles, but that was life. No one has a perfect love life.

"Really? Because I'm still worried," Kit said, her eyes glistening with apprehension. "You know how he feels about kids. And you know where I stand on that. I worry he'll feel cheated."

"You need to have more faith in Dean. And in yourself. Besides, we're beyond our childbearing years."

"*We* are, but Dean is younger than me and could certainly still father children at his age."

Kit paused, her eyes skirting away from Jackie's toward the lake and the public beach where they'd spent so much of their teen years. Jackie remembered the summer when Kit would try to convince everyone to stay well past when they should have gotten out of the sun, because she hated to go home. She never knew when her mother would be there, or what shape she'd be in. By their last years of high school the woman had all but disappeared.

"I know it's hard for you to come back here, but I'm so glad you did. I bet Grandma Hazel will be happy to see you, too." Jackie gave Kit's left hand a squeeze, then lightly tapped the shiny gold band. "This is a good thing. You'll see."

Nodding, Kit pulled her hand away and refastened her seatbelt. "That's the trouble with old friends—they know all your old baggage. I hope you're right. But Dean is a thousand miles away on a work trip, and you need to get home. Didn't you say your mother was making pot roast?"

Jackie adjusted her own seatbelt and put the car into gear. "Why is it the minute I roll into town I feel like I'm seventeen years old again and my mother is pulling my strings?"

Kit clicked on the radio, searching for and finding the old station they'd listened to as kids. An ad was playing for the local hardware shop. Both women laughed at the familiar words.

"That's the exact same jingle they used thirty years ago!"

"Hey, if it ain't broke, don't fix it," Jackie said as she pulled back onto the main road that would take her back in time, careful to keep an eye out for speeding motorcycles.

CHAPTER TWO

U NLIKE KIT AND HER search for the scent of their youth, Jackie didn't have to use her imagination to conjure up the smell of her childhood home. It assailed her the minute she reached the porch steps. The aroma of roasting meat danced over the softer perfume floating up from her mother's flowers. A riot of fragrant, colorful blossoms rimmed the porch and dangled from hanging baskets.

Memories coursed through her at the once familiar scent of a home-cooked meal. When Jackie was a girl, she had been convinced the only things her mother knew how to do were cooking and cleaning. The woman spent her days preparing meals for her demanding husband and two children. If her mother had spent any time with friends, she'd done her socializing during the day, when Jackie was off at school.

Jackie loved her mother. But she also pitied her. The woman had always lived in the shadow of her father's forceful personality. They all had, at least until that pressure blew her family apart.

With a shake of her head, Jackie did her best to banish those memories to the deepest corners of her brain. At least *she'd* done everything she could to make her father happy. Her big brother, Ronnie, made things so much harder for all of them. If only he'd done as their father asked, like she'd always tried to do; life behind their home's closed doors could have been more peaceful.

She heard the splash of running water and the muffled sound of a television as she reached the door. She hoped the pulsing energy of her childhood home had finally mellowed with time, especially since Ronnie wouldn't be around to stir things up.

Despite the strict boundaries she'd fought to put into place, she'd come back here again. Hadn't she always done what Dad wanted? It was easier that way.

Uncomfortable to walk into a house that no longer felt as familiar as it once had, she tapped her knuckles against the screen door instead of letting herself in. The noise sparked the shocking sound, somewhere deep inside, of a high-pitched yet faint barking.

A dog?

The only thing that could have shocked her more would have been if her long-lost brother had greeted her at the door—and he'd left home almost thirty years earlier. She was sure he'd never come back here.

Footsteps approached, along with the *clickety-clack* of the mystery dog's nails across hardwood floors. Her mother stepped into view wearing a bright smile and a familiar apron. She pushed open the screen and stepped outside instead of holding the door open to welcome Jackie in. The screen door banged shut.

The two women faced each other, looking the other up and down, and then her mother caught Jackie up in a hug.

The flowers on the porch competed with the floral notes of her mother's perfume that enveloped her with the hug. Slightly different from the scent she'd worn while Jackie was growing up. The old brand was no longer produced.

Must change be the only constant in life?

Jackie allowed the hug for a second longer than she was comfortable with before wriggling out of her mother's embrace. She stepped back just as a fluff of noisy dog skidded to a stop inside the screen door. Its feet stopped, but its greeting didn't.

"You got a *dog*?" Jackie said, still struggling to process the presence of a dog in her mom and dad's home. Unable to help herself, she opened the door, went inside, and sank to her knees in front of the tiny dog, leaving her mother on the porch. "Hello," she cooed to the vibrating animal. "What's your name?"

"Hoover," her mother offered, coming back inside.

"Hoover?" Jackie echoed, scooping the animal into her arms before standing up. Nikki had never been small enough for her to comfortably hold. The dog's fuchsia collar suggested the pup was female, but her fur was so soft and dense that a hasty glance toward the more definitive anatomy of the animal told her nothing. "What kind of name is *Hoover*?"

"Actually, an appropriate one. She keeps my kitchen floor cleaner than any of those new-fangled circular vacuums that creep around the house on their own ever could."

Jackie laughed, earning a lick on the nose when she nuzzled the animal.

"I see you haven't lost your touch with dogs."

"I still love them to pieces, Mom," she said, settling Hoover on her hip. "But I can't believe Dad actually overcame his aversion to one, long enough to let you bring this little gem into the house."

"Follow me," her mother grunted before heading back toward the kitchen. "What makes you think she's mine?"

Jackie wasn't sure she'd heard her mother correctly. "*Obviously* she has to be yours."

The familiar opening soundbite to the nightly news reached her ears, causing her stomach to rumble. She'd grown up knowing that sound meant they'd sit down to their evening meal in thirty minutes. The steam rising from a pot of boiling potatoes on the stove suggested her mom and dad's daily habits hadn't shifted.

"I did *not* bring that dog into this house, although now I can't imagine life without her."

The dog fought Jackie's hold when the older woman opened a lower cupboard next to miniature food and water bowls emblazoned with the name HOOVER in the same color as the dog's collar. The bowls sat where the garbage can used to be.

"*Dad* brought her home? No way. I can't believe that."

"Believe what you want," her mother said, removing a canister from the lower cabinet and scooping kibble into one of the bowls. "No one was more shocked than me. One of Glen's golfing buddies dropped dead of a stroke, and when there was talk of the dog ending up in the pound because she's getting older and there was no one to take her, your dad brought her home, complete with those personalized pet bowls and enough kibble to feed her for a year. I knew then that this would not be a temporary arrangement, despite his grumbling. And now he's crazy about her."

Jackie set the new mystery pup down and watched her bolt to the food bowl, snarfing down its contents as if she hadn't eaten in a week. "Good lord, don't you feed her enough?"

Her mom laughed as she poked at a boiling potato. "That feeding frenzy is a twice-a-day event. Trust me, Hoover gets plenty of food, treats, and attention."

She shook her head in disbelief. They'd only had one dog while she was growing up, a red setter named Fitz that Ronnie claimed to have rescued from a cardboard box on the side of the road. Jackie never quite believed that part of the story since Bruce, one of her brother's best friends, also had a dog that looked an awful lot like their Fitz. But she never called Ronnie out on it because Fitz quickly became Jackie's favorite family member. Her brother's interest in the rambunctious young dog waned, but hers never did.

Her father claimed to hate having a dog in the house, but because she loved Fitz so much, always feeding her on time and walking her every day, he allowed the dog to stay. Jackie tried hard to be a model kid—partly because she feared her father and partly because she knew he'd gladly use any misbehavior on her end as a convenient excuse to get rid of the dog.

It wasn't until Jackie was much older that she came to understand the impact Fitz had on the way she moved through her teenage years. She'd been terrified to screw up and make her father angry. At first it was because she feared losing Fitz, but even after they lost the dog to cancer, she was so accustomed to being the good girl that it stuck.

"So why a dog? That's totally out of character for him."

Her mother winced as she used hot pads to drain the vegetables. "It *is* out of character. But that dog has done more to soften his demeanor than anything I've tried over the past fifty years. She seldom leaves his side. Actually, you'll notice pretty quickly that Hoover isn't the only change in your father these days."

Jackie wondered if her mother's shoulder was still giving her trouble as she dug the potato masher out of the drawer and pulled butter and milk from the fridge. She was also curious about what she'd said about her father, but Jackie would need to witness this *softening* for herself before she believed it. "What is going on with Dad? You mentioned he wanted to talk?"

"He insists he wants to be the one to discuss it with you," her mother said, her cryptic comment revealing little as she busied herself with the final meal preparations.

Jackie expelled a frustrated breath. "Mom, I'll never understand why you insist on doing everything his way. Do you always have to let him run the show? I mean, I know I did a lot of that growing up, too, but what choice did I have? Ronnie didn't, and we both know *that* didn't work out well. But you're his wife."

When her mother didn't respond, Jackie pulled down the potato bowl from the cupboard next to the fridge, slamming the door harder than she meant to. Hoover skittered across the kitchen. Instantly Jackie regretted taking her frustrations out on an innocent cupboard door and scaring the equally innocent dog.

From the doorway, someone cleared their throat.

Jackie set the heavy stoneware on the island's butcher-block countertop, giving herself a beat before raising her eyes to meet those of the man filling the doorway.

When she did look up, she felt an odd sensation at the first glimpse of her father in over a year.

The man didn't come close to filling the doorway anymore.

He appeared inches shorter now, a slight stoop to his spine at least partially contributing to the loss in stature. He was narrower, too. Gone was the mass of flesh that used to fill out his rangy form. Her father had never been fat, but muscular and thick, making him that much more intimidating to both his daughter and the students at high school under his rule as principal. The red mop of hair that used to hint at his simmering ill temper had tipped from an ombre mixture of gray and russet to a pearl white since she'd last seen him. The ruddiness in his cheeks was also gone. An unhealthy pallor remained.

He looked sick.

This was what her mother hadn't said.

"Hello, Jackie. I see you've met my Hoover."

His first words, tinged with affection for the surprise pup, confused her already overloaded brain. Should she walk over and hug this man? Or stand her ground? He'd never been a fan of physical displays of emotion—unless he was hauling a wayward teen down to the office by the scruff of the neck.

"She . . . she's cute," Jackie stammered, glancing at the dog now sitting at her father's feet. He was barefoot, probably in deference to the hot July day.

"She's a sweet old gal," her father agreed. "Glad you're home. Charlotte, is it about time to eat?"

"Just about, Glen. Hoover ate, so why don't you take her out while Jackie helps me set the table?"

He nodded, gifted his daughter with a small smile, and shooed the dog toward the backdoor.

When they were gone, Jackie sought her mother's gaze. "Who was that, and where did my father go?"

Charlotte wiped her hands on her apron before carrying three dinner plates to the table in the breakfast nook off of the kitchen. "I told you. He's changed."

Jackie grabbed a stack of napkins and followed close on her mother's heels. "But you didn't tell me he was sick!"

"That's for him to discuss with you, not me. Grab the glasses and silverware. The food will get cold."

Jackie simmered in frustration but did as she was told. She recognized that tone. Her mother would share nothing more on the subject no matter how hard she prodded.

They'd set the last of the meal out when her father and his diminutive sidekick shuffled back into the room. "Smells good in here."

Her mother smiled at the compliment, motioning for daughter and husband to sit. Once settled, her father helped himself to a small scoop of potatoes, then passed the bowl to Jackie. She helped herself to a larger serving. Her mother's mashed potatoes were unequaled.

"You look good, girl. A little older, maybe, but who doesn't? It's been a while."

Her hackles inched up at her father's comment, but she refused to rise to the bait. Maybe he wasn't even trying to bait her. He'd just paid her an off-handed compliment, a rare event where he was concerned. Besides, he wasn't wrong. The last five years had been difficult, and Jackie knew they'd left a mark, despite her best efforts to minimize the inevitable impacts of aging.

"Thank you, Dad. It *has* been a while. I wish I could say you look good, too, but you taught me to never tell a lie."

The second the harsh truth slipped from her lips, Jackie held her breath, unsure how this near stranger would take her comment. She wasn't trying to be mean; her father was barely recognizable, a fact he surely knew.

And yet her words seemed to take the old man by surprise. He froze, a heaping spoonful of peas suspended over his plate. Then the husky sound of laughter filled the air. Charlotte smiled, and Jackie tilted her head. There was a unique quality to this laughter; a looser sound, as if verbalizing joy wasn't so foreign to him anymore.

"I know I look awful. And yes, I always tried to instill in you the importance of speaking truthfully, no matter how hurtful others might find it. I can see you've learned that lesson well."

Jackie stabbed a piece of meat, transferring it to her plate before adding a large dollop of ketchup. "Always speaking my truth has caused me more heartache than you could ever imagine, Dad, but I'm glad you're enjoying the irony of it."

If her father heard the hurt in her words, he ignored it. "A person can never go wrong with the truth."

Sighing at her father's recitation of words she'd grown up with, Jackie bit her tongue to halt her retort. What was the old saying about not being able to teach an old dog new tricks? She'd save her breath.

They ate in silence. The only sounds were Hoover's soft nuzzling as she scrounged for dropped scraps and the clink of silverware.

"This is great, Mom. I was starving. My plane was late, and Kit had already waited for me for over an hour, so we headed out as soon as I picked up my bag. I haven't eaten a thing since I left home this morning."

Before her mother could add to the conversation, her dad set his fork down and looked at Jackie. "How are my granddaughters? Were they excited about the big change? I can't believe they're starting college."

Jackie looked at her mother in bewilderment.

"Glen, the girls are starting their *second* year of college," her mother said patiently. "Remember? It was a year ago in early June when we flew out to attend their high school graduation."

Jackie noticed her father drop his eyes to his plate while carefully chewing a bite of roast. It seemed he was more intent on pushing the food around his plate than actually eating it. When she was a kid, he used to heap his plate full with everything her mother set out on the table.

"Right. Lost a little time there. Sorry," was all he said before scanning the floor, likely searching for Hoover.

Jackie ate the last delicious bite of her potatoes, losing the string of conversation over her dad's apparent confusion. As she considered a second helping of her favorite dish, a memory of her girls peeling a mound of potatoes in their kitchen back home danced into her mind. They loved the side dish, too.

"The girls are doing great, Dad. Hailey is working as a CNA and will probably take the nursing track. Mack isn't sure what she wants to do yet, but she still has plenty of time to decide."

Charlotte pushed away from the table and plugged in the coffee pot. When she returned, she was shaking her head. "I wish you wouldn't refer to our sweet Mackenzie as *Mack*. That is not a fitting name for such a beautiful girl."

Jackie shrugged. "Everybody calls her Mack. You can call her whatever you like, Mom. It doesn't matter."

The look her mother shot her said she disagreed, but Jackie let it go.

"This is the first summer the kids aren't living at home. It's so quiet. In fact, I'm thinking I'll end up moving. My house is too big for just me and Nikki."

"Nick? Who's Nick? What about that Ben fellow? I thought you two were living in sin."

Jackie abandoned the idea of a second helping of potatoes. At her father's mention of Ben, the little bit of her appetite that remained deserted her. "Dad, don't you remember Nikki? She's my border collie. The house would be way too quiet without her. In fact, if I'd known you were allowing dogs in this house again, I'd have brought her with me. I hate that I had to kennel her."

"That would have been tough on an airplane," her father said.

Jackie couldn't tell whether he actually remembered the dog he'd met when they'd visited for the graduation celebration for her twin daughters or not.

"You would have had to drive," he continued. "Do you think she'd get along with my Hoover?"

For one disorienting moment, Jackie felt as though she'd been dropped into an alternative universe. At her mother's cough, she refocused on their conversation. "I'm sure the two dogs would get along just fine."

"And Ben?"

Jackie could see she was going to have to give her dad enough of an answer where her ex was concerned for him to move on to a less anxiety-inducing topic. "Ben and I aren't together anymore. We split up two years ago."

Her dad shook his head. "No. That isn't right. He was at the graduation party you had for the girls."

"He was. But that was because he still has a close relationship with Mack and Hailey. Even though we're not a couple anymore, he's more like a father to them than Todd ever was."

Glen chewed another small bite of meat, then dropped his napkin over his plate, the age-old sign that he was finished. Jackie noticed he'd barely eaten anything.

"You certainly have a complicated love life."

"Glen," Charlotte said, a warning in her voice.

"What? Jackie isn't stupid. I suspect she finds the whole situation complicated, too, if her daughters consider her ex-boyfriend more of a father than their real dad."

Charlotte shook her head, exasperation clear in her expression. She faced her daughter. "Never mind him. Now, what is this business about moving? Have you sold your house? Where would you go, dear?"

"You must have decent equity built up by now," her father said. "Don't be rash."

Jackie pushed her chair back far enough to cross her legs. "Nothing is definite . . . *yet*. But circumstances might require it."

"What does that mean?" her mother asked.

"It means she might move for her job again," her dad said, eyebrows raised. "Am I right, Jackie?"

Shoot. She hadn't meant to tell her parents about the job prospect until she was sure she'd gotten it. She should hear soon. This promotion was important to her. It was the role she has been coveting for nearly ten years. There'd be more pay, more responsibility, more of everything. The only drawback was more travel. That would be problematic with Nikki.

But she'd earned this one. If she didn't get it, she didn't know what she'd do. And suddenly, irrationally, she felt that telling her parents about it now might jinx the outcome.

She stood and cleared the table, wanting to create a distraction from the topic at hand. "Enough about me. When are we going to discuss you, Dad? Mom said something was up but refused to go into any details. You've lost weight since I saw you last."

"I've lost more than weight, kid," he said, picking Hoover up and settling the tiny dog in his lap. "According to your mother, I'm losing my mind."

Her mom grunted at this.

Jackie poured her mother a cup of coffee, doing her best to keep her hand from shaking over the shock at her father's words. "I'm serious, Dad. What's wrong?"

He sighed, setting the dog down again, and rested his forearms on the spot where his plate had sat a moment earlier. "Unfortunately, I'm serious, too, Jackie. They're still working to diagnose exactly what is happening, but they're fairly certain it's dementia. So, see, I *am* losing my mind. Literally. That is why I asked your mother to encourage you to come home. I knew you'd enjoy seeing old friends at your class reunion, and I wanted time to sit down with you while I still have all—or at least most—of my faculties. No saying how quickly this will progress."

Jackie sank into her chair, the dirty stack of dishes forgotten. "Does Ronnie know?"

Color flushed her father's cheeks, making him appear more like himself. "That boy is no concern of mine."

"That *boy* is fifty-two years old, with an amazing wife and three nearly grown children you've never met. Dad, if the doctors are right, don't you think it's about time to let bygones be bygones?"

Glen stood quickly, causing his chair to skip back a few feet across the wooden floor. He pulled his shoulders back in a poor attempt to mimic the stance he'd habitually taken when confronting someone as a younger, healthier version of himself.

"I have to go to the bathroom."

Jackie might have snickered if the current situation wasn't so serious. So sad.

Her father was losing himself.

How long would it be before she lost him, too?

CHAPTER THREE

J ACKIE NEEDED FRESH AIR. She slid open the tiny bathroom window, and the lilting call of a songbird helped lift a sleepy veil of fog from her brain. She'd always loved the sound of tiny brown wrens on a summer's day. She searched the large elm on the north side of the house but couldn't spot the bird responsible for the morning serenade. The wren, hiding somewhere amongst the tree limbs, was nowhere to be seen, nor was the treehouse that used to nestle in the branches of the mammoth tree. She remembered how her heart had ached after a strong summer storm blew that treehouse down.

The house was quiet. It wasn't too stuffy, thanks to the two air-conditioning units installed after her last visit. She doubted her parents were up yet.

Stepping into the shower, her feet recognized the tacky feel of the decals her mother had stuck to the bottom of the tub after Ronnie fell and suffered a skull fracture during bath time. How could those little orange butterflies and pink tulips stay adhered to such a slick surface for almost fifty years, yet the shelf liner in her cabinets back home couldn't last a single year?

Hot water hadn't yet reached the upstairs bathroom, but Jackie didn't care. She ducked under the icy stream and felt cleansed of the stickiness she'd endured since waking to yet another dreaded episode of night sweats, followed by the inability to fall back asleep.

She hadn't planned to wash her hair, but she couldn't face the day, out and about in her hometown where she'd probably run into plenty of people she knew, with bedhead. Her teeth were chattering by the time hot water arrived. Thankful she'd thought to stock her shower the night before with the color-safe shampoo she'd packed, she lathered up her freshly cut and dyed hair. The dollar-store brand her mother stocked the guest bath with would have stripped her chestnut locks, leaving her hair mousey brown with gray strands peeking through. By the time her forty-year class reunion rolled around she might be brave enough to allow her hair to go *au naturel*, but she wasn't there yet.

Refreshed, she finished her morning routine and eased quietly out of the house. Hoover didn't give her away, leaving her with a sneaking suspicion that the little dog was sleeping with her parents. This entire business with her father bringing home a rescue dog cracked her up.

She dug through her purse for the keys to the rental, but then paused. More birds were twittering in the trees lining the boulevard, and the rising sun hadn't yet dried the dew from the grass. It was cool, despite the weatherman's promise of high eighties by the afternoon. Her sleeveless blouse, capris, and flats would allow her to walk comfortably for the twelve blocks to downtown. She might even wear off a portion of the calories she'd consumed when her mother brought her that late-night chocolate sundae on the porch swing.

That snack was probably the culprit behind her sleepless night. Her doctor had warned her of the dangers of sugar. She also confirmed Jackie was indeed making her way into the dreaded land of menopause, something Jackie had feared ever since her mother had driven them all crazy with her own mood swings.

She started off with an aggressive pace, but after her toe caught an edge of pitted concrete thanks to a massive tree root causing the sidewalk to heave, she slowed. There was no reason to hurry. She planned to treat herself to a fresh cup of coffee at the Crystal Café, say hello to the old gals she was sure still worked the counter there, then meander around downtown before stopping by the high school to say hello to Annie.

Given that the reunion would kick off the following evening, there was no way dear Annie was having as relaxing of a morning as Jackie. But that's what Annie got for staying in Ruby Shores, teaching at the same high school they'd all graduated from, eventually moving up the ranks to take over the role of principal—just as Jackie's father had done so long ago. Aside from her sporadic summer duties, Annie would have plenty of time to enjoy the Minnesota summer and all the lake activities around here. Jackie, on the other hand, only had two weeks off this summer. So, while Annie may have to work hard this week, Jackie wasn't going to feel too sorry for her old friend.

As she turned the corner onto Breconwood Road, a familiar yet updated house came into view. A warmth flooded through her as she thought of Owen, another of her old friends. Studying the brick colonial, she stopped. The once white shutters were now black, and the old arbor she'd sat under with Owen while they worked on their homework—or at least Owen had—was gone. A new pergola stood in its place. Jackie felt a twinge of regret that their old study area was no more, but she had to admit its replacement looked amazing. It appeared to be fashioned out of driftwood, probably salvaged along the shores of the local lake. The entire property had a modern aesthetic now.

She wondered what had become of Owen and his family. Would he be at their reunion?

She had felt so close to her studious young friend in grade school, but by the time they'd reached their high school years they'd drifted apart. She couldn't remember if something caused a rift between them, or if it was just the way of kids. Until ninth grade, she'd often referred to Owen as her best friend.

She felt a pang as she remembered his calm, mature nature. When they were young, he was shorter than she was and wore round little glasses that made his eyes look even bigger when he gazed through them in wonder. Owen was always intrigued. It didn't matter if it was something he'd discovered in a book, a movie they watched together, or a topic they discussed under the shade of that rickety old arbor. He was a curious boy.

A car drove by. The driver tapped his horn and gave her a little wave. She waved back, although she didn't recognize him. He may have honked as a not-so-subtle reminder that this was a small town, and neighbors looked out for each other. She probably looked odd, standing there, staring at Owen's old house. She moved on, thinking she would ask Annie if she knew what ever happened to her old friend.

Other familiar homes of past friends and acquaintances spurred memories as she walked the final few blocks to downtown. It was disconcerting, this feeling as if she'd only just walked these streets a month ago. And that sense of déjà vu only grew stronger as she reached the downtown area of Ruby Shores.

These were her old stomping grounds. Tourists were already dotting the streets. If it had been September, things would still be quiet this early in the morning, but the months of June, July, and August brought much needed traffic to the area. The small shops lining Main relied on business from their many tourists in order to survive the other nine months of the year. Ruby Shores wasn't far enough away from larger towns, so it was a constant struggle to compete against the pull of the more metropolitan areas.

Jackie felt relief when she spied her favorite ice cream shop on a corner. She hoped the pink-and-white fabric that created a unique canopy inside still stretched from one side of the interior to the other, setting a quaint backdrop for the wrought-iron table and chair sets she'd cursed when she used to have to clean them as a teenager. Scooping hard ice cream proved to be tough work for her summer job between her junior and senior years of high school.

The theater was still there, too, and since the movie listed on the marquee was current, it must still be in operation. She could practically smell the popcorn and feel the sticky floors of her youth as she passed by the entrance.

The Crystal Café was across the square, and it would be a shorter walk if Jackie cut through Emerald Park. The shortcut wouldn't be a hardship. She could already hear the gurgle of the old fountain, even though lush, flowering bushes hid it from her view.

The ringing of her phone, deep inside her purse, caught her attention. She considered letting it go to voicemail, but then worried it might be one of her daughters. She dug it out, freezing when she saw the call was coming from her boss.

"This is it," she muttered.

She glanced around for a bench she thought she remembered being close by. She needed to take this call sitting down, and hated the tremor in her hand as she answered. This wasn't the time to let doubt rear its ugly head again. She peeked around to make sure she was alone.

"Hello, Sam," she said, sinking down on the found bench.

"Hello, Jackie. Enjoying your vacation?"

They exchanged small talk for a minute or two, then Sam's voice lowered an octave. Jackie had worked with him long enough to know this meant he was finally getting down to business.

"Listen, Jackie, I'm sorry to disturb you during vacation, but you made me promise to call once we reached a decision about the position, no matter what. So that's why I'm calling."

A nervous laugh bubbled up in her chest, but she squelched it. "I figured as much. What have you decided?"

She heard rustling through the phone, as if he was referencing something or switching ears. "You should know this wasn't a simple decision."

The shout of a young child caught her attention, and she watched a toddler waddle off the sidewalk onto the grass near her bench, his finger extended toward a fluttering butterfly. She turned her back to him and cupped her hand around her phone, trying to listen but already knowing in the depths of her stomach that she wouldn't like what was coming.

"Jackie, you are an indispensable member of this team, but . . ."

And there it was. They were giving the job to someone else.

Jackie turned as the little boy screeched. A woman had scooped him up and was hurrying him away. Her eyes followed the back of the woman as she wondered what they were doing out and about so early in the morning.

She blinked. She needed to give Sam her attention.

". . . outside, a fresh perspective. I'm sure you understand. You've been in this industry long enough to know companies often get their biggest boost when they bring in new ideas."

"You're bringing someone in from the outside to fill the role?" she said, pretty sure she'd heard him correctly.

"Right. Right. But who knows, Jackie, another spot could open up in a year or two. You can always try again."

In two years? She'd be fifty.

"It's my age, isn't it? You were afraid I couldn't handle the demands of the job."

The man stammered at her question. Normally she toed the company line pretty closely, seldom questioning his directives. Her father, after all, had raised her to be obedient.

"Don't be ridiculous. This has nothing to do with your age. But the woman is already familiar with a new software system we plan to switch to. It'll take you some time to get up to speed with the new technology."

Heat rose in Jackie's cheeks. The powerful temptation to tell him exactly where he could shove his new technology shot through her mind, but she didn't voice it. If she'd learned anything growing up with her father, it was to bite her tongue until she was able to reply in what would be perceived as an acceptable manner.

Sam's voice was on the rise again, indicating he was ready to wrap up the call and end this uncomfortable conversation. Jackie couldn't argue with that. She thanked him for giving her the opportunity to interview for the role and for their consideration and then hung up, grateful he couldn't see her face or read the insincerity in her expression.

She could picture him now, sitting in her old office—the one she'd worked out of back when she'd hired him into the company. Now he was weighing in on decisions that would have long-lasting implications to her life. She'd even agreed to cut her vacation from her initial three weeks down to two so he could go to the eastern shore with his family.

Ungrateful little twerp, she thought, shoving her phone back into her purse and dropping her head into her hands.

After allowing herself a minute or two to grieve the news, Jackie straightened her shoulders—much as her father had done the night before—slipped on her sunglasses, and got back to her feet.

I will not allow this to ruin my vacation, she promised herself, walking toward the Crystal Café. She needed that cup of coffee now more than ever. Her steps brought her to the old fountain where she used to make wishes. Coins glistened against the tiled bottom of the fountain's blue pool, fed by the continuous trickle of water that flowed from the angel's outstretched palms.

Jackie closed her eyes, allowing her mind to wander back to another summer day. It was the day of her high school graduation. They were going out after the ceremony, but Lynette insisted they stop and toss a coin in while making wishes for their futures.

Those four girls thought the moment they shifted their tassels from one side of their graduation caps to the other that their lives would burst forth into all kinds of amazing adventures.

Jackie could see now that they'd been partially right. Each of them would encounter plenty of adventures, but not all of those adventures would be amazing. Some would downright suck. She'd learned that life was more of a rollercoaster of both highs and lows instead of the explosion of excitement they'd all expected.

This morning felt like yet another milestone for Jackie. All she'd focused on for the past eleven months, ever since she'd packed her twins up and escorted them off to their college dorm rooms, was her job. Her nest may be empty, but her career was supposed to be the thing that would see her through. Her track record with romantic relationships was dismal, but no one could fault her commitment to her career. That was the one thing in her life within her control.

Or so she'd thought. Until that phone call.

She fished a coin out of her purse and glanced at it, surprised to see it was a token from the amusement park she'd visited with Hailey and Mack. The summery handbag she was carrying had ended up on the top shelf of her closet, shoved there the day she'd arrived back home without her twins. At the time, she'd worried she would never survive their absence. But over the next few weeks, she remembered how she started to feel more like herself again, in a way she supposed most other mothers eventually did, too.

She'd spent more and more time at the office, because why rush home? Nikki didn't appreciate her late nights, but the collie had a high-end dog run in the backyard, giving her access to both the outdoors and a roomy garage.

Jackie had survived the transition period because she'd set her sights on big career moves and got busy making them happen. She'd planned to make her girls proud. Show them independence was a good thing.

A flutter of orange near the second tier of the fountain caught her eye. The butterfly was back. It might not be the same one the little boy had chased, but Jackie wanted to believe it was the very same, back to check on her. It floated in her direction, its tiny wings flapping hard then pausing, allowing it to glide. She imagined the colorful creature enjoyed its freedom. It flew high above her, then swooped down, landing ever so gracefully on her shoulder.

She froze, shocked. She barely dared breathe, certain any movement would cause it to float away. She didn't want the magical moment to end.

It reminded her of the way a monarch butterfly flitted around a park ranger during summer camp. She'd been so young, only twelve. That was the summer she'd first met Kit.

Too soon, a light breeze brushed past the fountain, ruffling the water's surface, then up Jackie's bare arm, sending the weightless insect up and away.

As her eyes trailed after it, she told herself she'd look at this as a time to transform into something different, too, much like her butterfly would have done when it transitioned from a lowly caterpillar into a flying rainbow.

Even now, the colorful butterfly might set its wings and travel some place faraway. That magnificent creature would never allow a round of dream-squashing news delivered by a low-level manager to clip its wings.

Jackie turned her back to the angel, closed her eyes tight, sent her wish skyward on the wings of the butterfly, and let her amusement token fly.

CHAPTER FOUR

A LEATHER STRAP LINED with sleigh bells jangled behind Jackie as she allowed the door to Crystal Café to shut behind her. She'd wondered where all the early-bird tourists were headed, and now she had her answer. They were all inside the café, scarfing down plates piled with eggs and hash browns, and drinking coffee from white ironstone mugs.

"It'll be a few minutes before a table frees up for you, hon, but sit tight. It shouldn't take too long," a woman assured her. She wore black polyester from head to toe, MARGE embroidered over her heart in gold thread.

As she'd expected, Kit's aunt was still working the morning rush, and in her haste, she hadn't recognized her niece's old friend. Jackie watched as the older woman handed menus to one table, poured coffee at another, and dropped a check off at a third. The woman had serious organization skills.

We all have a plethora of valuable skills by this age, Jackie thought. *Though others usually fail to appreciate all we have to offer.*

Another group pushed in behind her, and she stepped closer to the register. She thought she recognized a few faces in a knot of men at a table along the windows. She made eye contact with one of them, and recognition dawned on his face.

"Jackie! Get over here!" he hollered across the crowded restaurant.

Let the reunion begin, she thought, shouldering her way around others who were also waiting, toward the full table of what looked like mostly old classmates. As she approached, Elliott Garrison, the man who'd waved her over, stood and caught her up in a quick bear hug. Elliott had added a notch or two to the end of his belt since Jackie last saw him, but he was as friendly as ever, and she was happy to see him again. He'd actually been a year behind them in school. He reintroduced her to the other men at the table, all of whom had indeed graduated in the same class with her.

Marge sashayed up to the boisterous group, waving a stack of menus. "You boys about ready to move on out? I've got paying customers waiting for tables."

"We're paying," the man sitting next to Elliott piped up, then pushed at the younger man's shoulder. "Actually, *he's* paying today."

Elliott dug out his wallet and dropped cash on the table, elbowing the guy in the chest. Jackie suspected the man was ready to get out of the tight-fitting booth before Elliott squished him. They rose as a group, made Jackie promise to save them all a spin around the dance floor on Saturday night, and headed for the door. Elliott waved goodbye to Jackie as they left. The noise level dropped noticeably following their exit, despite the crowds still inside.

"You are a sight for sore eyes, Jackie Turner," Marge said, scooping Elliott's cash up and stepping aside to give a long-haired busboy room to clear the table. "Kit mentioned you might stop in. Sorry I didn't recognize you right away. Not sure how I missed it. You haven't changed a bit."

Jackie dipped her head and smiled at the waitress, noticing a smudge of what must be butter down the front of her chest. "And fibs like that are why you always were my favorite in here," she said, winking.

"Still as full of baloney as ever, I see," Marge laughed. "You girls always knew how to sweet talk me. Here, I'll get you a table." She grabbed Jackie's wrist and pulled her toward the north side of the café.

Jackie, a solid four inches taller than the waitress, scanned the tables. "But they're all full."

"Not for long. Hank, you about done with that paper of yours? Can't you see we've got a boatload of people waiting for a place to sit down?"

A man wearing thick black-rimmed glasses and a tie looked up from his newspaper, then checked his watch. "Hell, Marge, I don't have to be at the bank until eight thirty. I've got another ten minutes."

"Not today you don't. Come on. Grab your paper and go."

I'm sorry, Jackie mouthed to the businessman as he gathered his things and huffed away.

"Marge, you didn't have to—"

"Never mind him. He sits there twiddling his thumbs like that every morning. It won't hurt him any to get to work ten minutes early for once. Coffee?"

Jackie sank gratefully into the chair at the small table. Someone must have cleared the man's table earlier, as all that remained was a half-filled coffee mug, and Marge made that disappear in short order.

"Yes. Might as well bring a pot."

"Been that kind of morning already, has it, hon? That father of yours giving you guff? I know he can be a prickly one."

Jackie laughed. Her friends used that word to describe her father, too, back when they were kids. She wondered if Marge knew her dad wasn't as prickly as he used to be.

"No. Work stuff. In fact, if you have any champagne and orange juice, I'd be happy to drown my sorrows in a mimosa."

"Sorry, sugar. I've got the juice, but plum out of the bubbly. Why work? Aren't you supposed to be on vacation?"

Like magic, a full cup of coffee appeared in front of Jackie, and she took a blessed sip of it before responding. "That I am. But I made my boss promise to call me as soon as he had news about a job I applied for."

Marge nodded, a knowing look in her eye. She'd likely listened to hundreds of sob stories from customers over the years. "And let me guess. The bubbly isn't for celebrating."

"Sadly, not today," Jackie confirmed. "But you're swamped. I better let you get back to work. When you have a minute, if you could put in an order of dry wheat toast for me, that would be perfect."

Marge added a splash of coffee to Jackie's nearly full cup, then patted her on the shoulder. "Oh, I can do better than dry toast, honey. I'll fix you right up."

Jackie doubted she'd ever consumed that many calories by nine in the morning before. If she didn't watch out, she'd negate the pounds lost during her recent month-long crash diet and the clothes she brought for the reunion would be too tight.

As a teenager she'd hated it when people like Marge knew her favorites. It felt as if she had no privacy in this small town. Now she appreciated how comforting it was to be treated like a real person by a familiar face—especially after the morning she was having—instead of just another obscure customer.

She welcomed the quiet as she exited the still busy diner, continuing on down Main Street. It felt good to walk after so much food.

When Ruby Shores High School came into view, Jackie felt a rush of nostalgia. Had she even stepped foot inside since she'd graduated? She'd thought she would, given her father had worked there for some time after, but now she couldn't remember any specific visits.

Her eyes continued to take in familiar sights as her feet carried her up to the front. She paused at the three heavy sets of double doors that still sported wire mesh glass windows. Little seemed to have changed, aside from the color of the doors. Hadn't the metal been a faded red, way back when? The shiny black paint was new.

Then, suddenly, she remembered one visit to the school, years after she graduated. She'd come back to town for her father's retirement party. They'd held the festivities at a room in the local civic center, but she tagged along with him when he came down to clean out his office.

She did some quick math. That would have been about thirteen years ago. She wondered if she'd changed as much as her father had in the years since that last visit.

The first set of doors she tried was locked. Probably because it was summer break, but maybe it was a sign of the times. She hoped one would open; she wanted to surprise Annie with a quick hello.

When Annie had called her two weeks earlier, Jackie had heard the relief in the other woman's voice at her promise not to skip this year's class reunion. Annie might still be irritated with her for skipping their twenty-year, but Jackie hadn't been able to bring herself to make the trip. She'd brought her new husband to their ten-year reunion, showing him off just like so many of her other classmates. That first reunion had consisted of too much posturing to suit Jackie, even though she now realized she'd acted the same way. Todd was out of the picture by the time their twenty-year rolled around, and part of her was ashamed to show up single. When she added in all the summer activities of her then nine-year-old twins, she felt she had a valid excuse to skip it.

The last set of doors was unlocked, and she let herself into the hushed and shadowed main hall of her past.

The tiled floor gleamed where weak patches of sunlight stole in through open classroom doors. She stepped inside and her footsteps echoed, marking her advancement toward the offices, while she drank in her surroundings. The lockers looked much the same as she remembered. A coat of paint did little to hide the countless dents caused by wayward backpacks, hip checks, and even the occasional fist thrown against them in frustration over a failed test or fizzled romance. New, however, were the matching padlocks hanging from each locker.

What was her old locker number? She remembered how happy she'd been when they assigned Kit a locker two down from hers for their senior year, until she'd realized they had that snarky Fran Wood between them.

"You had number 539 and Kit was 541."

Jackie jumped at the disembodied voice that knocked her out of the flashback.

"You know the school is closed today, don't you?" the voice came again, and Jackie could hear, even if she couldn't yet see, the smile on Annie's face.

She spun toward the voice, hiking the strap of her handbag onto her shoulder and skipping toward her friend's silhouette outside the school offices, delighted to find Annie in the building.

"Those rules never applied to me," Jackie said.

Light flooded the hallway, and Annie hurried toward her. They caught each other up in a hug, punctuated with screeches and giggles that could have come from two high school girls instead of the school's principal and her forty-eight-year-old friend.

"I wasn't one hundred percent convinced you'd show," Annie said, stepping back and grasping both of Jackie's hands. "You look amazing, girl! How is it you never gain an ounce? I'm thinking I'll be as wide as I am tall before long if I'm not careful."

Laughing, the two women took a second to size each other up.

"Don't be ridiculous. You are radiant, Annie!" Jackie insisted, and she meant it. While her friend was indeed curvier than she used to be, the weight sat nicely on her short frame. "And after what I ate for breakfast, I won't be able to eat another thing all day."

Annie released her hands and threw an arm around her waist, steering her back toward the office. "What brings you down here to the school this morning?"

Jackie put her arm over Annie's, but paused as they passed the old trophy case.

"So many memories . . ."

She inspected the many photographs and awards layered inside the case. It was like stepping into a time warp. The oldest trophies were now more blackish than silver, tarnished with age. She remembered the oldest ones dated back to the early 1900s. Someone had organized them in roughly chronological order. Through the years, the type of trophies morphed away from silver winning cups into more garish versions: combinations of plastic and marble and gold plate. There was a time in the 1950s when this school could boast of a football dynasty. Jackie's own father had been part of that dynasty.

She'd always wondered if that was part of the reason he'd stayed here, moving up from teacher to administration to principal, because he didn't want to leave what he would have considered his glory days.

It still felt strange to Jackie that their little Annie, one of her oldest friends, now occupied the office chair from which her own father once ruled.

She was reminded again that change was life's only constant.

"How are your teams doing these days?" she asked, glancing at Annie.

Her friend motioned to the lowest shelf in the cabinet. "Not well. The kids with the genuine talent are opting to attend the larger schools within driving distance. When school boundaries have been a hurdle, some families have even picked up and moved. Boys and girls rarely play for the fun of it anymore. It's all about winning state championships and nabbing college scholarships."

Jackie didn't think that sounded much different from their own experience back in the late '80s. "Do you remember how so many of our social outings as kids revolved around sports? Not even just the ones we played, but the ones we watched, too. Basketball, football, and hockey games were the social events no one wanted to miss."

With a sigh, Annie used a tiny key hanging from a larger keyring at her waist to unlock the cabinet. Sliding the large glass door open, she reached inside and picked out one of the older, tarnished cups. "You're right. And without that school spirit, nothing feels quite as magical around here as it used to."

Jackie snorted, turning the trophy Annie held so she could read the inscription. "I would never have used the term *magical* to describe our high school experience."

"Really?" Annie countered. Jackie could read the challenge in her eyes. "Think about it, Jack. The community showed up in droves to watch us and our friends play. They packed the stands when you were running track. It wasn't only about winning and losing, either. Even when our teams had a terrible season, or a longer dry streak, people still showed up. Remember how thrilling it felt when our little school made the state semifinals in basketball when we were seniors? It was like we were on top of the world. I remember a picture of you, screaming your lungs out from the stands, that made the front page of the newspaper. When was the last time you got that excited about anything?"

Memories, spurred by Annie's questions, flooded her brain. Blurs of color, strains of music, and the blare of loud buzzers whirled, all hyped by an excitement level like no other. "Those were special days, weren't they?"

Annie used the bottom of her blouse to rub away the smudge Jackie's finger had left on the trophy before she put it back and locked the cabinet again. "That's what I mean. Magical. I don't know about you, but for me life certainly doesn't have that kind of sparkle anymore."

Little warning bells went off in Jackie's head. Something more than a lack of school spirit seemed to be on Annie's mind.

But, for the first time, Jackie wasn't comfortable coming right out and asking her old friend what was wrong. They'd been so close back in their school days. But their interactions in the decades since, while always fun and touched with a hint of magic of their own, had become less and less frequent. They'd need to find their way back to each other before they could expect to fall into the soul-deep conversations they used to enjoy.

Instead, she'd stick to the surface level, until they found their footing again.

"It really is great to see you, Annie. I just stopped in to say hello and see if you needed any help with preparations for this weekend. Oh, and I wanted to invite you over this evening. A little wine with cheese and crackers on my childhood porch seems like the perfect way to kick off the festivities. Kit and Lynette are coming. Kit is spending the day with her grandmother, and Lynette hasn't gotten to town yet, but she hoped to get in by four. We need to catch up."

Annie shrugged, and the rest of the glow Jackie noted seemed to ebb away. "That sounds amazing, Jackie. Really, it does. And enjoying wine *on* your mom and dad's porch, instead of hidden in our sleeping bags in your basement during one of our sleepovers, would be a nice change of pace. But I'm tied up tonight."

It disappointed Jackie that Annie wouldn't be able to join them. This was supposed to be a time for them to all reconnect. "If you have too much to do for the reunion, let me help. We can get to work now, so you can stop over tonight."

But Annie shook her head. "I have a pretty good handle on the reunion prep. All that's left are the last-minute things that will keep me busy tomorrow. No, this is family related. I have plans with Henry and Relic tonight. I'd reschedule if I could, but I just can't."

Henry was Annie's second husband. Relic was her youngest of three children. She'd had her older two with her first husband.

"Relic is going to be a senior this coming year, isn't he? That's hard to believe. Weren't we just that age?"

"Some days it feels like it. Other days it feels like our childhood never even happened. Here, come in my office. I know you haven't seen Relic since he was a little guy. We just got his senior pictures back this morning. I was actually looking at them on my computer when I heard you come in."

She followed Annie into the administrative offices. It still felt strange that Annie's office once belonged to Jackie's father. She used to come here when she needed money to run to the Crystal Café for lunch with her friends. Back then, they could eat for two dollars apiece, sharing heaping plates of French fries while enjoying their favorite milkshakes.

"Could you imagine my father having a computer on this desk?" she asked as they entered the familiar office.

Annie laughed. "No. Computers were never in your father's wheelhouse. But he knew how to run a tight ship around here. I sometimes wonder what it would be like today if we could still drag students down to the office by their ears when they misbehaved. What if the threat of calling their parents still struck the fear into them? Now most of them want us to call their parents so they can help get the kid *out* of trouble."

Jackie dropped into the chair alongside Annie's desk. She would have sworn Annie's chair was the same one her father inhabited all those years ago. "Despite your small stature, my friend, I'd put my money on you in a tussle. Those kids don't know how tough you really are!"

"And then I'd be looking for a new job. One misstep in the disciplinary arena these days and you'll find yourself out on the street. Things have really changed, Jackie."

Jackie could see her attempt at humor had fallen flat. "You're right, Annie. And I admire you. It can't be easy to run a high school in this day and age. Do you sometimes feel like they stacked the deck against you in your efforts to help kids prepare for the real world?"

"Every day, Jackie, every blasted day. But enough of the doom and gloom. It's a beautiful summer day, we have a fun weekend ahead of us, and the Kaleidoscope Girls will be back together again!"

Just like that, the gap she'd felt between Annie and herself evaporated. "Oh, wow, how could I have forgotten we called ourselves that? The Kaleidoscope Girls . . . we were inseparable! You know, I saw a monarch butterfly this morning, and it reminded me of camp. Do they still hold that same summer camp out by the falls that we went to as kids? Talk about magical. *That* was a magical time!"

"No, unfortunately. Those type of summer camps are a thing of the past. The summer my Ava turned twelve I made tons of phone calls hoping to find something similar, but all I could find were sports camps. Those are completely different."

"What were the names of those two camp counselors who were so much fun? They taught here, too, right?"

Annie stood to pull a book down off the shelf behind her. It was a school yearbook—similar to the one she'd hoped to bring home, but more recent. "Yes! They were twin sisters, remember? They both taught here for a while, but Stella moved away. Wendy is still here, though."

"They must be retired by now, aren't they?"

"No," Annie said, laughing. "I know when you're a kid, adults always seem so old, but they were only, like, twenty back then. Wendy is still teaching all of our art classes."

"You're right! My favorite year at camp was the year Kit moved here. We were twelve. If Wendy and Stella were twenty, they would have only been eight years older than us. I don't know about you, but I don't plan to be retired in eight years."

"Not unless this job gets to be too much," Annie said, flipping open the yearbook. "I think Stella left the summer of 2013, so five years ago. This would have been the last yearbook she was in."

Jackie strained to see the photo Annie was pointing to, but it was no use. "I have to use these stupid reading glasses now," she grumbled, digging a pair out of her purse. "My eyes aren't what they were back when we were twelve."

"Nothing is as crisp and clear as when we were twelve. But look at her. Don't you think she looks the same as she did back in '82?"

Jackie had to agree as she studied the photograph. "I hate people like that. They never age."

"No one could hate Wendy. She is one of those people who glides through her days, making everything brighter. But what are you talking about? You haven't aged, either."

Jackie tilted the book to cut the glare on the paper. "I've aged plenty. I try to fight it, but it can feel like a losing battle. You're right, though—I could never hate Wendy, no matter how timeless she might be. She had a way about her. Even when we were kids. Remember how she took us all out to the water's edge when the moon was full? The water thundered into the pool at the base of the falls, and the moonbeams sparkled like diamonds."

"And then the next day she showed us how to make homemade kaleidoscopes," Annie said, nodding. "She thought the sparkles from the night before would inspire us. She had tubes from old gift wrap she'd saved, crushed glass, and those little mirrors she got from her aunt who sold Mary Kay."

Jackie kept it going. "Actually, I think it was Avon. And do you remember what happened when Wendy sent Kit and Lynette to the office? That was terrible."

Nodding, Annie got back up and pulled a small brass tube down from another of her shelves, handing it to Jackie. "I actually have a decent number of kaleidoscopes at home. I've loved them ever since that summer. One year, for Mother's Day, my kids gave me that one you're holding. Believe it or not, I even kept the one I made at camp."

"No way!" Jackie cried. "I doubt mine lasted the summer."

Annie laughed. "It didn't. Remember? When we all got home, you insisted the treehouse in your backyard would be our club house. Your dog . . . shoot, I can't remember her name . . . she was going to be our mascot. And your kaleidoscope sat on the makeshift desk you made from a busted side table your mom was throwing out."

Jackie nodded along as the memories came back. "And I forgot to bring it inside over the winter. By the time I climbed back up there in the spring, all that remained was a tiny pile of crushed glass. The tube was long gone, probably lining a squirrel's nest somewhere in our neighborhood. The mirrors were on the floor, cracked and unusable. Ronnie went up there with me, and when he saw the broken mirrors he swore it meant I'd have seven years of bad luck."

Annie sank into her chair, dropping her head back and staring at the ceiling. "I used to think Ronnie was so cute."

"What?!" Jackie shouted. "You aren't serious!"

"I'm dead serious. But he never noticed me. I was just a friend of his kid sister. Then, after he graduated, I don't remember seeing much of him. It was like he disappeared. How's he doing?"

Jackie couldn't believe she'd never noticed Annie paying any extra attention to her big brother. She supposed she could understand it. Her brother had been cute, and athletic, and a bit of a trouble maker. It made for a heady combination for younger girls just starting to experience the early pangs of puppy love.

"I think he's doing well," she said. "I don't talk to him as often as I'd like. We're both busy with our own families and careers."

Annie gave her a knowing glance. "I use that excuse, too, when I'm feeling guilty about not talking to my big sister often enough. But wasn't there a big tiff between him and your dad? I remember Glen was never willing to talk about Ron much after he graduated from college."

Jackie didn't want to try to explain something she didn't even understand herself. "Men can be so obtuse sometimes."

She noticed her friend's eyes flick to the framed photograph of her husband, Henry, and her three kids, perched on the corner of her desk. "That they can."

Yep, something is up, Jackie thought. A topic for another day, when there was plenty of wine involved.

The phone on the desktop jingled, but Annie ignored it.

"Are you sure there isn't anything I can help you with today?" Jackie asked again, handing the kaleidoscope back.

Annie shut the yearbook and stood to return both items to their rightful places on the shelves. "I'm sure. But I appreciate your offer."

The desk phone rang again.

"And that's my cue to get out of your hair," Jackie said, getting to her feet as well. "It really is great to see you again, Annie. I can't wait to catch up more, and I'm sorry you can't make it tonight."

She turned to leave, but then remembered her friend's photos of her son. "Shoot. You didn't show me Relic's pictures yet!"

The phone continued to ring.

"I'll show you tomorrow night, promise. But I better get this. Duty is literally calling."

"I will hold you to that," Jackie said, then took her leave to allow Annie to get back to work. "I'll see myself out. I know the way!"

As she headed back out into the hallway, she flipped off the light and strode toward the front doors. She didn't need the buzz or illumination from the fluorescent lights above.

Her stubborn mind tried to flip back to the disturbing call with her boss earlier that morning. The disappointment burned deep.

"No!"

The forceful word echoed around the wide, dim hallway. She'd promised herself not to dwell on her stalled career until after her vacation was over. There would be time for that later. She needed to treat this week like the sacred blessing it was.

Kind of like the two weeks she used to spend at summer camp as a girl.

Few things in her life were ever as much fun as those camps.

At the end of the hallway, on the floor in front of the outer doors, a pool of sunlight splintered into a rainbow of colors.

They reminded Jackie of Annie's beloved kaleidoscopes.

As she stepped outside into the bright sunlight, she thought of a much younger Kit, her childish, unprocessed hair the color of the sun. She couldn't help but wonder if Kit had managed to keep the kaleidoscope she made at their first summer camp together, the one where they'd become the best of friends. Thankfully, their enduring friendship was one thing that hadn't changed.

new friends

SUMMER CAMP

1982

CHAPTER FIVE

K IT HESITATED IN THE center of Cabin 7. Where was everyone? Her battered suitcase slipped from her fingers, hitting the scarred floorboards with a heavy *thud*. She took in the messy state of three sets of bunk beds. A fourth set looked untouched.

She shivered at the unnerving sight, closing her eyes. The bunks reminded her of that other place and time. She'd kept her eyes squeezed tight then, too, as she'd lain on a similar bed, doing her best to block out a room full of castoffs like herself. The pillow she'd used to quiet the near constant squeak of those metal bunk beds did little to block out the nightmare she was living. She'd promised herself that night, as she feigned sleep while surrounded by strangers, that she'd never, ever end up in a place like that again. It was why she'd finally agreed to move in with her grandparents.

How could they send me away like this, *too,* she thought, chewing her lip and blinking fast, refusing to give in to tears.

Arriving at this stupid summer camp late only made matters worse.

Not bothering to pick her bag up from the middle of the floor, she strode over to the messiest set of beds, drawn by the black button eyes of a stuffed bear. It felt as if the bear was seeing right into her soul, discovering her secrets. He knew she didn't belong here. The bear's fur was brown, like everything else in the cabin, but worn. Patches of light fabric peeked through. Despite its ratty appearance, the toy looked well-loved.

Lucky bear.

Kit snorted. "What twelve-year-old brings a stupid stuffed animal to camp?"

The only answer was the twitter of a bird outside the open window. She wanted to hate the silly bear, but she felt compelled to pick him up, to hold him tight to her constricted chest. Something inside her loosened, and she dropped a quick kiss on his head before putting him back the way she'd found him.

Curious about what other campers may have brought from home, she grabbed hold of the upper bunk, set one tennis shoe on the rail of the lower bed, and hoisted herself up to see if anything interesting rested atop the patchwork quilt. Old wood creaked in protest, and her weight caused the unit to tilt toward the center of the room.

"What do you think you're doing?" a voice echoed through the cabin's interior.

Kit froze, guilt flushing through her. Her mind registered the accusation and the precarious tilt of the two-tiered bed simultaneously, and she jumped down, the heavy bunk crashing back into place. The lamp on the bedside table rattled.

"Who are you and what are you doing in our cabin?"

Kit braced for a lecture and spun around, expecting to see another camp counselor standing in the doorway. But there was only a girl, roughly her own age, hands on her hips and fire in her eyes. The dark eyes reminded her of the threadbare teddy on the bed behind her, as if she, too, could see that Kit didn't belong here.

Refusing to be intimidated, Kit straightened her spine and tilted her head so she could look down her nose at the girl. "Wendy sent me in here."

"Wendy sent you in here to snoop through our things? I doubt that."

Kit sighed, picking up the old suitcase her grandfather had dug out of storage for her the night before, then straightened to eye her cabinmate. "Chill. I wasn't snooping. I was just trying to figure out which bunk to take."

The other girl relaxed her stance enough to cross her arms while narrowing her eyes, weighing the truth of Kit's claim. "You must be Katherine. Wendy said there'd be one more of us, but she didn't know why you weren't here yet. Get lost?"

"Call me Kit. I don't answer to Katherine. And no, we didn't get lost," Kit said. Only her father called her by her given name. And she didn't owe this snippy kid any explanations. She'd already told Wendy the actual story behind her tardiness. "What should I call you? None of the words that come to mind describing you right now would be very nice."

"Is that so?"

Kit paused instead of quipping back. A lifetime spent butting heads with her own mother meant she'd learned to recognize when a conversation was stuck. If she convinced this girl she was sorry—even though she really wasn't—she might go away and leave her alone.

She turned toward the only set of beds in the cabin that wasn't mussed. "I'm sorry, okay? It doesn't look like anybody is using this bunk over here, so should I just take this lower one?"

The sound of footsteps running and sliding outside floated through the open window, followed by a high-pitched voice. "Jackie, what's taking so long? Did you find your mitt?"

The girl tossed an "I'm coming!" over her shoulder and hurried across the cabin floor toward the bunk Kit had indeed been snooping around. She scrambled up the foot of the beds, grabbed a softball mitt from up top, then scrambled back down, jumping the final few feet.

"Bottom bed is Wendy's. The top one's open. Take that. If you brought a ball or mitt, grab it. And hurry—we need to go kick some fourteen-year-old butts or we'll never hear the end of it, just like last year."

And as quickly as the girl had appeared, she was gone, footsteps and voices fading away until all that remained was the constant twitter of birds.

"Hello to you, too, Jackie," Kit said, plunking her suitcase at the foot of her newly assigned bunk. "Nice to meet you."

But sarcasm wasn't effective in an empty room.

She dropped to her knees and wrestled with the sticky latch on the right side of the suitcase. When she finally popped the top, she rummaged through the contents. The stack of books inside was the hefty culprit, and Kit piled them onto her mattress, out of the way and away from prying eyes. With any luck, she'd get through at least three of them before heading home at the end of these dreaded two weeks.

After finding the teddy bear, she wished she'd tucked her favorite blanket into her suitcase. It would have been easy enough to stash the well-worn thing under a pillow. But it waited for her back on her new bed, in her new room, at grandma and grandpa's home.

Would she ever think of it as *her* home?

Kit sighed. She'd promised her grandma she'd be a good sport, and *she* always kept her promises, so she peeled out of her jeans and sweatshirt and pulled on cutoffs and a favorite T-shirt. She stowed her suitcase and forced herself out the door, softball in hand, toward the sound of screaming girls.

Even though hiding away in Cabin 7 with her new books held far more appeal than approaching a gaggle of noisy twelve-year-olds, she might as well get this over with. She'd promised.

Jackie eyed the orange-haired snoop meandering in their direction. She still couldn't believe the new girl's nerve. Who digs around in other people's things? And that hair of hers. It had to be fake.

"Are you sure she was snooping? She probably thought the bunk was open."

Jackie shook her head as she glanced between Annie and the late-comer. "She was snooping. I'm sure of it. She better not have stolen anything."

"Jackie! You can't go around accusing people like that! You don't have any proof she did anything wrong." Annie stood, dropped her glove on the bench, and headed in the redhead's direction.

Jackie watched in surprise.

"Who's that? Tell me she's on our team. She's tall."

Jackie glanced at Lynette, standing on the other side of the fence with a softball bat, ready to warm up. Her free hand shielded her eyes from the sun as she stared after Annie and the new girl.

"That's the girl I told you I found snooping around in our cabin."

Lynette shrugged. "Give the girl a break, Jackie. Jeez, you're as prickly as your dad."

That stung. She was nothing like her father. It was just that her stomach had been bothering her all day, and the sun was giving her a headache. "Fine. I'll give her a chance. And you're right—she *is* tall. Wendy can put her in the lineup. Maybe she can at least bat a single and get on base. Then I'll clean up. We have to beat the Hornets. Teach 'em they don't sting as hard as they think they do."

Jackie caught her friend's eye-roll before she backed away from the fence to take some practice swings. Intent on proving Lynette wrong about her being anything like her father, Jackie dropped her mitt on top of Annie's and ran over to the two girls. She could be a team player.

"I see you brought a softball along. I hope that means you know your way around the field," she said, offering what she hoped was a sincere enough smile and nodding to the scuffed ball Kit was tossing into the air as she walked. The fact the girl didn't drop it was promising.

Kit gave her a wary look. "I've played a few games."

More than a few, by the way you handle that ball, Jackie thought, but she didn't push.

The older girls were taking the field in their brand-new mustard-colored shirts that sported a fancy logo. The previous summer that same team of girls had trounced Jackie's team, and she was humiliated. When she got home from camp last year, she'd insisted her big brother take her out to practice. She'd been able to help her softball team back home win a tournament the weekend before camp.

Would she be able to carry her camp team to victory this year?

As the trio reached their dugout, Jackie linked her fingers through the chain fence and eyed the competition. She didn't like what she saw out on the field. These didn't look like a bunch of pimply faced, flat-chested girls. While a year hadn't seemed to change the build of Jackie or her friends all that much, the Hornets, with their long, shiny ponytails hanging down their backs, looked curvier and stronger than they had last year. As they snapped their bubblegum and pounded their mitts, Jackie knew her team, made up of the twelve-year-olds in her cabin and the cabin next to theirs, was in trouble.

"Okay, girls, gather up. Thanks for hustling out here so fast, Kit," Wendy, Jackie's favorite camp counselor, said, waving them all into a tighter group. "Who's ready to have some fun?"

Jackie snorted. "I'm ready for some redemption."

Annie eyed the field, shaking her head slowly. "I don't know, Jackie. This might be a repeat. They're tough. Why can't *we* have team T-shirts? That's not fair."

Wendy shrugged. "I think one of their dads provided the shirts. But come on. Shirts don't matter. You girls know it isn't all about winning. Camp is supposed to be about making lifelong friends and enjoying nature. Now, grab your bats. Here comes Pratt. We'll start soon."

Jackie turned her back to Wendy so the older girl wouldn't see her make a gagging motion. She liked Wendy, and her happy-go-lucky attitude kept things light and fun, but the older girl still hadn't learned how important it was to win. Pratt understood. She wasn't sure if Pratt was the man's first or last name, and it didn't matter. Pratt was all about the competition. He was the one who set up all the camp games, and there were always winners and losers. Last year, when he gave blue ribbons to the cabin of girls with the best winning record and a younger camper complained about not getting a ribbon, he reminded them all that real life doesn't offer awards simply for being alive. Even though Pratt wasn't as old as Jackie's father, he was in charge of all the other counselors.

He was strict, a fact Jackie was happy about. She didn't think she could handle two weeks of annoying girl drama.

It was clear to Jackie that Wendy wasn't a fan of Pratt, even though the friendly counselor would never come right out and admit as much. Wendy's twin sister, Stella, always seemed to suck up to the boss. Jackie saw nothing wrong with that. It was never a bad idea to be friends with powerful people. At least that was what her father was always saying.

Cheers for Lynette pulled Jackie's mind back to the game at hand. "Come on, Lynette! You got this!" Jackie chimed in, clapping her hands and offering encouragement.

Her friend needed all the encouragement she could get. Lynette never even made it to first base last year. But when she stepped up to the plate and tapped the bat against her left foot before swinging it gracefully into position, Jackie felt a surge of hope. Lynette swayed ever so slightly, seeming to possess a new level of confidence as she shifted her weight from one foot to the other, waiting.

The burly pitcher pinned Lynette with a look meant to intimidate.

Jackie held her breath.

The first pitch sailed over the plate, fast and straight, thudding into the catcher's mitt.

Jackie flinched, but Lynette didn't. As the catcher tossed the ball back to the pitcher, Lynette adjusted her stance, bending her knees to crouch lower.

Lynette swung at the next pitch, connecting a tad late with the ball and sending it high above, only for it to land with a reverberating *bang* on the dugout's tin ceiling above her team's heads.

Two strikes.

Lynette flicked a stray black curl out of her eyes, resumed her position, and waited.

The pitcher, looking confident in her ability to sit her first batter down, grimaced with effort as she burned one toward the plate.

But this time Lynette was ready, and with the *crack* of the bat, Jackie was on her feet with the rest of her teammates, screaming, as the ball sailed for the surrounding pine trees and Lynette blasted toward first like a rocket.

The bubble-blowing Hornets might have come into the game with a smidge too much confidence, because by the bottom of the seventh and final inning, they were only up by two. Jackie was relieved that they weren't getting trounced, but a win was going to be tough.

Lynette was looking antsy on second, just waiting for someone to get a hit so she could score. Fran, a girl Jackie had known since kindergarten, had just struck out. Annie was in the batter's box. Jackie was pretty confident that Annie could get on base. Kit would be up after Annie, then Jackie.

Jackie bent her neck to the left then the right. Her head was pounding, and her stomach was cramping so badly she wasn't sure she'd be able to deliver a much needed hit for her team. She shouldn't have eaten that second hotdog last night. It had tasted off. But she always cleaned her plate when sitting next to Annie. The girl insisted that none of them throw perfectly good food away, stating that there were starving children in Africa.

After the first pitcher for the Hornets caught a fly on the nose, they changed pitchers. The new one lacked the same speed. Annie lopped one over the shortstop's head and raced for first, her short legs pumping fast but failing to cover much ground with each stride. The entire team held their collective breath as her left foot touched the base a heartbeat before the ball slammed into the mitt of the girl playing first.

Jackie swilled a gulp of icy water and crushed the paper cup in her hands, dropping it in the plastic barrel as she grabbed her favorite bat and took her place on deck. She accidentally bumped Kit, and the other girl's bat dropped to the ground.

"Careful," Kit spat, her eyes jumping with nerves when they met Jackie's.

"Sorry," Jackie said, barely registering the exchange. She needed to concentrate.

But as Kit straightened back up with her bat in hand, she grabbed Jackie's arm, pulling her close.

Jackie backed out of Kit's grip. "What?!"

But Kit grabbed her arm a second time and, with her lips close to Jackie's ear, hissed, "You need to go sit down."

"Are you crazy? Get out there. You're up."

The girl wasn't giving up, but she kept her voice low. "Jackie, stop. Go back into the dugout. There's blood on the inside of your thigh."

Jackie didn't understand. But Wendy was suddenly at her side, holding the towel she kept handy for wiping away disappointed tears or bloody scrapes.

"Jackie's bleeding," she heard the new girl whisper to Wendy.

Nodding, Wendy pried the bat out of Jackie's fingers.

"Time out!" Wendy yelled.

Her sister waved back. Stella was coaching the older team.

Pratt, acting as the umpire behind home plate, threw his hands up in exasperation.

Jackie noticed a look pass between Wendy and Kit, and the two stood in front of and behind her, ushering her into the relative privacy of the dugout. Their actions heightened her anxiety.

"I don't understand," she said, but a fresh wave of cramps hit and she sank onto the bench.

Kit pressed a fresh cup of water into her hand.

"Did I pass out? I don't feel so good."

The new girl bent toward her, whispering only loud enough for Jackie to hear. "No, dummy, you got your period."

Wendy sent another girl out with a bat to warm up in Jackie's place.

Horrified, Jackie met Kit's understanding gaze.

"Be cool and no one else will notice what's really happening," Kit whispered, before hurrying back out to the batter's box.

People's focus returned to the game once Wendy assured Pratt and Stella that her batter was just dizzy from the heat.

Kit hit a single.

With the game back on, the counselor took a seat next to Jackie. "You okay?"

Jackie nodded, but she felt far from okay. She'd known this would happen eventually. Why had she ignored the signs? Her mother had even tucked a supply of pads in her suitcase while they were packing on the off-chance Jackie would get her first period while away at camp.

She stole a peek at the ground beneath her, horrified at the notion that blood may be dripping between her feet even now. But there was only powdery gravel and discarded sunflower seed shells.

Another crack of the bat pulled everyone's attention to the field, and Jackie's teammates jumped to their feet, pounding on the metal chain-link fence, cheering Jackie's sub and the other runners on. The softball climbed high between center and left field. The two outfielders rushed toward it, their eyes on the sky. They crashed into each other, the ball bouncing onto the field between them. Lynette, fast as a gazelle, sailed across home base. Annie rounded third, never slowing, her short legs pumping fast.

But as the screams of her teammates filled the air, Jackie could already see from her seat on the bench that it was all going to be for nothing. One of the scrappy outfielders had already launched the ball for home, and the perfectly poised catcher would snag it before Annie could get there.

They'd come so close. They'd lost. And it was all Jackie's fault. She'd let her team down. She was the only one who could have gotten a solid enough hit to bring them all in and beat the Hornets. She'd practiced so hard.

But she'd failed.

"I'm so sorry, Wendy," Jackie whimpered as she tried to get comfortable in her bunk, a rubber hot water bottle resting against her cramping midsection. "Do they all hate me now?"

Wendy shook her head while tying the plastic bag containing Jackie's clothes that she'd offered to run through the washing machine. "Don't be ridiculous. It was a good game. Those girls are two years older than you. You knew it would be tough. And we almost won!"

"We *would* have won if I hadn't got my *period*!" Jackie bit out, averting her eyes to watch an ambitious spider weave an intricate web in the top corner of the window next to her bed. Spiders didn't scare her. Bleeding did. "Do they all know what really happened?"

"Of course not. As far as anyone else knows, you suffered from heat exhaustion out there and almost passed out. Jackie, it's ninety-two degrees today and there's no wind. Two girls on the other team had trouble with the heat themselves. And I admire your confidence, but no one likes a bragger."

Jackie adjusted the hot water bottle—Wendy had insisted it would help with the cramps—and propped her head on one hand to face her counselor again. "Yeah. I know. Sorry. And thank you for helping me, Wendy. My mom tried to tell me what to expect, and I know Lynette has been getting her period for, like, two years now, but I didn't know it would hurt like this. Man, it sucks to be a girl."

Wendy dropped the plastic bag by the door and walked over to Jackie's bunk. "I know it feels like that right now," she said, pushing a lock of Jackie's hair from her sweaty forehead. "But the aspirin I gave you will help, and the cramps will probably be better by tomorrow. Although I'm afraid you might not be able to go swimming until next week."

Jackie flopped onto her back. "I can't miss the race!"

Wendy nodded. "I know swimming is your favorite. But the race isn't until the middle of next week, and your period may have stopped by then. Or, if you like, I can talk to the nurse about showing you how to use a tampon."

A fresh wave of horror coursed through Jackie. She'd suffered enough embarrassment for one day. They'd learned about tampons and pads and periods in Life class the year before, but Jackie wasn't up for a demonstration. "No. I don't want anyone else to know."

Wendy gave Jackie a comforting pat on the arm. "I understand. And trust me, Jackie, this isn't the end of the world. In fact, it's really a miracle. It's a new beginning. You are becoming a woman. Now I need to go help in the kitchen. You girls are going to be starving after all this activity today. Will you be all right?"

Jackie wanted to groan from pain and embarrassment, but she was tougher than that. "I'm fine. Go. If supper is late, too, because of me, the girls will hate me even more."

"Oh, stop. No one hates you," Wendy said, grabbing the bag of Jackie's clothes before swinging open the door. "But you should probably thank Kit. She saved you from some embarrassment today."

Once Wendy was gone, Jackie's eyes sought the spider again. It was still busy weaving its web, oblivious to her catastrophe. Summer camp was ruined.

"This is the worst thing that could ever happen to me," Jackie seethed.

A tear leaked from the corner of her eye as she punched her pillow. Her head was feeling better, but a wave of homesickness washed over her.

"Mom, I need you."

CHAPTER SIX

K IT'S EYES FLUTTERED OPEN. It surprised her to see watery light inching into the room around the checkered curtains that hung from the windows, chasing shadows back into the far corners. Lumps on the other beds meant she wasn't alone. Plus, someone was snoring. No one else appeared to be awake yet. Despite the early hour, the air in the cabin already felt heavy and hot. Thunder rumbled off in the distance. Kit kicked her legs out from under the flowered top sheet, wishing for a breeze to stir the curtains Wendy had pulled shut over their open windows the night before, but the fabric hung as straight as a door.

Falling asleep had turned out to be easier than she'd expected. This place wasn't as bad as the group facility they'd tossed her in after removing her and her little brothers from their mother's care.

She'd been dead beat by the time a trumpet blared to signify the end of their first day. Her emotional arrival at camp, softball under a blazing sun, an impromptu water fight to cool off, and dinner in a noisy mess hall had all combined to wipe her out. When Wendy finally shooed them all toward the showers, Kit could have hugged her.

The bathroom was constructed of white cinder blocks, and its tiny stalls sectioned off with flimsy plastic shower curtains offered minimal privacy. Kit hated the way the curtains provided a peekaboo show of sorts, but the cool stream of water proved refreshing. She did her best to ignore the hum of mosquitos, easy to spot against the sea of white.

Jackie had joined the other six girls of Cabin 7 to eat, but begged off when it came time to shower. Kit guessed she'd showered earlier, after leaving the game. By the time the rest of the girls returned to the cabin, Jackie was back in her bunk, covers pulled up to her chin.

When the other girls pressed her, Jackie insisted she got overheated and her head still hurt. Kit didn't understand what the big deal was about getting her period. Obviously, based on the way she was acting, this must be Jackie's first. Kit had been dealing with hers almost every month for a year and was pretty regular now. Her mother said most of the girls in their family developed early.

Some others in their cabin probably had their periods by now, too. It was simple biology. Not something to be ashamed of, or scared of. Although Kit realized Jackie was probably missing her mom right about now.

Not that Kit missed her own mother, even though she hadn't seen her mother for more than ten whole minutes in the past six weeks. Why should she bother to miss someone who always reminded her and her two younger brothers that she was just never cut out to be a mother?

Kit couldn't argue that point.

At least she'd had her father. He was the more capable parent of the two.

But that all changed after the accident.

She gazed around at the sleeping mounds of the other campers, doubting any of them had a father in prison. They probably all came from families with two-point-five kids and both parents still in the picture.

Kit's family picture had looked like that, too, once upon a time. But looks can be deceiving. She could barely remember a time when her mother wasn't painfully unhappy, often drinking by breakfast. By midday, she'd be falling-down drunk.

After multiple instances in the last two years of almost losing Kit and her brothers permanently to the foster care system, her mother finally convinced her own parents to take the kids so she could get help.

A tiny part of Kit always wanted to believe her mother loved her and wanted to overcome her addictions, but she knew better.

But then it was her *father* wasting away in a jail cell for killing someone while drunk behind the wheel. She'd never once seen him drunk. It made little sense.

Kit hated that she'd dared get her hopes up again when her mother left them with her grandparents to go to treatment, praying this would be the time she'd clean up her act. If her mother could stay away from the booze, Kit could go back to her old school, their old house. She didn't even know if her grandparents were in touch with their daughter while she was at the treatment facility.

No one told Kit anything.

Until yesterday morning, as she was begrudgingly preparing to leave for summer camp. Looking back now, she couldn't believe the shock she'd felt finding her mother at the door, reeking of alcohol and begging her parents to let her come inside.

Why was she surprised? Her mother never kept her promises.

Kit cringed, remembering the awful scene. It got so loud that a neighbor had called the police. If any of her fellow campers found out the real reason she was late getting to camp, she'd be mortified.

Not that she cared what any of them thought of her.

It wasn't like they were her friends.

It was yet one more betrayal in a long string of them. Kit couldn't give that woman any more second chances. It hurt too much when her mom flaked out. And she always flaked out. Yesterday was proof of that.

The blare of a trumpet, bookending their first night, caused her to bolt upright and nearly smack her head on the ceiling. The rhythmic snores cut off with a cough and a groan, and the bulges on the beds slowly came back to life.

The cabin door swung open and Wendy entered, looking fresh and much too peppy for this heat and the early hour. Kit had thought the counselor was still asleep in the bunk below her.

"When did you get up?"

"An hour ago. And I've got a surprise for you all . . . banana and chocolate chip pancakes! But if you don't hurry, they'll be gone! And one more thing. Wear your tennies this morning."

Kit's stomach rumbled. She missed the mouthwatering pancakes her dad used to make.

Chaos ensued on the heels of Wendy's announcement.

At this rate, Kit wouldn't get any reading done.

Kit tossed her napkin onto her empty plate. It stuck to smears of sticky syrup. Either the camp cook had a pancake recipe that rivaled her father's, or it had been too long since she'd eaten a plate of his fluffy concoctions. Despite Wendy's warning, there'd been plenty, and she was feeling comfortably stuffed after seconds.

Breakfast in the narrow, log-sided hall was a far cry from the light-in-fused, tension-filled breakfast nook of her youth. Back then no one dared make too much noise, regardless of how many funny faces her father made or how hard he tickled them, because her mother was always either fighting a hangover or starting on a new one. A mimosa was her usual weapon of choice.

The mess hall pulsed with noise and laughter. Her mother would have hated it. Kit wasn't sure how she felt about it herself.

"Is this the first time you've come to a camp like this?" the girl across the scarred wooden tabletop asked.

"It's that obvious, huh? You're Renee, right?"

The girl nodded. "Right. This is my first camp, too. Well, kind of. I've stayed at a lake with my family before, but it was nothing like this."

"It's intense," Kit said, looking around. "I thought I'd hate it. And I kind of do. But I promised my grandma I'd try to be a good sport about it."

"I know what you mean. I was so disappointed when my dad couldn't get time off this year for all of us to go back to my aunt's resort. He felt guilty and thought this might be the next best thing for me."

Kit downed the rest of her orange juice, even though it was already lukewarm in the early morning heat. "I know it's only been one day, but what do you think so far? Was he right?"

The girl shrugged, brushing her feathered bangs back from where they kept falling over her right eye. "I don't know anyone."

This surprised Kit. "I guess I thought everyone in our cabin went to school together besides me. Ruby Shores is only ten minutes from here. Wendy mentioned that most of the kids live there when I checked in yesterday. I think she was trying to make me feel better. I told her we just moved there in June after school got out."

Renee tapped her fork against the tabletop. "I don't think Dad realized most of the other girls would already know each other when he signed me up. He's a teacher, and he found out about this camp through his school connections. He knows Jackie's dad through work. You know, Jackie, from our cabin?"

Kit nodded, although she barely knew her, of course.

"Most summer camps fill up early. Our trip to my aunt's resort got canceled kind of last minute. But because Dad knows Mr. Turner, they pulled some strings and got me in. I'm not sure yet if all this was such a good idea," Renee said, motioning toward the rest of the campers at their long table.

Kit picked at her napkin, tearing it when part of it remained stuck to the plate. "Do you know if the others in our cabin are all in school together?"

"Yeah, they are. Well, kind of," Renee said, pushing a piece of bacon fat around on her plate. "I sat next to Nancy at supper last night and she filled me in. She's twelve, but she's one class behind the rest of them. All five of them go to the same school. She thinks Jackie, Annie, and Fran have gone to school together for forever. Lynette is a little newer to town, but she's lived in Ruby Shores for at least a couple of years."

"That explains why they all seem kind of tight."

A shrill whistle cut through their conversation. The umpire from their softball game stood in the center of the room, clipboard in hand. Kit thought his name was Pratt.

"Quiet! Quiet down, ladies! Now that we have everyone jacked up on sugar and carbs, we'll be spending the morning on our annual hike. Hope everyone remembered their hiking boots!"

Kit exchanged a worried look with Renee. "Hiking boots? Wendy said to wear our tennies."

"I'm sure he's kidding," she said, but she didn't look convinced.

"I said quiet!" the middle-aged man yelled when the energetic clusters of girls failed to give him their full attention.

Jackie, sitting near the center of their table, shushed them with a slap on the table and a stern glare.

"Who does she think she is?" Kit whispered, bending forward toward Renee. "The camp police?"

Renee giggled but lowered her eyes.

"The buses are ready and waiting, so if all you prima donnas are ready to cooperate, we'll be on our way shortly. Wait for your table to be excused, scrape your plates, then head for the parking lot. Oh, and for God's sake, use the bathrooms on your way out if need be. All you'll find at the nature conservancy where we'll be hiking this morning are primitive outhouses. Last year I almost had to send a girl home when she had a breakdown over having to use an outhouse."

Kit felt torn over Pratt's announcement. "Wonder what kind of nature we'll see? It must be a semi decent place if they're going to the trouble of bussing us there."

Renee finished her apple juice. "I hope they have water for us. It's so hot already. I could even tolerate an outhouse if it meant we wouldn't die of thirst."

Kit pushed back from the table. "Where does he get off treating us all like a bunch of whimpering girls?"

"I agree." Renee stood when Wendy motioned for their table to file out. "Let's go make the most of this, and vow to only complain to each other if it sucks. We don't want to prove him right."

Kit liked Renee. She followed her to the oversized trash bins so they could scrape their breakfast plates. Unlike the outspoken Jackie, or even the flaky Lynette, Renee didn't seem to seek drama. Too bad she wouldn't be in her class come September. She had a feeling she was going to need a friend or two.

Kit fell back a step when Lynette cut in line, wedging her body in behind Renee as they all jostled their way toward one of three buses. Dismayed, she watched as the dark-haired girl plopped into the seat next to Renee. Just when she felt like she was getting to know one person at this stupid camp, Lynette—a girl with plenty of other friends—zeroed in on Renee.

Seats were filling up fast, and someone bumped Kit from behind, shoving her forward. She grabbed the back of the seat behind Lynette's head to hold her ground and caught Jackie's eye. The spot next to her was still empty. Kit considered grabbing it, but wasn't sure she'd be welcome.

Jackie glanced behind Kit toward the stream of girls still entering the bus, then tapped the seat next to her. "Quick. Sit here."

Relatively sure Jackie was speaking to her, Kit spun and grabbed the spot, deciding a bus trip next to her wouldn't be as bad as striking up yet another conversation with a complete stranger. Besides, Jackie owed her.

"Hey," she said, knotting the arms of her light jacket tighter around her waist. Despite the heat, storm clouds on the horizon hinted at the possibility of a welcome rain shower.

"Thank God," Jackie said, gathering her shoulder-length hair into a ponytail with the neon-colored scrunchy she pulled from her wrist. "If I have to listen to Fran blather on about how amazing it'll be when we all start junior high this fall, I'll throw up."

Kit caught the glare Fran gave her as she passed by, heading for one of the few remaining seats in the back.

"You don't like Fran?"

Jackie shook her head. "A little of Fran goes a long way. We got stuck on the same softball team this summer, and she thought that made us besties again. Sharing our cabin with her is almost more than I can stand."

"But I heard you and Annie and Fran are best friends."

Jackie snorted, then stood to wrestle the top window down next to her seat, lowering it a few inches. The girls opposite them took note and mirrored Jackie's actions. Kit had to admit, the resulting breeze felt wonderful.

Their green pleather seat expelled a musty puff of air when Jackie dropped back down next to her. "I suppose you could call me and Annie and *Lynette* besties, but not *Fran*. We aren't good enough for her most of the time. All she cares about is being part of the popular group at school. She only wants to hang out with us when she doesn't have a better option. Plus, she's a complete jerk to my friend Owen."

Kit did her best to follow Jackie's tirade, wanting to understand the dynamics at play around her, but another part of her brain remembered her vow to not get sucked into girl drama.

Lynette may have heard Jackie's comment about besties, because she glanced back at them and smiled. Kit could feel herself smiling back, despite her irritation with Lynette for butting in line. While Kit still hadn't decided whether she liked Jackie, given her forceful personality and bossy attitude, Lynette was different. She didn't put Kit on edge. She seemed like a genuinely nice person, even if she acted a little spacey. Kit even suspected it had been Lynette she'd heard gently weeping right before she dozed off the night before. Someone was homesick, and the sound had seemed to come from Lynette's bunk.

Kit sighed. Drama was probably going to be unavoidable during her camp experience. She turned her attention back to Jackie. "Did you say Owen? Is he your boyfriend?"

Jackie tightened her bushy ponytail. "No. I'm not allowed to date until I'm fourteen. But it's not like that with Owen. He's like another brother to me. Ronnie's my actual brother, but he's so busy with all his sports, and he's four years older, so he doesn't have time for me."

"Does Owen live by you?"

"He lives a few blocks away. He's just fun, you know? And he's super smart, so he's always helping me with my homework."

"So, he's a boy, but he's not really boyfriend material," Kit said, curious. Her mom always told her boys didn't make good friends. "Is he ugly?"

Jackie stared at Kit, frowning. "Why does it matter what he looks like? He's my friend. I always know I can count on him to do what he says. He's got my back. Who cares what he looks like?"

Kit shrugged. "I'm sorry. He sounds great. Don't be mad. My mom just always told me that boys are only good for one thing, and it isn't friendship."

A smile tugged at one corner of Jackie's mouth. "Your mom did *not* say that. Did she?"

"I think Mom sometimes forgets I'm just a kid. She tells me things she probably shouldn't."

Jackie leaned closer, lowering her voice. "Do you think she meant men are only good for *sex?*"

Kit felt her cheeks flame. "I think she meant money. At least that's what I'm going to keep telling myself. I don't even want to think about sex and my mom in the same sentence."

Shivering, Jackie nodded. "Yeah, I get that. I like to believe the stork dropped me and Ronnie off in our backyard. What's your dad like?"

"He's not around," Kit said, frantic to come up with a new topic. She had no intention of telling anyone the truth about her father. "Feeling better today? I know I usually feel better after the first day."

It was Jackie's turn to blush. "I suppose. And I should probably thank you for yesterday. You didn't tell anybody, right?"

"No, I didn't say anything. It's not a big deal, you know. The way the human body works is pretty amazing. Especially for girls. Don't let it embarrass you."

"It's not feeling so amazing right now," Jackie said, turning to gaze at the blur of trees rushing by. "It feels like I have a pillow stuck between my legs. And my stomach still hurts a little, but not as much as yesterday."

"Yeah, that part sucks. But you'll be good as new in a few days."

"Until the next time."

Lynette spun around to face them. "What are you two whispering about? You sound way too serious. Hey, Jackie, do you think that cute park ranger will be there today?"

The bus bounced over a rough patch of road, and Kit felt herself lift an inch off the seat before slamming back down again. "Are we even sure we'll make it to where we're going?"

"We'll make it. The road is just super bumpy." Lynette grinned. "Remember how that little girl threw up on the drive back to camp last year?"

Jackie moaned, holding a hand to her lower stomach.

"Is there something you want to tell us, Jackie?" Lynette asked, a suspicious glint in her eyes. "Or is the heat still bothering you?"

Before Jackie could respond the bus jolted again, but this time there was a tilt to it. The wheels were slipping off the gravel road. Frightened screeches erupted up front. Kit sat tall in her seat, trying to get a glimpse of what was happening. She saw their driver turn the oversized steering wheel hard to the right.

It wasn't enough.

The bus shuddered, then stopped, kids bouncing forward against the seats in front of them. Two or three even tumbled into the aisle a few rows back from the front.

"What happened?" a girlish voice hollered from the back of the bus.

Wendy popped up, hauling a fallen girl to her feet, motioning for her to take her seat again. "I think this might be the end of the road for now, ladies. The gravel is soft from too much rain. We're only about half a mile from the science center, so grab your jacket if you brought one. We'll walk the rest of the way."

Her order generated a mixture of whines and whoops. Kit didn't mind walking if it meant getting out of this stuffy bus. She stood, glancing out the window at the water pooled in the ditch.

"This might be a buggy, muddy mess," she muttered.

But before she could get too discouraged, a doe peeked out from behind a large pine. The graceful animal looked right at her, ears twitching. Kit held her breath, expecting the animal to bolt, but instead she took three graceful steps toward the ponded water in the ditch, dipping her head to drink. It wasn't until the screech of the bus door cut through the din of excitement that the doe's head shot up, her large, tan body taut with awareness. She looked straight at Kit again, gave a quick head bob and bleat, then spun on her hoofs and trotted back into the camouflage offered by the surrounding brush.

No one else gave any sign they'd spied the doe.

The animal reminded Kit of the many times she'd watched *Bambi* as a little girl with her father. A shudder passed through her as she remembered the fate of Bambi's mother. But this was a refuge, land specifically set aside for the safety of animals like that doe. She may even have her own fawn nearby.

Kit realized in that moment that these two weeks at summer camp could be a refuge for her, too; a place where she could forget about her shattered family, if only for fourteen days.

CHAPTER SEVEN

J ACKIE CAUGHT A GLIMPSE of Annie's lime-green T-shirt in the press of girls exiting one of the two buses that didn't get stuck on the side of the road. The counselors on those buses must have kept the lucky campers in their seats until the sorry saps from the bus mired in the mud could catch up on foot.

"Annie! Wait up!"

Annie must have heard her, because she stepped out of the group of girls and stood under the black RUBY SHORES PUBLIC SCHOOL lettering on the side of the bus. Jackie grinned as Annie jumped up and down, her head temporarily blocking Ruby as she struggled to find Jackie in the crowd. Annie could get impressive height, and might have been a prime recruit for their seventh-grade basketball team if she'd been anywhere near five feet tall. Not that Annie wanted to play basketball. She was the town's star gymnast, spending as much time at the gym as Jackie's brother did on the football field. Annie probably wouldn't get her first period until she was fifteen. She still looked like a little kid—at least until her ripped abs and long, lean muscles in her arms and legs were on display when she wore her bikini. She could even get away without wearing a bra when she wanted to.

Finally, Annie spied her, waving her over.

"Why weren't you on our bus?" Jackie asked, jogging over to her friend.

"The stupid girls in Stella's cabin were so lazy." Stella oversaw the other cabin of twelve-year-olds. "Some of them didn't even scrape their trays before leaving the mess hall. Can you believe that?"

"I can believe it. Some of them are spoiled brats. But what does that have to do with you?"

"I couldn't very well leave Stella and Wendy to clean it all up by themselves."

Jackie dropped her head, dismayed. "Annie, Stella and Wendy work here. Cleaning up messes is their *job*. Should the brats have put their own dishes away? Of course. But the fact they didn't was not your problem to solve."

Annie shrugged. "I just didn't think it was fair, so I helped. No big deal. But by the time I got out to the buses, the other two were full."

Jackie caught sight of the counselor for the youngest campers as she stepped off the bus. "You probably fit right in with the ten-year-olds," she teased.

Annie punched her in the arm, hard. "Shut up, Jackie. They're harmless kids. But someone needs to explain the value of deodorant to them. Besides, I bet none of them are missing out on swimming at camp because they got their period."

Jackie froze. "You know?"

Annie shrugged again and looped her arm through Jackie's, forcing her to turn toward the science center. She may look like she was ten, but Annie was probably stronger than most of the Hornets they'd almost beat in softball the day before. "Jackie, I've known you your whole life. Sunshine never bothers you. Besides, it's bound to happen to all of us some day. Now, come on. If I get stuck in the back at the presentation inside, I won't be able to see a thing."

Relieved that Annie knew her secret and trusting her oldest friend not to say anything, Jackie allowed herself to be dragged toward the flat-roofed building ahead. She knew from last year's visit that it would be cool and dark inside, and she hoped they'd learn something interesting again. Last year's presentation about wolves had been pretty neat.

Once inside, Annie said, "Lynette hopes that cute park ranger will be here again this year. Let's go find her."

Someone yelled their names, and Annie changed direction. "There's Wendy and the rest of our group! Come on!"

"Ladies, you know better than to go off on your own. I thought I'd lost you," Wendy said, waving them over.

"Sorry. I needed to find Annie."

Wendy's nod told Jackie she wasn't mad. "Hey, thanks again for helping clean up after breakfast, Annie. Sorry you had to ride on a different bus. Let's stand over in this front corner so everyone can see."

When Jackie snorted, Annie elbowed her in the ribs. "Shut up or I'll tell everyone your secret," she threatened, but Jackie knew she'd never do that. They both had secrets about each other that they'd sworn they'd take to their graves.

Because that's what best friends do.

Lynette was craning her neck, which meant, Jackie knew, that she was trying to see who would give today's presentation. That was always how they kicked off their hikes through the preserve. Someone started chanting when the overhead lights clicked off. A cloak of shadows dropped over the throngs of girls. Spotlights lit the makeshift stage area that spanned the front third of the room. Red ropes further delineated the area. It took a second for Jackie to decipher what they were chanting as more and more girls joined in, clapping their hands.

"Justin! Justin! Justin!"

Leading the chant was a group of older girls, no longer wearing their Hornets T-shirts but still recognizable by their long, flowing ponytails, and sunglasses perched on the tops of their heads.

"Sounds like Lynette isn't the only one hoping that cute ranger, Justin, is going to talk to us again today," Jackie said, her voice raised so Annie would hear her.

A woman stepped into the light with her hands raised to the crowd of rowdy girls. The screech of a whistle sounded, and the girls quieted. Even though they couldn't see him in the dark, they recognized Pratt's order to quiet down.

"I'd like to welcome all of you lovely ladies from Camp Barefoot to the Habitats Nature Preserve! I'm sorry to disappoint, but the illustrious Ranger Justin has moved on to a new gig, working with the wolves in far northern Minnesota. You get *me* today—Ranger Ruth."

The disappointed moans of the crowd nearly drowned out her last sentence. Somewhere in the darkness, Pratt's whistle issued two short blasts, quickly settling the group again.

"Poor Stella," Wendy laughed, pointing a finger at her twin in the far front corner of the room.

Jackie giggled. "Stella might have been the only one who had a chance with Ranger Justin."

A different, shriller whistle cut through the noise, pulling everyone's attention to the front once more, where Ranger Ruth stood with two fingers jammed in her mouth, her face red with exertion. When all was quiet, she dropped her hand and grinned.

"Now, why don't we get down to business? Mother Nature seems to be a little ornery today, and I don't want you getting caught out on the trails in a downpour."

"Maybe Mother Nature is on her period, too," someone whispered in Jackie's ear from behind, the words hot against the side of her face. She glanced back, relieved to see it was just Kit, the new girl. Her teasing grin told Jackie her secret was still safe with her. "Sounds like I missed out, not getting to see this Justin guy last year."

Wendy shushed them, and Jackie turned to face the front again, curious what the older woman, looking official in her tan uniform and ranger hat, planned to tell them about. Based on the steel-gray curls, bursting out from under her hat, and the wrinkles lining her face, the woman probably had forty years on Justin, but she was handling the noisy girls with style.

"Did any of you notice any butterflies as you walked in today?" the woman began, and a few mutters in the affirmative floated toward her from the crowd. She nodded. "Good. And if you didn't notice any, it's because you weren't *looking* for them. I hope the things you learn today will make you much more aware of these amazing creatures."

Jackie shifted her weight from left to right, noticing the glass-fronted cabinet next to the ranger. Bright-orange butterflies fluttered around inside, popping in and out of view, sometimes hidden behind branches and leaves. Someone had built a habitat of sorts inside the cabinet.

"I'm going to share some fascinating facts with you, and then I'll turn you loose. I hope each of you will find examples of these butterflies in all their different life stages, as well as the things they eat, and even what they disappear into when transitioning from caterpillars. How does that sound?"

A few random claps were all the encouragement the ranger needed to proceed. She bent toward the cabinet, opened a small wooden door in the top, slowly put her hand inside, then pulled it back, with a colorful orange and black butterfly standing on the pointer finger she'd recently used to issue her whistle.

Enthralled now, Jackie held her breath, afraid the fragile insect would flitter up and away into the darkness. But the butterfly remained there as Ruth kept her finger suspended a few inches above her head.

"Monarchs are the only butterflies in North America that migrate south in the autumn to avoid colder temperatures," Ranger Ruth began. "The monarchs in Minnesota travel all the way down to the Sierra Madre mountains, west of Mexico City."

"That's a long way," Wendy said, loud enough for the ranger to hear. Jackie knew they encouraged the counselors to ask questions and interact with the staff at the Habitats so the campers would warm up to the idea of making this an interactive presentation instead of a lecture.

"Indeed, it is. They'll travel approximately three thousand miles, always taking the same route, helped along by natural air currents and moving as fast as thirty miles an hour. They migrate in large groups, often referred to as 'swarms.' "

"That's faster than my grandpa drives," Kit whispered from behind, and Jackie had to bite her lip to keep from giggling.

"How do they find their way?" someone asked.

Ranger Ruth nodded. "Good question. It's not like they can carry a map in their pockets, can they?"

This question elicited a few chuckles—and moans. The butterfly on the ranger's finger fluttered up to hover above the cabinet, but then floated back to her finger again.

"Scientists believe these little beauties follow the positioning of the sun and the earth's magnetic field. It's somewhat of a mystery, but isn't that part of the beauty of nature?"

Jackie caught herself nodding. She'd never given much thought to butterflies, other than that they were pretty and free.

"These large swarms of butterflies travel at night, and often roost in trees by the thousands during the day. If you ever witness this phenomenon, it'll leave you breathless. The theory is they travel in such sizeable groups for a few different reasons. One is probably for warmth, and another is the simple fact that there is always safety in numbers."

The ranger paused, letting the information sink in.

"How far do they travel in a day?" a male voice asked.

Even Pratt finds this interesting, Jackie thought. She'd been wondering the same thing.

"As far as fifty or even one hundred miles a day," Ruth answered. "Their scientific name is *danaus plexippus*."

A girl a few feet to Jackie's left, standing along the red rope, raised her hand. When the ranger nodded at her, the girl cleared her throat. "So the butterfly on your finger flew all the way to Mexico last winter, then came all the way back here when it got warm out again?"

"Not exactly," the ranger said, softening her answer with a smile. "It's quite complicated, but most of these butterflies only have a lifespan of about one month. I'll explain how that month plays out in a moment. There can actually be three, sometimes even four, different groups of butterflies born in Minnesota each summer. Only the last swarm, born later in the summer, goes through a special process called 'diapause.' That process slows down their metabolism, allowing them to live much longer so they can reach Mexico before they reproduce and die off. All that is probably too much to get into today, but if you are curious, be sure to take your science courses in high school, where you can learn lots more on the topic."

The ranger's butterfly took flight again, but this time, just as Jackie had feared, it disappeared into the darkness. Unconcerned, the ranger stepped away from the cabinet toward a small pedestal table that held various plants. Jackie noticed, somewhere far off in the distance, a low rumble of thunder. The ranger must have heard it, too.

"I better keep moving. I still want to fill you in on what butterflies eat, and give you a quick rundown on the process of metamorphosis."

Jackie recognized the term, but was eager to hear this knowledgeable woman's version of how a caterpillar transforms into a butterfly. The ranger held up a large glass jar with holes poked in its lid. It looked like the huge pickle jars the lunch ladies served from in the cafeteria in grade school. The image made Jackie think how much she was hoping the food would be better at the junior high.

"If you look closely, you can see what is called a *chrysalis* hanging from this branch," the ranger said, holding the jar higher so more people might see. "I found this example on one of the nature paths this morning."

"Is there a *butterfly* in there?" a younger girl asked, straining against the red rope for a better look.

The ranger laughed. "Kind of. If you'll give me a minute, I'll explain how it works."

The girl nodded, never taking her eyes off the jar.

"The butterfly I was holding earlier was actually a male. You probably couldn't see from where you are standing, but he had a black scent gland on both of his back wings. A female doesn't have those. A mature female butterfly will lay lots of eggs, sometimes as many as four hundred. The eggs are white and no bigger than the tip of a pencil. Within a couple days an egg will hatch and a tiny caterpillar will emerge. You can recognize it by its yellow, white, and black stripes. It will actually eat its own shell. The only thing it eats after that is a plant called milkweed. A caterpillar can grow to two inches long. Then it will build its own little house, called a chrysalis. Like this."

Everyone strained to see the contents of the glass jar.

"It builds the house by attaching it to the underside of a branch or leaf, and it hangs upside down for five days. During that time the caterpillar's body is enduring massive changes. Again, I could get more technical, but I don't really have time to go into detail today."

Kit bumped Jackie in the shoulder with her arm. "See? It's like I was saying," she whispered. "Simple biology. We aren't so different from butterflies. Our bodies go through big changes, too. It's nothing to be embarrassed about."

"Good point," Jackie whispered back, surprised by Kit's insight.

"For those of you in the back, the chrysalis is made of a shiny, light-green silk. When I'm finished with the presentation, you can stop up here and have a look so you know what to watch for when I turn you loose."

Above, a soft tapping on the roof caught Jackie's attention. It was raining. While she'd dreaded today's hike when her cramps were at their worst, now she was excited to head out onto the trails to search for signs of the butterflies. Hopefully the worst of the weather would hold off so they could go out.

The ranger glanced up, too, then set the jar on the table. She picked up a black pot with an unusual plant in it. Jackie recognized that kind of pot from the nursery where she always went with her mom in the spring to pick out flowers for their front porch.

"This is milkweed. Do you remember how I said milkweed was the only plant this type of caterpillar will eat? That's why these plants are so important to the butterfly ecosystem. Some people think it's a weed, and admittedly it can spread easily and cause problems for farmers, but if you get rid of the milkweed, you essentially get rid of butterflies."

Kit had stepped forward and was standing side by side with Jackie. She noticed the taller girl nodding, as if she was also getting a lot out of the presentation.

"This is pretty cool, isn't it?" Jackie whispered.

Kit didn't even look her way, her eyes trained on the ranger. "Fascinating," she whispered back.

After the ranger explained more about the milkweed, and the seeds inside the pods that grew on the plant, she got back to the most important part—at least in Jackie's opinion.

"After about five days, the caterpillar has transformed into what is called a *pupa*. When it breaks free of the chrysalis, it is finally in the ultimate form of the butterfly, and it will live for another few weeks. All in all, as I said before, the butterfly lives for about a month. Except for the special batch that flies all the way to Mexico."

"What do the adult butterflies eat?" Wendy's twin sister, Stella, asked.

"The butterflies suck nectar from flowers. Nectar is about twenty percent sugar, which gives them energy."

Wendy laughed. "Kind of like the way we fed all of you plenty of pancakes and syrup this morning so you'd have energy for today!"

Amid soft laughter, the ranger paused again, tilting her head to listen. Nodding in satisfaction, she put the milkweed plant back on the table and rubbed her hands together.

"It sounds like the rain has stopped for now, so I think I better wrap this up and not push our luck. I'm told many of you have been here before, but I still need to give you a rundown on what is, and isn't, allowed on the trails."

Jackie only listened with half an ear, straining to see the tiny caterpillar house the ranger claimed was inside the jar. A glare from the spotlights reflected off the glass jar, making it impossible to see anything inside other than a bunch of twigs and leaves.

People were getting restless, so the ranger gave another of her finger whistles. "I know. It's getting hot in here, and you want to get outside. Here's your assignment. I want each of you to find examples of the striped caterpillar and chrysalis. Keep your eyes open for any group-ings of monarchs, in addition to single insects. Look near bunches of milkweed. You'll recognize the plants by their pinkish flowers. Your counselors will talk with you about what you find, during your bus trips back to camp. We have another group coming through here in an hour—otherwise I'd have loved to talk with you after you explore on the trails."

Girls started turning toward the exits, but the ranger gave one last whistle.

"Ladies! Before you go, pay attention. The most important rule of the day is 'do not touch'! Look, but don't touch! Got it? And stay with your groups. We don't need anyone getting lost out there."

CHAPTER EIGHT

W ENDY LED HER GIRLS toward the trail on the far western edge of the Habitats. "It's rougher going, but that means there isn't as much activity and we might see more wildlife."

No one argued. The brief shower that had moved through during the ranger's presentation had cooled the air, and once they got outside they coated themselves with bug spray.

Jackie took a deep breath, thankful for the fresh air. Her stomach didn't hurt anymore, and she really wanted to find examples of those little caterpillar houses. She couldn't remember the official name for them, but she'd inspected the jar before heading outside, so she thought she knew what to look for.

Kit seemed committed to their nature-based treasure hunt, too. "Come on. It looks like Wendy's sister and the girls from her cabin are heading this way. I want to stay ahead of them."

Jackie glanced back, seeing Fran's face among Stella's crew. She'd rather stay ahead of the other girls, too.

"Mind if we scoot ahead, Wendy?" Jackie asked, picking up the pace.

"Just stay where I can still see you."

"We will," both girls promised in unison as they brushed past the rest of their group.

In no time, Jackie spotted what looked like milkweed growing along the tree line up ahead. "There!" Jogging ahead, she made a beeline for the plant with the pink flowers.

Kit easily kept up, her longer legs covering more ground with each stride. "That does look like milkweed," she agreed, sliding to a stop and bending at the waist for a closer look. She reached a hand toward the pink flowers.

"Stop! We aren't supposed to touch, remember?"

"Fine," she said, dropping onto her bottom in the dirt to look at the plant from a lower angle. "I want to see if any of those little caterpillar deals are hanging from it."

Jackie knelt beside her, looking under the bushy flower tops, too. "Wow. There's at least three of them hanging under here!"

"Yep. Sure are." As Kit scooted closer, she slapped a spindly branch out of the way and her hand caught on a leaf, accidentally pulling it off the milkweed plant. "Oops. Didn't mean to do that." She held up the leaf, inspecting the underside. "Didn't the ranger say the monarch eggs are white and tiny? Do you think this might be one?"

Grabbing Kit's wrist so she could see, Jackie held the leaf closer. "I'm almost sure it is."

"Find anything?" Annie asked, dropping onto the ground next to them.

As Jackie pointed out the milkweed plant to Annie, she noticed Kit tuck the leaf with the egg on it under a clump of grass and another milkweed plant. Smart girl, not wanting to get in trouble if Wendy caught her holding a leaf. The egg might survive down there, too.

The rest of their friends caught up with them.

Lynette pointed toward a trio of fluttering butterflies above their heads. "My mom believes butterflies carry wishes and prayers to the Great Spirit."

Jackie stood, brushing dirt and grass from her knees. She spotted the butterflies Lynette and Renee were watching; the colorful wings of the insects stood out against the greens of tall bushes and stubby trees. "The Great Spirit? Like, God?"

Lynette inched closer to the trees, looking for more butterflies in the leaves. "I don't think so. Mom said it was Native American lore."

"I like that idea," Renee said, nudging a nearby milkweed plant with the toe of her tennis shoe. She jumped back with a giggle when two white butterflies danced out of it. "Guess it isn't just monarchs that like milkweed."

"What are you girls finding?" Wendy asked as she reached them, tapping a short stick that rattled with dry leaves against her thigh. "Anything interesting?"

A flash of movement behind the counselor caught Jackie's eye. Stella's girls were gaining on them. A gust of wind whipped strands of hair from her ponytail across her face. They needed to keep moving. "Lots! And we'll tell you all about it. But we still have more trail to see and I think the rain might start up again, so we better keep moving. We'll tell you all about it on the bus."

Wendy nodded, studying the sky. "You may be right. Maybe we should turn back the way we came. I hate to get too far away from the bus if we get hit with a storm."

That meant meeting up with Fran and the others. It was more fun to keep trying to avoid the other group. It felt like a game. "Don't be a wuss,

Wendy. We won't *melt*. I haven't heard any thunder since we came back outside. Please, can we keep going?"

Wendy glanced between Jackie, the cloud bank moving in, and back at Stella, now less than a hundred yards behind them. "Think we should go back?" she called out to her sister.

"Nah," Stella yelled. "We'll be fine! It's nice right now."

Wendy didn't look convinced, but she conceded. "All right, but if we want to get all the way through, why don't we jog? I bet we'll find a bunch of butterflies in that field about a quarter of a mile ahead. Last year it was full of wildflowers."

"Sounds good," Lynette said, turning and taking off at a slow jog. "I hope we see a blue butterfly, too. Mom says those have extra magic!"

Renee laughed, running away with Lynette, while Annie and Wendy were close on their heels. While Nancy bent to tie her shoe, Jackie turned to Kit. "Let's go!"

Kit looked up from where she still sat next to the milkweed plants. "Go? Why? There's plenty to see here."

"Jackie, wait up!" Fran yelled.

Giggling, Jackie nudged Kit on the shoulder. "Come on, we have to stay ahead of them!"

Awareness dawned on Kit and she sprang to her feet. They sprinted toward Wendy and the others, laughing. If Nancy wanted to keep up with them, she'd have to hurry.

"That was a good idea to check the field of wildflowers, Wendy," Lynette said as they headed back toward the parking lot. "I bet no one else found as many butterflies as we did. There had to be at least a hundred of them in the one tree alone!"

Kit stopped, then looking around said, "Didn't we come from that way?"

"We did. This is a shortcut," Jackie replied. "Don't worry. Wendy knows her way around here. She's been here lots of times. But be careful. It does skirt alongside this one low area that sometimes floods, and with all the rain we've had, it's probably full. Lynette named it Black Cat Pond last year."

They walked on in silence, a few yards behind Wendy and the others. Kit seemed to be watching for something.

"What's the matter? Are you afraid Big Foot is out here, hiding in the trees?" Jackie teased.

"There's no such thing as Big Foot."

Jackie spotted a flat rock, about the size of her hand, and picked it up. She'd skip it across the pond if it was full of water. "I know. But you're looking for something."

"Just a doe. I saw her when we got off the bus. I hoped I'd see her again. Hey, what's the deal with Lynette? Is she into witches or something? She keeps talking about magic and stuff."

Jackie laughed. "Yeah, I guess she kind of is. Her mom is, too. I think her mom studied different religions and beliefs of different societies in college. I don't really think much of it anymore. That's just how Lynette is."

"Magic is silly, if you ask me. I much prefer cold, hard facts. I want to be a scientist."

Given the conviction in Kit's voice, Jackie decided not to argue about it. Personally, she thought Lynette's openness to different ideas, like the possibility of magic and spirits, was what made her friend so interesting.

The faint path under their feet angled to the right, and Jackie recognized the massive, ancient oak tree ahead. "Down there is Black Cat Pool." She pointed. "And I hear splashing. We'll have to walk through water."

Up ahead, Wendy and the others were slipping off their shoes. Back here, dark water lined the path on the left. Swarms of mosquitoes pulsed above it, and there was a musty smell.

Kit followed hesitantly. "I'd hate to fall into that. Yuck."

"Me, too. But don't worry. The water up ahead isn't stagnant like this. I'd never walk through this stuff."

Then Jackie heard something. A rustling. Grasses to the right of the path swayed suspiciously. The clumps of green grew higher than her waist—tall enough to hide someone.

She heard a low giggle.

Then everything happened at once. A blur of movement as something popped up out of the grass, close enough that Jackie jumped back in surprise, even though she'd spotted the pranksters a half a second earlier. Kit reacted instinctively, grabbing for the figure that rushed at her and pushing it off the path, toward the brackish water.

Immediately there was a bloodcurdling screech, followed by an unmistakable splash as something—or someone—crashed into the water.

Fran and another girl caught up to them and stood between Jackie and Kit, doubled over in laughter, not seeming to hear someone screaming from a few feet away.

Kit was wild-eyed, still unsure of what had just happened. But Jackie knew. The screams were coming from Ivory, who was now standing in waist-deep water, sludge streaming from her hair and plopping off her fingertips.

Ivory was not a girl to be messed with, and Kit had just thrown her into the sludge. Not that it was Kit's fault, but that wouldn't matter. It wouldn't matter that Ivory was probably the instigator behind the whole thing, thinking it would be hilarious to scare Jackie and the new girl.

All the other girls from both Wendy's and Stella's cabins suddenly surrounded them, yelling and laughing, while the counselors helped Ivory climb out of the smelly water.

Jackie watched as Ivory zeroed in on Kit, and even though Stella held the mud-covered girl back, Jackie already knew things had taken a dark turn. Kit deserved to be warned. She needed to know what she was up against.

CHAPTER NINE

E VEN THOUGH IT FELT like hours had slowly ticked by since
lights-out, Kit was still awake, sweating on her top bunk. The
irritating sound of wings beating against a window screen went on and
on, moths drawn to the muted beam of Jackie's flashlight.

What was she reading under her sheet?

Kit wished she'd brought a flashlight, too, so *she* could read under the
covers. Instead, she closed her eyes and her brain formed an image of a
big swarm of moths, hovering white and ghostlike, outside their cabin.
The insects organized and coalesced, and the outline of a small child took
shape. The child stepped closer, arms coming up and hands cupping
the side of its head, allowing it to peer through the screen, glowing eyes
seeking her out.

Something slammed up against her back, jolting her.

"What the . . . ?"

"Kit," Wendy whispered. "You were having a nightmare."

She leaned over the edge of her mattress and searched the shadows
below, seeing the white glow of their counselor's T-shirt and mussed
blond hair. "You kicked me?!"

In the darkness Kit could see Wendy push up on her elbows and shake her head. "Shh! I didn't kick you. I nudged you. I didn't want you to wake everybody up," she said, keeping her voice low.

"I doubt any of us can sleep in this heat anyway," Lynette said, her voice floating through the shadows.

"I know *I* can't," Renee chimed in.

Footsteps padded across the cabin floor in the dark, wood creaked, and suddenly the beam of Jackie's flashlight hit the cabin's ceiling. Annie's head was level with Jackie's, her left hand gripping the headboard and her feet planted firmly on the edge of Lynette's mattress, almost like she was perched on a balance beam. She'd ripped Jackie's covers back.

"For Pete's sake, quit reading and turn off that blasted light, Jackie! You're keeping everybody awake!"

Jackie peeked around Annie's head, scanning the cabin, the flashlight illuminating the large room. "I wasn't keeping *Kit* up."

A moan came from Fran's bunk, under Renee's. "What is happening?"

"Get away from me, Annie," Jackie said.

Kit held her breath as Jackie pushed at the other girl, but Annie jumped back, landing on her feet like a cat. Kit thought back to when she'd stood up on that bunk the same way, but she'd practically tipped it over. Why couldn't she be coordinated like Annie?

A lamp clicked on, softening Jackie's flashlight beam. Wendy sat on the edge of her mattress, leaning outward so her hair wouldn't get tangled in the springs under Kit's bed. "I know this heat makes it hard to sleep. I wish we had a fan. What would you ladies say to a moonlit walk down to the beach?"

Kit, now wide awake, thought it sounded like the best idea she'd heard in a long time. She scrambled down.

Annie turned. "But it's after hours. We aren't supposed to leave our cabins."

Wendy laughed as she stood, adjusting her T-shirt and shorts as if she'd been tossing and turning, too. "You aren't supposed to leave your cabin without *me*. Come on. Get up. It's too hot in here."

"A moonlight swim would be perfect," Lynette said, rolling out of her bed.

"Walk. I said *walk*. I can keep track of all seven of you on foot, but not in the water."

Lynette grinned, pulling shorts on over her baby-doll pajamas. "I had to at least try."

"Be sure to put your tennis shoes on, everybody. I know this is Camp Barefoot, but I don't need anybody cutting open a toe."

Minutes later, Wendy held the door so the girls could file out. "Keep your voices down. We don't want to wake the whole camp. And keep an eye out for Dyani."

"Who the heck is Dyani?" Kit asked, hopping off the wooden platform in front of their cabin onto the shadowed grass. Blades tickled her bare ankles, and she regretted her decision to go sockless. Her feet were already slippery with sweat inside her Keds.

Wendy pulled the cabin door shut, careful not to let the screen slap. She snapped on a flashlight. "Dyani is the ghost that keeps watch over the waterfall."

Kit grinned. A nervous giggle escaped one of her cabinmates. This was so much more fun than sweating on her bunk.

"A ghost, huh? Why haven't you mentioned her before?" Jackie asked, the beam of her flashlight bobbing along in front of them while Wendy brought up the rear.

"She was news to me, too. My grandma used to tent next to the falls with her family when she was a little girl, long before this camp was here. This spring, I visited her in the nursing home after my finals, and when I told her I was coming back here again for my summer job, her eyes took on this faraway look. That expression usually means her next question will be to ask me who I am. She forgets things. But what's weird is she remembers lots from when she was a young girl."

Kit understood. She was noticing something similar with her grandfather. It was unnerving when someone who's known you your whole life looks at you as if you're a stranger.

An owl hooted off in the distance.

"So your grandma told you something about this Dyani?" Fran asked. "Did she know her?"

A soft breeze, like the whisper of a ghost, tickled the baby hairs on the back of Kit's neck. She'd twisted her hair into short braids before bed, hoping she'd feel cooler with her hair up, not caring that she looked like a redheaded porcupine.

"No. Dyani was an Indian priestess, or so the story goes. According to my grandmother, Dyani was assigned the task of protecting countless diamonds that encircled the once bottomless pool at the base of the falls. The diamonds were magical, and they twinkled so brightly in the moonlight, strangers were drawn here from miles away. If Dyani failed, and even *one* diamond was snatched away by a stranger, all the jewels would tumble into the pool and be covered with silt and dirt so deep that no one would ever find them again. Their magic would be lost forever."

"That must be why they're called Diamond Falls!" Kit recognized Annie's voice but couldn't see her in the darkness that was only punctuated at random by the flashlight beams. "I always wondered about that. Has anyone ever found diamonds around here?"

"I asked Grandma that. She wasn't sure, but she did swear she saw Dyani's ghost for herself, late one night when it was too hot to sleep."

"Kind of like tonight," Kit muttered, slapping at a mosquito when it nipped her shoulder.

"She told me she snuck out of her family's tent and wandered over to the water's edge," Wendy continued. "She sat on the bank, dipping her toes into the cool water. It was so peaceful. Stars glowed in the heavens and moonlight sparkled on the surface of the water like diamonds. Grandma swears she heard a young woman's laughter, and when she searched the face of the falls, she saw her, standing tall and proud, up top, moonlight glowing on her long, shiny hair. Her fingertips glittered, as if dripping with diamonds."

Kit suspected the "ghost" was probably nothing more than a short pine tree at the top of the falls that resembled a person in the moonlight. Maybe lightning bugs to add extra twinkle. But she was still enjoying the story.

"Your grandma probably fell asleep on the bank and *dreamed* the whole thing," Annie said.

Wendy's flashlight beam danced up the trunks of the tall evergreens that lined the path to the lake and Diamond Falls. "That's possible, I suppose. But Grandma was pretty adamant about what she saw. I'm going to choose to believe her. Who doesn't love a good ghost story?"

"I think ghosts and fairies and sprites are very real."

"Of course you do, Lynette," Jackie chimed in. "You still believe in the tooth fairy."

Someone stepped on a twig, the *snap!* only added to Kit's enjoyment of their walk, through dark woods flavored with the talk of ghosts. It didn't frighten her. She was a skeptic, convinced that science could explain everything. People's fears of the supernatural had always fascinated her.

"I don't believe in ghosts, but let's talk about those diamonds." Kit wasn't sure, but she thought it was Fran that was speaking. "Are you telling us there are diamonds in the pool below the falls?"

Wendy laughed. "I wish, Fran. I've never found any *actual* diamonds, nor did my grandmother. Maybe someone did, way back, and that's where the falls got their name. But wait just a few more minutes, and I think you'll agree that, as long as the moon is positioned just right and there aren't many clouds, moonlight makes it look as if diamonds are cascading down inside the waterfall."

The path they'd followed from their cabin, the one that looked so different at night, widened, and the ground beneath their feet transitioned from dirt and trampled grass to flat shale, crunching under the soles of their shoes.

"Careful now, ladies. This shale can get slippery. Save your flashlight batteries, Jackie. We don't need them now. The moon is so bright. It isn't far. Annie and Jackie, you know the way. We'll follow you."

The beauty of their surroundings stole Kit's breath away. Moonbeams created a stark contrast, bathing everything they touched in a soft white while the rest of the world lay in shadow. Tall grasses along the water's edge swayed like white flags of surrender. Soft waves ruffled the water's surface, shimmering. As they followed the path to their right, walking between what looked to be a steep bank down to the water on one side and tall trees on the other, Kit heard the tumble of water but couldn't yet see the falls. They'd traveled this path two days earlier during the heat of midday. Everything looked different under the light of the moon.

The other girls walked in front of Kit, only Wendy was still behind her. Something shimmered off to her right, a few feet off the ground. For a moment it reminded Kit of her dream, of the moths transforming into the shape of a child—the child that still haunted her. But her logical mind quickly took hold, and she smiled as lightning bugs danced along the tree line.

The girls up ahead angled right, and Kit watched for what she knew lay beyond the curve. Would she see the mirage that Wendy promised? A magical vision that looked like diamonds spilling over a cliff and raining into a moonlit pool below? It might make up for the countless mosquito bites she was sure she'd suffer from in the morning.

Honey, you don't have to be so serious all the time, Kit's father's words danced up from some forgotten place in her brain. *It's okay to let the magic in.*

Closing her eyes for a split second before reaching the curve in the path, she obeyed her father, trying to remember when her life used to have moments of fun, of joy, of magic. Before—

"Hey, careful!" Lynette said, stumbling a step or two ahead when Kit ran into the back of her.

"I'm sorry," Kit said. Everyone had stopped to admire the view. She took a step back and to the left so she was directly behind Annie and able to see the falls.

The murmur of the falls had risen to a roar now that they were close. The shoreline wove inward, forming a wide cove. A tall cliff face formed the back of the falls. In the daylight, the nearly vertical surface sported rainbow hues of green, but night brought shadows. The plunging waters absorbed the moonlight, concentrating it into twinkling orbs of light, blanketing the falls in what could be described as falling stars.

"Diamonds," Kit whispered, her eyes drinking in the sight.

"It looks magical," Renee whispered.

Her words pulled Kit's eyes to her new friend, standing off to her right. She'd forgotten Renee was even there, she'd been so quiet throughout their walk. Kit could see she felt as awed as she did.

"My dad would say this place is pure magic."

Renee met her eyes in the moonlight, a broad smile on her face. "Your dad sounds like a smart man."

CHAPTER TEN

K IT COULDN'T STOP SCRATCHING. Mosquito bites circled both
ankles, and there was a big one on her cheek that looked like a
massive zit. Their moonlit walk to Diamond Falls had helped her sleep,
as Wendy promised—they were all so tired by the time they got back
to their cabin that night, they crawled into their bunks and drifted off
before the stuffiness or fresh bug bites could keep sleep at bay—but now
Kit was paying the price.

She'd woken from a gauzy dream of a sunny morning back home,
where the scents of pancakes on the griddle and her father's aftershave
floated in the air, to a noisy group of girls preparing for their day. She'd
longed for the wavy image in her dream, but it bled away and lost its
potency to the reality of morning, much as the magnificent power of last
night's waterfall dissipated when it hit the pool, its power scattered.

A morning trip down to the lake to get cold water on her bug bites
after breakfast would have helped with the itch, but Wendy insisted they
complete a silly craft project before they could swim. One cabin was
assigned to the empty mess hall each morning so the girls could work on
their summer craft projects.

"I hope you picked something easy this year, Wendy," Jackie said,
plopping down at the table next to Kit.

"Did you have to make something complicated last year?" Renee asked, taking the seat across from Jackie.

Annie laughed. "No. It wasn't hard. We made friendship bracelets, but we ran out of supplies because we all wanted to make them for each other."

"This year's project might be a little more complicated," Wendy chimed in. She was pulling supplies out of a cardboard box on a table perpendicular to the three where the campers had grabbed seats. "And you each can only make one. But I think they'll be really cool when we're done. If they work, I know you'll want to take these home. Shoot, I forgot the box of cardboard tubes in the office."

Kit bent down to scratch at her right ankle again. One of the clusters of bites itched so badly she'd already scratched open her skin.

"What are you doing?" Jackie asked, inching down their shared bench, away from Kit. "Your hair tickled my arm!"

"Sorry." Kit could feel her face flush. "Aren't you all bit up and itchy?"

Jackie shook her head. "Nah. Mosquitoes don't like me."

"Kit, Lynette, I need you to run over to the camp office and grab the box of cardboard tubes. They're on the floor, under one of the windows," Wendy said, flinging her left hand toward the front entrance of the camp. "And Kit, grab a bottle of pink calamine lotion. That bug bite on your cheek looks itchy. It'll help, I promise. The first-aid supplies are in the closet in a back storage room."

Lynette, who'd been sitting next to Nancy, stood. "Sure, Wendy. But first you have to tell us what we're making."

Wendy shook her head as she removed a glass jar full of something sparkly. "Go grab the box first. *Then* I'll tell you."

Kit got to her feet, giving her ankles one last scratch. "I'm not sure where the office is."

"I know! Follow me." Lynette skipped out of the hall, her gauzy blue sundress billowing behind her. Everyone else dressed in cutoffs and halter tops, but Lynette seemed to have a style all her own. A clunky silver mood ring twinkled on her right hand, and she'd clipped a white silk flower into a rhinestone-covered barrette that held her black curls back above one ear.

As she hurried to keep up with the light-footed Lynette, Kit caught a reflection of herself in the glass window of the door leading into the camp's office. She felt like Bozo the Clown in her red-and-white-striped halter, light-blue jean shorts, and red hair. The bug bite on her cheek made the resemblance even stronger. She couldn't start at her new school looking like this. She'd need to do some serious clothes shopping before school started—even though she had no idea where the money would come from for a new wardrobe.

"Anybody home?" Lynette yelled, crossing through a short hallway into a messy office area. Two cluttered desks filled most of the small space, but nobody was there. Lynette pointed toward the window. "That must be Wendy's box."

Kit tagged after her, both of them peering into the tall cardboard box. It reached their waists and was about three feet square. "It's kind of big, but it doesn't look heavy."

"I think I can carry it," Lynette said, hoisting it into her arms.

"You sure?"

"Yeah, it's light. Let's hurry. I'm curious what Wendy is going to have us do with these. The cardboard tubes look like they were inside wrapping paper in another life. Plus, it's already hot and I want to swim."

"Me, too," Kit agreed, heading out ahead of Lynette so she could hold the door.

"What did you think of the falls last night? Weren't they pretty? I was disappointed we didn't catch sight of Dyani, though. Summer camp would be so much better with ghosts." Lynette switched the tall box from one hip to the other as they crossed the lawn area.

"If that's getting too heavy, I can take it," Kit said, watching the ground for any tripping hazards Lynette may not see.

"I got it. Oh man, Kit, that bite on your cheek looks like it's getting worse!"

"Crap." Kit skidded to a halt, scratching at her cheek. "I forgot the lotion."

"Just get the door to the mess hall for me, then run back and grab it. You know where it is now. I think the closet with the Band-Aids and stuff is back in that far corner, past where we found the box. We'll get things set up, but we won't start without you."

Kit's ankle twinged again. "Yeah, I better, or I won't have any fun with whatever project Wendy has for us. These bites are driving me crazy. Be right back."

By the time Kit rejoined the others, Wendy was dividing supplies into piles on each table.

"There you are, Kit. Did you find the lotion?"

Kit showed her the bottle, then took her spot next to Jackie. "What are we making?"

Jackie shrugged. "She still hasn't told us yet. She was waiting for you."

"Come on, Wendy, tell us what we're making," Annie said, picking up one of the long tubes next to the pile of supplies on their table and holding it up to her mouth. "Are we making some kind of instrument?" The tube magnified her question and the other girls laughed.

Wendy picked up a ruler and scissors from the head craft table. "Good guess, but I don't think we need anything that would make you girls even noisier than you already are. Anybody else have a guess?"

Kit glanced at the items on their table, surprised to see a stack of narrow mirrors. Beside them, Wendy had poured the glittery contents of her glass jar into white bowls. She suddenly knew. "We're making kaleidoscopes, aren't we?"

"Ding, ding, ding!" Wendy said, waving the scissors in the air. "You're right, Kit!"

Annie moved the tube from her mouth to her eye, looking through the cardboard cylinder. "Really? I didn't know you could make homemade kaleidoscopes."

"What's a kaleidoscope?" Jackie whispered in Kit's ear.

"You know . . . those toy things you aim at the sun or a light, then you look through it and turn it. Funky patterns appear." When Jackie still looked confused, Kit said, "You've never seen a kaleidoscope?"

"Guess not. But they sound neat."

Kit ran her fingers through the glittery contents of the bowl in front of her.

"Careful—those may be sharp," Wendy warned as she approached.

"I thought they were glass beads."

"Not exactly. It's crushed glass that's been tumbled, so most of the sharp edges are gone, but you still need to be careful." She picked up the tube from Kit and Jackie's table, waving it in the air. "We'll cut these down so each of you will have a twelve-inch tube. Then we'll follow the steps to make our kaleidoscopes."

The seven campers got busy. Kit was excited about the project, liking the idea of using the mirrors and getting them set to the proper angles inside the tubes so light would reflect, making the colored glass sparkle. She'd been worried they'd have to do some dumb little kid craft project. So she was glad this felt more complicated.

Wendy flipped on a boombox in the corner, and Joan Jett's current hit, "Crimson and Clover," filled the room. Some girls sang along, while others swayed to the music and concentrated on the task at hand.

"I can't believe I've never seen one of these before," Jackie said, aiming her nearly complete kaleidoscope toward a window. "I love the way the patterns shift inside when you twist it."

Kit nodded, adhering one more piece of decorative trim around her cardboard tube. "It'll look even better out in the sunshine. The mirrors are the trick."

Wendy wandered over to their table. "What do you think? Are yours working?"

"I'll tell you in a sec," Kit said, twisting her body to face the window and copying Jackie's actions. "Yep. It works. Where did you get all these long, skinny mirrors?"

Wendy grinned as she picked up an extra mirror. "You know what Avon is, right?"

Kit grimaced. "Yeah. My mom sold it for a while. They had a bubble bath for kids that smelled like grapes. We used it every day. I got so sick of the smell that I'll never eat a grape popsicle again."

"Your mom sells makeup?" Jackie sat back down and picked a few large plastic jewels out of the pile in the middle of their table. "Mine doesn't even *wear* makeup. I'm jealous."

Kit sighed. "She only did it for about a year. I think she used more than she actually sold."

Wendy pulled the conversation back to the original question. Maybe she sensed Kit's unease around the subject of her mother. Kit was grateful. "My aunt has sold Avon for years. Every time I hear a doorbell ring I think of her. You know their old slogan? 'Ding-dong, Avon calling'? I was helping her clean out her basement one day this past spring, before my job here at camp started. In fact, it was the same day I saw Grandma and she told me about the diamond legend. Anyway, I found a box of old supplies. My aunt must have had at least fifty of these little containers. They were supposed to hold a lipstick in a lady's purse. But they changed the design of the lipstick tubes, so she didn't have a use for the outdated containers anymore. I asked if I could have them for the mirrors inside. I figured we could do something with them for a craft project. When I mentioned about them to Stella, she suggested kaleidoscopes. She had a physics class last semester, and they used the mirrors inside of kaleidoscopes to study angles and reflections."

"Is physics a math class or a science class?" Kit asked, curiously.

Wendy set the mirror back down. "It counts toward your sciences in college. But you use math to answer physics questions. Why do you ask?"

Kit shrugged. "I like both math and science. Just wondering."

"You sound like Stella. She wants to teach science someday. To high school students, if you can believe that."

Jackie rubbed her fingers together. "I'm making a mess with this glue. My dad says they can always use good science teachers."

"Your dad teaches?" Kit asked.

"He used to," Jackie said, glancing at her while she worked. "But now he's the principal. I'm already dreading going to a high school where my *dad* is in charge. Yuck."

Kit could understand Jackie's feelings, but now that her own dad was practically dead to her and her brothers, she'd have given anything to go to a school where he worked.

"Your dad was a wonderful teacher," Wendy said. "He helped me get through my one and only chemistry class. But, oh boy, was he strict. That's probably what makes him an excellent principal, too. Personally, I'm not much for the sciences. Give me a paintbrush over a Bunsen burner any day."

"You want to be an artist? Is that what you're going to school for?" Kit asked.

"Hey, Wendy, can you give me a hand? I can't get these mirrors quite right."

"Be right there, Renee," Wendy said. "Yes, I'm studying art history in college, Kit, but I already call myself an artist. I don't need some teacher telling me I need to learn this technique or that before I can create art. Remember that."

After helping a struggling Renee, Wendy turned to the group and clapped her hands. "Take about ten more minutes, ladies, then we'll clean up our mess. Be sure your name is on your kaleidoscope, and set it carefully in the flat box on the head table. Once your area is clean, we'll be ready to eat a quick lunch. After lunch, we'll head back to our cabin, you'll put your suits on, and run to the bathroom if you need to. I'll meet you in front of the cabin, and we'll all walk down to the water together. I'll bring the box of kaleidoscopes, because I want you to try them down by the lake. I hope they'll sparkle as much in the sunshine as the water did in the moonlight last night. In the dark, the sparkles in the water looked like diamonds, right? Well, *these* should make the crushed glass look like a treasure chest full of jewels!"

Chapter Eleven

B Y THE TIME THEY reached the water, the beach was crowded with other campers. Jackie supposed it was too hot to do much else.

She waded into the lake, relishing the cool water enveloping her shins and then her thighs as she stepped in deeper. Swimming was her favorite part of camp, but getting her stupid period had kept her out of the water for the whole first week.

A splash of icy water hit her back, and she spun to find a laughing Annie a few steps behind her.

"You looked hot!"

"And *you* look too dry," Jackie said, springing forward to grab her friend by the wrists. Annie was slippery and strong, but Jackie held tight, taking backward steps and pulling them both into deeper water. She let go once the water started reaching their chins, and the two kicked up their feet so they could float on their backs.

"This feels good. I don't remember camp being this hot before."

"Better than good. This is heaven!" Jackie used her arms to help balance her body, closing her eyes against the scorching sun. "Did you see Ivory and her cronies over by the ropes? It looks like they're practicing for the race."

"Yeah, I saw. Do you think you can beat her this year?"

Jackie considered Annie's question. Every time she'd crossed paths with Ivory since the whole nasty business at the conservatory, the girl had glared at her. "I have to beat her. She's acting like *I* pushed her in the mud, when it was Kit."

Annie kicked her feet and moved her arms in a similar fashion to Jackie, floating on her back. "Kit didn't push her. Ivory tried to skirt around her and she slipped."

With a sigh, Jackie allowed her feet to sink, and she switched to a doggie paddle to keep her head above water. "Technically Kit *did* throw her in, but that was after Ivory scared her! And when have you ever known Ivory to take responsibility for her own screw-ups?"

Annie turned onto her side and slowly floated around Jackie. "Never. And I wouldn't want to be on the receiving end of that girl's revenge. Remember when she tripped over me at the roller-skating rink in first grade and knocked out her front tooth when she fell? Her mother had the nerve to call my mom and tried to insist we pay for Ivory's dental bill."

Jackie leaned her head back, enjoying the heat above and the chill below. "I was glad your mom stuck to her guns. We were *all* losing our front teeth back then. Ivory just sped up the process a little."

"Did you warn Kit to watch her back?"

Jackie turned to scan the beach, looking for Kit. Her flame-bright hair wasn't hard to miss. She was sitting on a towel next to Renee, deep in conversation. "I tried. But she didn't seem too concerned. What do you think of Kit?"

Annie shifted so she was doing the sidestroke in the opposite direction. "I like her. She's kind of quiet. But I'm sure it's hard to be new here when most of us already know each other. She'll be going to school with us this fall."

Jackie slicked her hair back. "I bet she's smart. A little nerdy, even. Do you think she'll want to hang out with us once we're in school?"

"You ask that like it's a bad thing."

"No. Not *bad* . . . I just get a different vibe from her. I wonder why she moved to town. She won't talk much about her family."

Annie gave up on her sidestroke and turned onto her back again, using her feet to kick toward shore. "Not everyone has a normal family like us, Jackie. I think she's nice. Now, come on. Wendy promised we could try our kaleidoscopes out here in the sun, and I see her with the box, up there by the grass, talking to her sister and Pratt."

"Fine, but then I want you to race me a few times before we have to head in to eat supper. We can't let Ivory and the rest of their cabin beat us. They may rule the school, but out here, the trophy is ours for the taking."

By the time the two girls reached their towels, Wendy was already there with the box containing their kaleidoscopes. She waved Lynette and Nancy over.

"Anybody see Fran?" Wendy asked, scanning the beach and water. "She knows she isn't supposed to go off by herself."

Jackie caught an edge to Wendy's tone. Something was up. "She's probably over with Stella's group. If she had her way, she'd be in their cabin instead of ours this year. We aren't good enough for her anymore."

Annie shook off some of the water still streaming out of her hair and down her arms, then pointed. "There! She's out in the water with them. She's fine. Can we see our kaleidoscopes now, Wendy?"

"Dry off first. These tubes are made out of thick paper, and if you get them wet it'll ruin them."

Kit and Renee pulled their creations out of the box while the other four girls toweled off. Jackie wrapped her towel around her long hair for extra protection.

"Go like this," Kit said, closing one eye while holding her beribboned kaleidoscope up toward the sun.

Once Jackie was confident her hands were dry, she followed Kit's example with her own scope. "Wow, this is amazing! Way better than when we looked through them inside. These have to be the best project anyone has ever done at camp. Thanks for the idea, and the supplies, Wendy."

"I'll pass your thanks on to my aunt. Without her stash of mirrors, these wouldn't have been possible."

Jackie looked between Wendy, who was still not her usual cheerful self, and her sister, Stella, still talking to Pratt. Another camp worker, an older woman Jackie often saw in the mess hall and sometimes during the different contests, had joined them.

"Did something happen, Wendy?" she finally asked, her curiosity peaked.

Wendy shook her head. "Hopefully not. Something might be missing from the office, but I'm sure it was just misplaced."

"It wasn't the lotion you told Kit to grab, was it?"

Laughing, Wendy sank down into the grassy beach sand beside the nearly empty box. "No. No one would miss a bottle of calamine lotion. I think they buy that stuff by the case around here. The mosquito is practically the state bird of Minnesota. Like I said, I'm sure it's just a misunderstanding. Don't worry about it. If it turns out to be a problem, we'll talk about it tonight. Is everybody's kaleidoscope working? Try pointing it at different things. You should notice a big change in the pattern, because part of it is the reflection of whatever image is getting bounced around inside by the mirrors. It isn't just about the crushed glass."

A trio of younger campers walked by, eyeing the girls and their kaleidoscopes. One girl bent to look through the front end of Kit's scope and asked, "Did you guys *make* those?"

It startled Kit and she jumped back. "What are you doing?! You scared me. I didn't hear you come up."

The girl giggled as she straightened, pushing her glasses back up from the tip of her nose. "Sorry. Can I try?"

Jackie could see Kit hesitate. Not that she blamed her. The kid might drop it.

"Fine," Kit finally agreed, handing it to her. "But just for a minute. And be careful."

The girl took the offered scope with a reasonable amount of care, but it didn't take long before the other two girls started grabbing for it. Wendy jumped to her feet and intervened, taking it away and holding it in the air, out of their reach, shooing the girls on their way.

"Thanks, Wendy," Kit said. "Can you put mine back in your box for now, please? Didn't you say we have to go back up at five? How much time do we still have? I wanted to take a quick swim."

After stowing Kit's kaleidoscope, Wendy checked her wristwatch. "Forty-five minutes. If anybody else is planning to swim today, follow Kit."

Still wanting to get some practice in for tomorrow's race, Jackie put her scope away, too, and headed back for the water. "You a fast swimmer, Kit?"

Kit shrugged, stepping gingerly across the hot sand. "I can cover some ground with the breaststroke. But I can't do the crawl. Why?"

"Because we race tomorrow. And we *have* to win."

Kit scrunched up her face and cast a doubtful glance at Jackie before nodding toward Fran and the girls she was hanging out with, that were still swimming out by the ropes. "I was watching them. They're pretty fast. Especially that one you told me to watch out for. What was her name again?"

Jackie squinted, checking out the competition as she reached the edge of the water. "Ivory. And she'll be gunning for you. You want to be prepared."

"Jackie, nothing I can do in the next forty minutes will change anything if she's already a faster swimmer than me. Besides, she doesn't scare me. Bullies are usually nothing more than scared little kids, acting all tough just to cover up their insecurities."

"Suit yourself, but don't say I didn't warn you," Jackie said before executing a shallow dive under an incoming wave. She'd done what she could to warn the new girl, but if Kit wouldn't listen there wasn't much more she could do about it.

Except she could brush up on her own strokes. If her cabin lost again tomorrow, this time it wouldn't be *her* fault.

Jackie pulled the cabin curtains closed. Since they'd all showered after swimming, and it would be lights-out in half an hour, some girls were changing into their pajamas. "Ladies, have you no modesty?"

"Quit trying to act like Wendy, Jackie. You are *so* bossy."

Jackie took a deep breath, ignoring Fran instead of setting her straight. She wasn't bossy. She just didn't think girls should change clothes with the windows wide open and lights on inside the cabin. Anyone walking by could see right in. She dug out her last clean pair of pajamas and stood in the shadows at the end of her bunk, changing as quickly as possible.

Fran pulled her tank-top off, removed a dog-eared paperback from under her pillow, and dropped into one of the two overstuffed chairs.

"Nice bra, Fran," Lynette said, though her tone wasn't complimentary. "The lace is pretty. Is this our first big-girl bra? I seem to recall you still wore a prissy white training bra in gym this spring."

Jackie did her best not to laugh.

Fanning through her book, Fran shrugged. "You're just jealous because your mom could never afford to buy *you* a bra like this."

Gasping, Jackie picked up her pillow and flung it toward Fran, knocking the paperback out of her hand. It slid across the floor, its cover catching and ripping off.

"*Now* look what you did! This is my big sister's book! She's going to *kill* me now," Fran cried, scurrying out of her chair to recover the damaged novel.

Jackie got a better look at the cover: a bare-chested man with a woman bent backward over his arm, her breasts spilling out of her dress. "Of course your sister would read a smut book like that. I suppose that's where she learns all her tricks."

Fran scooped up the book and cover, spinning on Jackie. "Take that back!"

"I will not. If you're going to be mean to Lynette, you better be prepared to get it dished right back at you. Besides, we all know your sister likes to date lots of boys. And I mean *a lot* of boys."

Fran tucked the novel back under her pillow, mumbling something Jackie couldn't hear.

"What did you say, Fran?"

"I said you're just mad because your brother has a crush on my sister but she'd never lower herself to go out with the likes of him."

That did it. Jackie kicked off her sheet and scrambled for the end of her bunk, intent on smacking some sense into Fran. She needed to be knocked down a notch or two.

"What the devil is going on in here?!" Wendy cried, the screen door slapping shut behind her. "I could hear you the minute I stepped outside the dining hall! What are you trying to do, get me fired? It's my job to keep you in line, ladies, but clearly I've been too lax with all of you."

Feeling ashamed, Jackie scooted back up on her bed, leaning forward so she could sit without knocking her head on the ceiling.

"Fran, get dressed," Wendy said. "We don't walk around here in our underwear, no matter how fancy it is."

Nodding, Fran pulled her nightgown off the headboard. "I was just changing, Wendy."

Liar, liar. Jackie glared at Fran, but the girl didn't look her way again.

"Sorry, Lynette," Fran said. "I was just teasing. I shouldn't have said that about your mom."

Lynette didn't respond, but Jackie saw her wipe a tear away. They all knew Lynette was sensitive about her family's financial situation. How dare Fran throw it in her face.

Wendy changed into the shorts and sleep shirt she wore to bed. Jackie supposed the counselors needed to be at least partially dressed at all times, just in case there was any trouble, even in the dead of night.

"Ladies, I know everyone's tired, and it's almost time for lights-out, but there is something important I need to tell you. Remember on the beach today when I mentioned a problem in the camp office? I didn't think it would be anything, but it does seem like we might have a real problem on our hands."

Seven sets of eyes turned to Wendy.

The trumpet blared outside, and when Renee reached to turn off the overhead light, Wendy stopped her. "This will just take a minute, then I'll turn everything off."

With a shrug, Renee crawled into her bed.

"What's going on, Wendy?" Annie asked.

Wendy rubbed her right temple, as if a headache was forming behind her eyes. "It seems the cash box in the office disappeared today."

No one said anything for a beat.

"Someone *stole* it?" Annie asked.

Jackie's mind barely registered the question. She glanced between Kit and Lynette, an awful thought dancing unbidden into her brain. The campers seldom had reason to go in the camp's main office, but Wendy had sent the two girls in there to get the box of supplies and the itch lotion.

Without an adult present.

As she watched, the thought seemed to register with others, too.

But only Fran would be cruel enough to give voice to the notion. "Well, isn't *that* interesting? Kit, weren't you in the office today?"

Kit sat up in her bed, assuming a similar angle as Jackie to avoid the low ceiling. "What are you implying, Fran?"

Fran grinned, pushing the white eyelet sleeves of her nightgown up as high on her arms as possible. "I'm not *implying* anything. Just trying to help with the chain of events."

"Screw you, Fran," Kit bit out before lying down again, her back to all of them.

Wendy sighed as she walked over to the light switch. "There won't be any finger-pointing around here. Do I make myself clear? We'll let the senior camp counselors figure out what really happened. You were bound to hear it from someone, so I wanted to be the one to tell you. I need every one of you to know I have the utmost faith in your integrity. I feel terrible that this is happening. Now, try to get some sleep. I'm sure they will straighten this out by morning."

CHAPTER TWELVE

D ESPITE WENDY'S ASSURANCES, NOTHING was straightened out by morning. Jackie heard the furtive whispers and felt the eyes on her back as fellow campers scanned their table, suspicious that their group was behind the missing money. Fran didn't even sit with them, opting instead to skip to Ivory's table when they waved her over.

"Why is Fran so intent on hanging out with those girls?" Kit asked. "They remind me of a group at my old school. My mom called them 'mean girls.' Snotty and rich, always thinking they're better than everyone else. Has she always been like that?"

"Not always," Annie said, peeling her orange. Jackie could smell the tang from across the table. "But Fran likes to be the center of attention. She thinks hanging out with them will get her that."

Jackie pushed her cereal bowl away, the leftover milk splashing the tabletop. "Forget about Fran. Talking about her is exactly what she wants us to do," she said, wiping up the mess she'd made with a napkin. "How's everybody feeling about the swim race today?"

Annie cracked her knuckles and smiled. "I'm ready."

"Is it a relay race, or how does it work?" Renee asked. "This is all new for me. And for Kit."

Jackie nodded. "Yeah, it's a relay. Each cabin enters a team of four. If everyone wants to swim, we can enter two teams, and someone just has to swim for both. Does everyone want to race today? Because I'd be happy to race on both teams. How about you, Annie? Fran probably won't want to swim with us, so we might need two of us to double up."

A tap on Jackie's shoulder interrupted her recruiting work. She glanced up to see Pratt standing over her alongside a woman who worked in the camp office.

"Sorry to interrupt, ladies," Pratt said. "But we'd like to ask all of you to meet us back in Cabin 7 when you're finished with breakfast. There's something we need to discuss with all of you."

Jackie didn't like Pratt's tone, convinced this discussion would be related to the missing cash box. "But we have to warm up for the race after breakfast!"

"There will be time for that," the woman stated. Jackie sensed she couldn't care less about a swim race.

Wendy stepped up to their table, her face flushed. "This is nothing to worry about, girls. We just need to help figure out what happened. Maybe one of you saw something that might be a clue. There was over a thousand dollars in that missing box, so this is serious."

Wendy's words gave Jackie pause. She didn't want to doubt Kit's innocence, but a thousand dollars was a lot of money, and Lynette got back to the mess hall with the paper tubes before Kit returned, which meant Kit may have been alone in the office. She knew there was no way Lynette would steal money, even though she and her mom always struggled to make ends meet. Lynette was too honest for that. But what did they really know about Kit? She thought back to the first day of camp, when she'd walked in on Kit snooping in their cabin after arriving late.

Annie met her eye with a questioning look of her own. Was she having doubts about Kit's innocence, too?

No one was eating, and Jackie suspected everyone had lost their appetite under the weight of suspicion that hovered over their table. She got to her feet and took charge. "Let's go get this over with, girls. We know that none of us had anything to do with this. The sooner we tell them everything we know, the sooner we can get down to the lake."

As her cabinmates gathered their dishes and headed out, she hoped she sounded more convinced than she felt.

"I understand two of you were in the office yesterday morning," Pratt said, standing just inside the door to Cabin 7, arms crossed over his barrel chest. "Who was that, exactly?"

Kit and Lynette each raised a tentative hand. Jackie could tell they both felt intimidated by the man, and she was relieved when their counselor jumped in.

"That's right," Wendy said, walking over to stand behind the two, hands on their shoulders. "I sent them to the office because I'd forgotten a box of supplies in there, for our craft project. And Kit needed some calamine lotion. She was miserable from too many mosquito bites."

The woman next to Pratt nodded. Jackie still couldn't remember her name. "You felt comfortable sending them to the office without an adult?"

"Of course," Wendy shot back without hesitation. "They're twelve. And there were two of them. It wasn't like they were going to get lost walking across camp in broad daylight. Besides, I've never known the office to be left unattended."

The woman shuffled her feet. It was her turn to look uncomfortable.

"Is that true, girls?" Pratt asked, looking directly at Kit and Lynette. "Was the office unlocked and unattended?"

Both girls nodded.

"I remember thinking it was kind of weird that no one was in there," Kit added.

"What time was that?"

"I sent them over at about ten," Wendy answered on their behalf. "They weren't gone long, not more than ten minutes."

Jackie wondered if Wendy remembered that Lynette got back before Kit. She certainly wasn't going to be the one to offer that clarification, even though it might be important. She didn't like the way Pratt and the woman were acting like they suspected Kit and Lynette of having something to do with the missing box.

Annie raised her hand. Jackie grinned despite the seriousness of the situation. She was always the good girl, and always quick to jump to the defense of someone she felt was being wronged.

"Yes, Annie? Do you have something to add?"

Nodding, Annie cleared her throat. "I don't see how you can stand here and imply Lynette and Kit had anything at all to do with the missing money. Yes, it's true they were in the office yesterday, but they were only gone for a few minutes. When they came back, all they were carrying was Wendy's box of craft supplies and Kit's lotion. Kit was wearing a T-shirt and shorts. Lynette had on a sundress. It's not like they could have hidden a box holding that much money in their clothes. And neither would have had time to stash a thousand dollars of cash, or a box of it, in that short of time. I haven't known Kit for long, but I've known Lynette for years, and she's one of the most honest people I know."

"It's nice of you to stand up for your friends, young lady," the woman said, and Jackie could see Annie bristle under the woman's condescending tone.

This time when Annie raised her hand, it was to silence the woman and not to ask for permission to speak. "If you, or someone else that works in the office, left it unlocked and unsupervised, which we know is a fact, then isn't that where you should be focusing your time? That sounds very irresponsible to me."

"We aren't accusing anyone of anything," Pratt said, rubbing the back of his neck in frustration. "We just wanted to give you a chance to tell your side of the story."

"We're on different sides now?" Annie challenged. "We may be kids, but even we know it isn't okay to assume anyone is guilty without hard evidence. And unless someone saw who took the box, or you find it in someone's possession, I'm wondering if your lack of proper controls might mean you'll never be able to solve this."

Pratt stared at Annie, his mouth slack for a moment. "If you're done, I just have a few more questions to ask."

Annie gave a sweeping motion with her right hand. "Ask away."

Jackie tried to hide her smile, but it couldn't be helped. Annie would make a great lawyer someday.

Pratt cleared his throat, then turned his attention back to Lynette and Kit. "The missing box is dark gray and made out of metal, about yea big," he said, miming the shape of a rectangular box with his hands. "Did you see anything like that sitting on either of the desktops?"

"Someone left the box sitting out?" Kit asked, eyes wide. "*I* didn't see it."

"I didn't either," Lynette said, shaking her head. "But we didn't pay much attention to stuff in the room once we found Wendy's box and Kit grabbed her lotion."

Jackie noticed Lynette didn't mention that the two of them separated at one point, either.

"Did either of you notice anyone else in the area?" the woman asked, her expression still sour. She couldn't be happy that they weren't getting any helpful answers.

Both girls shook their heads again.

Jackie wanted to ask the woman how long they left the office unattended, but figured it would be better to keep her mouth shut.

Pratt looked around the group of girls. "Anyone else see anything suspicious at all yesterday?"

Shrugs and mumbles were all he got. Jackie was thankful Fran hadn't come back to the cabin with them, going off instead with Stella's group of girls. If Wendy or anyone else noticed her absence, no one mentioned it. Jackie was sure Fran would have spouted off about Lynette arriving back first, without Kit. Anything to be the center of attention. The adults would have appreciated her help, and Fran would have felt so important.

"Will there be anything else?" Wendy asked, clearly eager to get Pratt and the woman out of their cabin.

"Suppose not," Pratt conceded, opening the screen door. "But if anyone remembers seeing something . . . anything . . . out of the ordinary yesterday, or if you hear any talk, be sure to let me know. I promise to keep your name confidential."

As the door closed behind the two, Wendy gathered Lynette into her arms. Jackie hadn't noticed how hard the girl's shoulders were shaking.

"They think we stole the money," Lynette squeaked out, her eyes shut tight in Wendy's embrace. "That's not fair! We—I mean, I—would never steal."

"Well, *I* wouldn't either," Kit assured them all. "It sounds to me like it could have been anyone."

Jackie watched Kit's face but saw no flickers of indecision or guilt. The girl held her shoulders back, her spine straight. Unlike Lynette, she was strong, and Jackie's gut told her the new girl was telling the truth.

"They need to investigate this from all angles, and not just grab at the easiest answer," Jackie said, pulling her suitcase out from under a bed and fishing out a clean swimsuit. "Actually, it's kind of like our kaleidoscopes. You need to turn them and look at them with different light to see *all* the patterns. They should do that with the case of the missing money, too, instead of jumping to conclusions."

Annie nodded, tapping her cheek in thought. "I like that, Jackie. In fact, you just gave me an idea! From now on, I think we should call ourselves the Kaleidoscope Girls. We are bright, multidimensional young women, and we won't let anyone dim our shine. And that includes accusing us of something we didn't do!"

Lynette pulled away from Wendy, a timid smile transforming her worried expression. "I *love* that name. And I love all of you for standing up for me, and for Kit."

"Hey, that's what friends do," Renee said, walking over to the box of kaleidoscopes Wendy had set against the far wall. She removed her scope. "Old or new, it doesn't matter. Friends trust friends."

All the other girls followed her example except Jackie, retrieving their scopes from the box.

"Let's take these outside and use them by the big flower garden at the camp entrance," Nancy suggested.

"But shouldn't we get ready for the race? We have to decide on the teams," Jackie said, watching the others skip out the cabin door.

No one paid any attention to her question.

Wendy held up the two remaining kaleidoscopes. "Take yours. Go have fun! There's time before the race. And besides, building memories with friends who aren't focused on competition can be more rewarding."

Jackie took her scope, not appreciating Wendy's advice. "That one's Fran's."

Nodding, Wendy put it back in the box. "I noticed she wasn't here. That was probably a good thing. She has a flair for the dramatic. She might have been too indiscriminate in casting blame. I hope she learns to work on that. It isn't an attractive trait."

Jackie turned to go, but stopped. "Wendy . . . do you think Kit or Lynette may have taken the money?"

"I don't," Wendy said, her voice confident. "My gut tells me they had nothing to do with it."

"Good. So does mine," Jackie said, and she smiled as she followed the sound of Annie's shrieks. "Sounds like I'm missing out on the fun!"

Jackie rolled her head from side to side, then stretched her shoulders out the way she'd watched her brother do so many times. She had spent many afternoons next to her parents on hard bleachers, in the heat and humidity of indoor pools, all throughout the state for his swimming competitions. She'd been relieved when he gave it up to focus on football and track, but she did remember that one good stretching trick.

She'd swim the anchor position for their cabin's team. Only Annie, Nancy, and Kit wanted to race, so they'd have just the one team. Lynette and Renee promised to cheer as loud as possible, and Fran was still showing support for the enemy camp.

Noticing that some of the other teams had given themselves fancy names, Jackie submitted their team as the Kaleidoscope Girls. Something told her that nickname was going to stick—no matter how the race turned out.

"Tell me again how this is supposed to work," Kit said, coming up behind Jackie. "I've only ever raced in a pool before. Racing in a lake can't work the same, right?"

Jackie laughed. "Be prepared. It gets a little chaotic out there. There aren't technically any lanes, but the rules are pretty simple. Six teams will race at a time. They've added an extra rope across the swimming area. See it? About halfway between shore and the outer safety rope that's always out there?"

Kit shielded her eyes from the bright sun, looking for the additional rope. "There! I see it. But what are the colored flags for?"

"They'll assign each team one of six colors. You line up in the same order as the flags. Each swimmer has to swim out to the rope, tear off one flag in their assigned color, and bring it back to shore. As soon as the girl drops it in her team's sand bucket, the next person wades in as fast as possible and swims off."

Kit continued to scan the swimming area, frowning. "Without lanes, don't the swimmers run into each other?"

"Sometimes," Jackie said, dropping to the ground so she could stretch her hamstrings. "The judges watch to make sure they don't crash into anyone on purpose. It gets pretty subjective. That's why I said to be prepared. Be careful. Especially for Ivory and the rest of the girls on her team. I bet she's coming for you."

"I hope she won't swim against me . . ."

Jackie switched legs and bent deep to stretch her hip flexors along with her hamstrings. "I decided it would be best if you swim third. Ivory always swims last. Let's hope our swimmers can keep up with their team, so I'm the one swimming against her. I know her tricks."

A cap gun sounded.

"It's showtime! Let's go find Nancy and Annie at the starting line."

The teams quickly found their places.

"Huddle up, girls," Jackie said, holding her arms out wide. The others followed her example, forming a wheel shape with their arms, and their heads in the middle, voices lowered. "I know it sucks, but the fact that we are right next to Stella's team might be an advantage. Watch the one you are swimming against. That way we'll know how we're ranking."

The cap gun sounded again. "Swimmers, take your mark!"

"What color are we again?" Annie asked, checking the buckets on both her left and her right. One was red, the other blue.

"Red!" Kit, Nancy, and Jackie all hollered simultaneously.

"Okay, no need to shout!"

A third *crack!* split the air.

Annie burst forward, slipping smoothly under the water. When she resurfaced, now many feet from shore, her arms picked up a smooth rhythm and she jumped out in front of the other swimmers. She still held the lead when she dropped her flag in their bucket and Nancy headed out in the number two spot.

Jackie and Kit stood poised on the edge of the water, clapping and yelling encouragement as their teammate swam neck and neck with the swimmers on either side of her. By the time Nancy stumbled up on shore with her flag, she was out of gas.

Kit rushed in, and when the water reached her waist, she mirrored the dive Annie had executed, cutting through the waves with sure strokes. She reached the rope quickly, but wrestled with the flag. Jackie forgot to breathe as she watched Kit struggle. By the time she'd turned, Ivory's team had a small lead. Kit headed for shore, arms pumping faster and not even coming up for air as she fought to close the distance. She swam fast, but with her head down in the lake water she must have lost her bearings, and she ran right into the swimmer from Stella's cabin.

The other girl looked disoriented for a beat after the collision, and Ivory screamed in frustration. The second Kit dropped her red flag in their bucket, Jackie rushed into the water, ahead of Ivory. Later, Jackie would hear how Kit stumbled in exhaustion, blocking Ivory from getting into the water for an extra second or two.

The time by which Jackie would come in ahead of Ivory.

The Kaleidoscope Girls had won . . . but at what cost?

CHAPTER THIRTEEN

KIT HAD TO SIT on her grandpa's old suitcase to get it latched. Why did dirty clothes take up more room than clean clothes? If she hadn't brought the three thick paperbacks—which she'd never had time to read, anyway—it wouldn't have been a problem. The only new thing she was taking home was her kaleidoscope, but she'd have to carry it; it would break if she tried to fit it in her luggage.

She heard Jackie laugh at something across the room, and looked up to see Annie sitting next to Lynette on her bed, helping her sew one of her teddy bear's eyes back on with a needle and thread. Kit thought back to how lonely she'd felt on the first day of camp, when she'd arrived late to an empty cabin. She'd been so sure it would be a terrible two weeks.

Instead, she'd made a bunch of new friends. Life was so much better with friends.

Kit didn't think starting at her new school in September was going to be so bad after all. The transition would be a big one for all the seventh graders in Ruby Shores. Everyone had to move from their smaller grade schools and the watchful eye of a single classroom teacher to the larger school building that housed both the junior and the senior high.

She doubted she was the only one worried about getting lost in the hallways.

Things would go even more smoothly if no one at school knew her family's history. She hadn't told anyone, but word might still get out. Ruby Shores was her mother's hometown, and her grandparents had lived there for forever, so she wasn't sure she'd be able to keep it a secret.

The cabin door opened and Wendy came in, carrying her trusty clipboard. "How's the packing going, girls?"

"It's going," someone muttered.

Kit smiled sadly. No one seemed to be in a big hurry to leave. While they still had a full day of activities scheduled before their families arrived at four, the end of their summer days at camp felt bittersweet. They'd discussed it on their way back to pack after breakfast.

"Wendy, can I run to the office?" Fran asked. "I need tape. The cover ripped off my book, and I need to fix it."

Kit noticed the girl held the damaged novel behind her back. Wendy wouldn't have approved of a twelve-year-old reading such a sexy book.

"Are you packed?"

"Almost. I need to fit this book in my suitcase, but I can't go home with it like this."

Wendy hesitated before nodding. "As long as you'll be ready to head over to the awards ceremony in twenty minutes, I suppose that's fine. I'm sure someone will be there to help you. Do you know the way?"

"Sure, I know where the office is," Fran said, skipping out the door.

After the screen slapped shut, Wendy checked her paperwork. "Nancy, did you remember your father is coming to pick you up early? He'll be here soon."

"I did," the girl said, pulling her fitted sheet off. Campers had to strip off their linens and fold them neatly in a pile on top of their mattress. Staff washed everything after the campers left, then set the cabins up for the next round of kids. "I hate to miss the tug of war . . . but my cousin is getting married tonight, so I don't have a choice."

"Is there going to be a wedding dance?" Annie asked, yanking off her own sheets from the bunk above Nancy's.

"There is! With a live band and everything. And the bride has a really cute younger brother. He's a junior groomsman. I'm going to ask him to dance."

Jackie snorted. "You're excited to dance with your cute *cousin?*"

"No, dummy!" Nancy said, tossing a pillowcase in her friend's direction. It fell harmlessly to the floor. "The *groom* is my relative, not the bride."

"Oh, well, that'll be fun then." Jackie picked up the pillowcase and folded it before adding it to Nancy's stack. "Here, give me a hug. I'll miss you, Nancy. It sucks that we won't see you at school in the fall."

Nancy allowed Jackie to pull her into a quick embrace. "That's what happens when you have a July birthday and your mom keeps you home for an extra year. You guys will have so much fun in junior high. I think I'll miss the boys in your class as much as I'll miss you. The boys in my class are so immature!"

Wendy dropped her clipboard on her own bare mattress. "Believe me, all boys are immature, no matter how old they are."

The small wooden deck on the front of their cabin creaked under heavy footsteps and someone rapped on their screen door. "Everybody decent in there?"

Kit eyed the door in surprise. The only male voice she'd heard in two weeks was Pratt's, and that definitely wasn't Pratt.

Wendy ran a hand through her hair, and Kit noticed how pink her cheeks looked. She must have gotten sunburned at the swim race the day before. "We're decent. Come on in," the older girl replied.

The screen squeaked open, and all conversation stopped.

"Hi, Scott. What are you doing here?" Wendy asked. Kit thought her voice sounded higher than normal. "The girls are just packing."

The young man grinned, and Kit felt herself grinning back. Who was this Scott guy, and was she the only one who thought he was gorgeous? Pulling her eyes away from the tall guy named Scott, Kit looked around the room. No, she was definitely not the only one who thought he was cute.

"I know I'm early. I apologize. But I didn't have anywhere to stow my gear. Plus, I hitched a ride up here, so I couldn't be picky about the timing. Mind if I just leave my pack over in a corner? Then I'll get out of your hair."

Jackie left Nancy's side, moving over to stand next to Kit. She bent close enough that only Kit would hear and whispered, "He can get in my hair anytime he wants."

Kit choked back a laugh, and Jackie blushed a deeper shade than Wendy's sunburn. "Oh God, did he hear that?"

Wendy picked her clipboard back up, using it to fan her face. The blush wasn't a sunburn after all, Kit realized. Wendy thought this Scott guy was cute, too.

"Sure . . . just put it anywhere. You and your boys are in here again this year, right?"

"I think so."

Renee, who had been quietly packing, set her suitcase on the floor next to her bed and turned to Scott. "*Boys* stay in here, too? I thought this was just a camp for girls."

Scott nodded. "Girls only for the first half of the summer. From now until late August, us boys take over."

Renee thought about this and turned to Wendy. "Does that mean you're done working now? I figured you were staying until the end of the summer."

"I hope she's not leaving," Scott said. Kit thought she saw him wink at Wendy. "We have some catching up to do."

Not looking in Scott's direction, Wendy walked over and checked to see if Renee had left anything behind. "I switch to working in the camp office for the rest of the summer."

Annie stood and stashed the needle and thread she'd been using back in the drawer where they'd found it. Lynette tucked her repaired teddy bear in the overnight bag on her bed.

"I sure hope you do a better job keeping track of things in the office," Lynette said. "That whole mess took some of the fun out of camp for me this year."

"Was there a mess your cabin was involved with?" Scott asked, adjusting his baseball cap.

"I'm sure you'll hear all about it soon enough," Wendy told him, then turned to Lynette. "I really am sorry, Lynette. If I wouldn't have sent you to the office in the first place, you probably wouldn't be feeling this way."

The screen door opened again, and Fran came in, her book still clutched behind her. She skidded to a stop when she saw the guy standing in the middle of their cabin.

"Did you find some tape?" Wendy asked, but Fran kept staring at Scott, giving no sign she'd heard the question.

"Doesn't look like it," Renee said, nodding toward the book. Kit wasn't able to see it from where she stood next to Jackie.

"Who are you?" Fran asked. Kit had assumed Fran was acting strange because she was shocked to find the handsome stranger in their all-girl's cabin, but her tone sounded almost accusatory.

"I'm Scott, the counselor in this cabin for the new kids coming in. The boys arrive tomorrow, but I came early. Pratt trains us in, but this isn't my first summer here, so I'll probably just hang out until the actual work starts."

"Fran, did you get your book fixed?" Wendy asked again. "Let me see it."

Fran shook her head. "No, the office was locked. But it's no big deal. Really. I'll just fix it at home."

With that, Fran shoved the book into her suitcase, holding it upside down so the cover still wasn't visible. "Can I run over to Stella's cabin now? Please?"

Wendy sighed. "Next year we'll probably need to make sure you're in the other cabin. You haven't been with us much."

"That would be nice," Fran said, shifting from side to side like she had to go to the bathroom. "Can I go, please? I'm packed."

Wendy glanced at Fran's empty area around her assigned bed. "Fine. But check in with me at the tug of war. You're still my responsibility, not my sister's."

"I will. Bye, everyone!"

Scott turned and watched Fran go, frowning. He tossed his large duffel bag onto an empty spot along the wall, then nodded to the rest of them on his way out the door.

Once he'd left, Jackie clapped her hands. "Well, that was fun. If the rest of the boy counselors look like Scott, I'm kind of sorry it's time to go home today. But you're glad you don't have to leave, aren't you, Wendy? I'd call *you* the lucky one. He seemed interested in you, too!"

Wendy pulled a suitcase out from under her bed and loaded her things into it. "Don't be silly, Jackie. He's a friend. I haven't even talked to him since last summer. He may be handsome, but we have nothing in common."

"That's not true," Kit said. "You both work here. He looks like he's about your age, too."

Wendy scoffed. "And he took my sister out on a few dates last summer."

Jackie threw her arms into the air. "Oh no! That is definitely a deal killer! I'm sorry, Wendy."

"What are you sorry for? It's not like I like him or anything."

Kit caught Jackie's eye, and she could see they shared the same idea. Wendy was totally into Scott. But no one wants to share someone with their sister!

A crowd of girls huddled around a white, rickety scoreboard where Pratt had stapled the results of the various contests they'd all participated in over the course of the two-week camp.

Kit watched Jackie jostle her way to the front, then weave back out of the fray with disappointment etched into her features. "We're in third place. We have zero chance of getting to first, regardless of how the tug of war goes."

"I don't see what the big deal is," Kit said, frowning when Jackie kicked a clump of dirt as they walked away from the results board. "It's not like there's a big prize for first or anything, right? Don't they just get blue ribbons? I bet you already have a million blue ribbons at home."

Jackie looked at her, eyebrows raised, like it should be obvious. "I don't like to lose. Neither does Annie."

Annie, hearing her name, left a group of girls she'd been talking to and joined Jackie and Kit. "What don't I like?"

"To lose."

Annie looked back at the results board with a shrug. "You win some, you lose some. Come on, Jackie, didn't you have fun this year? I know I did. And you're going home a changed girl. Or should I say . . . *woman?*"

Kit winked at Annie. If Jackie wasn't going to relax about the topic, they'd poke fun at her instead.

"I saw that wink, Kit. You two promised not to tell anyone!"

"How many times do I have to say it? I haven't told *anyone*. Annie figured it out on her own. And, remember, I'm the one who saved you from extreme embarrassment at the softball game."

"Fine." Jackie sighed. "Heck, we might as well skip the tug of war. We can't win anyhow."

"I didn't take you for a quitter, Jackie," Kit teased.

A commotion near the results board caught their attention. Pratt was giving high fives to everyone within reach.

"I wonder what's got *him* so excited," Kit said.

The woman who had come with Pratt to their cabin after the money went missing was standing next to him. The pinched look was gone from her face, replaced by a grin from ear to ear. In fact, all the counselors near the two of them wore expressions of relief, too.

"I bet they found the money!" Jackie said.

Annie's head swiveled between Jackie and the excited group of staff. "Wouldn't that be great if they did? No more doubts over who might have taken it."

Kit raised her eyebrows, relieved. "That would be the best news ever. I still feel like I was one of the prime suspects."

Lynette skipped over to the trio. "Did you guys hear? They found the money!"

"We wondered if that was what everyone was so excited about. Where was it?"

"Don't know. But there's Wendy, talking to that other counselor, the cute one from our cabin. She probably knows the story."

All four ran over to where Scott and Wendy stood huddled in a hushed conversation.

"Is it true?" Lynette asked, grabbing Wendy's upper arm. "Did they find it? I *told* you we had nothing to do with the missing money."

Instead of responding, Wendy looked around them, as if trying to spot someone else. She didn't look as excited as Kit would have expected her to be if someone had indeed solved the mystery of the missing money. "Have you guys seen Fran?"

Annie nodded. "She's here. Don't worry. I saw her with Ivory, signing up for the tug of war. She'll probably come find you. She said she'd check in with you, didn't she?"

"Did you four sign up already?"

"Not yet," Kit said, noticing Jackie squirm. She'd just as soon skip the final competition, but Jackie looked like she was struggling with the idea of bowing out, even knowing they couldn't win.

Then she wondered again: Why didn't Wendy look more relieved?

"I'll go talk to Pratt," Scott said to Wendy before jogging off.

"They found the money, didn't they?" Annie pressed. Wendy still hadn't answered Lynette.

"Right," Wendy said, as if distracted. "Yes, it showed up. Now, why don't you guys go get signed up? I need to find my sister."

They watched Wendy walk away, that distracted look still on her face.

"We might as well go register," Jackie said, though Kit could tell her heart wasn't in it.

"Do we have to?" Lynette whined. "I'd rather go sit in the shade and chill until it's time to go. I feel so *relieved* that they found the money. I just want to relax."

Jackie looked conflicted. "But what will Wendy think?"

"Jackie, can't you see something is still bothering her?" Kit said. "She won't notice one way or another if we do the tug of war."

Jackie shrugged, finally giving in. "Lead the way to some shade then, girls. I wish we knew what *really* happened with the money, and if that's what's still bothering Wendy."

Kit headed for the nearest stand of trees. "We may never know. I'm just glad the spotlight is off of us."

After the tug of war and awards ceremony concluded, the five remaining girls met again inside Cabin 7. Nancy had gone hours before, and Fran was probably off with Stella's girls.

"I wonder what Nancy decided to wear to the wedding tonight?"

"Who cares what she wore?" Lynette said. "I wonder if she'll get up the nerve to ask the bride's brother to dance!"

Wendy yelled through the screen door, "Renee, your folks are here! Grab your things."

Turning to Lynette, Renee caught her hands. "Remember, you promised to write. If you hear from Nancy, find out what happens tonight at the dance and let me know. I bet she dances with him."

The two girls hugged, then Renee gave Jackie, Kit, and Annie each a quick hug as well. "I'll miss you guys! I wish we could do this every summer, but I'll probably go back to Whispering Pines with my family again next year instead. I hope I'll see you again someday!"

After reuniting Renee with her parents, Wendy came back inside.

"Thanks for everything, Wendy," Annie said. "The kaleidoscopes were a great idea. I can't wait to show mine to my sister! None of our families are here yet? Not that I'm in a big hurry to leave. Camp was great this year."

Wendy sank to the floor, her back resting against her stripped mattress. "They aren't here yet, but I'm sure it won't be long. I wanted to talk to you four, though, before you go. Sit down, will you?"

They all joined her on the wooden floorboards, exchanging curious glances.

"What's up?" Jackie asked. "I'm surprised you don't seem more relieved that they found the money."

Wendy nodded. "That's what I wanted to talk to you about, actually. There's been a strange twist to the story. I'm not sure what to make of it, and I'll only tell you if you all promise not to run out of here and blab about it to anyone else. I feel like you have the right to know, but this has to stay between the five of us. Can you promise me that?"

All four nodded solemnly, assuring Wendy that whatever secret she had to share was safe with them.

"Friends keep each other's secrets, Wendy," Jackie declared. "And you've always been more than a counselor to us. You've been a good friend."

Wendy reached over to tap Jackie's foot, smiling at each of them. Kit saw the worry in her features melt away. Finally, she took a slow breath and said, "Fran turned the money in."

Kit wasn't sure she'd heard Wendy right. "Fran?"

Wendy nodded. "Scott saw someone set a metal box down outside the office door a few minutes after he'd arrived. He didn't think the girl noticed him, and she ran off before he could ask her what she was doing. He tried the office door, half expecting it to be locked, but it wasn't. Since the box was locked, he thought it might be something important, so he set it on a desk inside. Justine came out of the back storage room just then and screamed when she saw the box. Scott didn't have a clue what was happening. He'd only just arrived, so he didn't know anything about the missing cash. At first, Justine thought *Scott* may have taken it, but it couldn't have been him, since he'd just gotten dropped off minutes earlier."

Kit was trying to follow the timeline. "Was that before or after he brought his duffel bag here?"

"Before, but he didn't want to ask me about it or bring it up in front of all of you. You see, when Fran ran in here, Scott recognized her T-shirt. He was certain she was the same girl who left the box by the office door."

"How did Fran have the box in the first place?" Lynette asked, looking as confused as Kit felt. "Wait . . . did she *steal* it?"

Wendy shook her head. "We confronted her about it, and she swears she found the locked box behind the mess hall."

"And you believe her? Fran seems like the type of person who'd love to take credit for turning in the missing money. Unless, of course, she stole it in the first place," Kit pointed out.

Wendy blew out a sigh of frustration, her bangs puffing up from her forehead. "I don't know what to believe."

"I bet she took it because she wanted to make me look bad."

"We can't assume something like that, Kit," Wendy said.

But Jackie was nodding, staring at Kit. "She did it because Ivory was mad at you, and if Fran got you in trouble, that would make Ivory happy."

"But what about me? Why would she want to hurt *me*?" Lynette asked. "I didn't do anything to Ivory *or* Fran."

Jackie thought for a moment, then her eyes grew wide. "Fran was making kaleidoscopes with us. She saw you come back from the office without Kit. She probably figured you wouldn't get in trouble."

Wendy looked uncomfortable with the turn in the conversation. "Ladies, we don't have any proof that happened. Why would Fran return the money if she took it in the first place?"

Kit shrugged. "Guilt, maybe?"

"What's going to happen to Fran now?" Lynette asked.

"Let me worry about that," Wendy said.

The evasive answer frustrated Kit. She had a bad feeling about it. "Don't tell me they're treating Fran like the hero here." When Wendy refused to meet her eye, Kit feared she was right. "Is Pratt really that gullible?"

Wendy got off the floor with another heavy sigh. "Ivory corroborated Fran's story."

"I wouldn't exactly call Ivory credible," Annie chimed in, scowling.

"She may not be credible, but her daddy is the mayor back home, and the park board employs Pratt," Jackie said with disgust.

Wendy snapped her fingers. "Bingo."

"Well, that just *stinks*," Lynette spat out, jumping to her feet.

"Anybody home?" a woman's sing-song voice floated through the open window.

"And that's my mom."

Wendy grabbed Lynette's hand. "Remember, you promised to keep this between us. We might not agree with how this is being handled, but for all we know, Fran is innocent. Pratt made Fran and Ivory promise not to say anything either."

Lynette rolled her eyes, then hugged Wendy. "I'll keep it to myself. But I doubt Ivory can keep her big mouth shut."

The screen opened and Lynette ran into her mother's outstretched arms.

"Hi, Mom! I missed you."

"Tell me you didn't cry yourself to sleep every night this year, Lynette," her mother teased, her arm staying wrapped around her daughter's shoulders.

Kit watched them, sure it had been Lynette she heard crying softly at night.

Lynette introduced Kit to her mother before they left, and then, just like that, only Jackie, Kit, and Annie remained with Wendy in Cabin 7.

"I'm sorry to drop this on all of you just before you leave," Wendy said. "I know it's hard to hear. But I really need you to keep quiet about this."

Kit hated the worry that had crept back into Wendy's eyes. She didn't think Fran and Ivory would keep quiet about it either, but she could. "We won't say a word. I promised to keep quiet, and I always keep my promises." She picked up her grandfather's battered suitcase, grunting with the weight of it.

Wendy looked between the three girls, as if deciding for herself whether or not she could trust them.

"Wendy? Are you in there?"

She picked up her clipboard from the bedside table and pointed at each of them, winking her acknowledgment of their promises, before going outside to see what her twin needed.

Jackie picked her suitcase up, too, then nodded toward the door. "I guess that's that then. We better get going."

Kit nodded, but she hated to leave things open where Fran was concerned. "Are we really going to let Fran get away with this?"

"Of course not." Jackie smiled. "She'll pay. But we won't breathe a word of this to anyone. Because we promised."

"We'll find a way to make things right," Annie added.

Kit returned their grins, relieved her two new friends weren't willing to let it go, either. "School is going to be interesting, isn't it?"

Jackie laughed. "Welcome to Ruby Shores, Kit. I have a feeling summer camp is only the beginning of lots more fun adventures."

reunion with friends

BACK HOME IN
RUBY SHORES

2018

Chapter Fourteen

"There's weather moving in. I can feel it in my bones," Glen declared. "You girls may want to take your wine to the basement tonight. Or better yet, I hear that new restaurant downtown is offering free appetizers on Thursday nights."

Jackie snorted at her father's less than subtle hint as she stood to clear the dishes. "Don't worry, Dad. We have plenty of reminiscing to do about our many adventures, but I promise we won't keep you up all night with our giggling. We aren't teenagers anymore. And since when did you turn into one of those old men who use their body as a barometer?"

Charlotte sighed. "Don't tease your father, dear. You may be the only one in the world who can get away with calling him old, but that doesn't mean you should."

Her mother was right. Jackie didn't appreciate when someone made her feel old either. Her early morning phone call from Sam had been a tough reminder of that fact. The news had left her depleted, but her visit with Annie had helped, and the upcoming evening with Kit and Lynette gave her something to look forward to.

"Guess where I was this morning, Dad?" she said, hoping to cheer her father up instead of hurting his self-esteem some more.

He shrugged, one hand absently petting Hoover as she sat patiently in his lap. "I suppose you stopped in at the Crystal Café."

"You're right, I grabbed breakfast there, but I was referring to my stop to see Annie Pierce. Your old office hasn't changed much."

Charlotte cleared the last of the dishes while Jackie filled Hoover's bowl with kibble and set the excited dog down before she could jump off Glen's lap and hurt herself in her frenzy to reach the food. With nothing left to hold on to, Glen rubbed his hands together then tapped the tabletop. He never had been good at sitting still.

"You mean she hasn't painted everything pink and put vases of flowers all over the place?"

Jackie felt torn. Part of her wanted to scold him for saying something so stupid, but another part of her was relieved to see him get a little of his spunk back. "No. But you knew she wouldn't do that. You're just being ornery. The only big change I noticed was the computer."

He snorted. "I hate those things. Principals should be out among the students and staff, not sitting in an office typing away on a computer."

"I'm afraid she doesn't get to pick between one or the other. The only way she can do the job nowadays is to be competent at both."

Charlotte snapped her dishcloth after drying the dishes that hadn't fit in the dishwasher. She threaded a corner of the cloth through a drawer handle, then motioned to her husband. "It's a good thing you retired when you did, dear. Now, come on. Your show starts in five minutes, and Jackie has company coming. Let's take Hoover back to the family room with us so the girls can have some privacy."

Jackie checked the clock, surprised to see it was so late. She opened the fridge and retrieved one of the two bottles of wine she'd purchased earlier that day.

At the doorway, Glen slapped his hand against the trim. "Hear anything on that job?"

She grabbed the second bottle.

"Maybe I'll get a call tomorrow." She hated to lie, but she really didn't want to get into that discussion with her father at the moment.

The doorbell rang.

"I better skedaddle before your mother comes back for me," he said, disappearing.

Kit stood on the opposite side of the screen, a vase of pink roses in one hand and another bottle of wine in the other.

"You shouldn't have," Jackie said. As she reached for the bouquet, she remembered her father's comment about Annie filling his old office with flowers, and smiled.

"I didn't," Kit said, handing her the bottle instead. "These are for Charlotte, courtesy of Hazel."

Laughing, Jackie held the door for her. "I have some munchies back in the kitchen. Help me bring everything out here to the front porch, will you?"

Kit grimaced, waving a hand in front of her nose. "It smells like tuna in here. These roses will either help with that, or make for a nasty combination that your mother will not appreciate."

Jackie chuckled as she tucked one bottle of wine into the crook of her arm, then laced her fingers around the stems of three wineglasses and picked up a large tray of meat, cheese, and crackers. Balancing these precariously, she nodded to a bag of chips she couldn't carry, then wrestled the screen door open with one foot. "My folks had tuna hotdish tonight. With peas."

Kit made a gagging sound. She grabbed the chips and quickly followed Jackie back to the porch. "No wonder it smells like the old cafeteria in there. Did you eat any of it?"

"God, no! But apparently it's now one of my dad's favorite dishes. Speaking of the cafeteria, guess where I went today?"

"To see Annie?"

"Right! It was weird to be back in the school. Things looked the same." She set their refreshments on the old steamer trunk that served as the porch's coffee table.

"Oh, Annie . . . I can't wait to see her again."

The sound of a lawn mower firing up nearby irritated Jackie. She didn't want to have to compete with the noise, but she also refused to go inside on such a beautiful evening. "You'll have to wait a little longer. She can't make it tonight."

Kit scooped the corkscrew off Jackie's platter before sitting in one of the three wicker rockers. She propped the bottle between her thighs for leverage. "That's disappointing. We all have lots to catch up on."

"How are things over at your grandmother's?"

"Things have been better." Kit grunted when the cork let loose, then tossed the bottle opener and stopper onto the trunk before filling a glass for each of them. "It feels strange, drinking wine out in the open at your house."

"It's almost like drinking Boone's Farm in my basement again, but we don't have to hide it from my parents anymore."

"At least this vintage tastes better," Kit said, raising her glass. "To coming home, and the good, the bad, and the ugly all of that entails."

"Hear, hear!" Jackie agreed, tapping her glass to Kit's.

"You ladies better not be starting without me!" another voice joined theirs, raised to be heard over the grind of the lawnmower. Jackie spotted their friend sauntering up her mother's flower-lined sidewalk, hands tucked inside a billowing skirt.

"Lynette!"

She set down her glass, sloshing wine onto the scarred wooden trunk top in her haste. Kit mirrored her actions—minus the spill—and together they rushed down the stairs, arms extended.

"You look amazing," Kit said, holding one of Lynette's arms up as she inspected her.

Jackie echoed her words, taking in Lynette's carefree appearance before shooting an angry glare at the noisy neighbor. A flash of lightning lit up the dark horizon behind the two-story house next door. With luck, the approaching weather would force him inside.

She turned back to Lynette, noticing the thick bands of silver weaving in and out of her once jet-black curls that still trailed down her back and shoulders. "You look like a middle-age gypsy!"

Lynette tossed her hair back over her left shoulder, frowning. "Well, shoot. I was going for a *witchy* look."

"If it was an old crone you were hoping to mimic," Kit said, running a finger down one of Lynette's silver streaks, "you look too sexy to pull that off!"

The reunited trio turned back toward the porch, their arms wrapped around one another's midsections in sisterhood as a breeze ushered them on. Sprinkles of rain stained the concrete in front of them, and, just as Jackie had hoped, the annoying purr of the lawnmower cut off.

"When did you get to town?" Jackie asked, watching Lynette as she settled into the third rocker. The bohemian-style print of her voluminous skirt was a vivid contrast to her gauzy, low-cut white blouse. An assortment of silver necklaces, nestled against the burnished skin of her bare neck and upper chest, disappeared into her cleavage. Silver bangles jingled as she accepted a glass of wine from Kit.

"A few hours ago. We drove all night. Or, I guess I should say *Wyatt* drove all night. I mostly slept. We relaxed at the hotel, then I freshened up, and he dropped me off so I wouldn't have to drive home later, since you mentioned an abundance of wine when we talked last week."

"Dang, girl, you should have saved that ensemble for tomorrow night," Kit said, motioning at Lynette's outfit with her left hand. If Lynette noticed the sparkle of the new diamond on Kit's ring finger, she didn't mention it.

Laughing, Lynette tugged at a silver chain, pulling an egg-shaped crystal out from between her breasts. "Do you like it? It's from my spring collection."

Jackie thought of the conservative sundress she planned to wear to their reunion dinner the following evening, now hanging in her childhood closet upstairs. Why was everything she owned so boring? "Like it? I *love* it! Things must be going well for you then. I want to hear all about it."

Lynette reached for an almond on the platter, chunky silver rings flashing as she popped the nut into her mouth. "Where's Annie?"

"Tied up with something. I was hoping to see her tonight, too—but at least there will be more wine for us," Kit joked.

Jackie glanced at Kit, wondering what sorrows her friend might want to drown. "I swung by the school today and we had a quick visit. Whatever she had going tonight, she couldn't reschedule, but she's eager to see you both tomorrow."

Lynette sipped her wine. "I still have a hard time picturing her behind your father's old desk, doling out punishment and guidance as the principal."

"It is strange to see her sitting at the same desk," Jackie agreed.

Her friend's words conjured a memory of the time they'd all ended up in that office, along with Lynette's mother. The contrast between that Lynette and the modern-day one sitting in front of her now was striking. That girl had been a curious mixture of a mama's girl and teenage rebel. This woman exuded self-confidence and poise.

Had *she* changed as much as Lynette?

Kit poured herself a second glass. "You mentioned Wyatt. Who is he?"

Lynette kicked off her strappy sandals and tucked one foot up under her other leg, considering the question. "We don't really believe in labels. We met on a photoshoot. He's very talented with a camera. That was last summer. We enjoy each other's company, but beyond that I don't know what you'd call us. 'Boyfriend and girlfriend' sounds so juvenile."

"Lovers?" Jackie offered, grinning.

"Yes, but even that sounds too narrow. Suffice it to say we complement each other in every way that's important."

"Leave it to you to be in a hard-to-define relationship," Kit said.

Tilting her glass toward Kit, Lynette winked. "That seems to be my modus operandi, doesn't it? Speaking of relationships, how long have you and Dean been engaged?"

Kit dropped her left hand into her lap, spinning her ring so the diamond nestled against her palm. "For a few months. We haven't set a date or anything."

"Did he come home with you? It would be great to see him again."

Jackie noticed the way Kit shook her head and tried to turn the conversation to Lynette's thriving online clothing business, and again she wondered what might be bothering her friend.

"I'm so thankful Mom survived her cancer to see our business grow," Lynette was saying.

When Lynette almost lost her mother to breast cancer, Jackie remembered feeling a surprising jolt at the idea of her own mortality. "How involved was she in getting your business off the ground before she got sick?"

"Our business wouldn't exist without Mom."

A gust of wind rattled the wind chimes hanging beneath the corner of the porch roof, just beyond the screening that kept troublesome mosquitos at bay.

"I wonder if we're going to get a storm," Kit said, leaning forward to catch a peek of the darkening sky.

Lynette fiddled with the large silver ring on the middle finger of her right hand.

"Is that one of the pieces you sell?" Jackie asked.

Nodding, Lynette held her hand up so she could study the ring. "Mom designed it. I never took it off when she was sick. She has a matching one."

Kit kicked her shoes off, too. "I've always envied the close relationship you share with your mom."

"I know I'm lucky. But when I was younger, I felt like the odd ball, since it was just me and her. Most of the time we were so poor we barely scraped by. You two, and Annie, all headed off to college after high school. That was never in the cards for me. There wasn't any money."

Lynette touched her left cheek, her fingers tracing a scar that reached from her temple to her jawline. The mark was faint, faded with time, but Jackie knew it would never completely disappear from Lynette's body or memories.

"Traveling the world like you did gave you the kind of education Kit and I could only dream of," Jackie said.

"I can see that now," Lynette conceded, "but at the time I thought I was being punished."

"And *now* look at you! A successful business woman, playing by your rules, coming to your high school reunion to show off your beautiful outfits with a sexy cameraman on your arm."

Lynette laughed as she poured herself another glass of wine. "I never said he was sexy, and you've never met him, so how can you say that?"

"He's dating *you*, isn't he? I've never known you to date anyone who wasn't incredibly hot." Jackie stood. "I'll go grab another bottle of wine."

Conversation and laughter continued behind her as she went inside. Hoover came running at the sound of the screen door. Jackie had to smile. Even her bark had a sassy ring to it.

Her cell phone buzzed on the kitchen island just then. A quick glance told her it was Ben, checking to see if she was enjoying her time at home.

What was she going to do about Ben? She'd told her father the truth when she'd said they'd broken off their relationship two years ago. She had been the one to end it, and while the breakup marked a painful time in her life, she'd initiated it because it felt like there was something lacking in their relationship. But ever since he'd dropped in on her four months earlier, he'd been persistent about wanting to give it another try. Her daughters weren't helping, either, both insisting that Jackie give him a second chance.

She wanted what Lynette always seemed to have—handsome, edgy men who kept her on her toes—and probably curled her toes, too, when it came to sex. Maybe it was too much to ask for at her age, but that didn't mean she had to settle for Ben. He was kind, and it was hard to let him go, but she wanted passion. And if she couldn't have passion, she was fine being alone.

"Where's that wine?" Kit yelled.

She'd deal with Ben later. Just like she'd deal with the job she didn't get later. Jackie flipped her phone back over and scooped up Hoover in one hand, their second bottle of vino in the other.

"You need to meet Kit and Lynette, little lady. They will not believe you're *Dad's* dog."

CHAPTER FIFTEEN

J ACKIE TOOK A SIP of tepid water, the curves of the squat glass still familiar to her hand. Was it possible these were still the same glasses as when they were students?

She used the evening's program to fan herself, but neither the artificial breeze nor the aged cooling unit in the old school were a match for the sweltering summer evening pressing against the cafeteria's windows. A bead of sweat meandered down Jackie's back. Good thing the multicolored flowers strewn across the cotton fabric of her sundress would mask her discomfort.

The sleeveless shift she'd finally decided on didn't conceal her less-than-toned arms, but she'd have melted if she'd worn the navy number. She'd have to remember not to wave at any old friends. At least the cut of the dress was flattering, though she wished again that she'd ordered an outfit from Lynette's company, one with a looser, cooler fit.

Next time, she promised herself.

Lynette and Annie stood beside their table, catching up. Annie, upon learning her other three friends were coming alone, left her husband at home, too. He wasn't local, so he was happy to sit the first night of his wife's class reunion out.

Jackie gave up trying to fan herself. "Nothing like a class reunion to challenge a woman's self-confidence," she muttered, setting down her glass and tossing her program onto the white linen tablecloth.

"You've got to be kidding," scoffed Kit, sitting across the table from her. "You've never lacked confidence, Jacqueline Turner."

Jackie eyed Kit. "How did you know I was considering dropping Henning and taking my maiden name back?"

Kit threw back her head in a bark of laughter, and Jackie's concern over her flabby arms and sweaty back faded away. Time with Kit, as well as with Annie and Lynette, was the only reason she'd agreed to come home for this silly reunion.

"I didn't know, but I'll always associate the name Henning with your ex, and since that part of your life is thankfully far back in your rearview mirror, I'm just going to go back to Turner for you now, whether you make it official or not."

"But what about my girls? We'd have a different last name if I drop Henning."

Kit shrugged, unconcerned. "They're practically adults. They could change their last name, too, if they ever get married and choose to take their spouse's name. Regardless, unless you think it would hurt your career, I'd change it."

"I don't care about that."

This tidbit caused Kit's smile to falter. "Since when doesn't work figure into almost every decision you make?"

"Since yesterday morning," Jackie admitted. "But I don't want to talk about it now, okay?"

"Did you lose your job?"

"No . . . but seriously, not now. Please?"

"Fine, but you *will* tell me later." Kit scanned the crowd milling about. "Now, who can we gossip about in here?"

Jackie wasn't terribly interested in catching up with anyone else in attendance at the weekend's events. Just Kit, Annie, and Lynette. The intensity of their friendship had ebbed and flowed through the decades—partially because of the normal demands of busy lives, but also due to neglect—and it was time to rectify that. They'd promised each other that the Kaleidoscope Girls would be forever friends. The rest of her life might crumble around her, but these women would always be her rocks.

As she watched Kit scan the room, it occurred to her that these three beautiful souls might not know how important they each were to her. When was the last time she'd bothered to tell them? Life could be cruel, and she'd learned you don't always get a second chance to tell someone how much they mean to you.

She caught a waiter walking between the tables with a bottle of wine and asked him to top off their glasses. "Would you mind bringing her a glass, too?" she asked, noticing Lynette wasn't holding one, but her friend waved the request away, insisting she didn't care for one. Jackie acquiesced with a shrug. Maybe she was battling a migraine. She'd suffered from them when they were younger. Or the vintage may not be to her liking. Lynette's taste in wines had no doubt matured beyond the bottles they'd swilled around bonfires in high school.

Jackie raised her glass and the other three followed suit once Annie and Lynette each took a chair.

Lynette giggled as the light from the candle on the tabletop revealed the cloudy state of her water glass. "Annie, tell me these aren't still the same glasses we drank out of in high school. I swear, they look like they could be the same ones, but with an extra thirty years of use."

Annie rolled her eyes. "Two words, Lynette. *Budget. Cuts.* Now, quit busting on the tableware. I think our fearless leader has something to say."

Jackie felt three sets of eyes swing back in her direction. "You know I hate it when you say that, Annie." If these precious women knew the full extent of the ways she'd sabotaged her own life, they wouldn't look to her for any type of leadership. "All I wanted to say was how much I love each one of you. My life would be dull and lifeless without you. You've saved me from myself more times than I can count. And I'm sorry if I've never told you I love you before." She reached to tap her glass against each of theirs, no longer caring if the loose skin under her upper arms flapped like bat wings.

No one said anything for a moment as each lowered their glass and took a sip.

The base of Jackie's wineglass caught the edge of the butter plate when she set it down, and the spell broke as wine drenched the bread basket.

Annie moaned with dismay, half standing while peering into the basket of ruined rolls. "I've starved myself for the past two months leading up to this shindig so I'd fit in this dress, and I was finally going to treat myself to carbs tonight!"

Wine seeped from the bottom of the basket, darkening the cloth below it. "Since you *are* running this shindig, I think you could arrange for a new basket," Lynette pointed out between hiccups of laughter. Jackie was glad to see she mustn't have a headache after all.

Annie stood, using the napkin from her lap to cradle the dripping basket. "Be right back."

Kit leaned forward. "What's up, Jackie? Why are you getting all sentimental on us? Are you sick? Do *not* tell me you're dying. I couldn't take it. And why aren't you drinking, Lynette?"

Lynette's eyes dropped to the cover of the program she was fiddling with, then back to Kit. "I'm simply not drinking tonight." Her tone suggested she didn't plan to explain why.

Rather than press the matter, Kit picked up the silver water pitcher at her elbow and refilled Lynette's glass. Condensation dripped off the pitcher into the bowl of salad dressing.

"That thing is sweating more than I am" Jackie laughed. "And no, I am not sick or dying. I just want you three to know how much I appreciate you."

Lynette pulled her blouse away from her neck, glancing around the room. "And we love you, too, Jackie. Man, it is *warm* in here. Annie did a great job converting this place into something more than the smelly old cafeteria where we used to choke down those rubbery hamburgers though, didn't she? But I swear I can still smell that nasty vegetable medley they used to feed us every other day. Hey, do you remember that spectacular food fight in here? We watched it all from that corner over there. Those senior boys got suspended, right? Wasn't your brother one of them?"

Jackie's mind shot back to that infamous winter day. She hadn't thought about that horrible food fight in years. She could still picture the white blur of falling snow beyond the windows. Inside, a rainbow of colors and shouts filled the air. Orange cooked carrots, green lettuce, red Jell-O, and chocolate pudding rained down everywhere, staining clothes and making an awful mess.

She couldn't remember who or what started the fiasco, but she'd never forget how it ended. Her father, all six-foot-four of him, came gliding through the double doors. His wide shoulders filled the frame, and despite his silent entrance, some sixth sense pulled Jackie's eyes to his red face. As a lowly freshman, she was sitting with her friends at a table in a far corner, away from most of the action, but with a clear line of sight to what came next.

Even now, all these years later, she could still remember the way her blood iced over at the rage on her father's face; the vivid red of his cheeks and the tips of his ears signaled trouble. Their father's calm fury had always terrified Jackie. Inside a school that housed six grades and roughly five hundred students, he wasn't her father. He was Principal Turner, a man to fear if pushed too far.

His style of discipline would never work these days.

Unfortunately for Ronnie, Jackie's brother, there was no denying his involvement in the whole nasty affair. Their father caught him red-handed with a fist full of lettuce and a smear of chocolate pudding across his white AC/DC-emblazoned T-shirt. That day marked a turning point in the relationship between her dad and her brother. Whatever transpired between them happened behind closed doors, once they were in the privacy of their own home, and Jackie never knew the extent or details of the face-off.

Two weeks later, her big brother graduated from high school. Ronnie's college years were rocky. He was still in and out of the house, depending on his college schedule, but he no longer attempted to appease their temperamental father.

Once he finished with college, Ronnie left, and he never came back.

The food fight was a crazy, fun memory for most, but not for Jackie.

"The twinkle lights and greenery she brought in really soften things up," Lynette was saying, pulling Jackie back to the present.

"Our Annie has always had a magical touch," Kit agreed. "I know how disappointed she was when they couldn't hold this dinner at the Elks, but she made this work."

"Mom said this school wouldn't even still be operating if not for Annie," Jackie said, joining back in the conversation. She didn't want to dwell on painful family memories. The past contained a landmine of shadows and secrets she'd prefer not to face. She wanted a simple, fun night out with her besties. Surely that wasn't too much to ask.

Lynette nodded. "It's probably true. Too many things have closed in town already. If they lose the school, you might as well turn off the streetlights and take down the 'Welcome to Ruby Shores' sign out on the highway."

Annie reappeared with a fresh basket of rolls. "Here we go! Help yourselves. They'll be bringing out the salad and main course shortly. You didn't talk about anything fun while I was gone, did you?"

"Nothing other than Jackie assuring us she isn't terminally ill after her very moving declaration of love for all of us."

Jackie sighed. "Kit, are you ever going to get over your fear of displays of emotion?"

"Probably not, but remember, you love me regardless."

"That I do." Jackie helped herself to a fresh roll before passing the basket on. "And why don't we transition from all this serious talk to some good old-fashioned gossip? Since you probably know more than the rest of us, Annie, spill!"

Annie shook her head in mock horror as she held the bread basket away from the table.

"Cute. Come on, I'm serious! I'm sick of thinking about real life."

"Fine. Who do you want to hear about?"

It was Jackie's turn to survey the room. Her eyes caught on a solitary figure at a table in the far corner. The man looked engrossed in his phone. "How about that guy, sitting alone over there? Do you recognize him? I wonder what his story is. Why bother to come to a class reunion if you won't socialize?"

"Maybe he's a spouse, bored because he doesn't know another soul here," Kit said, squinting at the man Jackie pointed out.

Lynette had to turn in her chair to see who they were talking about. "Isn't that Owen Jameson?"

Jackie's heart sped up at the mention of her grade school friend. Until she happened by his house the previous morning, it had been a long time since she'd thought about Owen. "Really? If it is, I'd love to catch up with him. It's been too long. I can't believe I didn't recognize him!"

"Do you have your contacts in?" Kit asked.

"Those things feel like sandpaper in my eyes. I probably should have worn my glasses so I wouldn't be squinting all night, but . . ."

"But you're too vain."

"That's true!" Jackie admitted. No point in arguing.

She set her napkin on the table, thinking she'd go say hello to her old friend before their meal arrived, but a waiter slipped a plate of salad in front of her. At the same time a group of people were joining Owen at his table.

"I'll go visit with him after we eat. Do you have any scoops on him, Annie? Married? Kids? Rich? Career criminal?"

Annie pulled her chair closer to the table, picking up her salad fork. "Since when am *I* the one with all the dirt?"

"Since you are the only one who lives here, and since *you* sent out the invitations for this reunion. You would know if you addressed Owen's to Mr. and Mrs. or if his address included the word 'penitentiary.' "

Grinning, Annie reached for the salad dressing. "Fine. But I don't know much. And you have to pretend you don't know any of this when you actually talk to him, Jackie. Promise?"

Jackie stabbed a slice of tomato. "Cross my heart."

"I don't think he's married. Not sure if he ever was, but he has two grown sons."

"How do you know that?" Kit asked.

"Because, he still has a house in town, and I've run into the three of them a time or two through the years."

Jackie thought about the handsome arbor she'd noticed along the north side of Owen's old house during her morning walk the day before. "Their old house?"

Annie nodded. "Owen's parents are gone now. They lived there until first his father, then his mother, ended up in a nursing home. I thought the house might go up for sale after they passed. In fact, I might have bought it if it did. I've always liked the looks of that house, even though I've never been inside. But Owen kept it."

"Did you guys move?" Lynette asked.

Jackie tried not to show her frustration at the question. She wanted to know more about Owen.

"No, not yet," Annie said. "Anyway, I've always wondered what Owen does for a living, since he seems to spend most of his summers here, but I've never asked him. I just never knew him very well. He was part of our prom group our senior year, remember? But beyond that, we didn't run in the same circles. Not like you, Jackie."

"I'd hardly count being friends in grade school as running in the same circles, but I know what you mean," Jackie said, wanting to know more. "Is that all you've got? You aren't exactly the deep pool of juicy gossip I was hoping for, Annie."

Laughing, Annie set her fork down. "Well, there was a rumor floating around, but that's all it was, so I'm not sure I should mention it."

Lynette squealed. "Now you have my attention, too. Come on, Annie, you can't put that teaser out there and then clam up!"

Jackie hoped Annie was just hinting at some type of scandal to tease her, but she held her breath. Owen had been important to her, once upon a time, and she wanted to hear that he'd lived a good life, free of too much negativity. Not that it was easy for anyone to get to forty-eight years old without some drama and heartache.

"There were just rumors about where he got his money. Not only did he keep his family home, but he bought up some lakefront property a few years back. People expected him to develop it, but so far he hasn't done anything with it. Actually, now that I think about it, you guys know the land he bought up. It's where the summer camp used to be."

"*Our* summer camp?!" Jackie said, loud enough that conversations at neighboring tables quieted.

"Seriously?" Kit asked, looking as surprised as Jackie felt.

"One and the same," Annie confirmed. "It went into foreclosure because the previous owners couldn't pay the property tax. But they canceled the public auction. Come to find out later that somebody with deep pockets stepped up and not only paid the back taxes, but offered fair market value for the property. Eventually, word got out that it was *Owen*."

"When he is here in the summer, does he live out there, then?" Jackie asked. "There were quite a few cabins, at least when we were kids."

Annie shrugged. "No idea. There is activity at his old family house in the summers. I drive by there on Breconwood on my way to work. But whether he and his boys stay at the house, or out at the old camp, I couldn't say."

"That property has to be worth a lot of money," Jackie said, more curious than ever about her old friend. "I never thought his family had much money when we were growing up. If they did, they didn't spoil Owen with it."

Waiters appeared again and cleared their salad dishes, switching the plates out with their main course.

"This looks much better than the lunches in high school," Kit said, digging into her chicken Kiev. "Maybe Owen found the diamonds hidden in the waterfall out there."

Jackie smiled, remembering the tale their camp counselor, Wendy, shared with them about the Indian priestess who guarded the jewels that once purportedly lined the falls. She'd loved that story as a kid. Her mind conjured up a much younger Owen, with his round metal glasses and scruffy hair, climbing along the side of the falls, digging for rocks. Imagining him as a rock collector fit her old memories of him.

As she glanced over her wineglass, toward the corner of the room, she couldn't help but wonder about the type of man her childhood friend had become.

Chapter Sixteen

THICK, STEAMY AIR SURROUNDED Jackie as she stepped outside. Dinner had ended and the program would start in thirty minutes, giving her time to slip away to check in with her daughters. If Annie wasn't the emcee for the evening, she might have skipped it altogether. She loved catching up with Kit, Annie, and Lynette, but the truth was she was homesick. She missed Hailey and Mack. Summer hadn't been the same without her twins around. She also missed Nikki, and couldn't help but wonder how her dog was coping.

Wandering around the back of her old school, she spied an inviting picnic table perched under a familiar oak. The massive tree dwarfed the handful of others that dotted the back lawn. Jackie suspected this particular oak had provided the backdrop for countless snapshots on graduation days dating back even further than her own. The tree was old. The table was new. Her high-heeled sandals were flattering but painful, and it was an immediate relief to sit and kick them off. The grass caressed her bare feet. The breeze stirring the green leaves above didn't help ease the humidity, but their dance offered a calming effect nonetheless.

She tried Hailey first, since she was the daughter most likely to answer a phone call from her mother on a Friday night. Three rings and the girl's voice came through, but it was her voicemail. She resisted the temptation to use her phone to check her daughter's location, trying Mack instead.

"Hey, Mom! How's the reunion going? Is Aunt Kit there?"

Jackie smiled at her daughter's questions. While Hailey would have started the phone call with a detailed rundown of her own day, Mack was always more likely to inquire about her mother's life first. Whether it was because she was truly interested, or it was a way to avoid talking about her own life, Jackie was never quite sure. And what Mack didn't share, Hailey usually would, providing Jackie with a healthy amount of insight into the lives of her daughters.

"Yes, I met Kit at the airport and we drove here together. It's so fun to catch up. Oh, and I have news!"

"About Kit?"

"She's engaged!"

"Finally," Mack said, her relief evident in that one brief word. "Dean has wanted to get married for as long as I can remember. I never understood why Kit was so against the idea. I wonder why she finally changed her mind."

Jackie bent to pluck an acorn from the grass that her toes had found. "I'm not sure. To be honest, I'm also not sure she's as excited about it as she should be. But that's Kit for you."

"What about you, Mom? Have you talked to Ben lately?"

She sighed. The girls, Mack especially, refused to accept that her relationship with Ben had run its course. "Not lately, honey. You know we aren't getting back together, right? I know Ben's a great guy, and he's so much better to you and your sister than Todd has ever been, but sometimes that isn't enough to build a life together."

Jackie's phone beeped with a text from Kit.

Where did you disappear to?

She checked the time. She still had at least ten minutes before the program started. "But enough about me and my old friends. What have *you* been up to?"

They talked for a few more minutes, then Mack had to go. Her shift at the restaurant would start soon. Jackie knew she was putting in countless hours to earn money for next year's rent.

"Tell your sister hi for me, too. Love you!"

Jackie set her phone down and leaned her head back, eyes closed. She'd tried to keep busy enough with work that she could ignore the hollow ache she felt in her chest over the absence of her girls. Her marriage with Todd had never been strong, and it had finally fallen apart under the pressures of introducing two newborns into their household simultaneously. Raising them mostly on her own had resulted in a strong bond between the three. Ben entered the picture later, when the girls were already in middle school, and he'd slowly made inroads into their happy trio, until the four of them had felt like a complete unit.

It could have worked.

But, over time, Jackie realized there was something vital missing. The girls insisted she was skittish, scared to make things legal because of her first marriage. They kept hoping, even now, that she would find the error of her ways and go back to Ben.

"I'm not sure Annie will forgive you if you miss her program."

The words jolted Jackie out of her musings. She jumped to her feet and smoothed the front of her sundress, spinning toward the male voice.

Would she have recognized Owen if Annie hadn't put a name to him earlier while he sat in the corner on his phone?

Thirty years was a long time.

Or was it? His eyes looked the same, even though they were no longer blinking out at her from behind the round wire-rimmed glasses he'd worn as a kid. Their friendship had waned during junior high, and she remembered her surprise at the handsome figure he'd cut when a crazy set of coincidences landed him in their prom group during their senior year. The grown man in front of her now bore little resemblance to the cute boy in the white tux.

"Owen Jameson. It's been a long time. How are you?"

"Jackie Turner. It has indeed been a long time. I was hoping we'd have a chance to say hello."

Her phone vibrated with an incoming text on the table behind her. The program would be starting. She ignored it.

"I thought about you yesterday."

He raised his eyebrows. "And here I assumed you hadn't given me a moment's thought in years."

He wasn't far off, but it would be rude to admit as much out loud. "It was such a beautiful morning, I walked downtown for a cup of coffee and to pop in to see Annie. Wandering down Breconwood Road felt like a trip down memory lane. I saw your old house. So many memories . . ."

"Good memories, I hope."

"The best," Jackie assured him.

The memories hit her all over again. It was a shame they'd drifted apart.

Her phone vibrated again. "We better get back inside. Annie won't start late."

He shook his head and took a step backward, pulling a set of keys out of his pocket. "Don't let me hold you up."

"You aren't leaving, are you?"

He took another step back, wagging his phone in the air. "My son was driving over for the weekend, and his car is giving him trouble. He thought he'd make it to town if he took it easy, but he's still twenty miles out and there's steam rolling out from under his hood."

"Oh, heavens, you need to go," Jackie agreed. The mother in her hated the idea of anyone's son being stranded alongside the road.

Owen turned with a wave, but paused after a few hurried steps, turning back to her. "I really would love to catch up. Could I talk you into a cup of coffee Sunday morning? Or will you be leaving first thing?"

"I'm here until later next week, actually. But won't you be back for the dance tomorrow night? We could talk then."

"Sorry. I've got another commitment with my boys. I'd hoped to make my rounds tonight, catch up with a few people, including you. But, well, duty calls."

A surprising sense of disappointment settled in her gut. She considered her schedule over the next few days. "Annie is taking us out on the lake on Sunday afternoon, but I should be able to get away in the morning."

He grinned, and his face transformed into one that looked much more familiar than the adult version that had surprised her minutes earlier. "Great. How about nine? I'll get there a little earlier to grab us a table."

Feeling a flush of excitement at the chance to catch up with her old friend, Jackie returned his grin. "It's a date!"

Owen's phone rang.

"Go! Don't keep your son waiting."

"And don't forget *your* phone." He spun toward the adjacent parking lot and jogged off.

Jackie scooped up her phone, noticing a text from Hailey.

> Sorry I missed your call, Mom. Hot date tonight. I'll tell you all about it tomorrow. Well, maybe not all about it, but you know what I mean.

Hot date, indeed, she thought, hurrying back toward the school. She wondered what her daughter would say if she told her *she* had a hot date, too. Not that coffee with Owen was a date, exactly, but she found that she was already looking forward to seeing him again.

"I was starting to think you ditched us," Kit said, pulling out the chair next to her and tapping the seat. "Sit here so your back isn't to the stage."

"Where did you run off to?" Lynette asked, leaning forward to see around Kit.

"I wanted to catch the girls quick. I haven't talked to them since I got here."

"How are those two little sweethearts?"

Kit snorted. "They aren't so little anymore. They're going to be sophomores in college this fall, right?"

"That is not even remotely possible," Lynette said, grinning. "I still feel like I'm twenty instead of pushing fifty."

Kit slapped her knee. "How dare you? You're not allowed to say the f-word."

Lynette laughed. Didn't turning fifty bother her? Jackie wished she felt the same regarding their next big milestone birthday, now a mere two years in the future.

Tap, tap. "Is this thing on? Can you hear me?"

Lynette brought her head around, clapping at the sound of Annie's voice. "We can hear you!"

Annie held up a hand against the spotlight's glare. "Well, good, but I can't see you! Can someone turn that blasted light a little? You're blinding me."

The obnoxious beam swung away from Annie's face. A bit more comfortable, she straightened a pile of notes on the podium, folded her hands together, and leaned on her elbows, surveying the crowd in front of her. Jackie grinned at the sudden realization that Annie must be standing on a stool.

"Think she's nervous?" Kit asked.

"Nah," Lynette said. "Annie was born to do this. I bet she speaks in front of large groups all the time."

Jackie wasn't so sure. Addressing a room full of adults you used to know as kids would be much harder than talking in front of a group of students, something Annie surely did on a regular basis.

"I want to thank everyone for coming to help us celebrate our thirty-year class reunion," Annie began, giving a mock shudder.

Or maybe the shudder was all too real, Jackie thought. Three decades? Where *had* all those years gone?

"I'd also like to thank Marge and her crew over at the Crystal Café for catering tonight's event. The food was superb, and since many of us spent our lunch hours during high school sharing plates of your famous fries, it's only fitting that our class continue to support you!"

"Burgers and fries would have been easier to serve tonight," a voice shouted from the back of the room, drawing laughs.

"I can't believe Aunt Marge has kept that old place running for all these years," Kit said. "Too bad her sister didn't inherit the same work ethic."

"Marge is the best," Jackie said, glancing hesitantly at Kit. Her friend tended to get lost in a spiral of dark thoughts anytime she brought up her estranged mother. Hoping to divert the conversation, she referenced the open program on the table in front of them. "What else does Annie have planned for us tonight?"

"She told me she's keeping it short," Lynette said, checking her own copy of the evening's schedule. "There's a slide show, and a speaker or two."

Jackie was glad to hear the program wouldn't last long. The heat was getting to her, causing her head to ache.

"We thought it would be nice to hear from all of you," Annie was saying. "Get some updates!"

Kit leaned back in her chair and crossed her legs. "She's nuts if she thinks I'm getting up there to say anything."

"No, that isn't what she meant," Lynette said. "She thought it would be fun to find out who traveled the farthest to come here, who might have the most grandbabies already, that kind of thing."

"Well, that's a relief." Kit smiled. "I'm safe, given the perfectly boring, uneventful life I've lived up to this point."

"Unless one of her questions is who from our class is most likely to become a crazy cat lady."

Kit gasped, throwing a napkin at Jackie. "How dare you? I've only ever had two cats at a time, and I may be many things, but crazy isn't one of them."

"I'm not sure Dean would agree," Jackie said, laughing as she remembered Kit's story of how long it took them to figure out he was allergic to her cats. "Wait—are the *cats* the reason it took you so long to accept his proposal?"

"Ha-ha. Be quiet and listen. Annie is talking."

Winking at Kit, and hoping she hadn't offended her, Jackie turned her attention back to the makeshift stage.

"But first, I thought we'd share a slide show tonight. A big thank-you to Fran and Ivory for helping me unearth boxes of photos from both the school newspaper and the yearbook groups."

Jackie noticed Kit shudder at the mention of the two girls who'd tried to make her first years in Ruby Shores miserable. They were mostly unsuccessful, but she knew that Kit still held a grudge.

"Are those two bitches here tonight?" Kit hissed low, scanning the room.

"Easy, girl, pull those claws in," Lynette said, though she didn't look too pleased at the mention of the two, either. "I told you after they pulled that crap at summer camp that they weren't worth our energy. You have to let that stuff go."

"Did *you*?" Kit asked, looking doubtful.

"Mostly."

"I haven't seen them," Jackie said.

She was morbidly curious if they were both still attractive and annoyingly popular. But what did "popular" even mean at their age?

There was a section in their old yearbook that she'd forgotten all about until she paged through it before coming to the reunion. They'd voted for classmates in categories such as "best-looking," "best body," "most likely to succeed," and so on. She cringed at how inappropriate it all felt now. Those kinds of contests weren't likely to make it into modern yearbooks, surely. Unfortunately, social media now served a similar purpose, times a thousand. The world would most likely never embrace true inclusion, Jackie thought grimly.

"Oh, wow—I think that *is* Fran! And there's Ivory, too, standing near the doorway."

Jackie followed Kit's finger, holding her breath. Was it immature of her to hope both had aged poorly? When she spotted them, she expelled the air in a sigh. How had she not noticed them before? Neither had changed much, and Jackie hated them all over again.

"Wait until our forty-year reunion. I bet they'll both be stooped-over old hags by then," Lynette said, grinning.

"We look every bit as good as those two do," Kit said, crossing her arms in front of her chest. "And, Lynette, why don't you put one of those witchy hexes on them? Raise some warts. You know."

Lynette choked on the water she was sipping, her shoulders shaking as she tried to keep quiet. Once she got a handle on herself, she wiggled her fingers at Kit. "Last night I said I was going for a witchy look. I didn't say I *was* a witch!"

Kit shrugged, unconvinced. "I've always wondered about you."

Jackie grinned at their antics while secretly hoping Kit's statement about looking as good as the two women by the door was true. She still felt like she could be in high school—aside from the hot flashes and night sweats—so why couldn't she look like it, too?

As the lights dimmed for the slide show, her mind jumped back thirty years to the final few months in this very school.

promises between friends

RUBY SHORES
HIGH SCHOOL

1988

Chapter Seventeen

J ACKIE TIPTOED PAST THE door leading into the high school offices. She didn't want her father, or anyone who worked for him—he had spies everywhere, to catch her skipping track practice. With all the slamming locker doors and noisy conversations in the halls, she probably could have walked past the doorway in wooden clogs without anyone noticing, but she wasn't taking any chances. This was the only day that she could shop for prom dresses with her besties. Her father would never consider that a legitimate excuse to miss practice. If it were up to him, nothing short of a grave illness or loss of a limb would qualify.

Once she cleared the office, she skipped around the corner—and slammed right into the captain of the boy's track team. The stack of books she was carrying punched right into his solar plexus, knocking him back a step. Her books crashed to the floor. He dropped his notebook. His other hand still held his letterman's jacket draped over his shoulder. Horrified, Jackie dropped to her knees, restacking books and papers as quickly as possible.

"I'm so sorry, Nathan! I was in a rush and I didn't see you. Are you okay?"

He used his free hand to help her up, then picked up his notebook. Even though she was sure her face was as red as the prom flyer that had flown out of one of her dropped books, she forced herself to look at him, horrified to realize he couldn't catch his breath. She balanced her book stack on one hip and slapped him on the back with her other hand.

He twisted out of her reach, holding up a finger. "Just give me a second," he squeezed out, bending at the waist until he was able to suck in some air. When he could finally talk again, he grinned. "Practice doesn't start until four. What's the rush?"

She averted her eyes. Nathan wouldn't be any more understanding of her desire to skip practice than her father. He was the most dedicated athlete on the team. He was also the cutest, and Jackie harbored a secret hope that he might ask her to prom. They'd sat together on the bus for the ride back to the school after an out-of-town meet the week before, and they'd hit it off. At least Jackie thought they'd clicked. But there was also a track meet scheduled for the first Saturday in May, the same date as prom. For all she knew, he wasn't even planning to go to the dance.

"I'm not going to make practice today," she fessed up, trying to act as if it wasn't a big deal. She didn't want to tell him what she was doing instead.

The toe of his shoe kicked the prom flyer she'd failed to scoop up with her other things. He bent to pick it up, giving it a cursory glance before handing it back to her. "I hope you're not missing practice because you're coming down with something. I remember you said you wanted to break the school record for the 110-meter hurdles."

She wondered what he'd say if she told him the truth. He'd probably be disappointed in her lack of dedication. Most girls who planned to go to college on a track scholarship would put the sport first during the last season of their high school careers. Instead, she was planning to skip practice to go shopping.

"It's a family thing," she said instead, then bit back a groan over the lame excuse.

He rubbed his stomach, then nodded at the flyer on top of her books. "Are you going to prom? A bunch of us guys were talking about it at practice yesterday. It sucks that we have that big meet earlier the same day."

It was like he knew why she was *really* ditching track. She shrugged. "I want to go."

He shuffled his feet and bit his lip. Jackie realized he suddenly looked apprehensive—shy, even.

"Do you . . . have a date yet?"

A glimmer of hope blossomed in her chest. "No . . . not yet."

"Would you want to go with me?" he asked, his expression earnest. "I thought about asking you on the bus last week, but there were too many people around. And then I was worried someone would beat me to it."

Jackie grinned. It wasn't like they were alone now, but she wouldn't point that out. "I guess it was fortunate we ran into each other today. And yes, I'd love to go to prom with you."

Two other boys from the track team walked by just then, knocking Nathan in the shoulder, and she noticed his expression change to a cool mask of indifference. He nodded to the pair, then turned back to Jackie. "I'll call you then, when it gets closer, and we can make our plans around the meet."

Jackie tried to appear as nonchalant as Nathan, tossing her hair and moving her books back in front of her chest, wrapping both arms around the stack again. "Sure. Sounds good. We'll talk later."

Stepping around him, she headed for her locker. Her insides shook with excitement, but she fought to appear calm on the outside. Her shopping buddies were already gathered near her locker, but she stopped when Nathan yelled her name.

She looked back over her shoulder and he gave her a wink. "Have fun shopping."

Jackie climbed into the front of Kit's faded red Mustang that was parked in its usual spot along the curb directly in front of the school. Annie was already in the backseat. She had to yank the door hard so the latch would catch when she closed it. Kit's grandmother had given her the car the summer before their senior year as an early graduation gift.

The motor rumbled to life when Kit turned the key and worked the foot pedal. A group of eleventh grade boys walking by on the sidewalk gave whistles and catcalls, along with a couple of indecent hand gestures.

"In your dreams, boys!" Kit yelled out her open window before sliding her sunglasses on and pulling away from the curb.

Jackie, no longer fazed by the spectacle Kit's car created, spun in her seat so she could better see her friends. "Which one of you was blabbing around about us going prom dress shopping today?"

Kit shifted the car into drive, glancing her way. "Why?"

Jackie recognized that smirk. "I think you already know why."

Annie sat forward, her hands draping over the front seat between Kit and Jackie. "What's up? What are you two not saying? And why isn't Lynette riding with us?"

"I think Jackie got herself a prom date," Kit said, stopping for a red light on Main.

"Already?" Annie cried, knocking her fist against Jackie's shoulder. "With who? Am I the only one looking at prom dresses today who doesn't have a date yet?"

"Nathan asked me."

Annie's eyes grew wide. "As in cute, track captain Nathan? I didn't know he even knew you were alive."

Jackie slapped Annie's hand away. "What kind of thing is that to say? Jeez, Annie, you can be such a downer."

Annie sat back, crossing her arms in a pout. "Right back at you, Jackie."

"Oh, knock it off, you two," Kit said, driving again when the light changed. "She isn't trying to be mean, Jackie. You know what she meant. Nathan is part of the 'in' crowd, while we barely qualify for the fringes."

It was a conversation they'd had many times, and it wasn't something that bothered any of them. Much. Jackie sighed. "I met him through track. We sat on the bus together last week."

Kit nodded. "You told me that. And you had a silly grin on your face the whole time you were giving me the rundown of everything you two talked about during your forty-five-minute bus ride. I could tell you liked him. He sits behind me in homeroom. I *might* have mentioned we were going dress shopping today when I passed the stack of prom flyers back to him."

Jackie vented another sigh. She should have known Kit was behind the invite. Some of the elation she'd felt over what she'd thought was an unsolicited invitation ebbed away.

Kit pulled into an open parking spot near the Bumble Bee Boutique, the only women's clothing store in town that sold formal dresses. Prom was still two months away, but the girls wanted to pick out their dresses before others got all the good ones, or they'd have to drive into Minneapolis for more selection.

The motor kicked and sputtered when Kit shut it off. She must have noticed something in Jackie's body language or expression, because she grabbed her hand, squeezing it. "I swear on my dead grandpa's grave that I did not tell him to ask you. I was just making conversation."

Jackie gave her a side eye. "I hate it when you say that. Your grandpa was a sweet old man."

"He certainly was, and I'd never lie when I swear on his grave."

"I've known you for a long time, Kit. You never lie, period. Even when the truth hurts."

Kit tossed the keys in her purse, checking her reflection in the rearview mirror. She picked at her teeth with a fingernail. "Believe me when I tell you I had almost nothing to do with him asking you to prom."

Jackie took a deep breath. Kit was the most honest person she knew, and believing her meant Nathan might have actually come up with the idea to invite her on his own. "Wait . . . what did you mean when you said everyone would have a date except you, Annie?"

Annie slapped the backseat. "Kit has a date, you have a date. I don't know about Lynette. Where is she? No one answered me earlier."

"Working. She can skip her study hall during final period if it's for a job, and they're short over at Joey's Pizza, so they'll take her anytime, even if it's only for an hour or two. She promised to be here by four thirty. She said we can start without her."

Jackie held up a hand. "Wait. Kit. Who are *you* going to prom with?"

"You say that like it's shocking that someone would ask me," Kit said, sticking her bottom lip out.

"Oh, stop. That isn't it and you know it. It was like pulling teeth to get you to agree to shop for a dress today. You said you didn't even want to go."

Kit shrugged. "That was before my grandma told me she had an envelope of cash saved up to buy me a prom dress, and when I tried to refuse, she said she wouldn't take no for an answer. I can't disappoint her."

Jackie thought again, for the millionth time, of how lucky Kit was to have the support of her grandparents. Even though her grandpa was gone now, her grandma was still working hard to provide the best possible home for Kit and her brothers.

"My lab partner asked me if I wanted to go with him."

Annie leaned forward again. "He's been crushing on you all semester. It's sweet."

"Do you like him?" Jackie asked.

"I like him for his brain. If I had to partner up with some of the idiots in our chemistry class, I'd pull my hair out. We're going as friends. I will make that clear," Kit insisted.

"Heartbreaker," Jackie teased. "Should we go in?"

Kit squinted at a paper sign hanging on the store's door. "It looks like they're closed for a coffee break. It says 'Back in ten.' "

Annie sighed. "Lynette is sure working a lot lately, even for her. What gives?"

Jackie grabbed her backpack from the floor and dug around for her lip gloss and comb. If they had to wait, she might as well clean up a little. Her hair was probably a mess after a long school day—and her collision with Nathan. "I asked her that. She didn't want to say, but I pushed. I know money is always tight, and she has no time to study because she's working so much. Her grades are suffering for it. She finally admitted that her mom has a new boyfriend, and he's always hanging around the house."

"That isn't anything new. Being short on money, I mean," Kit said, eyebrows raised.

Jackie shook her head. "I think this is different. She said the guy makes her really uncomfortable. He goes out of his way to touch her, and the perv even had the nerve to ask her when she turns eighteen."

"Why doesn't she just tell Donna? Her mom has always put Lynette first. She wouldn't stand for that, if she knew."

Someone tapped on Jackie's window, sending all three girls into shrieks. Lynette mushed her face against the glass, infuriating Kit but causing Jackie and Annie to laugh so hard that tears streamed down their cheeks.

Kit rolled up her window and got out of the car, slamming her door and rushing over to push Lynette away so she could wipe the marks off with the bottom of her shirt.

"Chill!" Lynette laughed. "Why are you all sitting in the car?"

Kit pointed toward the store, but the sign was gone. "They were closed. We must have missed them coming back."

Jackie and Annie got out of the car, and the foursome headed inside.

"Please tell me you don't have a date to prom yet. I don't want to be the only one," Annie begged, looping her arm through Lynette's. "You smell like pizza. I'm starving."

Lynette shook her head as the two led the way to racks of formal dresses in the back. "No date for me. I've been so busy, I haven't even thought about it. I'll just ask one of my coworkers to go with me if I don't find a date at school."

Annie released her arm and all four girls started browsing through the dresses.

"Hey, doesn't Owen work there?" Annie said. "You know, Jackie's old friend? Ask him."

This caught Jackie's attention. She and Owen used to be close, but she barely saw him anymore.

Lynette pulled a long, dark navy dress covered with silver stars off the rack. "Owen is super nice. A little too nice for me. No, I have someone else in mind."

Jackie took the dress out of Lynette's hand and held it up to her. "This would look amazing on you. It has a witchy vibe."

"Perfect! I'll try it."

Miss Sherman, the lone clerk in the store, approached the girls with a smile, before helping them select possible dresses to try on and getting them each a dressing room. Since it was one of the few places to shop in town, the stylish woman had been helping all four girls pick out clothing since their early teens.

"If it isn't hideous, we have to show each other," Jackie said, poking her head out from behind the curtain of her assigned room.

Annie was the first one to step in front of the three-way mirror. The clerk stepped forward to zip up the back of the dress.

"That's a nice color on you, Annie," she said. "It would need to be hemmed, but that'll be the case for any dress you select."

"I know, I know, I'm still short."

The clerk laughed. "You may not be very tall, but you've certainly filled out nicely. I'm not sure your momma would approve of all this cleavage."

Jackie stepped out of her dressing room, wearing a bright-purple confection that set off her chocolate-colored hair. "That looks beautiful on you, Annie! And she's right. Where did those boobs come from? I don't think you had those last week!"

Annie squirmed, trying to cover her chest. "They were there last week. I've just never worn anything this revealing."

"Let me see," Kit said, as she stepped out from behind her curtain. Jackie wrinkled her nose at Kit. "I know. Pink does nothing for me. I thought I'd try it, but this one is a definite no. I have a royal blue one I'll try next. Annie, that is fabulous on you! And I like the purple, on you, Jackie."

Annie did a slow spin, checking out the back of the dress in her reflection. "I do like the bright color. Here, I'll get out of the way so someone else can see. Hey, do all these vivid colors remind you of anything?"

Jackie stepped up to the mirror. The dress was a definite possibility, but she wanted to try on more. "No. Why? What do the colors remind *you* of?"

"Come on," Annie prompted, a saucy hand on her hip. "I'll give you a hint. Summer camp."

Kit grinned. "I know where you're going with this! It's about our science lesson today, too, isn't it?"

Annie nodded.

"What are you guys talking about out there?" Lynette said, still in her dressing room. "I can't figure out how the straps work on this one."

"Come out and I'll help you," Miss Sherman said. "There isn't anyone else around, just me and your friends."

Lynette came out holding the bodice of the dress against her chest, a mess of straps dangling in front of her. "Oh my God, Annie, you're a knockout in that dress! You look a lot like Millie."

Annie spun in a circle. "I'll take that as a compliment. Millie has always been the pretty one at our house."

"But you are the *nice* one," Jackie countered.

"Only the oldest of friends can say something like that to another girl without worrying about offending her," Miss Sherman said, doing her best to untangle the mess Lynette had made with her dress.

"Jackie knows. My big sister is pretty, but she isn't always the nicest. Don't get me wrong, I love her. But sometimes I don't like her much. Like last night. She has the sweetest boyfriend, his name is Liam, and they were supposed to go to the movies. But Millie bailed on him when her girlfriends invited her to a party. He deserves better."

The clerk grunted. "I've got one of those sisters, too."

Annie walked over to Kit. "Can you unzip me? I have a bright pink one to try, too."

"You could ask *Liam* to take you to prom," Kit said, lowering the zipper on the red dress. "Don't you get your braces off soon? Millie better watch out. It won't be long and you'll pass her over in the looks department, and if she doesn't treat her guy better, you could swoop in and steal him."

Annie shivered, catching the dress as it fell away on top. "Gross. I wouldn't do that." She disappeared for a few minutes then reappeared in a bright pink dress. "This one is pretty, too."

Kit, who'd slipped into the royal blue dress, shook her head. "It's pretty, but you have to get the red. You forgot to tell Jackie and Lynette what we found out about in science today. All that talk about Liam distracted you."

"Shoot! Right. Remember what we called ourselves at summer camp?"

Lynette nodded. The clerk had fixed the straps on the dress she was trying, and Jackie thought it looked beautiful on her. "Sure. We're the Kaleidoscope Girls!"

Kit nodded. "Yep. And what was the other cool thing we learned about at summer camp, that same year we made our kaleidoscopes?"

Jackie thought back, struggling to remember.

"The monarch butterflies," Annie said, smiling.

"Oh, I get it!" Lynette said, spinning in her nearly black dress, the silver stars sparkling under the overhead lights. "Both monarchs and kaleidoscopes are beautiful because of their bright colors. So you want us all in bright dresses because it fits our name."

"It gets even better," Annie said, clapping her hands. "We learned today that sometimes groups of monarchs are actually called *kaleidoscopes*."

All activity stopped. None of the girls moved a muscle. They almost looked like butterflies, dressed in their bright dresses, poised on a branch, just before flitting off.

"No way," Jackie said, shaking her head.

Kit grinned. "Yes way."

"I love the idea, but I also love this dress," Lynette said, her expression torn. "It's not bright."

"That dress works, too, because it looks like you're covered in diamonds."

Lynette laughed, executed a little moonwalk, and raised her arms up high. "From now on, you all must call me Dyani, Diamond Protector of the Falls!"

"If any of you decide on any of those dresses," Miss Sherman said, "bring them to the till and I'll either ring you up, or hold them for you if you need to have an adult stop in to purchase them." Then she walked away, shaking her head and mumbling something about crazy kids.

Once the four of them were alone, Jackie waved them into a circle. "Ladies, this is it. We made it. Only three more months and we'll all flitter off, just like the monarchs. But no matter what happens, we'll forever be the Kaleidoscope Girls!"

CHAPTER EIGHTEEN

K IT COULD HARDLY BELIEVE they'd be starting college in less than six months, but the tour they were taking made it feel real.

She'd left Jackie in the bedroom portion of the dormitory suite they were exploring, under the guise of checking the bathroom. She'd planned to room with Jackie, but the idea of sharing a living space with three other girls, instead of just one, did not appeal to her. She needed her own space. Since she only had younger brothers, Kit had always had a room to herself. College would be different, and she could accept that, but she'd agreed to room with Jackie specifically because she thought her old friend understood her need for solitude. If housing stuck them with a pair of obnoxious girls in tight quarters like these, Kit doubted she'd survive it.

Jackie bounced into the bathroom. "Come on, Kit, why do you look so nervous? Living here would be fun! College is supposed to be a new experience, a time to meet new friends, and enjoy some much-needed independence. I'm afraid if it's just the two of us together in a dorm room instead of a suite, it'll be harder to meet new people."

Kit wasn't interested in expanding her social network. She was more intrigued about the classes she'd register for, come summer. Would it be a mistake to room with Jackie? She loved the girl, but she'd also heard plenty of horror stories of ruined friendships when shared living conditions went bad.

"I wonder if they have any single rooms . . ."

Jackie froze, her expression crestfallen. "You're bailing on me?"

Kit jammed her hands in the back pockets of her jeans, kicking herself for uttering the words out loud. She hadn't wanted to get into this today, but her reservations were growing. "I didn't say I'm *bailing* on you. I'm just getting a little worried that you and I want different things out of our college experience. Don't take it personally. What if you get *bored* living with me? And what if I can't study as much as I'll need to? I can't afford to lose my academic scholarship. I'll need to keep my grades up. You just need to keep running fast to keep yours."

"I beg your pardon?" Jackie said, narrowing her eyes at Kit. "Are you implying that I won't work hard on my classes? You know I don't really care much about the track team. But if they want to give me money to pay part of my tuition, why wouldn't I take it?"

Jackie's voice notched up with each word until she was practically yelling. Kit could hear another group entering the suite. Grabbing Jackie's arm, Kit led her out into the hallway, not wanting to make a scene.

"Keep your voice down!"

Once out of the sample suite, Jackie yanked her arm away and stormed down the hallway. Kit was torn between feeling bad for upsetting her friend and thinking Jackie's reaction was an example of exactly why she was worried.

She followed Jackie at a slower pace, imagining what this narrow, painted cement hallway might feel like come September when it was teeming with countless other freshman girls. Since it was spring break, few girls were around now. Most of the doors were festooned with cutouts and stickers that Kit thought belonged in a kindergarten class-room instead of a college dormitory.

A door slammed behind her, and she turned to see a tall, thin boy scurry down the hall in the opposite direction, the hood of his sweatshirt pulled low over his face.

"Great," Kit whispered. Not only would she have to deal with a bunch of hormonal and emotional girls, but horny college guys would be sneaking in and out at all hours, too.

She was pretty sure she wasn't cut out for dorm life.

Once outside, she welcomed the warmth of the early spring sunshine. A few patches of dirty snow still nestled up against the south-facing wall of the dormitory, but stubborn shoots of fresh green plants poked up through the sludge. Winter and spring were in a battle for dominance.

"Kind of like me and Jackie, trying to figure out which dorm to pick," Kit said, looking both left and right for her ticked-off friend. "Where'd she go?"

"She hopped in the car and insisted Ronnie take her somewhere for ice cream," an older boy standing against a nearby tree said.

Kit jumped, so caught up in her own thoughts that she hadn't noticed Bruce standing there. He was one of Jackie's brother's best friends and had come along for the ride. "They *ditched* us?"

"Nah, they'll be back." He pushed away from the tree and sauntered over, dragging one foot to dislodge a chunk of mud he'd picked up with his shoe. "Man, I'll be glad when things dry up. Messy time of year."

Kit was ready to get on with the change of seasons, too, but not because she minded the mud that was always part of springtime in Minnesota. These last few months of high school were full of too many big events, none of which she was excited to take part in. She'd agreed to go to prom only because it was what her grandmother wanted. What if her mother crashed her graduation ceremony? If she did, would she behave? Kit would gladly skip the next twelve months of her life, if only that were possible. That would put her past all this fluff, and maybe she'd even be gearing up to move off campus by then.

"What are we supposed to do in the meantime?" Kit asked, irritated that Jackie would leave her with this virtual stranger while going off with her big brother to pout. Not that Ronnie would tolerate much pouting. No one in Jackie's family tolerated pouting.

Ronnie's friend shrugged. "Want to see the new wing they added on the library last year? I used it all the time last semester. Lots of huge windows and natural light, plus plenty of quiet study areas. If you're like me, I need quiet to study."

"I am very much like you then, Bruce, at least in needing my space and plenty of quiet. Yes, I'd love to see the library. If they have trouble finding us when they come back, that's on them."

With a nod, Bruce turned left and headed toward the center of campus. He was tall, and even though Kit was one of the taller girls in her class, she had to hustle to keep up with him. They walked in companionable silence for a block, but she had so many questions about campus life. "I know you said you're graduating in June, once you finish your student teaching back in Ruby Shores. You don't still live on campus, do you?"

"No way. I hated dorm life. I only tolerated it for the first year. Most of the guys only cared about parties and drinking. They were a bunch of slobs. For my sophomore year, I rented a house with a handful of other guys. It was a few blocks from campus."

He held an arm out in front of Kit to stop her before she could step out on the crosswalk. A guy on a bicycle buzzed past. He might have run her over if Bruce hadn't stopped her. Bruce barely seemed to notice, as if crazy bicyclists were a normal part of campus living.

"To be honest, that first house wasn't much better. Still too much noise and partying. After that, I found a small studio apartment, and I've been there ever since. That probably sounds incredibly boring to you. Not exactly the typical college experience, at least during my junior and senior years, but it's worked for me."

Kit skipped up a curb, still hurrying to keep up with him. "Actually, I'd rather jump right to that kind of living arrangement if I could. But it probably isn't in the cards."

He glanced her way with a knowing nod. "Let me guess. You told that same thing to Jackie when you were touring the dorms, and now she's pissed off."

"Something like that. But now I feel bad. I wish I hadn't said anything to her. We've been planning on rooming together for nearly two years."

They'd arrived at a large, sleek building sporting brass letters marking it as the library. Bruce held the door wide for Kit, allowing her to enter in front of him. She accidentally brushed against his broad chest, and she realized this friend of Ronnie's who somehow got roped into tagging along on this college tour was more man than boy.

Unlike the rest of her friends, Kit's interest in boys had been minimal, almost to where she'd worried there was something wrong with her. She didn't see what all the fuss was about.

But now, as she walked through the marble-floored lobby of a university library, hoping no one would realize she was actually a high school senior just touring the place, she understood. There was nothing wrong with her. She just hadn't met the right boy yet. Or man.

Too bad this one was off limits.

"You can just drop us off at Shoreline Pizza. It's late, and you guys probably have better things to do than hang out with us after two days."

They'd already agreed the four of them would grab pizza when they got back to town, so Kit could have kicked Jackie for trying to get rid of Ronnie and Bruce. Especially Bruce.

"Nice try, sis," Ronnie said, glancing at them both in the rearview mirror. "Shoreline was part of the deal. You're buying, remember? I drove your ass all the way to college and even tolerated a night at Mom's sister's house—which, by the way, the basement where she stuck me and Bruce reeked of mold. You two lucked out getting the spare room upstairs. Not to mention having to listen to your bellyaching about your roommate drama. You aren't even in college yet, and you two are already arguing? You better figure that mess out, or it'll never last."

Bruce peeked back at the girls, winking at Kit.

She hoped he had no idea how her stomach flipped at his half grin.

How was she going to act normal when she saw him in the hallways of her high school as a student teacher? She'd allowed herself to fantasize that he thought of her as an equal, when he'd given her a tour of the library and then walked with her to his studio apartment. But she wasn't his equal. He was nearly done with college and working as a student teacher. She was still one of the students.

It had turned out that, unbeknownst to her, he'd known all along that Ronnie and Jackie would be waiting at his apartment, Jackie having cooled down, and suddenly she felt more like Bruce had been her babysitter.

Jackie crossed her arms, shooting a death glare at the back of her brother's head. "You agreed to the trip because Mom bribed you with a hundred bucks, and it gave you an excuse to sneak out last night to see that girlfriend of yours."

"Hah," Bruce said, shoving at Ronnie's shoulder. "*Told* you someone would hear you leave."

"Why didn't you just stay at college over spring break?" Kit asked. She hadn't realized Ronnie was seeing someone. It made her wonder if Bruce had a girlfriend, too, even though he'd never mentioned one.

"Because he brought all his dirty laundry home for Mom to wash," Jackie said. "And we have to go to Grandpa's eightieth birthday party at the nursing home tomorrow."

"And I just tagged along because there's not much to do in Ruby Shores anymore," Bruce said. He looked to be getting a kick out of the brother-and-sister sparring going on between the front and backseat. "I needed to grab a few things from my apartment, too. But I'm glad I did."

Jackie glanced at Bruce, face pinched. "Why?"

He shrugged. "I forgot to do anything about my plants, and since I've been working in Ruby Shores and staying with my folks since Christmas, they were all dead. I tossed them."

Kit thought that sounded like a lame reason. She hoped maybe he'd actually had fun hanging out with them.

"You're as weird as Ronnie," Jackie said, rolling her eyes as her brother pulled the car into the pizzeria where Lynette worked. "Fine. Come on then. We're here and I'm hungry. Might as well go in," Jackie grumbled, then perked up to add, "I hope Lynette is working."

"All she does is work, remember? She'll be here," Kit said, climbing out of the backseat.

Inside, Lynette greeted them, playing the hostess role. She sat them at a big table in a back corner. "My shift is up in a half hour, so I'll join you when I'm done. Annie is coming in, and we were planning to go to that keg party out by the lake later if you want to come along."

"I think we're a little too old for a high school kegger." Ronnie tossed his jacket on the back of a chair and held his hand out for the menu Lynette offered. "Besides, the rules don't allow Bruce to hang out with his students."

Like Kit, Lynette had spent plenty of time around Jackie's big brother through the years, and she playfully smacked him over the head with the menu before handing it to him. "The invite was for Jackie and Kit, you moron, not you two old geezers. It's almost ten. You probably need to get home to bed pretty soon."

"Ouch," Bruce cried, grabbing at his chest in mock dismay. "That hurts. We may be old enough to order a beer, but I wouldn't call us geezers yet. Speaking of beer, please send over someone old enough to take our drink order."

The camaraderie continued as everyone took their seats, placing their food and beverage orders. Kit found herself seated next to Bruce, which she didn't mind at all. Annie showed up minutes later, breezing in looking fresh and ready for fun. When she smiled, Kit choked on the sip of water she'd just taken.

"You got your braces off!"

"I did," Annie said, grinning broadly to show off her unadorned pearly whites. "Thanks for noticing. And I got a perm! Do you like it?"

The additional transformations in Annie were striking. "You look amazing. Millie will be jealous!"

"Are you Millie Boyd's little sister?" Bruce asked. "You kind of look like her."

"I am. And you are . . . ?"

"Sorry," Ronnie said, setting down his beer. "This is Bruce. He grew up around here, too, but we got to know each other more at college. He's student teaching at the high school now."

Annie thrust her hand in Bruce's, giving it a vigorous shake. "Nice to meet you, Bruce. What do you teach? I'm thinking I might want to teach Government someday."

Kit marveled at how easily Annie was able to strike up a conversation with Bruce. She'd felt tongue-tied around the older boy for the past two days.

Lynette brought over a tray of appetizers. "These are on the house. Storm told me to bring them over. He's going to have to toss them at the end of the night if no one orders them, and since we close soon, he figured you guys might as well eat 'em up."

"Storm?" Kit asked, looking back toward the partially walled-off kitchen. "Is that someone's name?"

"Sure," Lynette said, pulling napkins out of her apron pocket. "He's the assistant manager on duty tonight."

"Well, thank this Storm guy for us, would you?" Ronnie said, helping himself to a chicken wing.

The door opened and a boy walked in. He looked familiar, but Kit thought he may be a grade behind them in school. He made his way over to their table.

When Bruce saw the boy approach, he raised his glass to him. "Oh, hey, Elliott! Thanks for coming to get me. We just ordered. Want some pizza?"

"That's a stupid question," the newcomer said with a smirk, grabbing the empty chair next to Annie.

"Everyone, this is Elliott, my brother. I let him use my car while we were out of town. I called him from the gas station on our way back, told him to meet us here."

They said their hellos and made introductions all around.

"I *thought* you looked familiar," Annie said, flashing him a big smile.

The new guy looked stunned at her words—or, more likely, her smile. Kit wondered how long Annie would walk around smiling like a jack-o'-lantern to show off her new teeth.

Various conversations flowed around the table. Ronnie and Bruce talked about people Kit didn't know, but she still kept one ear on their conversation. Their two-day road trip had turned out better than she'd hoped, despite the little tiff she'd had with Jackie. Mainly thanks to Bruce's friendly nature. She hated to see the trip come to an end.

Lynette returned a short time later, minus her apron, holding a large pizza high in the air. Another waiter followed behind carrying a second large pie.

"Hey, guys," the waiter said, using his free hand to clear a space for the pizza on their table.

Jackie smiled when she noticed who'd brought out their food. "Well, hello, Owen! Long time no see!"

The girls all greeted their classmate, though Jackie was the only one who had ever really known Owen very well. Kit remembered the two were close friends when they were younger, before she'd moved to town, but like so many grade school friendships, things had changed.

Lynette sat down to eat with them, but Owen begged off. He was still on the clock and had cleanup to do in the back.

"Owen, tell Storm I'll pop back there quick before we leave, will you?" Lynette asked, and then, as if she'd only just thought of it, she stopped him. "Hey, we're going to that kegger after this. Want to come with?"

Owen looked uncertain, glancing between Jackie and his coworker. "You want *me* to go with?"

"You can come, too, Elliott," Annie offered.

Both boys looked surprised by their invites.

"I don't have a car," Elliott said, and Kit noticed the pleading look he sent Bruce, as if silently begging his older brother to let him keep his car for the rest of the evening.

"Sorry, bud, I've got a date," Bruce said, catching Elliott's drift. "And for God's sake, would you all please be careful and don't get caught? You know you're all minors, right?"

Kit's heart sank, even though she knew she had no right to be disappointed that Bruce was seeing someone. He was way too old for her anyway, not to mention a teacher at their school. Even if he was just a student teacher, it would still be way too weird.

Not that he'd ever be interested in someone like her.

"I can give everybody a ride," Owen offered, and suddenly their group had grown by two.

CHAPTER NINETEEN

K IT NURSED THE WARM beer in her solo cup and watched her friends. Jackie wasn't drinking—she'd be in huge trouble with her track coaches, and her father, if she even got caught at the keg party, let alone drinking alcohol. Annie, on the other hand, was on her third cup of beer, which was strange. She was normally the goody-two-shoes of the bunch. Maybe she was taking this whole Millie thing a step further, doing more than just trying to look like her. Millie seldom missed a party.

Young Elliott seemed to hang on Annie's every word. Kit recognized similarities between Elliott and Bruce, though the age gap between the two brothers seemed bigger than four years. But then she remembered Elliott was only a junior, so there was *five* years between them.

Kit closed her eyes, imagining what it would be like to be on a proper date with Bruce right now, instead of sitting on the tailgate of Owen's pickup, surrounded by a bunch of high school kids, most of whom were trying way too hard to impress each other.

"Penny for your thoughts," Jackie said, leaning into Kit.

Sighing, Kit glanced at her friend. "I think I'm just an old soul."

Jackie laughed. "You think? You've been old since I first met you at summer camp, and we were only *twelve*!"

"Is that how long all of you have known each other?" Elliott asked. He seemed eager to be part of the conversation.

"That's where we met Kit," Annie said. "Jackie and I have known each other since we were babies. And Lynette moved here in third grade. The four of us have been tight for a long time."

"How about you, Owen? Do you just know these girls through Lynette, since you work together?"

Owen, who'd been sitting quietly in the bed of his truck, a beer bottle dangling from his fingers, shook his head. "Nah. Jackie here used to be my bestie. But she's too good for me now."

Kit grinned at his words. There was no bite in his tone. "She usually thinks she's too good for all of us, too. Especially now that she's going to prom with Nathan, Mr. Track Captain and Perfect Hair Boy."

Jackie grabbed Kit's half-empty cup, took a swig from it, and gagged. "Gross, that's warm! And that's not true, Kit. I don't think I'm better than anyone else."

Kit noticed she didn't address Owen directly.

Lynette returned just then, juggling four cups of keg beer, an older guy Kit didn't recognize following behind her. "Good thing I work in a restaurant, otherwise I wouldn't be able to carry all of this."

Once she'd handed cups to Elliott, Annie, and Kit, she motioned behind her. "Look who drove up when I was getting more beer. Everyone, this is Storm. The guy who gave you free appetizers tonight!"

Kit studied the man standing behind Lynette, thinking his strange name was a good fit. His hair was long, and either wavy or straggly, she couldn't tell in the shadows. They were a long way from the enormous bonfire, their only light coming from the bright moon above. Kit frowned. She thought he looked a little old for a party like this.

"Lynette forgot her keys at work," Storm said, holding a set in the air and shaking them. "She wouldn't have been able to drive home when you bring her back to her car at Shoreline."

Shame rose in Kit for judging him so quickly.

"Would you like my beer, Storm?" she offered, holding the full cup out to him. She had no intention of drinking it.

He hesitated, then shook his head. "Nope. But thanks. I should probably be going. I don't want to crash your party, kids."

"We're hardly kids," Lynette said, grinning up at Storm. "You're only a year older than most of us."

"Really?" Jackie said, staring at Lynette's boss in surprise. "Only a year?"

He smirked. "Or two. And Lynette, have Owen drop you at home if you drink any more, okay? You can get your car in the morning."

"He's so sweet," Lynette said, leaning back against him. "Which is why I've talked Storm into being my date for prom."

Kit dropped her beer. Elliott jumped back to avoid the splash. "Sorry," she mumbled, still more shocked at Lynette's announcement than concerned about spilled beer. "Lynette, are you sure that's a good idea?"

Lynette gave Kit a look that clearly said to zip it, they'd discuss it later. Storm was still behind Lynette, so he couldn't see 'the look.'

Storm nodded at Kit. "I know, right, Red? This chick's bonkers, but I'm always up for helping out a friend."

A few people had tried to call Kit by that name in the past, but she'd never allowed it, and she wasn't about to start now. Jackie, clearly seeing her annoyance, spoke up first.

"Her name is Kit," she clarified before turning her attention to Lynette. "Are you sure they'll let you bring him as your date? There's an age limit, and anyone older that comes is usually in college."

Everyone stared at Jackie. Kit was shocked she'd say something that rude.

"What, I'm not college material?" Storm came back, his tone mocking.

Lynette looked hurt. Jackie wiggled off the tailgate, jumping over to Lynette's side. She wrapped an arm around the stricken girl, walking her over to the tailgate. Storm took two steps forward, and Kit got a better look at him. He wore black boots, dark jeans, and a plain black shirt with the sleeves pushed up to his elbows. Tattoos covered both forearms.

He looked like trouble.

He looked like someone Donna, Lynette's mother, might have brought home.

Someone brushed against Kit's arm, and she was surprised to see Owen had slid forward, out of the box to the edge of the tailgate, taking over Jackie's spot.

"Should we be worried?" Kit whispered to Jackie's grade school buddy, knowing he also worked with Storm.

"Not unless you ladies keep egging him on," he whispered back before raising the bottle he'd been nursing. Kit noticed he'd barely drank anything. Probably because he'd driven them all out to the party. He turned his attention back to his boss. "Nice to see you, Storm. Thanks for bringing Lynette's keys out. You still up for fishing tomorrow? I heard the walleye are hitting it hard just off that point out there."

Lynette's prom date looked to Owen, as if noticing him for the first time. He may not have been able to see him sitting in the back of the truck bed. "Hey there, Owen. Yeah, I'm up for it. I'll meet you at the arena. What time? I have to be at work by five."

Owen and Storm finalized their fishing plans, and then he left, disappearing into the shadows.

No one spoke. The only sounds were that of Def Leppard, crooning about pouring sugar on him from the pickup's radio, and partiers having fun, off in the distance around the fire.

When the song ended, Jackie faced Lynette in the moonlight. "Are you sure it's safe for you to go to prom with that guy? He seems . . . I don't know . . . old. And a little scary."

Lynette squared her shoulders and met Jackie's eye. "Storm is a decent guy once you get to know him. He's been helping me out with some stuff at home. I trust him. Ask Owen. He's decent."

Jackie looked to Owen, but all he did was shrug.

"Hey, at least she has a date," Annie said, swaying a little. Kit wasn't sure if her friend was dancing to the new song that had come on the radio or if the beer was hitting her. "I'll probably end up going alone. Can I dance with you guys if I'm all by myself?"

Kit couldn't help but smile at the whine in Annie's voice. There was no way Annie wouldn't have a date by the time prom rolled around.

"You don't have a date yet?" Elliott asked, sounding shocked.

"Nope." She shrugged. "I'm just a little wallflower."

It was then that Kit realized she was witnessing Annie perform a masterful dance of manipulation.

"Would you go to prom with *me*?" Elliott asked.

The poor guy looked like a desperate little puppy, begging for attention. Kit held her breath, almost feeling sorry for Elliott and the rejection she knew was coming. There was no way Annie would go to prom with a junior she'd just met.

"I'd love to," Annie said, surprising them all as she moved over to Elliott's side and wrapped an arm around him.

Lynette clapped, clearly happy with Annie's answer. "That does it. We all have dates now!"

"Not so fast," Jackie said, eyeing Owen. "Do you have a date? When we were kids, we always talked about going to prom as some famous couple, like Spencer Tracy and Katharine Hepburn, or Humphrey Bogart and Lauren Bacall."

"Or Romeo and Juliet," Owen said, his expression unreadable in the shadows, even being so close to Kit now. "Jackie, that was just silly kid talk. Besides, you already have a dream date all lined up, right? I think I'll just cover for Lynette and Storm at the restaurant that night."

Kit only felt the tremor that passed through Owen because their arms kept brushing against each other. She thought he sounded sad, but if Jackie noticed, she gave no sign.

Lynette, however, had other ideas. She wagged her finger at him, shaking her head. "No way, Owen. You *have* to go to prom. We're seniors! This is your last chance."

"Who cares? Besides, since all of you beautiful ladies are taken, I'm out of options," he said, dumping out his beer and setting the empty bottle in the truck box behind him.

"Actually, I have an idea," Lynette said, raising even Kit's curiosity. "Do you guys remember Renee, from summer camp?"

"When we were twelve?" Annie asked, giggling. "Sure. She's our fifth Kaleidoscope Girl, but I haven't thought about her in a long time."

"The fifth what?"

"Kaleidoscope Girl," Annie repeated, an impatient hand on her hip at Owen's interruption.

"What about her?" Kit asked. She knew Lynette still kept in touch with the other girl through letters.

"Prom at her school is earlier than ours. She had plans to go with a guy she's been dating for like six months. Had the dress and everything, but . . ."

"Let me guess. They broke up," Jackie said.

Lynette gave a little bow. "They broke up. She's devastated. I told her maybe she should come to our prom. We could find her a date. Because, you know, we're going as the Kaleidoscope Girls, and it wouldn't be fair to leave her out."

Kit wondered how much beer Lynette drank on her way back from the keg.

"But none of us have even seen her for almost six years," Annie said, looking confused.

"That's not true," Jackie said. "I've run into her at basketball games."

Lynette pointed at Jackie. "She mentioned that in her letters! Anyhow, Owen, you should take Renee."

"You're nuts, Lynette. I've never even met the girl."

"What, are you afraid she won't be pretty enough?" Jackie said.

Kit wondered why Jackie was being so mean to Owen. He'd been nothing but polite to her the whole night.

"Don't be such a bitch, Jackie," he said.

So much for being polite. Not that Kit blamed him.

"No, actually, Renee is really pretty. She sent me one of her senior pictures," Lynette said. "And she's super nice. I think she'd appreciate having the chance to see everyone again. If I can get her to drive over and get ready with us, would you be willing to take her to prom, as a friend, Owen? We could all go together as one big group! Would everybody be up for that?"

Kit liked the idea of seeing Renee again. And a big group date sounded much better to her than an awkward one-on-one event with her nerdy date.

With plenty of encouragement from everyone—except for a surprisingly quiet Jackie—Owen finally agreed. "Fine. Get me her number and I'll call her tomorrow. But I swear, Lynette, if this turns out to be a disaster, you're going to cover every Saturday shift they give me at Shoreline for the whole summer."

"Deal!" Lynette agreed, shaking Owen's hand.

Their clasped hands froze at the far-off shriek of police sirens.

"We gotta fly, folks, toss the drinks!" Owen cried, grabbing his empty beer bottle out of his truck box and whipping it into nearby weeds. They wouldn't all fit in the cab, so Annie pulled Elliott by the hand into the back of the pickup, promising to lie flat and be careful. Owen jumped behind the wheel and Kit, Jackie, and Lynette all piled in beside him.

They were lucky to be on the opposite side of the bonfire, farther away from the blacktop road the police were racing in on with red and blue lights punctuating the darkness.

"Cross your fingers. I'm going to try to sneak out of here before they notice us," Owen whispered, turning the key.

The truck sputtered and complained, not starting right way.

"I shouldn't have left the radio on."

Kit held her breath and crossed her fingers that the truck would start.

The engine finally caught, and everyone exhaled a sigh of relief. He put the truck in gear and eased forward, bumping slowly over the moonlit field, his lights still off. They'd be home free if he could make it to the shadows of the nearby shelterbelt in time.

CHAPTER TWENTY

ANNIE TIGHTENED THE TOWEL wrapped around her head, then reached for another to cover the rest of her. She was behind schedule, and the steady *tick-tock* of the old windup alarm clock on the back of the toilet mocked her. The girls would be banging on her door any second. She'd planned to be in her robe with her hair blown dry before they arrived, but she'd smudged a nail.

The doorbell rang. Annie ran toward her bedroom to grab her robe but caught her pinky toe on the old phone stand in the hallway. Pain shot up her leg, and she dropped onto the stand's bench, squeezing her injured foot and fighting tears.

"Your friends are here!" her sister yelled from behind her closed bedroom door.

"Millie! Can you answer it? Please?!"

The bell rang again. Annie tried to hobble to her room on her injured foot, but it was slow going. "Millie! Please?! I hurt myself!"

The low thud of music flipped off and Annie's sister flung her bedroom door open. "Seriously? I'm trying to write my paper."

Annie knew there was no way her sister was writing a paper for her freshman English class on a Saturday afternoon, but Millie always responded better when she didn't question her. "I'm sorry, but I stubbed my toe, and I need to throw my robe on. I can't answer the door in my towel! Please?"

"Fine. I think it's cute all you little 'Cross-Eyed Girls' are getting ready for prom here before the boys pick you up."

Having reached her bedroom, Annie yanked her bathrobe from the hook on the back of her door. She bit her lip to keep from snapping at her sister. "It's the Kaleidoscope Girls, remember?"

"Whatever." She shook her fingers, fanning her nails as she passed by Annie's open door.

"Looks like you're doing an art project instead of writing a paper. You can't type with wet nails," Annie said, checking to see that her own bottle of red polish was still on her dresser. She needed it just in case she chipped a nail before they left. The shade was a perfect match to her dress.

"What did you say?"

"Nothing!"

The doorbell rang for a third time.

"Hold your horses!" Millie yelled, walking through the house toward the front door.

A murmur of fresh voices reached Annie as she tied the belt on her robe.

"Back here!" she yelled, sinking onto the end of her bed to check her still throbbing toe. "We can hang your dresses in my closet while we do our hair!"

"No need to shout," Kit said, swinging Annie's door all the way open. "We're right here. Your hair is still wet?" She did a double take, seeing Annie's foot. "What happened to you?"

Annie straightened, still holding her injured right foot. "Smacked my toe. I hope I can still dance tonight."

Lynette pushed past Kit, carrying a stack of dresses, each wrapped in a clear plastic garment bag.

"You brought Jackie's, too?" Annie asked, glimpsing bright purple silk in the pile.

"We did," Lynette said, hanging the three dresses in Annie's closet. "She's showering at the school once her track meet wraps up, then coming straight over here to finish getting ready with us."

"I'm glad you decided on the orange dress, Kit. It looks great with your hair."

Kit shut Annie's door and made a beeline for the closet. She tore the flimsy bag off her dress, then fingered the puffy sleeves. "I hope I don't look like a monarch butterfly in this getup."

Annie laughed, flexing her toe. The pain was fading. There may still be dancing in her future after all. "Butterflies are amazing creatures."

Someone knocked on Annie's door.

"Go away, Millie!"

"Did I hear something about butterflies?"

All three girls froze, then Annie bounced up from her bed, forgetting all about her sore toe. She ripped the door open. "Renee!"

A flurry of hugs and greetings commenced. Lynette took Renee's dress from her and hung the buttery yellow gown next to the others.

"Thank you, Lynette, for inviting me to go to prom with you guys! It's so great to see all of you again . . . in person. I've run into Jackie, but otherwise I've only seen you in pictures Lynette sent with her letters. Everyone looks so different from when we were twelve at summer camp! Where is Jackie, by the way?"

"She'll be here any minute," Lynette assured her, explaining about the meet.

"How was your drive?" Kit asked.

"Easy, but it took two hours, so thank you for letting me stay here tonight, Annie. And I'm sorry my mom called yours, but you know how it is. My folks even talked about driving over to watch Grand March, but I convinced them it would be boring, since they wouldn't know anyone but me. With my luck, they would have wanted to stick around town and bring me home afterward. This will be much more fun."

"It *will* be fun!" Annie assured her. "And Owen is a great guy. Jackie knows him the best, but any time I've been around him he's been super nice."

"He even kept us out of trouble when we all went to a keg party last month and the cops showed up," Lynette said, lowering her voice as if the walls were listening. "We almost got caught, but Owen was driving, and he snuck us out of there. I thought Jackie was going to have a heart attack. She had the most to lose if we'd have gotten caught."

Annie noticed Renee looked apprehensive over the tidbit about the party. "Don't worry. He really is nice."

"But does he like to party? Because I promised my parents I wouldn't drink tonight."

Kit was digging in the overnight bag she'd brought along, pulling out dressy heels and undergarments. "I really don't think so. It seemed like the beer he had in his hand at the keg party might have just been for show. I saw him dump it out. If you don't want to drink tonight, and you don't want him to, just tell him."

"I haven't even met him yet! I've only talked to him on the phone twice."

"Doesn't matter," Kit insisted. "It's always best to be upfront with people. Plus, I promise you I won't drink anything tonight either. I doubt my date will, but to be honest, I don't know him very well. We just have chemistry class together."

Renee looked marginally relieved. "Then I'm not the only one going with a guy who isn't my boyfriend?"

Both Annie and Kit laughed. "No. In fact, *none* of us are dating these guys," Kit said, placing her fancy heels on the floor next to Annie's bed.

"Well . . ." Lynette said, "I'm kind of seeing Storm."

Shocked, Annie spun on her. "*Tell* me that isn't true! I thought he just agreed to go with you because you didn't want to bother to find someone at school. Lynette, I'm sorry, but he doesn't seem like your type at all."

"And what exactly *is* my type? It's not like I've ever had a steady boyfriend."

"That's kind of my point. I'm not sure Storm is the kind of guy a girl should *start* with."

Lynette sighed. "You disappoint me, Annie. You never used to be so judgmental. You assume you know what kind of person he is because of how he looks. Now, if you'll excuse me, I need to pee."

Once the door closed behind her, Renee grinned. " 'Storm' is an interesting name."

Kit grinned back. "He's an interesting guy."

Annie scoffed, defensive. "I don't judge."

Kit shook her head. "Of *course* you judge. We all judge. It's human nature to be leery of the unknown."

"Just because you went on one college visit with Jackie doesn't mean you have to talk like a psych professor. Now, come on, ladies, I invited you over here to get ready, not to gab. We need to get in that bathroom and work some magic with our curling irons and mascara. Hope Lynette is done. We may not be dating these boys, but that doesn't mean we can't *wow* them."

Annie led the way, and the four of them crowded around the littered vanity, vying for space in the plate-glass mirror. Two curling irons were already filling the outlet above the vanity, so Annie plugged her blow dryer into the spare.

There was a *pop*, then nothing.

Muffled music cut out. Millie screamed her displeasure.

Annie sighed and rolled her eyes. She pulled open the window curtain, sacrificing privacy for light, and headed downstairs to flip the breaker. Her father had taught her exactly what to do, since overloading the bathroom circuits was a common occurrence with two teenage girls.

The foursome helped each other with their hair and shared makeup. It wasn't long before the air was hazy with hairspray. Their hair needed plenty of height and volume to be in style.

"Jackie should have been here by now," Lynette said.

Annie lowered her mascara wand, glancing between Kit and the alarm clock. Jackie *was* cutting it close. Their dates were due to arrive in forty minutes.

As if on cue, the doorbell rang.

"Your turn to let another one of your Cross-Eyed Friends in!" Millie yelled from down the hall.

Annie shoved her mascara wand back in the tube and dropped it on the counter. "Never mind her. She's an idiot. I don't think she can pronounce 'kaleidoscope,' so she pretends she thinks we call ourselves the Cross-Eyed Girls."

Renee laughed. "Sisters. You gotta love 'em. Kaleidoscope Girls . . . I forgot all about that name!"

"Hold that thought." Annie left the cloudy air of the bathroom. She returned a minute later with a flustered Jackie on her heels. "Make room, ladies. You already look fabulous. Jackie could use a little help here. We're running out of time."

Ten minutes later, they were all back in Annie's room, getting dressed. Annie was so excited to pose with the others. Millie had promised to take a few pictures of the girls outside in their finery before their dates arrived.

"Why were you so late, Jackie?" Kit asked, saying out loud what everyone had been wondering.

"There was a rain delay first thing this morning, so the meet was running at least an hour behind. I ran two red lights and had to swerve around an old lady crossing the street on my way over here!"

"You did not," Annie said, her eyes wide.

"Okay, I made up the part about the old lady, but the rest was true. I hope Nathan gets here on time. The boys were still competing when I ran into the locker room to shower."

Kit shrugged. "Even if he's a little late, we don't have to be to Grand March for three hours yet."

"Easy for you to say," Jackie replied between grunts as she wrestled with a strapless bra. "Didn't your date write out a whole itinerary for the evening? I doubt Nathan will even remember where we have our group dinner reservations."

"Most jocks aren't known for their brains," Annie said, adjusting her pantyhose.

Lynette looked up from the straps on her dress; she was having a hard time with them despite the instructions the store clerk gave her when she'd purchased it. "And you claim you aren't too quick to judge?"

Annie flopped onto her back on her bed, not caring how silly she looked in her underwear. "Ugh, you're right. I swear I never used to be! I think I'm just panicking about tonight. Whatever possessed me to say yes to a guy I barely know for my senior prom? And he's only a junior! I'm sorry, Jackie. And, Lynette, I'm sorry for what I said earlier about Storm." She sat up, crossing her arms over her bare midsection. "The Kaleidoscope Girls have to stick together."

"Oh my God!" Renee yelped, hurrying over to the shelves above Annie's small desk. "I can't believe you still have this! My little sister Val wouldn't keep her hands off mine after I got home, and she *broke* it. I almost killed her. Can I see if it still works?"

Annie turned and watched Renee carefully take her homemade kaleidoscope off the shelf. She nodded, smiling. "It works, but sure, try it. I bet if you pointed it at our dresses hanging in the closet, the patterns would be amazing. My parents got me that other kaleidoscope on the shelf below it last year for Christmas. I know Jackie's got ruined when she left it outside, but don't the rest of you still have yours?"

Only Lynette nodded. "Oh, my gosh, I almost forgot," she said, grabbing her bulky purse off the back of the desk chair. "I have a present for each of you! But you have to put your dresses on first."

Annie checked the time. "We need to get dressed anyhow. The guys are supposed to be here in five minutes, and we haven't even taken our pictures without them yet."

In a flurry of silk, tulle, and lace, all five Kaleidoscope Girls finished dressing, taking care not to get makeup on their fabric or disrupt their hairdos, still standing tall under layers of hairspray.

Finally, Lynette grabbed her purse again and pulled out five small jewelry boxes. "Renee and Annie, feel free to keep your necklaces on, but hopefully you are okay with layers. I have one final touch for all of us."

The doorbell rang again. This time, Millie was quick to yell "I'll get it!"

"Hurry," Annie said, clapping her hands.

Exclamations filled the room as the girls each took their little white box from Lynette and they all removed the tops, finding inside matching silver butterflies. Rhinestones outlined the tiny wings, sparkling in the light from the ceiling fixture.

"Tonight, the Kaleidoscope Girls will make memories to last a lifetime," Lynette said, throwing kisses to her best friends.

Kit smirked as she helped Annie take off her first necklace and put on the new one. "And even if tonight doesn't turn out to be all we've dreamed of—because, let's face it, we aren't exactly going into this on the arms of our Prince Charmings—I vow again to remain forever friends with the four of you!"

Annie squeezed Jackie's shoulders and leaned close, doing her best to hold her friend's attention. "Relax. He called. He promised to meet us here. Now *breathe*. He did not stand you up."

She could feel Jackie's shoulders shake as the girl did as she was told, trying to take deep, calming breaths. "And here I thought I was the one with the perfect date for tonight," she whispered, a tiny smile on her lips despite the moisture shining in her eyes. "At least all of your dates showed up on time for pictures."

"We can take more pictures when we get to the school before Grand March. Or after. You're going to have fun. I promise."

Annie released Jackie's shoulders and stepped back, her gaze skipping away in case her despairing friend noticed the lack of certainty in her own eyes. So far, their evening was off to a rocky start.

Charlie, Kit's date, had been the first to arrive. He'd brought Kit a wrist corsage that reminded Annie of a head of lettuce in both size and weight, but at least he was acting the part of a perfect gentleman. A perfect gentleman with questionable taste in floral design, but a gentleman nonetheless.

Owen arrived with Storm, apologizing to Renee that he hadn't driven his own truck, muttering something about a hatched starter. Annie marveled at how different the two looked as they walked up the sidewalk to where the girls were gathered on her front lawn so Millie could take a few photographs.

Owen looked handsome in his white tux, sporting tails and a yellow vest and bow tie. He'd paid attention when Renee talked about her dress during one of their two telephone conversations. But he looked incredibly awkward as he approached the girls, nodding to his date but saying little after Lynette made introductions.

She wouldn't have described Storm as handsome, but there was something striking about him, dressed in black from head to toe. Unlike Owen, who wore shiny white dress shoes that matched his suit, Storm had on black boots with a heavy heel. If not for the narrow white tie and black sport coat, he'd have looked ready to stride into a biker bar.

Annie watched as he approached Lynette, wrapped his arm around her waist, and handed her a plastic container with a delicate wrist corsage of yellow roses inside. Owen slipped an identical one on Renee's wrist. She suspected Owen picked up two corsages to cover for Storm, but Lynette didn't seem to notice, her eyes glued to her date.

Her own date, Elliott, was the last to arrive—not counting the still absent Nathan. Elliott had brought her a pin-on corsage. It looked lovely and smelled delicious with a large blush rose encircled with miniature white roses and a sprig of eucalyptus, but she hated to pierce the red silk fabric on the bodice of her dress. Millie saved the day when she figured out a way to clasp the small arrangement onto the dress with one of her hairclips instead of using the pins.

Each girl had to pin boutonnieres onto the lapels of their dates. Kit had no trouble attaching Charlie's. Elliott's still drooped despite three attempts to tighten it up. Storm refused to wear one, and Annie hoped the droplets of blood on Owen's lapel from Renee's mishap would come out before he had to return the rental.

Their table wasn't ready when they arrived at the restaurant, despite their 4:45 reservation, but Storm had a hushed conversation with the manager on duty and they seated the prom group within minutes.

Annie still wasn't sure how she felt about Storm, despite her guilt at being so judgmental toward him. One minute she was convinced he was bad news for Lynette; the next, he did something mature, like take care of the lost reservations with ease, all while looking dangerously sexy in his black get-up and his blue-black, unfashionably-long and wavy hair. Storm made the rest of the guys in their party look like boys playing at being men, despite their prom finery.

"But what if he doesn't make it here before it's time to leave for Grand March?" Jackie asked, pulling Annie's attention back to the ladies' room and her friend's dilemma.

"He'll be here," Annie repeated. "Touch up your lipstick, and let's get out there in case they brought our food."

Grunting, Jackie slammed her jeweled clutch onto the vanity counter and snapped open the clasp. "I don't see why I have to touch up my lipstick when I'm going to eat it right off with my meal."

Annie grabbed a small strip of toilet paper out of the only open stall and handed it to Jackie to use as a blotter. "Because, I know you, and if Nathan doesn't get here until after your food arrives, you'll be too nervous to take a bite. You *should* eat, but you probably won't. And you want to make a good impression. You're a little pale right now."

Jackie glared into the mirror and slashed at her lips with a coral shade. "You'd be pale, too, if your date was late for *prom!*"

Nathan arrived at the restaurant minutes before they brought the food to their table. Annie thought his gracious apologies to Jackie and the rest of the group for his tardiness seemed sincere. He looked handsome in a well-fitted black suit, complete with a cummerbund that matched Jackie's purple gown. The only clue that he'd been rushed was his blond hair and shirt collar, which looked damp.

"The track meet must have run way over," Owen said, bending forward to address Nathan from down the table.

"It did. I was the anchor on the last relay race, and there were lots of heats. Then my buddies wanted to practice our handoffs afterward, since they sucked today."

Annie saw Jackie tense. "You stayed longer than necessary, knowing tonight was prom, to practice your handoffs?" Jackie asked, surprising everyone at the table with her direct, rather rude, question.

Nathan had the good sense to squirm in his chair. "Yeah, and that was probably a poor decision . . . I'm sorry, Jackie. But I was the only one actually going to prom tonight, and they can be pretty convincing."

Annie thought she better try to steer the conversation in a different direction. If they didn't start having some fun, this night might turn out to be a disaster for them all. "Anybody else excited about the DJ the student council brought in for the dance tonight? I heard he played over in Browning last weekend, and everyone was still out on the dance floor for the last song!"

All the girls around the table—as well as Elliott—showed obvious enthusiasm at the prospect of a full night of dancing. His response gave her pause. She wasn't sure if her date truly liked to dance, or if he was simply being supportive, but she'd find out soon enough.

Unbidden, her imagination conjured up a vision of her spinning slowly around the dance floor in her red satin gown, strong arms surrounding her, pulling her close. She had to look up to meet the eyes of her dance partner, given the heavy black boots he wore.

She felt a guilty flush stain her cheeks and she stole a glance at Lynette.

Charlie mumbled something about two left feet. Owen groaned at talk of dancing. Storm grinned, pushed his chair back, rested one ankle on his knee, and patted his boot.

"Not to worry, boys. I've got something stashed in here that will help loosen us all up on the dance floor."

Despite the way Storm kept stealing into her thoughts, Annie didn't like what he was implying. "What do you mean? What exactly is in your boot, Storm?"

Lynette made a cutting motion, begging him to stop talking, but Storm didn't take the hint. Instead, he reached inside his boot and pulled out a silver flask, giving it a little shake before stowing it away again.

"You can't take *booze* into Grand March!" Jackie hissed, glaring first at Storm then looking at everyone else as if to seek support. "My father is the principal at Ruby Shores High, and he'll be checking us all in at the door. If he smells one lick of alcohol on your breath or suspects you might be hiding something, he won't let any of us in."

The bad boy's grin morphed into a smirk. "Chill, girl. I'm not stupid. No one drinks until after we're all in. And he can't search me. That would violate my rights."

Annie felt torn, knowing she shouldn't feel one ounce of attraction for her friend's date, but unable to stop wondering what it would be like to spend an evening with someone like Storm.

"I'm with Jackie on this one," Nathan said, fixing Storm with a serious look. "Some of us are in spring sports and can't afford to get caught drinking."

"No worries there, slick. No one is going to force you to do anything you don't want to do. Now, eat up. We've got partying to do."

CHAPTER TWENTY-ONE

J ACKIE SEARCHED THE LINE of couples behind them, but she didn't see Renee or Lynette anywhere.

"It's probably a good thing they weren't here to line up with us," Nathan said, catching Jackie looking over her shoulder. "If that stoner of hers gets caught with booze, I don't want to be anywhere near him. You shouldn't want to be associated with them either."

Annie overheard. "Do you know for a fact that Storm does drugs?"

"I'd say there's a pretty good chance," he said, eyebrows raised.

Elliott stood near Nathan. "No kidding. Anybody who looks like that *must* do drugs."

Jackie shook her head. "There's no way Lynette would go out with a druggie. You guys are awful, assuming things like that."

At least she *hoped* Lynette was too smart to make that kind of mistake.

Her father's booming voice cut through the talk and laughter of the kids waiting in line. He stood next to the ticket table, looking intimidating in his black suit—the suit that only came out for weddings, funerals, and prom night. "If any of you kids were stupid enough to think you could sneak alcohol in with you tonight, I suggest you excuse yourselves from the line immediately and throw it in the waste basket outside. You get this one pass. I have a chaperone positioned out there, but we won't punish you for disposing of it. He is merely there so that no one thinks they can raid the trash later."

Chuckles rippled through the line, but Jackie wanted to go hide in the bathroom and never come out. She couldn't think of anything worse than having your father checking all your classmates into Grand March.

"However," he continued, and Jackie held her breath for fear of what he might say next. After a dramatic pause, he went on. "If I smell even a whiff of alcohol on you, not only will we remove you from Grand March and the dance, but we will also notify your parents. The march will start in five minutes."

She noticed a few couples slink out of line. Her heart beat faster.

Where is the rest of our group?

"Hey, Jackie, look who's here!" Kit grabbed her arm and pointed to the double doors each couple would walk through when the MCs announced them. "Mrs. Long is holding a microphone. And so is your brother's buddy, Bruce. Did you know they were reading names for the march?"

Jackie followed Kit's finger and spied the two. Outside of school, Mrs. Long would always be Wendy, the counselor from back in their summer camp days. But in school, Jackie's father required that she and her friends call the woman Mrs. Long.

"I wonder if Renee will remember her. Does she even know she works here?"

"Doesn't Bruce look handsome?" Kit said, swaying slightly from side to side.

Jackie almost laughed when she noticed Charlie stand on his tiptoes to see who Kit was so intrigued by. Needing a distraction from her dismay over her father's presence, she decided to have a little fun. "He certainly looks handsome, Kit. Say, you never told me what his apartment looked like when the two of you ended up there during our college tour. He lives alone, right?"

Kit, not picking up on her teasing tone, looked alarmed at her words. "Jackie, keep your voice down! Bruce works here as a student teacher. If anyone hears you talking like that, they might jump to the wrong conclusion. He could get in big trouble."

Even though Kit reprimanded her in low tones, Charlie was obviously doing his best to hear their conversation. "Are you guys talking about Mr. Davidson? He's the student teacher in my stats class. You know him? I mean, like, outside of school?"

"He's been a friend of my big brother, Ronnie, for years." Jackie kept her answer vague, knowing it might make him even more curious. "I used to have the *biggest* crush on him."

That last part wasn't true, but the way Kit hummed when Jackie said it brought a splash of color to Charlie's cheeks. Kit's date was jealous. Jackie wanted to pull him aside and let the poor boy down gently. If he'd thought he'd come out of tonight with some kind of romantic relationship with his lab partner, he was going to be disappointed. Jackie knew Kit had no interest in high school boys. But what if Charlie's suspicions about Kit liking Bruce were actually true? She'd never noticed Kit go googly-eyed over anyone before, but her friend couldn't seem to tear her eyes from the two staff members holding the microphones. Wendy wouldn't be the one capturing Kit's attention; they saw her daily in her creative arts class.

The line advanced, and Nathan put his arm around her shoulders, keeping her from moving forward. She had to stop herself from shrugging it off. It felt too heavy, too possessive. Back when they'd sat next to each other on the bus after the track meet, the notion of standing beside him in her prom dress had felt thrilling. But after his late arrival and apparent inability to talk about anything other than running and the track team, she wasn't feeling quite as interested in her date anymore.

"You really do look beautiful tonight, Jackie," he said, whispering into her ear.

The words tickled, raising goosebumps down her arms. She glanced up at him, seeing again how handsome he was, especially in his tux. His compliment went a long way in thawing her out, as did the envious glances she noticed at least two other girls send their way.

Nathan showed her father the proper level of respect at the ticket table, and the older man looked pleased to see the two of them together. Why wouldn't he be? Her father was really just like most principals, always showing favoritism to the star athletes of his school.

Before he turned his attention to the next couple in line, her father caught her hand, squeezing it. "You look pretty tonight, honey," he whispered, throwing her off kilter.

Her dad praised her often, and she knew he loved her in his own way, but this was the first time in a long time she felt like he was seeing her as his daughter, and not a stand-in for the son he fought with constantly.

She heard Wendy announce Annie and Elliott to the crowd packing the bleachers in what she knew would be a darkened gymnasium. Kit and Charlie entered next, and Nathan offered her his arm as they awaited their turn.

Closing her eyes, she decided to simply let herself feel the excitement. All girls dreamt of their senior prom, imagined dancing in the arms of the most handsome boy in school. And here she was, living the dream.

Maybe she was lucky after all.

"Have you seen Kit?" Charlie asked, catching Jackie as she returned from the bathroom. "She keeps disappearing on me."

Jackie didn't want to tell him she'd spied Kit talking with Bruce near the punch bowl five minutes earlier. "Kit isn't much of a dancer," she improvised, hating to hurt his feelings. Kit better be careful. People would talk. "Have you checked the tables in the back?"

With a shrug, Charlie headed in that direction, leaving Jackie to go in search of her own date. She'd danced the first few songs with Nathan, but then he left her to get them punch. That was at least thirty minutes ago. She walked the entire perimeter of the gymnasium again, hoping it wasn't obvious to anyone else that she'd lost her prom date.

First he's late, then he disappears.

"Jackie! Come sit with us!"

Lynette's voice. Relief flooded through her as she spied them at a table.

"There you guys are! What happened to you? I was starting to think you didn't get in!"

Lynette laughed, dipping her head back. That was when Jackie noticed she was sitting on Storm's lap instead of a chair of her own. Owen and Renee sat across from the lovebirds, looking uncomfortable.

"We had to make a little detour. When Storm realized how nervous you were about him sneaking a flask in, he offered to drop it off back at his place."

Storm shrugged and dropped a hand on Lynette's knee. "Anything to keep my girl happy."

Another giggle out of Lynette sent Jackie around the table, anxious to put a little distance between herself and the handsy couple. Owen gave her a cool nod as she approached, standing up and motioning for her to take his chair. He promised to bring them both back some punch. Happy to have a quiet minute with Renee, she scooted the chair so they could visit despite the loud music.

"It's so fun to see you again. It's been too long! Were you shocked to see Wendy—I mean, Mrs. Long—announcing?"

"I couldn't believe it! She hasn't changed a bit. Well, other than being super pregnant, but you know what I mean. She looked shocked to see me, too."

Jackie noticed Lynette get up off Storm's lap, and the two headed for the dance floor.

"Of course they go dance to a slow one," Renee said, looking deflated.

Noticing the sudden change in Renee's mood, Jackie leaned in. "Oh, no . . . what's wrong?"

Renee shrugged. "Nothing, really. It's just been awkward, that's all. Owen and I are strangers, and while Lynette is being very nice, those two can't seem to keep their hands off each other."

"I'm so sorry. I'd offer for you to come sit with the rest of us, but I can't find the others. I don't think Annie and Elliott have left the dance floor since the music started. My date seems to have vanished, and Charlie is having a hard time keeping track of Kit. So, to heck with all of them, let's catch up. Six years gives us a lot of ground to cover."

Jackie and Renee ended up having plenty of time to visit. Owen brought them punch as promised, but when two buddies swung by their table, he fell into an animated discussion with them about their engineering club, ignoring the girls. Not that either of them minded. Nathan didn't track Jackie down until the DJ announced his final set. The announcement brought everyone onto the dance floor, and the night ended on a more positive note.

After the final chords faded away and light flooded the gymnasium, Lynette and Storm were nowhere to be found. Renee and Owen had to catch a ride back to Annie's with Nathan and Jackie.

Once their dates dropped them off, the girls switched out of their dresses and into pajamas, but everyone was too wired to sleep.

Annie's bedroom faced the street in front of their house. Jackie pulled the curtain back again, checking for any sign of Storm's truck.

"I can't believe she took off with him like that," Annie hissed, pacing the floor near her bedroom door. "My mother promised all of your parents that we'd be in by now, and if Lynette gets caught we're all going to be in trouble."

"Do you think they are back at his apartment . . . having *sex*?" Kit said, not bothering to whisper.

"Kit, my parents might hear you!"

Kit gave a loud sigh and dropped onto her back on the bed beside Jackie. "Your mom and dad's bedroom is on the other end of the house, in the back. This is a big house, Annie. Didn't you just get done telling us Millie used to sneak out all the time during her senior year in high school and your parents never caught her?"

Annie huffed over to a sleeping bag she'd rolled out on the floor near her closet. "Fine. Yes. You're right. I'll try to relax. Now, back to your question about sex. If I was Lynette, I'd at least consider having sex with Storm. He's hot."

All the girls met this admission with hoots of laughter. Jackie hoped Annie's mother wouldn't come running to find out what all the racket was about.

Once things died down again, Renee sat up, crossing her legs on top of the sleeping bag she'd brought along. "I don't think they'd go to his place to have sex," she announced, piling her wilting hair on top of her head with her hands. "I expected some hole-in-the-wall bachelor pad when he wanted to swing by his home to get rid of the flask. It was actually a really pretty house on the lake. He told us to stay in his truck so we didn't wake up his baby brother."

Kit sat up. "No way. Here I was thinking they didn't go to his place because he had, like, four other bad-boy roommates. You just exploded the image of him I'd built in my head. Baby brother?"

"Yep. Plus, he said something about how hard it is now for his mom, since his dad is gone. I wasn't sure what 'gone' meant, and Owen didn't know either when I asked him."

They all took a moment to absorb this news. It was quiet except for the crooning of Meatloaf from Annie's boombox, turned down low, on her desk.

"Hopefully they didn't go to a hotel," Jackie said. She hated the idea that Lynette might let lust cloud her judgment. Her friend had made a big deal about waiting for the most romantic moment, with the perfect guy, before she'd give up her virginity. Jackie doubted Storm was that guy.

She heard a car on the street outside and again checked for Lynette, but the vehicle rolling to a stop next to the curb wasn't Storm's. As she watched, Annie's sister got out of the passenger side, stumbling and giggling as she approached the house. "Looks like Millie had a good time tonight."

Annie rolled her eyes. "Millie *always* has a good time. But I doubt her boyfriend did. She was supposed to go out with him, but I think she bailed on him to go out with friends again. Poor guy."

They listened as the front door opened, closed, and footsteps shuffled in their direction, cut off by a *thud* followed by muffled cursing.

"I swear, Mom refuses to move that coffee table just to make Millie regret coming home drunk. My sister has permanent black and blue marks on her shins."

Kit laughed. "I used to want to be like your sister when I grow up. She always seemed to have it all together. Now I'm not so sure."

Annie's bedroom door rattled.

"Millie, go to bed! It's three in the morning. If you don't be quiet, you're going to wake Mom and Dad. It won't matter that you're in college, they will ground your butt for coming home drunk!"

Millie's muffled voice came through the door. "I knew I should have lived in the dorms this year."

"Did you lock it?" Renee asked, giggling.

"Nope, she's just inebriated. This happens all the time."

The rattling stopped, and the footsteps moved on. AC/DC blared from the adjacent room, drowning out their Meatloaf. The noise sent Annie flying out her bedroom door.

"The next time I complain about not having a sister, remind me of tonight, will you?" Kit said, tapping Jackie's arm.

"Same," she replied. One older brother was more than enough drama for Jackie. "You have sisters, right, Renee?"

"Yep. But they're younger."

The music blaring from the bedroom next door snapped off and Annie reappeared. "Sorry about that."

Renee shook her head, giggling again. "Don't apologize. That was funny. In fact, it might have been the highlight of my night!"

Annie frowned as she dropped back onto her sleeping bag. "Was it that bad? Do you regret letting Lynette drag you over here for prom? We'd hoped you'd have fun."

"No, no, I didn't mean it was all bad. Catching up with you girls is great. And I'm not even mad at Lynette for ditching us. I get it. I was just . . . I don't know . . . hoping to hit it off a little better with Owen. I can tell he's a nice guy, but I think his heart belongs to someone else."

This was news to Jackie. "Really? Is he dating someone we don't know about? I've never known him to date anyone. He's always so busy studying, and working. I'm not sure he even does anything fun anymore. To be honest, I considered Owen one of my best friends in grade school, but we never hang out anymore."

"Yeah, he mentioned something about that." Renee shrugged. "He didn't come right out and admit that he likes anyone. But my gut tells me there's someone else. I'm sure I won't hear from him again. Which is kind of a bummer. He's super cute."

Jackie had to admit she, too, had noticed how handsome her old friend looked, dressed in his tux, his wire-rimmed glasses replaced with contacts. When Nathan was so late showing up, she'd even thought how much simpler it would have been if she'd just gone with Owen. It probably wouldn't be hard to pick up on their old friendship, despite all the time that had passed. She'd always think of Owen as one of her oldest friends.

"Could he be gay?" Kit asked.

"No way!" both Renee and Jackie cried.

There was a light tapping on Annie's door. Everyone froze.

"You girls better get some sleep in there," Annie's mother whispered through the door. "It's late. Or practically early. The sun will be up soon. I was just checking to see that Millie made it home."

"Will do, Mom," Annie whispered back. "Millie got home a little while ago. I'm sure she's sound asleep by now. We're all good."

They all held their breath, waiting, and Jackie bit her bottom lip to keep from giggling as Annie waved her crossed fingers in the air. If that door opened and Mrs. Pierce saw that Lynette wasn't there, there was no telling what would happen.

"I'll make breakfast for you all at eight," she said, before bidding them goodnight.

"Can we make it later, Mom? We're beat."

"Fine, but only if you girls settle down now and go to sleep."

As Annie's mother headed back to the other side of the house, a sound outside the window caught Jackie's attention. "Crap. It's Lynette. I'll run out there quick and make sure she's quiet as a mouse coming in. Annie, you stay, just in case your mom hears something and comes back."

Jackie tiptoed as quietly as she could out of Annie's room, thankful for the countless times she'd visited the house through the years, and for the moonlight streaming through the living room windows that allowed her to navigate her way around the coffee table. She had no idea what condition Lynette would be in, and she didn't want black and blue shins to show below the hem of her graduation gown.

CHAPTER TWENTY-TWO

K IT PULLED UP TO the curb in front of Elliott's house and cut the engine to the Mustang.

Annie grabbed Elliott's red bow tie off the dash. She'd slipped it around her neck during the dance, and forgot to give it back to him when he'd dropped her off the night before. He needed to return his rented tux, and he'd called Annie's house hoping she could drop it off. He said he didn't have a car he could use that day.

The other girls had already left by the time Elliott called, so Kit offered to drive her over. Given their late night, they'd lounged around in Annie's bedroom until almost ten that morning, then gathered around the table for a brunch of pancakes, sausage patties, and fruit. Renee couldn't stay to eat; she had to get home because her sister Jess was celebrating her birthday. Jackie hurried off to track practice after brunch. Shortly after that Lynette's mother called, insisting she hurry home for something.

Kit watched as Annie slammed the car door and hurried up the walk, and she wondered if Bruce was inside, too. A twinge of guilt niggled at the edges of her conscience. Had she spent too much time talking with Bruce at the dance the night before? He was supposed to be chaperoning, and Kit was there with Charlie.

Charlie had said little when he'd dropped her at Annie's the night before.

Elliott opened the front door and Kit could see him talking with Annie. Then they both waved at her to come in. She glanced at her watch, knowing her grandmother would start to worry if she didn't get home soon. But if Bruce was inside, she might get to talk with him again. *Sorry, Grandma.*

The first thing she noticed when she hurried inside was the heavy aroma of fried chicken. The second was Bruce, standing next to a stovetop, spatula in hand.

He half turned and noticed Kit inside the doorway. "Hey, Kit! Did you have fun last night?"

The sight of him standing there in a loose tank top and basketball shorts, hair mussed, made her mouth water more than the smell of the food. Last night, dressed in his suit and tie, he'd looked like he'd stepped out of one of her grandmother's soap operas, handsome and out of her league, due to both their gap in ages and their teacher versus student roles. Now he just looked like an older brother of one of her friends. *Sexy* older brothers, that was.

Annie bumped her arm. "Kit, what's wrong with you? Bruce asked you a question."

Kit yawned and stretched her arms over her head, hoping it hid the fact that she was struggling to string a comprehensive sentence together in his presence. "Sorry. I'm tired. It was a late night. But, yeah, I guess it was fun. Especially after the boys dropped us off. We stayed up most of the night talking."

"And waiting for Lynette to get home," Annie added, rolling her eyes.

Kit frowned. She didn't think Annie should have shared that with Elliott and Bruce. What if Bruce felt compelled to mention Lynette's escapades to someone?

"I thought you said you all had to go straight home after the dance?" Elliott said. "If I'd have known you could stay out later, we could have checked out that party we heard about at my buddy's."

Annie shook her head. "We were *supposed* to come straight home. Lynette chose not to, so we had to cover for her. I don't think my parents realized she missed curfew, or Mom would have already talked to us all about it over breakfast."

Bruce removed browned chicken pieces from the large fry pan onto a plate to drain. "I was hoping we could convince you two to stay for Sunday dinner. Our parents are at church. We got a pass this morning because of the late night. I wasn't out as late as the rest of you, but when I offered to cook, they didn't argue."

"We just ate, but thank you," Annie said, handing the bow tie over to Elliott.

Kit wasn't as eager to leave. "I don't know, Annie . . . that chicken smells awfully good."

Annie glanced her way, maybe seeing her friend's true intentions, then shrugged. "I guess it's been a couple of hours since we ate."

"Great!" Bruce wiped his hands with a rag and tossed it over his shoulder. "Anyone want to help me mash these potatoes?"

Kit was stuffed. First she'd eaten too many of Annie's mother's pancakes, because they'd reminded her of the ones her father used to make; then she'd eaten a helping of every dish Bruce served with the chicken, wanting to be a gracious, if unexpected, guest. Bruce and Elliott's parents had been surprised to find Annie and Kit in their kitchen when they arrived home from church, but they were welcoming.

After the girls helped clean up the mess, Elliott invited them to the park with him for a game of football with friends. Kit declined. She needed to get home before her grandmother went nuts with worry. That woman had lived through enough of that when Kit's mother was a teenager.

But then Bruce rubbed at his own stomach, complaining about how he'd eaten too much and needed some exercise. "I might tag along, if you don't mind, little bro."

"Come on, Kit," Annie said. "That sounds fun! If I go home, Mom is just going to put me to work around the house."

Three sets of eyes looked expectantly at her. The fact that Bruce appeared to want her to join them was the tipping point.

"I have to call my Grandma Hazel first. I haven't seen her since Grand March last night. I need to tell her where I'm at so she doesn't worry. Can I use your phone?"

"Sure," Elliott said, taking her to the telephone where it hung in the hallway, just off the kitchen. "I'm going to go change quick."

Kit dialed the number and wrapped the cord around her finger. Her grandmother was usually a reasonable woman, and if there wasn't anything pressing at home she probably wouldn't care if Kit went to the park.

But the anxiety in her grandmother's voice when she answered the phone didn't bode well. "Kit! I've been calling *everywhere* looking for you! What the devil are you doing? You told me you'd be home by noon today!"

Kit took a deep breath, considering how best to calm down her grandmother. "I'm sorry, Grandma. I lost track of time."

"Kit, I called over to Annie's house. I talked to her mother. She told me you left two hours ago! Then I called both Jackie's and Lynette's, but their mothers didn't know where you were, either."

She had to grit her teeth to hold back the urge to yell at her grandmother for involving all the moms of her friends. "You're obviously upset. Has something happened? Is it the boys?"

She heard her grandmother take a deep, shaky breath. "The boys are fine. Well, kind of. I need you to come home this instant, young lady."

The hairs stood up on the back of her neck. Her grandmother never talked to her like that. Something was definitely wrong.

"Are you coming, Kit?" Elliott shouted from the kitchen.

Ignoring him for a minute, she turned to face the wall in the hallway, lowering her voice. "Grandma, something's wrong. Tell me what happened. Is it Mom? Is she back?"

"No. Not this time. It's your father, dear."

Kit sucked in a breath, startled. "Oh no. Has something happened?" Fear pulsed through her. People experienced terrible things in jail.

Her grandmother didn't respond immediately, and Kit could hear voices in the background. Finally, the phone rustled and her grandmother spoke again. "Honey, your father is here. You need to come home right away."

The telephone receiver fell from Kit's fingers, smacking against the wall as it dangled from the twisted cord.

Bruce popped his head around the corner. "What's wrong?"

Ignoring the swinging handset, Kit met his concerned gaze. "I have to go home."

Kit pounded up the stairs and into her house on shaky legs. She'd dreamed of hearing those words for almost nine years. *Your father is here.* How could her father be here? His sentence was a minimum of ten years.

The morning pancakes had been a sign, surely. They always reminded her of her father, especially the banana and chocolate chip variety. Her grandmother, knowing they made her granddaughter miss the man even more, had gone so far as to stop making them.

"Where is he?" she demanded.

Her Grandma Hazel sat alone with a cup of tea at the dining room table. A shredded tissue surrounded the delicate porcelain cup. The woman took a ragged breath.

"Have you been crying?"

Her grandmother patted the chair beside her. "I need you to sit down for a moment, dear. We need to talk."

"But I want to see Dad!"

Nodding, she pulled the chair out a few inches. "And you will. But I need to talk to you first. He's out in the backyard with your brothers now."

Kit stepped toward the window overlooking the backyard, but Hazel's raised voice stopped her. "Kit. I will not tell you again. Sit."

"Fine. What's going on? I thought he had at least another year before he got out."

Hazel reached for the teapot and poured herself another cup. "Would you like one?"

Kit threw her hands up and groaned. "No. I don't want a cup of tea, Grandma. You know how long I've dreamed about Daddy coming home. Why won't you let me go see him?"

"I will, dear, but I want to prepare you first. I'm afraid maybe you've built up an image of your father in your mind, based on ten-year-old Kit's version of him. He's been gone a long time. He was gone because he did a terrible thing."

Kit dropped into the chair next to her grandmother. "He was wrongly accused of killing that little girl. He'd never drive drunk. He told me that before his sentencing. Momma said it, too."

Her grandmother's face contorted. "Since when has anything your mother told you been true?"

If the words weren't so accurate, her grandmother's harsh comment might have hurt. Instead it was like a splash of cold water.

"You never wanted to talk about what happened, Grandma."

Wrapping an icy hand over Kit's on the tabletop, the woman squeezed her fingers. "I didn't want to cause you any more pain, honey. I thought there was still time. Time when we could discuss this as adults. But I should have known that things never go as planned where your parents are concerned."

Kit placed her other hand on top of her grandmother's. "Why are your hands so cold?"

The woman chuckled, and the atmosphere in the room lightened enough for Kit to draw a much-needed breath. "Shock, I suppose, dear. Opening my door to find that man standing there, holding a bouquet of white daisies, almost bowled me over. He was always a charmer, that guy, and jail didn't steal the charm from him. He knows daisies are my favorite. But, dear, he's not the same man he was nine years ago."

Kit pulled her hand back and straightened her spine. "How can you possibly know that, Grandma? Didn't he just get here?"

Nodding, her grandmother wrapped her hands around her steaming cup of tea, as if to warm them. "About an hour ago, yes."

"And that's enough time for you to say he's *changed*?"

Eyes snapping back to Kit, her grandmother frowned. "You will not sass me, child."

"Grandma, I'm hardly a child. I'm eighteen."

"Be that as it may, you will never be old enough to sass me."

Kit hated the way the reprimand twisted her stomach, but her grandma was right. The woman had taken her and her two younger brothers in when her own daughter, Kit's mother, eventually spiraled out of control following the incarceration of their father.

Or was it the other way around? Had Kit's mother's vast problems sent her father over the edge?

"I'm sorry, Grandma. You're right. I didn't mean any disrespect. Please, can we talk so I can go see my father? What did you want to tell me?"

Hazel met and held Kit's gaze as she pushed her cup away. It clattered against the saucer. "You were young when they sent him away. It was a very stressful time, and your mother's problems only complicated things. You worshiped your father, and after the accident, I didn't see the point in ruining the picture you'd built up of him in your mind, since he'd be gone for so long."

"But now that he's back, you suddenly feel there are things about my father that I need to know about? Before I can even give him a hug after all this time?"

Grandma Hazel's eyes brimmed with tears. "He's not alone back there, Kit."

"I know, the boys are with him," Kit said, getting to her feet.

"True. But he had someone with him when he arrived."

Kit's stomach turned over. "Mom?"

"No, not your mother. It's another woman. I guess they wrote letters to each other while he was in prison. Kit, he claims she's his wife."

She couldn't have heard her grandmother right. "He can't have *two* wives."

"Your parents aren't married anymore, honey. Your mother filed for divorce a year after he went to prison."

If this heart-to-heart continued much longer, Kit was afraid she'd throw up. "Why didn't anyone tell me that?"

"I'm so sorry, honey. Like I said, I thought we still had time. Your mother didn't even tell me right away. And I haven't heard from your father since they took him from the courtroom. You and your brothers had enough to deal with . . . the way your mother kept popping in and out of your life, plus a father in prison. The boys were so young, and you were so convinced that your father was unjustly accused. I can see now how wrong it was for me to keep so much from you."

Kit's excitement to see her father was quickly becoming overshadowed by a sense of dread. "There's more, isn't there?"

Hazel picked up one of the shredded pieces of tissue, mangling it further with nervous fingers. "There's always more where your mother and father are concerned. Remember how I told you how your grandfather loved that Mustang I gave you?"

Kit had a bad feeling about what was coming next.

"The part I left out of the story was that the car was originally your mother's. We gave it to her for her high school graduation."

"My mother's? It wasn't even your car to give when you gave it to me for my birthday?"

Her grandmother shook her head and dropped the tissue into her half-empty tea cup. "We thought it was. Your mother signed the title back over to us five years ago, after you'd been living here for a while. It was the last time she showed up here, remember, on Thanksgiving? She needed money. Again. Your grandfather was tired of bailing her out. The car was in the garage out back. It had been under a tarp for at least ten or maybe even fifteen years. Way back when, she'd tried to run it without enough oil."

That sounded like something her mother would do.

"Despite your mother's many problems, she can usually weasel out of tight spots. I don't know where she got the idea, but she suggested she sign the title back over to your grandfather in exchange for a few thousand dollars. Your grandfather was already planning to fix up the motor so you could drive it when you were old enough. A clear title would simplify things. He hated to give her more money, but at the time it seemed like the best option. And we thought that would allow us to give you the car, free and clear."

Unable to help herself, Kit walked over to the window, searching the yard for her father and brothers. "Grandma . . . is Dad here to see us, or to take my car?"

She jumped when Hazel wrapped her arms around her middle from behind. She hadn't heard her get up. "Oh, honey, I'm sure he wanted to see you and your brothers. It's been so long. But you are right about the car. He alleges your mother gave it to him in the divorce proceedings, but he couldn't claim it because he was in jail. And now he says he needs it. He has no other assets. He's been in prison for so long. He wants to drive his new wife across the country to visit her parents."

The father Kit remembered would never show up here, out of the blue, and steal her car away from her. "Did you tell him you gave me the car?"

Sighing, Hazel released Kit and stood beside her. "I tried. I wish your grandfather was here. He could always stand up to Duncan. He never quite believed the charming mask your father always hid behind."

Kit missed her grandfather every day of the four years since his passing. But she'd never missed him more than today. How dare her father show up here, unannounced, and bully her grandmother?

Feelings welled up, and Kit turned from her grandmother's side, racing for the back door. Grandpa might not be able to stand up to her father anymore, but she could.

Ignoring her grandmother's calls, Kit ran down the back steps and across the longish grass toward the two adults and two young teenagers standing by the garage. At the banging of the door, her father turned her way. Kit's steps faltered, and she pulled up next to the tire swing her grandfather hung for them when they'd first moved in. Part of her wanted to run into her father's extended arms. But she kept picturing her grandmother's guilt-ridden expression, and she grabbed tight to the swing's rope instead. The old tire thumped against her hip.

"Look how you've grown, Katherine. Come, give your daddy a hug," the man insisted, wiggling his fingers at her.

He looked different than she remembered. The sweep of dark brown bangs he used to brush back with a toss of his head was now gone. All his hair was gone, in fact, his head shaved bald. He seemed shorter, but broader, too, and a massive tattoo covered his left bicep. The artwork reminded her of Storm.

She remembered her father as a handsome, boy-next-door type. This man looked like someone else entirely. He looked like a thug.

Kit stayed where she was, clutching the rope for support and eyeing her brothers to gauge their reactions to the surprise visitor. Pete, the youngest, had only been five years old the last time he'd seen their father. He was staring at the older man. Tony, just one year older than Pete, kept looking between their dad and the woman at his side.

Did her brothers know who she was claiming to be?

Feeling steadier after the initial shock over how different her father looked from the man she remembered, Kit released the rope and moved to stand between her father and her brothers. She understood that the protective instincts she felt for her two younger siblings were disproportionately strong, thanks in part to the man standing in front of them now. She'd been doing her best to protect them since they were born.

"It's nice to see you, Dad," Kit said, and a small part of her meant it. But she refused to hug him. "You should have swung by yesterday. You could have taken pictures of me in my prom gown. You could have met my date. But I guess milestones like that in your children's lives aren't that important to you. How long ago did you get out?"

"I—well—"

The way he stammered told her he hadn't expected this type of reaction from her.

The mystery woman at his side stepped forward, threading her arm through his. "We came as soon as we could," she said, snapping gum while meeting Kit's gaze with a challenging one of her own.

"I see. Your three children weren't your first stop then, huh, Dad? Even after all these years."

He stepped toward her, extricating himself from the woman's arm. She didn't look happy about it. "Honey, please understand. I needed her help with a few things first, but I'm here now. How about that hug?"

When she was younger, she'd fallen asleep every night for months on end, craving those exact words. Though that dream had died years ago, she couldn't help herself. She'd tried, but her years of missing him won out. She let her father hug her.

He lifted her off her feet, swinging her around as if she were weightless. At almost five feet eight inches, she knew she wasn't the lightweight girl he'd last hugged, but her eighteen-year-old size didn't seem to faze him. She supposed he had spent his time in jail lifting weights.

Her shield came back up, and she nodded toward the woman. "Grandma tells me this is your wife. Silly me, I thought you were still married to our mother."

He had the grace to look embarrassed. Both Tony and Pete whipped their heads around, and stared at her. They clearly hadn't heard the news. She hated that she'd been the one to share it with them, and in such a harsh manner.

She considered running back into the house, where she suspected her loving grandmother was still watching them from the dining room window. The woman's instinct would be to protect her and her brothers from their dysfunctional parents, just like she'd always done. Twelve-year-old Kit might have run inside. Eighteen-year-old Kit, however, could not, because she needed to be an adult. Her brothers needed her to be their buffer.

Kit inhaled deeply, summoning her courage. "One of you should have told us you'd divorced. Instead, you let us hope that someday, if you came back to us, maybe you could fix things with Mom, too."

Wife number two tried to take a step forward, but her spiky black heel sunk into the grass. "Your father deserves someone better than that awful woman," she said, wrestling to free her heel.

Kit eyed the woman with disgust. "A woman like you, I suppose?"

One of her brothers snickered, but Kit didn't look their way.

"Katherine, there's no need to be unkind," her father said, and Kit's mind flashed back to the time he'd scolded her for tossing her Barbie doll into the corner of her bedroom. She'd been playing house. The doll was her mother.

Would this man always pick less-than-ideal women?

Her grandfather had been right not to trust him. She finally saw that. How could she have cried so many tears over him, praying and wishing he'd surprise them and come home?

"We can't stay long, Katherine, but we'll be back. I promise. I'll do my best to be back in time for your graduation."

"Dad, you've been gone for almost nine years. Don't pretend you want to start attending our events now." She already knew why he'd really come, and where he was going, thanks to her grandmother, but she doubted Tony or Pete knew the truth.

Tony kicked at the ground, then crossed his arms to mirror Kit's stance. "We were doing fine without you, too."

"You kids surprise me. I thought I'd get a warmer welcome."

Kit waited, arms crossed, not letting him off the hook.

"Say, Kitty-Kat, I have a little something I need to talk to you about," he began.

She held up a hand. "First, never, ever call me that again. The man who used to call me that no longer exists. Second, no, you cannot take my car. Grandpa bought it from Mom years ago, and Grandma gave me that car for my birthday. Even you wouldn't be heartless enough to steal it from your only daughter."

Her father exchanged a look with his new wife. "Now, Katherine, you need to understand. That car didn't belong to your grandparents. It belongs to me. Your mother gave it to me in the divorce agreement."

Kit shook her head. "I don't believe you. Even she wouldn't be that heartless."

Her father stepped forward, taking hold of Kit's upper arm. If he squeezed any harder, he'd leave a bruise. "Your mother never had a big heart," he growled.

Kit tried to pull away, but he held fast.

The door banged open, much as it had when Kit rushed out. Hazel was heading their way, waving Pete's baseball bat above her head.

"Holy crap, Grandma!" Tony cried, laughing at the picture she made.

"Language, young man," the gray-haired woman scolded without missing a step. She brought the bat down, jabbing it toward her son-in-law. *Ex* son-in-law.

Later, Kit could mourn the loss of the father she'd thought she'd known. Right now, she needed to get rid of this nasty man before her grandmother did something foolish. "Dad, unless you have something legal and in writing that proves you own that Mustang, I'm going to have to insist that you leave. Without my car. If you aren't gone by the time I count to ten, I'm going to send Pete inside to call the police. I bet your parole officer wouldn't take kindly to that."

"I *told* you this was a bad idea, Duncan," the woman said. "Come on. Let's go find that paperwork. When we come back, we'll bring the cops with us. Then this little bitch won't have a choice. She'll have to turn the keys over."

Luckily Tony sensed his grandmother's rage. He took three quick steps in her direction and grabbed the bat on her backswing.

Everyone held their breath for a beat. Duncan gave Kit a pleading look, but this time she managed to turn her back on him and walk away. "Come on, Grandma. Boys. I've had enough of this. Come inside and I'll tell you all about my prom date last night."

Never turning around, Kit kept walking, her eyes locked on the back door of her grandma and grandpa's house, the house that had always felt more like home than anywhere she'd lived with her parents. She'd thought it was the end of the world when they'd forced her to move here at twelve years old. Now, after seeing the type of man her father really was, seemingly not knowing or caring where her mother had disappeared to, Kit finally understood that coming here had been her salvation.

CHAPTER TWENTY-THREE

K IT STUCK HER YEARBOOK between her knees and squeezed while she wrestled to shove her backpack, stuffed with the textbooks she'd turn in later that day, far enough into her locker that she could slam the door shut. She'd done her best to prepare for her finals over the past two weeks, but the disturbing visit from her father, and that awful woman, was never far from her mind.

How could she have wasted so many years missing him?

"Come on," Jackie said, appearing out of nowhere, her yearbook cradled against her chest. "Lynette and Annie are waiting for us in the gym. Do you have a good pen?"

Kit pulled her favorite four-color pen from the pocket of her jeans.

The girls had agreed to meet in the gymnasium after their last final so they could be sure to sign yearbooks for each other. Annie's sister, Millie, suggested they make an event out of it, warning that if they waited until after graduation, they'd never do it. They'd probably lose touch altogether, she claimed.

"I don't understand why we have to write a bunch of sappy stuff in each other's yearbooks," Kit said, testing her locker to make sure it wouldn't pop open.

Jackie shrugged. "I don't really understand it, either, but Annie wants to, so we might as well get it over with. Who knows? Maybe someday, when we're old, we'll get together over wine and cheese and read what we write today."

Kit laughed. "What do you consider 'old'?"

"I don't know. Like, sixty? Or maybe even fifty? Any milestone birthday after thirty sounds old to me right now."

Underclassmen crowded the hallways. They still had a few more days of finals to get through, but seniors always finished out the year ahead of the younger students. Kit watched them, hardly believing that after this week she may never set foot in this building again. "Doesn't it feel weird to you, knowing this is it?"

Frowning, Jackie nodded toward the school offices as they passed them. "Since my dad works here, I'll probably be back. But maybe you won't."

Kit pivoted around a trio of giggling girls. She didn't know any of them. They looked too young to be freshmen. "Were we ever that immature?"

"Never," Jackie said, breaking into a jog. "Come on, we're late!"

By the time they burst through the doors of the gymnasium, the bell was ringing. Groups of kids littered the bleachers. During most of the school year, teachers didn't allow students in here unless they had gym class, but they loosened the rules during the last week of school.

"Up here!"

Annie was waving to them from near the top of the bleachers. Lynette barely glanced their way, already hard at work, writing in what had to be Annie's yearbook. Jackie ran up the stairs, unfazed by the steep incline and number of steps. Kit huffed and puffed behind her.

"You ladies are late!" Annie said, but she didn't look upset.

The two of them got comfortable and passed their books to each other.

"Lynette, what are you finding to say?" Jackie asked. "You're writing away over there! I can't think of anything that won't sound stupid when we look back at these years down the road."

Lynette looked up and pushed her dark curls away from her face. "Don't overthink it. Just say what's in your heart."

"My heart is feeling a little black these days," Kit admitted, clicking through the colors in her pen.

"I bet. Any word from your dad? Did he steal your car yet?"

Kit could tell from Jackie's tone that she was teasing, but thinking about it still felt like a knife to her gut. "Not a word."

News of her father's return had spread through her small friend group like wildfire, since Annie had been with her when she called her grandmother from Elliott's house. They'd hashed through the painful details more than once in the weeks since the incident, but it still hurt to talk about it.

"He might not show up at graduation," Annie suggested. They all knew Kit was praying he'd stay away and not cause a scene.

Kit flipped through Jackie's book, looking for a blank page. "I'm sick of thinking about him. I hope he's halfway across the country by now, and he stays as far away from our graduation ceremony as possible. Let's get down to business here."

She racked her brain for somewhere to start, holding her pen against the paper. In the six years since she'd met these three at summer camp, they'd become the best of friends. How can you possibly summarize that in one stupid paragraph?

You can't.

Kit had an idea.

She hated the notion that they might lose touch, but people changed. The awful transformation her father went through had taught her that. Unless they didn't allow long gaps of time without seeing each other.

"What if we made each other a promise?"

Annie frowned and looked up from the page. "What kind of promise?"

"A promise that we'll never go a full year without seeing each other."

"I'm not sure that's realistic, Kit," Jackie said, tapping her pen against the book in her lap. "We may all head off in different directions, separated for some stretches of time, sure, but that doesn't mean we'll grow apart. What if we get married? Start having kids?"

Annie nodded. "You're probably right, Jackie. It might not be realistic to say we'll see each other every year. But, actually, my mom does something really cool with her old friends from high school. They just started a couple years ago, now that everyone's kids are older. They take a girls' trip once a year! No husbands. No men. No kids. Just them, and they have a blast! I heard her talking to her friend on the phone one night after they got back from last year's trip. She didn't know I could hear her. They laughed and yacked for at least an hour, and then they started planning this year's trip."

Kit considered this. An annual girls' trip did sound amazing, and her friends were probably right that they wouldn't be able to start that up right away. "We should do that, too! Annual trips, I mean. But when do you think we can start?"

No one seemed willing to throw out any suggestions, though they all agreed to the concept.

"Fine," Kit said, clicking her pen. "I'm putting this in writing. 'We promise we will start doing annual trips . . . just the four of us . . . no later than the summer we all turn forty.' "

Jackie shook her head. "I'm not planning to have kids until I'm at least thirty."

"Really?" This surprised Kit. But if she were being honest, she'd never even thought about what kind of timeline she wanted to follow for starting a family of her own. Did she even want kids? It wasn't like her mom and dad had taught her how to be a good parent.

"Better make it fifty," Annie suggested. "My mom is, like, forty-eight already. We can always start sooner, if it works for everyone."

Kit shuddered. "Fifty sounds *ancient*."

"Well, yeah, because we're only eighteen, but my mom keeps telling me the older she gets the faster the years fly by," Lynette said, joining the conversation.

Kit made eye contact with each of the other three girls. "Do every one of you promise that, no matter what happens, we will start taking annual girls' trips together when we are fifty, if not sooner?"

Annie placed her right hand over her heart. "All right, ladies. As a Kaleidoscope Girl, I promise to take annual trips with all of you, starting in the year 2020, when we are all fifty. Or sooner if we can swing it. Agreed?"

"Oh my God, 2020?! That sounds light years away," Jackie said. "I wonder what the world will even be like by then. Even thinking about the year 2000 feels crazy."

"It'll be incredible, I know it! Who knows what all of us will accomplish over the next thirty-two years? Hopefully each of us will contribute to world peace, or equality for all. And no more starving children!"

Kit grinned at Lynette, appreciating her optimism but harboring doubts. "That would certainly be amazing, wouldn't it?"

"Wait," Jackie said. "What about Renee? I know we barely ever see her, but she was one of the original Kaleidoscope Girls, too."

"We'll invite her, too," Annie said, making a note in the book she held. "Everybody write about this in whoever's yearbook you have right now. Then we won't forget."

Happy to have something to write, Kit started crafting her reminder in Jackie's book.

"Tell me we don't have to include *Fran* in our old lady trip, too," Jackie said, pointing over at the large group of girls on the other end of the bleachers. "She was in our cabin that summer, too, remember?"

Kit snorted. "She was never an official member of the Kaleidoscope Girls. We weren't good enough for her then, and now she isn't good enough to hang out with us. She's out."

Annie nodded. "Not only is Fran out, I think we still need to get back at her for the crap she pulled that summer at camp. Remember when she tried to frame you two for the missing money she took?"

Lynette slammed the book shut she'd been writing in. "How could I forget? But that was six years ago. Isn't it a little late to get back at her now?"

"Actually . . . tomorrow *is* senior prank day," Kit said, her imagination dreaming up all kinds of ways to get back at her old nemesis.

Jackie rolled her eyes. "What are we, twelve again? Fran screwed up. She made some poor decisions when we were younger, but I think she did it because she felt like we'd abandoned her. That doesn't mean we should stoop to that level now. We know better. Just let it go."

"Fine. I don't have time to dream up a prank that would be good enough to balance out what she did to us anyhow. But maybe someday she'll pay."

Lynette nodded. "Karma has a funny way of finding us, and I don't think there is an expiration date on that."

CHAPTER TWENTY-FOUR

Jackie tried to adjust the bobby pins poking into her head as the familiar strains of *Pomp and Circumstance* filled the gymnasium. She wobbled, finding it difficult to stay balanced on one foot while the crutches dug into her armpits.

"What are you doing?" Kit whispered from behind her. "If you keep messing with that, it'll fall off when you cross the stage."

"Millie made it too tight." She took a painful step forward, cursing the way her pantyhose caught on the gauze covering her skinned right knee. At least her gown covered the damage on her leg. It provided less concealment, however, of a similar scab on her right arm that spanned from wrist to elbow. A long-sleeved dress would have done the trick, but then she'd be too hot.

She closed her eyes and tried to will the pain away. After waiting nearly eighteen years to walk across that stage and receive her diploma, she was determined to enjoy it. It just wouldn't be the graceful glide she'd imagined.

The final week of her high school career had turned out to be so much more difficult than she could have imagined.

"Are you going to be okay?" Owen asked, leaning toward her.

Jackie found it ironic that they'd ended up standing next to each other in their graduation's processional line. Once they reached their assigned rows up ahead, she'd turn left and he'd turn right, heading to their seats on opposite ends of the gymnasium. She didn't miss the symbolism. She felt the bittersweet twinge of loss as her eyes met his, the concern there for her well-being apparent.

"I'll be fine," she whispered back. "I fell on the hurdles at practice. Now I can't run at the state meet next week. I think my dad is even more disappointed than I am."

"Will it impact your track scholarship?"

His question surprised Jackie. How did he know she was going to college on a scholarship? She didn't even know what his plans were after today.

"I hope not."

But as she uttered the words, she wasn't sure they were true. Initially, the offers she'd received to continue running for a variety of different universities were thrilling. The decision to pick the school where Kit planned to go, and to room with her old friend, had been easy.

What she hadn't considered was the university's focus on math and the sciences. The business department wasn't as strong. The economics class she'd just finished had exposed her to some fascinating concepts she wanted to explore further, but after their college visit where she'd talked briefly with an academic advisor, she was worried she'd picked the school for all the wrong reasons.

College track, after all, wouldn't ultimately turn into a lifelong career path for her.

Kit prodded her in the back. "You need to move, Jackie."

Gritting her teeth in an effort to ignore her injured knee, Jackie edged forward. Owen moved in concert with her. He'd grown taller, a fact she'd first noticed when he escorted Renee to prom. Part of her wished her two old friends had hit it off, but as far as she knew, he hadn't talked to Renee since that night.

She picked out her father, standing onstage with other important people, watching proudly as yet another class of seniors filed in. How many of these ceremonies had he overseen in his years as principal? She felt the connection when his eyes found hers. She was starting to realize how much of her life she'd organized around his expectations. He didn't even bother to hide the disappointment he felt over her older brother's life choices. It was why Jackie tried so hard to please him.

Would she live to regret her choices?

"Congratulations, Jackie," Owen said with a wink when they reached their rows, then turning opposite each other, they went to their seats.

The tiny gesture made her heart skip a beat as she felt one last touch of nostalgia for her old friend.

She scanned the crowded bleachers, trying to pick out her mother and Ronnie. She couldn't find them, but she knew they were there. Once seated, she looked at Kit, sitting beside her. She was also checking the bleachers, but Jackie knew her friend hoped she wouldn't find either of her parents in the crowd.

It had taken a long time, but was still early in their friendship, for Kit to share the actual story behind why her and her two brothers came to live with their grandparents. Jackie hated that Kit's father showed up the way he had that Sunday after prom. She knew her friend had held one version of her father close in her heart for all the years he was away. The reality of the type of person he was—or at least the type he'd become in prison—shattered Kit's illusion.

As the last notes of music floated around them, the ceremony commenced. She tried to pay attention, but her mind kept replaying her recent tumble over the hurdles. It happened the very afternoon she'd met with her besties in the gym to write in each other's yearbooks. Their talk of careers and families was still on her mind as she set the hurdles, her motions automatic, born of years of practice.

That's what happens when your mind is elsewhere, she thought, trying to focus on the ceremony. She knew better, then and now, than to let her mind wander. Her father had tried to instill the importance of focus in her.

When she went down, Nathan was one of the first at her side. They'd talked little since prom, both of them busy with the end of their senior year. Jackie hadn't felt the connection with him that she'd expected, so the fact that their initial date hadn't grown into something more didn't bother her, but she appreciated the way he'd helped her to her feet once she'd caught her breath. He'd supported her as she hobbled over to the trainer, blood running down both her leg and arm. He didn't leave her side to return to his own practice until he knew she was in good hands.

She hadn't broken anything, but there was a deep bruise on her leg, and her doctor insisted she allow it to rest and heal. Running in the state tournament was out of the question. She knew her father would still expect her to travel to the meet with her team, to show support to everyone still running. She'd rather skip it altogether and hang out at the beach with her girlfriends—even though crutches and scabs would be a horrible mix with the sand.

Her attention flitted back to the stage when someone tapped the microphone. It was her old friend-turned-enemy, Fran, preparing to give her valedictorian speech. *Enemy* was probably too strong a word, but the gap between now and the friendship she'd shared with Fran as far back as kindergarten was far wider these days than the one between her and Owen. How that girl ended up at the top of their class was a mystery to Jackie. What could she say that would offer an ounce of inspiration to their graduating class? Hopefully it would be short and to the point so they could get on with the handing out of diplomas and wrap this ceremony up. Jackie's nylons were sticking, and she worried that her knee was seeping again.

But as Fran delivered the speech—one she'd undoubtedly practiced dozens of times—Jackie was intrigued despite herself.

"It's time to focus our eyes on the horizon, on the unlimited potential each of us has before us, if only we have the courage to step into the unknown," Fran was saying, pulling Jackie in. "The skills we needed to succeed here, in high school, are not the same skills we'll need to pursue our best lives out there in the real world. It will take courage. It will take ambition. And it will take some luck."

Fran paused for effect, and Jackie could hear classmates shuffling uncomfortably in their chairs.

"But if that all sounds a little overwhelming to you, I have some good news. I would venture to guess that none of us have reached this milestone day without regrets. We've all done things we aren't proud of. I know I have."

She heard scattered chuckles following Fran's admission. She wondered if missing cash at summer camp was on Fran's list of regrets.

"So, here's the good news. When we walk out of here today, we can choose to wipe our slate clean. We *can* have a 'do-over.' I'd go so far as to say we *have* to give ourselves permission to start fresh. It's the only way. I hate that each of us has caused hurt and confusion in others during this path we've followed through childhood to today. We have done the hurting, and others have hurt us. It's unavoidable. But hopefully we've also learned from this journey we've all been on. No one arrives in this world knowing how to be a kind human. A good friend. Our experiences can teach us a better way. Some of us learn those lessons quickly, while others are still working on it. Sadly, not all of us have learned enough yet, and we'll struggle."

Jackie noticed the gymnasium was oddly quiet now, despite the size of the crowd. Fran had people's attention.

"Let it all go. Stop living your life for others. Decide which path interests you, go find the trailhead for that path, and take those first steps. Because today is the first day of the rest of your life. And when you inevitably reach your last days, only you will know whether you lived a life you are proud of. Not your parents, teachers, or even your friends. You get to decide. Now, go out there, and make good choices."

Applause erupted as Fran took a small bow before carefully making her way back to her seat on ridiculously high heels.

"I hope she has a big-ass eraser in her pocket," Kit said, not bothering to whisper given the continuing clapping. "Because that girl has a lot on her slate to wipe clean."

Jackie grinned, knowing Fran's words might not have landed quite as squarely for Kit. But she found some solace in Fran's encouragement and was glad she'd dissuaded her friends from pulling some kind of nasty prank on the girl. Yes, Fran had most definitely made mistakes through the years—the most notable one, in Jackie's eyes, being the way she'd sacrificed one set of friends for another back at summer camp—but it seemed she was trying to move past it now.

She'd just given them all permission to open a new door and move through it, slamming the old door on all their past heartache. Jackie loved the idea and planned to do just that.

Even if it proved to be harder than Fran made it sound.

"Here's a glass of punch and a cookie," Kit said, setting the refreshments in front of Jackie and dropping into the chair next to her. "God, I'm glad that's over with."

Jackie thanked her, eyes scanning the crowded lunch room. She wondered where Annie and Lynette had disappeared to.

"Are you looking for Nathan?"

"Why would I be looking for Nathan?"

Kit sipped her punch. "I wasn't sure whether you still liked him. I've barely seen you since prom, given all the crap that happened in my life since then."

Thinking back, Jackie realized it was true. Other than their conversation while signing each other's yearbooks, she hadn't chatted with Kit in weeks. They'd all gotten so busy with everything. Was this what the future would hold? Were they destined to drift apart?

Not if she could help it.

"You know, I'm not thinking about Nathan much anymore. I think I realized at prom that we don't have much in common after all."

Kit snorted. "That's not true. He runs. You run."

Jackie grinned, tapping one of her crutches where it balanced against the table. "Not so much."

"You know what I mean. You guys have sports in common. And he's handsome. I know he was late to prom, and you weren't happy about that, but remember what Fran said. Wipe the slate clean. Forgive him."

Jackie considered it, but the idea held little appeal where Nathan was concerned. "Nah. It's not that. I just didn't have any kind of connection with him. Does that make sense?"

"Actually, yes, it does."

But Kit sounded distracted. Jackie noticed her friend watching a group of teachers working the refreshment table.

"I'll hold our spots if you want another cookie."

Kit swung her eyes back to her. "What's that? A cookie? I can go get you another one."

Laughing, Jackie shook her head. "That's not what I said. What's going on, Kit?"

She glanced back toward the refreshments and noticed that Ronnie's friend Bruce had set out a fresh plate of cookies. Things clicked. Jackie suddenly remembered how she kept seeing Kit talking to Bruce on prom night. He was the chaperone. They'd both gotten to know him when he'd tagged along on their college visit a few months back.

"You like him."

"Who?"

"Bruce. You like Ronnie's friend Bruce."

Spots of color flared in Kit's cheeks.

Jackie laughed. "It's been years since I've seen you blush like that. You know he's too old for you, right? He's a teacher!"

"*Student* teacher," Kit corrected. "I know he's older than us, but does that really matter?"

Jackie considered this. It did matter when Bruce was teaching at the school where they were students. But the tassel dangling from the left side of her graduation cap reminded her they weren't technically in high school anymore.

"Look at Lynette and Storm. He's older. She doesn't seem to care," Kit said, nodding toward where their friend was standing with her boyfriend. They seemed to be locked in a heated discussion with Lynette's mom and a man Jackie didn't recognize.

"I wondered where Lynette had disappeared to," she said. "I'm still not sure Storm is good for her. Maybe her mom doesn't think so either. It looks like they're arguing about something. I wonder if it's Storm."

Kit studied Lynette and her family for a moment, too, before Jackie noticed her eyes flip back to where Bruce was helping with the cookies. "Bruce is nothing like Storm," she insisted. "Besides, it's not like my parents are around to approve or disapprove of anyone I might date."

Jackie couldn't help but wonder if that was actually why Kit seemed interested in Bruce. Did she unknowingly see him as the father figure she so desperately missed?

The scrape of a chair caught their attention.

"Hi, guys," Annie said, taking a seat at their table.

Elliott stood behind her, his hands full with two cups of punch and a napkin stacked with cookies. Once he set them on the table, he pulled out the only remaining chair and joined them. "Congratulations, ladies," he said, nodding to both Kit and Jackie. "You looked good up there today. Do you want some cookies? Bruce gave me a big stack. Said they still have way too many in the kitchen."

Jackie had forgotten Elliott and Bruce were brothers.

"Thanks, Elliott. I'm sorry you still have another year at this place," Kit said with a laugh. "Will you miss us?"

"I'll miss Annie," he said, bumping his shoulder against hers.

Just as Kit had moments before, Annie blushed. Jackie wondered if her and Elliott were dating. If they were, Annie had stayed quiet about it.

"I hear the three of you and Lynette are planning annual girls' trips as the Kaleidoscope Girls," Elliott said. "That's pretty neat."

Jackie narrowed her eyes at Annie. What was she doing, sharing their private conversations with this guy? Their pact wasn't a secret, but what else had Annie shared with Elliott?

"And I liked the kaleidoscopes you made at camp. Annie showed me hers. Pretty impressive. Do you all still have yours?"

Kit shook her head and grinned. "What have you two kids been up to? Annie keeps that old kaleidoscope above her desk in her room. I thought your parents cracked down on that kind of thing after they caught Millie with some guy, sans clothes."

"Her folks aren't always home." Elliott winked.

Jackie knew from the expression on Annie's face that she wasn't enjoying being the focus of the conversation. But before anyone could tease the girl further, raised voices caught their attention.

"I warned you to keep your hands off her!" a familiar voice growled, and Jackie twisted in her chair in time to see Storm step up to the man standing next to Lynette's mom and grab him around the neck.

Bruce was there quickly, doing his best to pull Storm off the man. Within a second or two, Jackie's dad also appeared, and between the two of them they restrained Storm and hustled him out the nearest door, with Lynette, her mother, and the red-faced man all close on their heels.

Annie jumped to her feet. "We need to go make sure Lynette is okay."

Jackie grabbed her crutches and hobbled after Kit and Annie, ordering Elliott to watch their things.

Chapter Twenty-Five

A s Kit paced a short stretch of empty hallway outside the school offices, Jackie wished she could do the same to help dispel the nerves she felt over the mystery of what was happening behind the closed door of her father's office.

Instead she said, "Would you sit down before you drive me crazy?"

"No. I will not sit down. And you wouldn't either if you weren't on crutches. What is happening in there?"

Jackie could only shrug. Snippets reached their ears, but not enough for her to tell what was being said. Her father's voice, deep and low, was the easiest for her to pick out, but it wasn't loud enough to decipher.

"I wonder what Storm meant about a warning," Kit said, moving to stand in front of the old cabinet that held the trophies from decades of school events. "I think that older guy is Lynette's mom's boyfriend."

"That would make sense. Lynette's talked about him, and I can tell she doesn't like the guy, but I've never actually seen him."

The door from the lunchroom opened and Annie rushed toward them, three purses in her hands. She was alone. "Anything yet?" she asked as she reached them, handing them each a purse.

"No. We can hear them in Dad's office, but we can't tell what they're saying."

Annie took the empty chair next to Jackie. "I wonder if they called the police on Storm."

"I hope not." Kit looped her purse strap over her shoulder without turning in their direction. "I think he was defending Lynette."

"Defending her? What do you mean?" Jackie asked, keeping a close eye on the office door.

Annie fidgeted next to her. "If I tell you guys something, do you promise to keep it to yourselves?"

"Like you kept our plans for our girls' trips to yourself?" Jackie asked. Even in all the chaos, she was still irritated by Elliott's earlier comments.

Annie collapsed against the back of the wooden chair, knocking her graduation cap askew. She moaned and pulled the mortar board off, her hair snagged in a mess of bobby pins that rivaled Jackie's. "I'm sorry about that. I didn't think it was a big secret, and Elliott is just so easy to talk to. I might have mentioned it to him."

"Obviously. Are you two dating or something?" Jackie asked.

Annie struggled to remove the bobby pins without a mirror, shaking out her hair. "I don't really know. Never mind about that right now. This is about Lynette. I feel like I should probably tell you something."

Kit followed Annie's lead and removed her own cap, a task made easier by her reflection in the trophy case glass. "What do you know, Annie?"

"I know she's scared."

"Scared?" Jackie repeated, forgetting all about Elliott. "Scared of Storm? Because I swear, if he's done anything to hurt her . . ."

Annie grabbed her knee, squeezing it to get her to stop.

"You're lucky that wasn't my *sore* knee."

"And you're lucky I'm more patient than you. Now, shut up and listen. No, Lynette isn't afraid of Storm. In fact, it's the opposite. She sees him as her protector."

Kit turned away from the glass, unzipping her graduation gown and shrugging out of it. "I got that vibe between them."

"What is he protecting her from?" Jackie asked, struggling to keep up. "Wait . . . is it that guy? Her mom's boyfriend?"

"It is. Lynette told me some things the other day, in private, and she made me promise not to say anything. But I don't think secrecy is a good idea in this case. Especially now."

As if to punctuate Annie's point, the door to the principal's office opened and the older man Storm had grabbed walked out. As he turned into the hallway, he noticed Jackie and the other two girls.

"You kids are more trouble than you're worth," he hissed, making a beeline for the door.

His words set off a flash of fury in Jackie, sending her to her feet. Her wounded leg couldn't hold up under her weight, and she stumbled forward. Luckily Kit was close enough to grab her before she went down.

"Let him go. We don't need another scene today," she said, her lips close to Jackie's ear.

Kit was right. The last thing Lynette needed was more drama.

Storm was the next to exit the office. When he spied Jackie and the others, he gave them a curt nod but didn't say anything. He headed for the same door as the first guy, and a small part of Jackie hoped Storm would catch up with him in the parking lot and beat him to a pulp. She had no doubt Storm was capable of it, and if that man had hurt Lynette, he deserved it.

Before Storm even reached the outer door, Bruce came jogging out of the office, following him.

"Ladies," he said as he passed them, his expression grim.

"He's going to go make sure Storm doesn't beat the crap out of that guy," Kit said, echoing Jackie's thoughts.

"Come on, let's go in and check on Lynette." Annie hurried into the principal's office, not bothering to knock.

Jackie hated this part of her life, where her father's job intersected with her life as a student. She struggled to her feet, making better use of the crutches this time.

Her father was on the phone. Lynette was sitting quietly in a chair, a pensive look in her eyes as she focused on something beyond the open window. Donna wasn't looking as stoic. Tears streamed down her face as she clasped tight to her daughter's hand.

"You girls shouldn't be in here," her father said, holding one hand over the mouthpiece of the telephone. But someone on the other end of the phone line must have said something, because he turned his attention back to the call.

Annie was already at Lynette's side, a supportive hand on her shoulder.

"What's going on?" Kit asked, taking in the scene.

Jackie sensed the charge in the air. Whatever it was, it was serious. They watched her father hang up the telephone with a heavy sigh.

"Donna, would you like me to ask the girls to leave so we can talk in private?" Jackie knew her father normally kept a more distant, formal relationship with the parents of his students, but the fact that Lynette had been one of her best friends since grade school meant he was more relaxed with her mother.

Lynette's mother shook her head. "No. She'll tell them everything anyhow, so they might as well hear it straight from us."

"Jackie, were you aware that man was bothering Lynette?"

She held her father's gaze, shocked at his question. "Of course not."

He turned back to Donna. "I wasn't able to find anything out yet. I passed on the information, and they're going to do some digging."

"They? Who are they?"

He frowned at Kit and cleared his throat. "The police. Some concerns came to light today, and we are looking into them."

Crouching in front of Lynette, Kit took both of her hands. "If he hurt you, I'll help Storm hunt him down and make him pay."

Donna gasped. The corner of Lynette's lip twitched.

"Not helping, Kit," Jackie said, watching her father. He wouldn't tolerate much more interference on their part. He surely thought this was a situation the adults should handle.

He'd forget they were *all* adults now.

"What should we do?" Donna asked him.

He stood. "I don't know what is really going on here, but I suggest you keep him away from your daughter until we learn more."

Donna nodded, getting to her feet and pulling Lynette up with her. Kit moved out of the way.

"I will. And please call me the minute you learn anything."

As Donna and Lynette passed her on the way to the door, Jackie caught her friend's hand. "Are you going to be all right?"

Lynette nodded, squeezing her fingers, and leaned close. "Meet me outside in ten minutes."

Once they were gone, Jackie's father rounded his desk and leaned his hip against it, arms crossed as he regarded his daughter and her two remaining friends. "If any of you know anything more about what might have been happening between Lynette and that man, I need you to be honest with me. I can't protect her if I don't know the truth. I'm not even sure there is anything going on. Keep an eye on her, will you? She needs her friends right now. And I'm not sure that boy she's seeing is the right person for the job."

It took some convincing, but Lynette was able to talk her mother into letting her leave the school grounds with Jackie, Kit, and Annie.

"Mom, I need time with my friends. It's our graduation day," she said as she stood beside her concerned mother in the parking lot. "Don't let him ruin the whole day for me."

Jackie felt a pang of sadness for Donna as her shoulders drooped at Lynette's words. For as long as she'd known them, the mother–daughter duo had seemed so close. Like it was the two of them against the world. Today would have been an emotional day for Donna, even without the added drama around the man she was seeing. But Lynette didn't seem inclined to give her mother a break.

"Are you sure, honey? I'd feel better if you came home with me, at least until we find out if Joe is dangerous. I want to keep an eye on you."

Lynette pulled away from her mother. "Trust me, Mom, he *is* dangerous. Grown men don't go around patting their girlfriend's seventeen-year-old daughter on the butt or copping a feel when they brush past her."

Donna shuddered. "Lynette, don't talk like that. It's that boy you've been seeing. I know it."

"Don't talk to me about the boy I'm seeing. Storm isn't the problem here."

Jackie could see this conversation wasn't going to get any more productive. She hobbled between the two of them, wishing she was more coordinated on the crutches. "Look, Donna, I think Lynette just needs a little girl time. Let her come with us. I promise we'll keep her safe. You know us. You can trust us. We'll grab food somewhere, try to get her mind off all of this ugly business. The late-night graduation party starts at eight and goes until one. The four of us will go to that together, then we'll bring her straight home. Would that be all right with you?"

She could see the indecision on Donna's face. "I wish I'd have gotten time off work to help at the party tonight. Are any of your parents working at it?"

Annie stepped forward. "Yes. My mom is helping. She'll be there."

Relieved—this tidbit clearly helped Donna become more comfortable with the plan—Jackie winked at Annie. She'd convinced her own mother not to help chaperone, insisting she didn't need her father running the graduation ceremony and her mother monitoring her at the after-party. A girl could only take so much.

Checking her watch, Donna finally gave her blessing. "My shift starts at the nursing home in twenty minutes. If you girls promise to watch my baby, I won't call in sick. I'm trusting you."

Another round of assurances was enough to send Donna on her way.

After watching her mother pull out of the parking lot, Lynette turned to them. "Come on. Let's go to the park. Storm promised to wait for us there. And he's bringing beer."

Annie and Kit looked as surprised at Lynette's words as Jackie felt.

"Lynette, we can't take you to Storm," Jackie said. "We just promised your mother to keep an eye on you."

Nodding, Lynette grabbed Kit's purse and fished out a set of car keys. "And that's why I invited you along to the park with me."

"But you don't even have a car, Lynette, and those are my keys."

Lynette tossed the keys to Kit and grinned. She didn't look upset, confusing Jackie even more. "I know. You have to drive. Let's go."

She skipped toward the red Mustang that Kit's father hadn't yet managed to steal, laughing back at her stunned friends.

"I think she's officially lost it," Annie said, frowning.

"And I was just stupid enough to promise Donna we'd keep her safe," Jackie pointed out, gripping the handles on her crutches tighter so she could hurry after Lynette. "Looks like we have our work cut out for us tonight."

The smell of antiseptic stung Jackie's nose. Her heart ached as her mind kept replaying scenes from their disastrous evening. She'd failed Donna. More importantly, she'd failed Lynette.

She agreed with Lynette that trauma impacts everyone in different ways. Storm survived an abusive childhood, but the experience hardened him. At least that was the story their friend had fed them during their drive to the park. As if that could excuse his behavior.

Aside from the detour to the park, the foursome had grabbed pizza for dinner and made it to the party ten minutes after it started. But it wasn't long after their arrival that things fell apart. Attendance at the party was lower than expected, and the initial games of bingo were lame. None of them even got a bingo, and they all cringed when Fran won the blackout round, the proud new owner of a television set donated to the event by the local Sears store.

Lynette hinted that they should sneak out. Annie insisted that would be a bad idea. Her mother was taking tickets at the door, and she'd surely tell Donna if she saw them leave. Music blared from upstairs, and most of the other kids headed up for the dance. Jackie didn't want to try to navigate the stairs on crutches, and the elevator was out of order. Kit complained of boredom, and Annie didn't want to dance since Elliott wasn't there.

"Come on, ladies, why don't we tell Annie's mom that Jackie's leg hurts so we're going to call it a night? We'll promise her we're all going back to my house, where we'll stay until Mom gets off work. She'll be too busy to check on us. Maybe we could find Storm and an actual party instead of this boring one. You guys could even stay overnight later."

Jackie was pretty sure Lynette wouldn't stick to the plan she'd just laid out. "Lynette, come on, I promised your mom that we'd keep you safe tonight."

Lynette dropped her forehead to the tabletop. A moment later, she sat up straight, then stood just as fast. "Fine. I'm going to the bathroom. You three figure it out, because this is too tame."

Jackie watched her walk away. "What's gotten into her?"

"My grandma told me once that my mom seemed to change overnight. She hinted that something bad happened to her, but she wouldn't tell me what," Kit said, frowning as she also watched Lynette leave. "She said it happened before she met my dad. I didn't believe that people could change that fast and I thought she was just making excuses for Mom. But maybe whatever happened to Lynette was bad enough that it changed her, too."

"Do you think Storm is behind the way Lynette's acting?" Annie asked.

Kit shrugged. "It has to be either Storm or Donna's boyfriend, right?"

"Do we dare leave?" Jackie asked, still feeling responsible. "I know this isn't much fun."

The answer to that one question would prove to be pivotal. Lynette didn't come back from the bathroom, and Jackie learned later that she snuck into the adjoining bar and used the payphone. By the time Kit, Annie, and Jackie could sneak past Annie's mother's watchful eye and head for the Mustang to go search for their friend, they heard an obnoxiously loud truck racing away.

Things were a blur after that. They'd driven up and down Main, and past all of the usual haunts they could think of, but they couldn't find any sign of Storm's truck or their friend. It was like they'd disappeared into the night.

Then, when they'd stopped for gas, they heard the scream of sirens, eerie in the darkness.

"No . . ." Jackie remembered whispering, dread filling her.

They followed the flashing lights from a safe distance, something telling them they'd find their friend when those lights finally stopped moving. Storm's truck rested on its roof at the bottom of a steep ditch. Annie tried to run down to the crash site, but a first responder grabbed her around the waist, holding her back.

Now their friend was somewhere behind the ominous doors of the emergency room. No one knew what had happened to Storm. They couldn't find him anywhere. Jackie's parents were conversing with Donna near the nurse's station, their expressions somber.

What was happening? Annie and Kit looked as devastated as Jackie felt, sitting across from her on a short couch, while they awaited news about their friend.

The double doors swung open and the two doctors went straight to Donna. Jackie's mother kept a supportive arm around the other woman's waist, and they listened intently to whatever the doctors were saying.

Jackie was tired of being left out of adult conversations. She was tired of not being able to get around on her gimpy leg. And she was tired of disappointing people.

After tonight, she was going to turn over a new page, wipe the slate clean like Fran had said.

But first, she had to know whether Lynette was going to be all right.

reminiscing with friends

RUBY SHORES

2018

CHAPTER TWENTY-SIX

J ACKIE SCANNED THE CAFÉ. It was as busy as it had been just three
days ago, that Thursday morning when she'd stopped in for breakfast
the day after her arrival. If Owen wasn't here yet, they might not even get
a table before she'd have to leave to go meet Annie.

Marge happened by, one arm expertly balancing three breakfast plates,
the fingers of the other threaded through three empty coffee mugs. "He's
back in the far corner, waiting on you, sugar," she said, nodding toward
the rear of the restaurant.

Thankful he'd kept his word, she headed in that direction, stopping
to say a quick hello to the elderly couple who lived next to her parents. It
was the neighbor whose mowing kept interrupting her wine and cheese
get-together on the porch with Kit and Lynette the other evening, at least
until the weather chased him inside.

By the time she reached Owen, Marge was there, refilling his coffee.
"Need a cup?"

"Absolutely," Jackie said, hoping for a potent brew. Her mother's
coffee was painfully weak, and all of the reunion activities had worn her
out.

"Have a little too much fun last night?" Owen asked, motioning for
her to take a seat.

"If you're asking if I have a hangover, then no. We had fun, but I'll leave the heavier drinking to my college-age daughters—even though I shudder to think about that."

They gave Marge their orders, and she disappeared into the crowd. Jackie noticed she wrote nothing down. "I wish *my* memory was still that good."

"Careful, now. Don't make me feel old. Doesn't she have a good twenty years on us?"

Jackie took her steaming mug in both hands and inhaled. "She does indeed, which would put her at nearly seventy. I hope I'm not still working as hard as she is when I'm that age."

"Do you work that hard now?" Owen asked. "*I* certainly don't. Waiting tables is a grind."

Jackie sipped her coffee and nodded. She'd waited tables in college. "That it is. Have you done it?"

He nodded. "I've always said everyone needs to have at least one job where they are at the mercy of paying customers. Best way I know of to build empathy for service workers."

"I agree. I reminded my daughter of that very thing when I talked to her Friday night, right before her shift. It's a tough gig, but she'll come out of it knowing how challenging waiting tables can be."

"I worked at a steak joint in the early '90s, and some of my best tippers used to wait tables themselves."

They both sipped their coffee, the small talk fading away to silence. Jackie searched for where to start. They had so much to catch up on and she only had an hour.

"Thank you for meeting me this morning. I've been looking forward to it ever since I ran into you on Friday night," Owen said, taking the lead. "I remember you have somewhere you have to be before too long, but I want to know everything. What have you been up to over the past thirty years?"

She laughed. When she'd driven down Breconwood Road on the way to the café, she'd eyed his house with apprehension, nervous about what she'd find to talk about with her old friend. But the butterflies had settled, and she realized she wanted to know everything about him, too.

"I'm not sure where to start," she admitted. "I've done a lot of living in those years."

Marge arrived with their food, slipping their plates in front of them. Owen picked up a fork. "I know. So, start at the beginning and give me the abbreviated version if you must."

"Only if you promise to do the same," she said, smearing strawberry jam on a triangle of toast.

They both talked and ate, interrupting each other with questions as they went along. She didn't even notice when Marge, or maybe another waiter, whisked their empty plates away.

"Are your boys already done with college then?" she asked, trying to picture younger versions of Owen.

"Not quite. They both finished their undergraduate degrees, but my oldest is still in his medical residency, and my youngest is going for his doctorate in archeology. One does his best to keep people alive, and the other one is set on digging up dead bodies."

Two men stopped at their table to say hello. Both were home for the reunion. When they moved on, she asked Owen about them.

"You wouldn't have known them. They were my friends in high school. We were all part of the nerdy group, the ones who liked chemistry and took part in the science fair instead of basketball or track. You were too popular to pay us any attention."

Jackie flinched at his words. Although he kept his tone light and he smiled as he teased, she sensed an undercurrent of something else.

"I'm afraid you have me mixed up with someone else. I was never part of the popular group. I was an outcast, just like you apparently think you were, back in the day."

He grunted. "You just keep telling yourself that, Jackie."

A young hostess stopped by their table, offering to top off their coffee. Jackie glanced at her watch, then held a hand over her cup. "If I drink any more coffee, I'm going to struggle on the pontoon this afternoon."

Owen checked his own watch. "Do you need to get going?"

"Not yet. This is fun, catching up with you. Now, where were we? Let's get back to your boys. Did your son get his car running again?"

He laughed. "For now. Logan isn't the most responsible of kids. I'm afraid he takes after his mother. And he's the complete opposite of Adam, my oldest. Now, that one could write a book on being responsible."

She still hadn't been able to glean the story about the mother of Owen's sons. She sensed Owen wasn't married to her—at least not anymore, if he ever was—but he shied away from the topic. Jackie, on the other hand, had spilled the condensed yet still unflattering story of her first husband. She was curious, but she didn't want to pry. He'd talk about it if he wanted to.

"Your boys sound like they are both at busy points in their lives. It's nice that they still make time to hang out with their old man," she teased. The man sitting across from her certainly didn't look old. *Distinguished* would be a better way to describe him.

"We are close. I'm lucky. What about your daughters? Twins, you said? I can't imagine. Are the three of you close?"

If she'd run into Owen two years ago and they'd sat down like this for coffee, the answer would have been an unequivocal yes. But now she was learning she had to start letting go a little. It was so hard. "We've always been close," she said, without offering more. "Are both your boys in town this weekend?"

"They are," Owen said, snatching up the ticket Marge slipped onto their table before Jackie could even react. When she frowned, he reminded her that coffee was his idea, before going on about his two sons. "As you know, Logan drove in Friday night. Adam actually flew in from Chicago early Wednesday afternoon. He rented a car and drove over from Minneapolis. It's been nice to have a couple extra days with him. He rarely gets much time off. Yesterday was my Uncle Joe's birthday, so the three of us spent the day with him. He's all alone now."

Jackie vaguely remembered an Uncle Joe. He'd seemed ancient even when they were kids. But then something Owen said clicked. "Wait. Adam flew in from Chicago on *Wednesday*? Which airline?"

"United, I think. Why?"

"Do you have a picture of him?"

Owen scoffed, pulling his phone out of the front pocket of his blue button-down. "What kind of dad would I be if I didn't have pictures?"

He turned the phone toward Jackie and she studied a picture of two young men. The slightly taller one had similar features to Owen, while the shorter one was blond with a slender build.

She tapped his screen, grinning. "I *thought* there was something familiar about him."

"Adam? What do you mean?"

"You won't believe this, but I'm sure this is the young man who sat next to me on my flight on Wednesday. There was some kind of medical emergency when we landed, and he offered to help."

Grinning, Owen turned his phone back to study the picture himself. "He told me about that. Well, not about *you*, he couldn't have known who you were, but about the emergency. Leave it to my kid to raise a hand to help. It is a small world, isn't it?"

"It sure is," Jackie said. Even though her coffee was cold now, she gulped down the rest. "I hate to say it, but I probably need to get going. But speaking of small worlds, I heard a rumor, and I've been dying to ask you about it."

A wary expression crossed his features, but she pressed on, too curious. "Annie said you bought a sizeable chunk of land, out by the lake."

He seemed to relax. "Annie's right. I did. I was in the right place at the right time."

"Do you know that's where I used to go to summer camp?"

He grinned again, wider than before. "Sure. Because that was back when we were still friends. You made it sound almost magical."

"We were always friends, Owen," she said, feeling a surge of guilt.

"Of a sort, I suppose." He looked unconvinced.

She moved off the topic that still caused a pang in the center of her chest, circling back instead to the land. "Are the old cabins still there? I'd love to go back and look around. See what things look like now."

Owen scooted his chair back. "Go check it out any time you like. We even mowed out there yesterday, my boys and I, after we finished up with Uncle Joe. If you and your friends are still in town tomorrow, see if they want to go look around with you. Didn't Annie, Lynette, and Kit all go to camp with you? There's a key under the flower pot in front of the cabin where the business offices were. Inside, you'll find a board with keys for all the buildings. Explore all you like, just be sure to lock up after you're done. But don't expect too much. No one has used the buildings in about a decade."

Jackie stood, reluctant to go, but she was already running late. "What are your plans for the property?"

Owen shrugged, palms out. "I'm still trying to figure that out."

Jackie made it to their old beach in record time, but she was still fifteen minutes late. This familiar spot is where they'd arranged to meet for a boat ride, but since she couldn't spy Annie and the pontoon yet, she gave herself a minute to catch her breath and pull her mind away from her visit with Owen. She'd hated to leave the café.

She tugged self-consciously at the bottom of her swimsuit as she made her way across the hot sand toward her friends, then wrestled with the beach chair she'd nabbed from her mom and dad's garage, finally dropping into it with a sigh.

Kit and Lynette were already settled in similar chairs, along with a man Jackie assumed must be Lynette's photographer-slash-lover who she refused to call a boyfriend. She couldn't help but grin. Lynette was right—why did they feel it was necessary to assign a label to everything?

"That's a cute swimsuit," Kit said. She tilted her head back so she could look out from under the wide brim of her sun hat. "Is it new?"

"I bought it a couple years ago for that trip we took the girls on to Hawaii." She wished she'd brought her hat down, too. She'd left it in the car, thinking it would blow off when they went out on the pontoon.

"We?" Lynette asked.

"Me and Ben," Jackie said. "Back when we were a 'we.' "

"Ah. I see." Lynette dropped her sunglasses down over her eyes. "Jackie, this is Wyatt. Wyatt, this is Jackie."

"Hey, Jackie, it's nice to finally meet you. Lynette's shared some of your escapades with me. It's nice to put a face to your name."

Jackie smiled at him, taking in his youthful appearance and firm abs. When Lynette talked about Wyatt over wine and cheese, she'd failed to mention he was so much younger.

Good for you, Lynette, she thought.

She was sick to death of the opposite so often being true. Her ex-husband had a tendency to date women closer in age to their twin daughters than to himself. Maybe she should try to find herself a younger man, too. But then she caught sight of an excess roll of flesh around her own midsection that the strategically placed ruching of her swimsuit failed to hide. On second thought, she didn't need a man. She had enough to juggle without adding a new romantic complication to the mix.

"What time was Annie supposed to get here on the boat?"

"Fifteen minutes ago," Lynette said, getting to her feet and holding a hand out to Wyatt. Together they wandered down to the water's edge, promising to keep an eye out for Annie and her husband.

"How does she always end up with the hot ones?" Kit asked, voicing Jackie's thoughts just like they were kids again. "How old do you think he is? Thirty?"

"I was just wondering the same thing," Jackie admitted. "Probably forty. I wonder when things flipped for her. When we were kids, she dated older guys. What was that guy's name she dated when we were seniors? The one who disappeared after she crashed his truck."

Kit groaned. "Storm. Yeah, he started out as her boss. He was kind of scary. You heard what the deal was with that, didn't you?"

Jackie racked her brain, but she'd lost track of Lynette in their twenties. "Not that I remember. All I remember is that awful accident and then Donna whisking her away, to who knows where. Lynette was lucky. All she got out of that was the scar on her face."

Kit dug a can of beer out of the cooler at her feet, offering Jackie one, then popping the top of one for herself. "We—or at least I—misjudged Storm. He didn't crash the truck that night. He wasn't even *with* Lynette. She knew where he kept his keys, and they never locked their house by the lake, so after she left our graduation party that night, she hitched a ride over there and took his truck without his permission. He was out with other friends."

"Huh," Jackie said, absorbing this bombshell. "How could I not know all this? *She* was driving?"

"Yep. Needless to say, Storm washed his hands of her after that. He really was trying to help Lynette with Donna's awful boyfriend. Anyway, her mother's guy was the real reason they left town for a while. To get away from him. Not from Storm."

Jackie watched as Lynette waded farther into the lake, playfully splashing water at Wyatt. The woman in front of them now was so different from the one she'd dissolved into during the latter part of their senior year.

"Whatever happened to Storm, then?"

Kit shrugged. "No idea. He was just the first in a long line of suitors where Lynette is concerned."

"She seems happy."

"She does, doesn't she? I'm glad. I worried about her when her mom got sick. They're so close. But she says Donna is doing better now, and Lynette seems to have embraced the lifestyle they've created with their joint business."

"Can I be Lynette when I grow up?" Jackie asked, only half kidding.

"Jackie, you have an amazing life. A job you love, and daughters who adore you."

"Not as much as I adore them."

Kit sipped her beer. "Obviously. I hope I don't regret never having children."

"You have your kitties."

"Cute," she said. "But, seriously . . . my parents were both so awful, I was afraid I'd inherited their worthless parenting genes."

Jackie sighed. She wondered how different Kit's life might have turned out if she'd had parents who cared about her. Her grandparents stepped up and did the best they could, and she knew Kit still thought of her grandmother as a second mother, but there were scars.

Kind of like the light scar on Lynette's cheek from the long-ago accident on graduation night.

Some scars are deep enough to alter life's path.

"There they are!" Lynette cried, waving to a pontoon that was pulling up to the shore on the other side of the rope that delineated the southern portion of the swimming area. "Grab your stuff, everyone, it's time to get this party started!"

Jackie scrunched up her nose. She could already feel the effects of too much time in the hot July sun. As a kid, worry over wrinkles never crossed her mind. At forty-eight, now she worried more about skin cancer than wrinkles. The wrinkles encroached regardless.

She inhaled the fresh lake air and let her mind wander back to their high school days. Back then, speedboats and water skiing were more prevalent than pontoons, but regardless of the type of boat under her, she'd always loved feeling the wind in her hair.

"I'd go out on this thing every day in the summer if I lived here," she said, lounging back against the white cushions of Annie's pontoon.

"That's what we thought, too, when we first bought it." Annie pulled the rim of her baseball cap lower so it wouldn't fly off. "But it's more work than you think, getting it in and out of the water. At least we have friends who let us keep a lift in front of their cabin. If we didn't have that, we'd probably only take it out over the Fourth of July."

"Give me another beer, will you, hon?" Annie's husband asked as he fiddled with the radio and skippered the pontoon.

Jackie thought she caught Annie cringe at the request, but she did as Henry asked, fishing through the cooler of icy water. Her friend had to be exhausted after all the work she'd done on the reunion.

"You did an amazing job planning everything for this weekend, Annie. Thanks again."

Annie sat up straighter at the compliment. "I was happy with the turnout, and other than the shouting match between Ivory's ex and her current husband, I dare say drama-free. Were you able to meet Owen for coffee this morning?"

"I was. It was fun to catch up."

Kit held up a hand. "What? Why am I just hearing about this now? You finally went out on a date with Owen?"

"You did?" Lynette pushed off Wyatt's thigh and sat up on the bench across from Jackie. "How was it?"

"First, I didn't *go out* with him. We met for coffee. At the Crystal Café on a Sunday morning, for crying out loud. That hardly constitutes a date."

Kit waved this away. "Semantics. Come on, dish. What's his story? Are you going to see him again?"

Jackie grabbed the hat off Kit's head and smashed it on her own. She flopped back against the cushions and hid behind the brim. "You guys are awful. Quit ganging up on me!"

"Fight! Fight! Fight!" Relic, Annie's seventeen-year-old son, chanted, clapping his hands. It may have been the first words he uttered since they'd left shore. Jackie had gotten the sense he'd rather be anywhere in the world except on the pontoon with his parents and his mother's old friends.

Kit stood and tried to wrestle the hat away from Jackie. Wyatt and Henry joined in with Relic, egging the women on.

"You two haven't changed much," Annie said. She shook her head, but a smile broke out on her lips despite the stern look she tried to maintain.

"And you look like Jackie's dad with that principal face of yours," Lynette said, pointing at Annie and laughing.

Annie opened up the cooler, scooped out a couple of floating ice cubes, and tossed them at Lynette. Her aim was true, and the cubes slid down her cleavage, out of sight. Their antics continued for another minute until Kit yanked her hat back and took her seat again. Somehow Wyatt suddenly had a camera in hand, and he was snapping away.

Jackie froze. "Lynette, you have, like, a gazillion followers on Instagram, and so help me God, if any pictures of me in this swimsuit show up online, I'll hunt you down and no one will ever find your body."

Lynette slapped at Wyatt's hand, and the camera disappeared as quickly as it had appeared. He made a crossing motion over his heart and promised to keep the pictures under tight wraps.

Winded, Jackie took a swig from her water bottle. She thought back to her breakfast with Owen. She wished Kit hadn't made that crack about her finally going out with him. Some of the shine from her fun morning had suddenly dimmed. But then she remembered one of the last things he'd said to her.

"I nearly forgot!" She dropped her water back into a holder by her feet. "I asked Owen about the summer camp land. Annie, you were right. He does own it now. I'm still having trouble wrapping my head around that fact."

Annie smirked. "Told you."

"Are the cabins still there?" Kit asked, her hat now safely back on her head, the safety strap snapped under her chin.

"Yes, but no one's used them in a long time. He said we could head over there and explore if we wanted to. If you guys aren't busy tomorrow, would you want to do that?"

"Heck yes," Kit said, raising her right arm. "I'm in!"

Annie glanced at her husband and then back at Jackie. "I'd love to. I'm taking tomorrow off, after all the hours I put in on the reunion."

"I should hope so. What about you, Lynette, can you make it?"

Lynette looked to Wyatt. "I know we talked about leaving tomorrow, but I'd love to join them. Would you mind if we stayed one more day?"

The man shrugged. "No problem, babe."

Jackie appreciated his easygoing attitude. Her stomach did a funny little roll at the endearment. It had been a long time since anyone had called *her* "babe." Lynette might want to hold on to this one.

She clapped her hands with excitement, then tugged at the strap on her swimming suit. "Perfect. I'll pick you all up at noon, and we'll take a picnic lunch. I think it's about time the Kaleidoscope Girls head back to summer camp!"

"The *what* girls?" Relic asked, looking confused.

"You mean you never told your kid why you have kaleidoscopes all over your house, Annie?" Jackie asked, laughing.

Annie grinned. "Nope. Some stories are ours alone. And I can't wait to go back and revisit some of ours tomorrow."

CHAPTER TWENTY-SEVEN

J ACKIE LEANED AGAINST THE split-rail fence surrounding what once was a wildflower garden, back when the area was home to their summer camp. She pushed against it and was happy to find it was still sturdy. The wood of the top rung was new, while the three lower rungs had weathered to a silvery gray. She didn't have to look far to see other structures had aged significantly as well.

"If I didn't keep my roots up, my hair would probably be as gray as this old fence," Kit said, resting a foot on the lowest rung as she stood beside Jackie.

Two monarchs danced and weaved above a twisted clump of purple thistle, flitting around as if they didn't have a care in the world.

"Those lucky little buggers get to spend their days out here at camp all summer long," Kit said when she also spied the butterflies. "I bet there's milkweed in there somewhere, too."

Jackie watched them dip and soar. She remembered a similar butterfly that landed on her shoulder her first morning back home just a few days before. It happened right after she'd taken that dreaded call from her boss, the one she had been trying not to think about.

"Did you know they are my inspiration?" Kit asked, and Jackie was happy to detour away from the direction her thoughts were traveling. Today would be a day of revisiting only happy memories.

"For your hair color?" she teased.

Kit bumped her shoulder with her own. "Ha-ha, you're a funny one. No, for my research. The vivid description that park ranger gave of the migration of monarch butterflies ignited a fire in me. Who would have guessed how much that first summer camp would influence my future career? And I didn't even want to come to this camp in the first place. My grandparents made me go."

Jackie took a deep breath, enjoying the familiar tang of pine-scented air. "I need to remember to thank your grandmother for that at lunch tomorrow. If she hadn't sent you here, I might have missed out on the best friend a girl could ever have."

"Yeah, you'd have been stuck with good old *Fran* if not for me." But Jackie knew from the soft smile on Kit's face that she appreciated the comment. Sentimental comments usually made Kit visibly uncomfortable.

"Remember when I caught you snooping in our cabin on that first day?"

Kit stepped away with a snort. "How many times do I have to tell you? I wasn't snooping!"

Lynette and Annie joined them beside the fence, each holding the handle of a cooler that contained a picnic lunch Annie had made. "Are you two talking about the time Kit went poking through our things? Maybe she really took that money from the office, too."

Over the years, the events of that summer had morphed into a story that grew beyond the reality of what actually happened. False accusations caused hurt feelings, fantastical what-ifs grew around the legend of diamonds in the falls, and dreams grew of travel to foreign lands, much like the path the monarchs would take.

"Hey, Jackie, wasn't that the same summer you got your period?" Annie asked, dropping her end of the heavy cooler into the powdery dirt.

Lynette followed Annie's lead, setting the cooler down. "I remember that. You tried to keep it a secret, but we all knew. Ironic how that was the beginning of our bodies transitioning into womanhood, and now hot flashes and night sweats are signaling a *new* transition."

"Don't remind me," Jackie said, but she could appreciate the synchronicity.

"Hey, Lynette, whatever happened to that old, threadbare teddy bear you brought to camp that summer? Are you a saver like Annie?" Kit asked.

Lynette sighed, hands on her hips as she surveyed the surrounding area. "Our lifestyle didn't really lend itself to keeping many possessions. But, believe it or not, that stuffed animal was about the only thing my mother kept. She has a spare bedroom in her apartment, and it still sits on the bed, ready to welcome me anytime I stay with her. It started out as hers when she was young, then she passed it on to me."

"Boy, it's hot," Annie said, lifting her hair off the back of her neck. "I vote we get out of this direct sun. Anybody else want to go see if our old cabin is still standing?"

Jackie suspected it was, based on Owen's comments about the general condition of the buildings. Then she remembered what he said about keys. "Wait. Before we head over there, Owen said there are still keys in the office. We might as well grab those first."

The foursome found the keys, then headed for their old cabin, Cabin 7, leaving the cooler until they were ready for sandwiches. And wine.

"There she is!" Annie cried, hurrying ahead. The door was locked, but she scooted along the side to peer through a window while she waited for Jackie and the key.

"Can you see anything?" Jackie yelled, her progress hampered by a rock in her sandal. "I can't believe we used to run around barefoot out here."

"Right?" Kit laughed. "My middle isn't the only part of me that's gotten a little soft over the years."

"We may be softer, but we are also a heck of a lot wiser than those four young girls," Lynette added. "Just think about how far we've all come since then."

"Yet here we are, right back where we started."

Jackie glanced at Kit. She had yet to find time for a one-on-one discussion since they'd pulled into town. She still sensed something was bothering her, and she hoped it wasn't anything more serious than the common middle-age dilemmas they all seemed to be grappling with, each in her own way.

Jackie stepped up onto the small platform in front of their old cabin; the still familiar groan of the wood planks brought a smile to her face. The only thing that looked new since their camp days was the lock on the door. There used to be a latch on the screen door that Wendy would use at night to prevent someone—or even an animal—from wandering into the cabin while they slept. The world was a different place now, in so many ways.

She didn't have any trouble with the lock—another sign that it probably wasn't thirty-some-odd years old. She pushed open the door and let the others file in. The bunk beds were all gone, as was everything else. She was sad to see the inside of the cabin so empty.

"Shoot!" Annie slapped her thighs. "I wanted to see if our initials were still visible in the bottom right corners of the headboards."

"Initials?" Lynette asked. She sounded distracted as she ran a hand lightly along the curve of one of the interior logs, knocking out a chunk of loose mortar.

"Yeah, remember? We used Jackie's fingernail file. Actually, I think that was the last year we came out here. The year you missed because you were off somewhere with your mother that entire summer."

"I know I was actually out here for camp two more times after that first summer, but it was my first year that really sticks out in my memory," Kit said, standing in the middle of the cabin. "I remember how I got here late because my mom showed up at my grandma and grandpa's house that morning. She ditched rehab, and there was a big, nasty fight. I thought I'd hate it here."

"But you didn't," Jackie whispered, old memories bursting forth in her mind, too.

"No. I didn't hate it."

Jackie watched Lynette wander over to the window, the one she used to look out of from her top bunk, and remembered watching an industrious little spider weave a web in its corner, while cramps racked her young body. Lynette tapped the glass. "Did Owen tell you why he bought this property, or what he plans to do with it?" she asked, glancing back at Jackie.

Jackie tried to remember Owen's exact words. "The topic of this place came up at the very end, so we didn't talk about it too much. He just said something like he's still trying to figure out what to do with it."

"Hmm, interesting . . ." Lynette turned back toward the center of the cabin. "Have any of the rest of you kept in touch with Renee?"

The name was another blast from the past for Jackie. "Renee? The girl we went to camp with that one summer? And Owen took to prom? I haven't. But I always liked her."

Kit shook her head.

"Sadly, no," Annie added.

"I actually have," Lynette said, crossing her arms over her stomach, her eyes ever moving around the interior of the cabin. "Remember how we agreed to be pen pals, way back when? We don't write letters anymore, other than an annual Christmas card, but we drop each other an email once in a while. She's had an interesting life, too."

"I sometimes forget there were actually *five* Kaleidoscope Girls, not just the four of us," Annie said. "Where did she ever end up?"

"Oh gosh, she's lived through a lot, just like all of us. She went to college, got married, had two kids, was widowed pretty young, and endured a less-than-inspiring career in some kind of corporate job."

Jackie tried to picture their old friend. She recognized some parallels between Lynette's quick synopsis of Renee's life and her own.

"But," Lynette went on, "she's had some exciting things happen lately. She got laid off, which sucked, but instead of just finding work in a similar role, she is rebuilding a lake resort that a rich relative left to her. Being here, in this old cabin, reminded me of her and her story."

"Wow, that's amazing," Annie said.

"You know," Kit said, "I remember talking with Renee about a resort one morning at breakfast. It must have been only a day or two into camp, because we were both feeling like outsiders still. She said she usually went to her aunt's resort in the summer, but they couldn't go that particular year. I don't remember all the details. I just remember thinking it was so cool that she had an aunt with a resort."

"It has to be the same place," Lynette said. She pulled her phone out of her skirt pocket, fiddled with it for a few seconds, then put it away. "No reception. I wanted to show you her website. I think the place is called Whispering Pines."

Jackie's mind started jumping with possibilities. "Is it anything like this place? Do they rent out cabins? And she can earn a living doing that?" It sure sounded like a lot more fun than a desk job.

Lynette laughed. "I haven't actually been there. I doubt it is as big as this property. When Renee emailed me to tell me about it, she mentioned some type of retreat she hosts there, too, with her sisters, to help supplement her income outside of the summer months."

"It's possible that the cabins aren't inhabitable in the winter," Annie said, rubbing her upper arms. "A person would freeze to death if they tried to survive in here over the winter."

Jackie thought that wasn't entirely true, given settlers probably lived in rustic homes very much like the one they were standing in, and Native Americans survived under even harsher conditions. She felt a pang of jealousy over Renee's good fortunes, but almost as quickly felt compassion for the path the woman must have had to follow to get to this point in life.

Her stomach rumbled. "Anyone else getting hungry? What do you think about taking our lunch down by the water? We could even walk over to the falls."

Laughing, Lynette said she thought that sounded like a fabulous idea. "And don't mind me, but I plan to hike my skirt up and do a little wading in the pool below the falls. I don't know about you ladies, but I wouldn't mind finding one of those legendary diamonds today."

"Leave it to Grandma Hazel to remember to send a blanket along for us to sit on," Jackie said, smoothing a wrinkle out of the brown wool beneath her. "Add that to the list of things I want to remember to thank her for."

Kit raised her acrylic wine goblet toward the sky. "I could never thank her enough for all the things she's done for me and my brothers through the years. Which is why this whole question about whether she should still be living on her own is so hard."

"To Hazel," Lynette said, tapping her drink against Kit's. "How old is your grandmother now?"

"She's eighty-eight, almost eighty-nine. My aunt stops over to see her every day. She comes up with a bunch of different excuses, but she's really just checking in to make sure Grandma is safe. And believe me, Hazel is on to her, and while she appreciates the occasional helping hand around the house, she's too prideful to admit there are some risks to living alone at her age."

Jackie leaned back on her palms, straightened her legs, and crossed her feet at the ankles. "What does your Aunt Marge think? It has to be hard to make time to check on her every day, especially if she has to pretend that she's stopping for another reason."

"It's complicated."

"How so?" Annie asked. She was just returning from wading into the water to cool off.

"Marge worries. Grandma has left an empty pot on a hot stove before. But there isn't money to put her in a home. If Grandma went into a nursing home, we'd have to sell her house to pay for it."

Kit's comment made Jackie think about her own parents. Given her father's health concerns, was this the type of conversation she'd have to have with her family before long?

"Would that be the worst thing?" Lynette asked. "Sometimes property can weigh a person down, hold them somewhere they don't belong anymore."

Kit drained the last of her wine and set the empty cup next to the blanket. "Spoken like a woman with the soul of a gypsy."

Lynette shrugged. "You know me too well. But I am serious. Neither you nor your brothers live here anymore, and if your aunt wanted to live in that house, I would think she'd have moved in with your grandmother by now—especially given how often she has to be over there anyhow. Even if your grandma didn't go into a nursing home, an apartment might be easier for her to take care of. I know my mom enjoys it, and she's only in her early seventies."

Kit nodded but said nothing else for a moment. The calming sound of the rushing falls a hundred yards away was the only sound, other than the call of a bird high above. "Marge and Grandma are both worried that if they try to sell the house—which has gone up a lot in value given how close it is to the lake—then my mom will show up looking for her piece of the inheritance."

Annie reached over and gave Kit's shoulder a reassuring squeeze. "How long's it been since you've seen your mother?"

"Not long enough," Kit said. Jackie thought the actual answer was about ten years, but it was next to impossible to get Kit to talk about it. "But, enough about me. Jackie, give us an update on your life. Have you adjusted to your empty nest?"

Jackie glanced at the wine bottle, propped up in the sand beside their picnic blanket. A second cup might help the discussion, but she'd limited herself to one since she was the day's driver. "I think I've sold my nest."

Kit's head whipped in her direction. "What?! You sold your house? Why? Are you moving?"

That wine did look good. Straightening, she pulled her legs in and sat cross-legged. "I really don't want to talk about this."

"Too bad," Kit countered. "There's no better place to hash through life's problems than sitting lakeside with a bottle of wine and your besties."

She had a point. "Fine. I thought I had a fantastic shot at a promotion. Said promotion would have required a move. Besides, my house is too big now that the girls aren't coming home much. So, I called my realtor friend. It was really just to put some feelers out. To get a sense for what I might ask for it. That type of thing. But . . ." She let her words trail off.

"But the housing market is hot in your area right now, and she was more than happy to show it to the perfect couple she was working with," Lynette said, a sympathetic look on her face.

"Exactly. And now I find myself potentially homeless in six weeks. I wonder if the girls would have room for me on their couch."

Annie grimaced. "If they are anything like my daughter, that would not go over well."

"I thought you and Ava were close," Jackie said, surprised.

"Oh, we are, but she's still trying to learn how to stretch her wings."

Jackie understood that, too. She sighed. "I didn't really mean that about crashing with the girls. I'll figure out something. But I didn't want to give it too much thought while I was here. Too depressing."

"What about the promotion? Has that come through?" Kit asked.

A white butterfly hovered near the wine bottle. Jackie thought of the monarchs they'd spied upon their arrival. She wanted to be like the butterflies, graceful and carefree, maybe even preparing to fly south in a few months. But then she remembered not all the butterflies live long enough to make that journey. It was just a select few that actually migrated.

"The house sale is happening. The promotion is not."

"Dang, girl," Lynette said. "What are you going to do? Buy a smaller house?"

Jackie plucked a thick blade of grass, wrapping it around her thumb as she considered Lynette's question. "Like I said, I don't know. Can I ask you guys something?"

After a round of assurances that she could ask them anything, she considered how best to phrase her dilemma.

"Screw this," Kit said, retrieving her own wine cup and Jackie's. "Another half a glass of wine isn't going to hurt anything," she said, splitting the remaining contents between them all. "I have a sense we are about to go deep."

Jackie couldn't help but laugh. "I just . . . I don't know . . . I feel unmoored. Do you know what I mean?"

"I know exactly what you mean," Annie said, swirling her wine. "Now that the reunion is over, I'm going to have to buckle down and get serious about Relic's senior year. I know Jackie might be the only one to understand this since you never raised kids, Kit and Lynette, but I am terrified of the day my last child leaves home. Then what?"

Kit considered the question. "Might I point out that you are a high school principal, Annie? I would think you'd be thrilled to go home to a blissfully child-free zone at the end of your workday. Once Relic flies the coop, that is."

Annie bobbed her head but didn't look convinced. "This is about Jackie, not me."

Jackie sipped her wine. Kit was right about the alcohol. A bit more couldn't hurt, and this might not be a quick discussion. "I thought, by the time I was nearing the end of my forties, I'd be in a better place. More secure in my career, coming home to a man who maybe liked to cook more than me and who definitely turned me on in bed. Can Wyatt cook, Lynette? Because I suspect he probably does fine in the sex department."

The joke earned laughs all around, but Lynette wasn't going to take the bait and let her derail the conversation again.

When it was clear her three friends were waiting for her to continue, Jackie's eyes sought the white butterfly again. It was back, landing on the empty wine bottle in the grass. "I've been putting extra effort in at work, knowing this opportunity was coming soon. No one puts in longer hours than me, or volunteers more than I do. I thought I nailed the interview, but when they gave it to someone else from outside the company, it was like I had an epiphany. I don't like what I do anymore. But that realization is depressing, too, because who wants to start over again at our age?"

Since it was more of a rhetorical question, no one said anything immediately. Then Lynette cleared her throat. "I think that's exactly what Renee did. And she seems happy. She might even have solved the whole *man* thing. She met a guy while she was on a trip somewhere tropical. They fell in love, and she married him last summer. I don't know if he can cook, but her Christmas card this last year was a picture from their wedding, and he is *handsome!*"

"Can I just *be* Renee?" Jackie asked.

"Nope. Each of us has to live our own lives. I think you're just stuck in a rut. No offense."

"None taken. Because you are absolutely right," she said, still watching the butterfly. "My rut is so deep, I can hardly see above the steep walls."

Kit, who had stayed unusually quiet for the past few minutes, snorted. "Are you done whining now, Jackie? Because it's time for a bit of a reality check. You have two strong daughters and an amazing dog. Your home is beautiful, and I bet you stand to make a hefty profit when you sell it. Am I right?"

"So far," Jackie said, bracing herself for what could sometimes be painfully direct observations from Kit. But she also knew this was what she needed if she wanted to get out of her funk.

"You are currently unattached romantically, and despite interference from your daughters, you've held true to your belief that Ben wasn't the right man for you. I count that as a win. You've learned not to settle in your relationships. You're bored at work. Big deal. It happens. Even if it's been a while since you typed up your résumé, I bet you'd have an impressive one."

"It didn't do much to get me the promotion I wanted."

Lynette shifted on the blanket, catching Jackie's eye. "But don't you see? That's just the universe telling you it's time to move on. Jackie, women our age have so much to offer. But unfortunately, we're programmed to sell ourselves short. To think that it's too late for us. That we've had our chance. It's an enormous problem, and personally, I'm sick of it."

Jackie watched her butterfly as it floated higher and higher, until she lost it against the backdrop of a fluffy white cloud high above. She let her gaze move to the top of the waterfall, searching but not finding the ghost of the Indian priestess their camp counselor had told them watched over the area, back when they were twelve years old. The priestess, whether she really existed long before their time or was nothing more than legend, would have possessed an internal fortitude as strong as iron. Jackie used to think *she* was made of tougher stuff, too.

Where had that strong girl disappeared to?

"I'm *so* sick of the boxes society wants to shove us into," she said. She remembered the rush of fury over her boss's condescending comments when he'd called with the news that she hadn't gotten the job. She'd made that little pissant, and now he was using her to advance his own career. He was even using her when it came to making his own summer vacation plans.

"What are we going to do about it then?" Kit asked. As she got to her feet and rested her hands on her hips, a leaf caught in her orange, spiky hair.

The sight made both Jackie and Annie giggle. Lynette tossed back the remnants of her wine and got up to stand next to Kit, a grunt escaping her lips when she accidentally stepped on her bohemian-style skirt. Giggles morphed into hoots of laughter, and the mock-stern look on Kit's face fell away, replaced with a satisfied smile.

Lynette held up a finger and waited until the other three women got themselves back under control. "I suggest two things. First, we're going to go search that dang water for diamonds. And second, when we get somewhere with cell service, I'm going to call Renee and get all of us into one of her retreats this fall. It's about time the Kaleidoscope Girls shed their cocoons and get back to living lives full of bursts of color and joy!"

CHAPTER TWENTY-EIGHT

J ACKIE KEPT HER EYES closed, imagining her old room as it looked while she still lived in her mom and dad's home. The posters on the wall, a shelf above her desk crowded with trophies, pictures of her friends rimming her full-length mirror. Her mother, always practical, had cleared out both bedrooms after her children graduated from college.

"You'll only come back for brief visits, and we need the space. Don't worry, the things I thought you cared about are in a box in the attic. I tossed or donated everything else."

She still marveled at the many inaccuracies in that simple statement. The woman couldn't possibly have known which items Jackie would have deemed worth saving, and besides, Jackie had never mustered up the courage to look into the boxes in the attic. On top of that, their five-bedroom house was more spacious than her parents could ever need for just two people. After Todd left Jackie and their daughters, the three had moved back here and stayed for nearly a year. She wouldn't call *that* a "brief" stay. And the most inaccurate assumption of all was that Ronnie would ever come back.

The slamming of a car trunk outside her window pulled her eyes open.

She'd barely slept, but this time her insomnia wasn't thanks to night sweats. Their discussion beside the falls the previous afternoon had her mind jumping in all different directions. Lynette was right, of course, and so was Kit. She had plenty to be thankful for, but somewhere along the line she'd stopped forging ahead. Working harder than everyone else wasn't the ultimate path to success. How had it taken her this long to learn that? More times than not, it just resulted in others taking advantage of you.

Ending her relationship with Ben had felt so monumental, and she kept patting herself on the back for her insightfulness. But she saw now that that should have only been the first step. She'd made zero effort in the two years since the breakup to find someone new to spend time with, and had nearly given in to the pressure to reunite with Ben—only because it was comfortable and what her daughters wanted.

Where did that leave her?

With a grunt that reminded her of Lynette when she almost fell on her face after tripping on her skirt, Jackie tossed her legs over the side of the bed and stood up. They'd done lots of walking the previous day exploring their old summer camp. She felt stiff and more than a little sore. As kids, they tore all over that property every day. They'd collapse into bed every night, thoroughly exhausted, but able to jump out of bed with nary a groan each morning, ready to do it all over again. Jackie was thankful today wouldn't include anything more strenuous than lunch at Kit's grandmother's house and some time with her own parents.

Then she remembered today was also the day she was having that big talk with her father. A second full day of walking all over Owen's property, out by the lake, suddenly sounded like more fun, despite her stiffness. But she couldn't avoid this discussion any longer.

"Are you going to sleep all day?" her father yelled, those hated words from her childhood floating up the staircase and squeezing through her shut bedroom door.

God, she used to hate it when he hollered that on Saturday and Sunday mornings. He usually roused them out of bed early on Saturdays so they could get their chores done before any of their extracurricular events started. Sundays had meant church. That was part of the reason she now avoided weekend chores like the plague and she seldom attended Mass, aside from Christmas and Easter.

"I wonder what my daughters blame me for these days," she said, her words bouncing off the boring taupe walls of a room that used to be her personal sanctuary. Not that her bedroom in her own home now was much better. She'd kept things neutral throughout the house, and that was probably one reason it sold so quickly. When everything is neutral and bland, people can easily picture themselves coming in and putting their personal stamp on it. But was it really any way to live, practically devoid of color?

Not according to Lynette. Especially for a Kaleidoscope Girl.

"Jackie, come down here and say goodbye to your mother. I want to talk to you."

"Adding some color back is going to have to wait," she muttered to herself.

She slipped into a relaxed outfit that would be dressy enough for her lunch plans but comfortable, too. It was a good thing she wouldn't be seeing Lynette; her stylish friend wouldn't have approved of her all-black ensemble. But since she'd promised to work on the whole *joy* thing, she slipped on the brightly painted bracelet she'd purchased at a flea market in Hawaii with her daughters, as well as the gold locket with their pictures inside. They were her two favorite pieces, always nestled in her jewelry pouch whenever she traveled.

Hoover met her at the bottom of the stairs. A bow was now clipped to her collar. Jackie was still unnerved by her father's about-face on dogs as pets.

"I see you put your jewelry on, too," she said, bending to pet the trembling dog. She wondered if the animal ever stopped shaking.

The welcome scent of coffee pulled her into the kitchen.

"Did Mom leave already?"

Her dad glanced her way, then turned his attention back to the crossword puzzle he was scratching at in the open newspaper on the dining table. "Yep. Sorry, you just missed her. She was taking a trunk full of things to the thrift store for donation. She does that most Saturdays. She thinks I don't notice that she sometimes drags home as much junk as she takes. It's just someone else's junk. I'll never understand that woman."

She poured herself coffee, checking to see if her dad needed his warmed up. His cup was still full, untouched.

"Did you eat anything?"

"Nah. Not much of an appetite today." He dropped his pencil, closed the newspaper, and folded it into a small bundle, then tossed it toward the garbage can, now in a new location at the end of a different bank of cupboards, since his dog's dishes took over the other spot. He missed.

"Guess moving the garbage can throw your aim off," she teased. But there was no smile in return. She took a seat across from her father. "I know you wanted to talk about things. Do you feel up to it now?"

He shrugged. "When I suggested to your mother that I sit down and discuss things with you, I'd only just received my initial diagnosis. I was still relatively clear-headed, and determined that I'd convince you to help me figure out how to beat this."

She sensed a "but," so she stayed quiet, giving him time to arrange his thoughts.

"Instead of waiting until now, when you were going to be here anyway, we probably should have jumped in an airplane and flown out to see you right away."

This surprised her. "Was there something we could have done right away, to help cure or at least delay things?"

Hoover whined at Glen's feet, and he picked up the little dog. He held her in place with one hand, petting her back with the other. "I suspect not. But at least I was feeling more optimistic then."

Jackie could sense the comfort the little dog provided her father, and was grateful for it. Better late than never. "And how do you feel now?"

He turned Hoover's collar to move the bow up from under her chin, where it was probably bothering her. "Resigned. Worried about what will happen with your mother. Regretful."

"Dad, did the doctors give you any estimates as to how quickly this will progress? Is there anything we can do to slow or reverse things?"

Hoover dropped her head back and licked his chin, drawing a smile out of him. "I'm afraid not. Nothing, at least, that could make a real difference. I'm not sure I want to slow the progression."

Jackie wasn't sure she'd heard him right. "Dad, you can't mean that."

"Can't I? Last week I took the garbage out, got turned around, and headed down the alley, sure I was walking back toward the house. Well, I wasn't. Then we went to see our banker—we're considering refinancing the house—but I couldn't follow what he was suggesting. And your mother is no help. I've always handled the finances around here."

Several alarms went off in Jackie's head, accompanied by an overwhelming sense of pity for her father. She knew better than to let him see that. "Why are you thinking about refinancing the house, Dad? You paid it off, like, fifteen years ago."

"Because there will come a time when I will probably have to move to one of those special care facilities. I can't expect your mother to take care of me when I get too bad. But I got so flustered, we didn't move ahead with anything yet."

"I'd be happy to help you in any way I can," she offered.

"I was hoping you'd say that. I want to protect your mother from as much of this as possible."

Jackie knew her father's concern for his wife stemmed from love, but bits and pieces of the discussion that she and her friends had, at the lake the day before, kept trying to intrude on her thoughts. If it applied to her and Lynette and the other Kaleidoscope Girls, why not her own mother, too?

"Dad, I appreciate that you want to spare Mom any pain, but I don't think that will be possible. I think the better option is to help her get a handle on the finances, and everything else that you normally take care of around here. She's a strong, smart woman. She doesn't need to be coddled. She needs to be allowed to step up and handle things."

Glen's ashen cheeks flushed with color. "Aren't you the sassy one today?"

"Sassy?" Jackie said, sure she'd never heard her father say that particular word before. "Why, yes, I suppose I am feeling sassy. And scared. I'm scared, Dad. It's hard for me to hear you talk about these things."

He set the dog down and stood, pacing over to the window. "I'd give anything to protect both of you from this."

Jackie hated everything about this. Hated seeing her strong father grapple with such a terrible diagnosis. Hated that he couldn't see that Jackie and her mother *would* be strong enough to handle what was coming, because they didn't have a choice. She also hated the way he never, ever referred to Ronnie anymore.

"Dad, I'm going to ask you one more time, and please think before you respond. Will you please consider calling Ron, or at least giving me permission to call him, to let him know what is happening? Regardless of what the two of you said to each other that proved to be so hurtful, so long ago, I think he deserves to know the truth about what's going on here now. We have some tough years ahead of us as a family, Dad, and I don't want to be the only one doing the heavy lifting. Mom needs to be involved, and she'll need to learn how to do some of the things that you have always handled. I suspect there will come a time when we'll need Ronnie's help, too."

She saw her father's shoulders shake as he drew in a deep breath. "Why would that boy want to help me now? After everything that happened? It wouldn't be fair to him."

Jackie suppressed a frustrated sigh. He made a valid point.

But then a memory from way back in her past wriggled to the surface. Owen's pet gerbil had died, and when she stopped over to play, he met her at the door with tears in his eyes. They'd been in third grade. Their classroom gerbils had had babies, and Owen talked his parents into letting him bring one home. She'd watched as he used a spatula from the kitchen to put the small animal's lifeless body into a shoe box. The gerbil's name was Star.

"Star was such an amazing pet," she'd whispered, tears streaming down her face, as much for the pain she knew Owen was feeling as for the dead rodent.

But as Owen tapped down the dirt on top of the tiny grave, he shook his head. "Jackie, don't you know life isn't fair?"

It was a common refrain their third-grade teacher would fling at them anytime someone complained in her classroom. He'd been serious when he said it, but something about his expression struck her as funny. It lightened their moods, and from that day forward, instead of repeating the standard "life isn't fair" quote, they'd remind each other that "Star was the best." It was code—people looked at them like they were crazy when they'd throw it into conversations when someone complained—but the truth behind it stuck with her.

Who was she to say whether it was fair to Ronnie to pull him back into their father's life at this stage?

This was one area where she decided she was done compromising. Her relationship with her brother wasn't one she'd term as *close*, but they were part of each other's lives to an extent.

"Dad, I honestly don't know what Ronnie will want to do when I tell him about your diagnosis, but I am going to loop him in, and I hope you understand."

She watched her father closely, but couldn't see any obvious reaction to her declaration. Then he started patting the pockets on his shirt and his pants. "Now, where did I put my blasted keys?"

"Your keys?"

"Yes. My keys. I need to pick up your mother from the hairdresser. Her car is in the shop."

Jackie realized the string of their conversation had slipped away from him, replaced with some vague memory of another time. She was going to have to research the best way to react when he had a spell like this. With nothing other than her gut to go on, she got up from the table and started pulling items out of the cupboard and refrigerator to prepare a light lunch.

She noticed a pill organizer on the counter. Was he due for his medication?

"You still have some time, Dad, before you have to leave to pick up Mom. How about some lunch?"

He met her eye, dropping his hands to his sides. His anxiety ebbed away and his shoulders relaxed. "Lunch? Can I have tuna and mayo on my sandwich?"

Jackie got busy, hoping there was a can of tuna in the cupboard. Her mother knew to be back home by noon so Jackie could head over to Kit's grandmother's. She knew her mother didn't like to leave Glen home alone anymore. Initially she thought maybe her mother was over-reacting, but now she agreed. If he was getting lost outside, in his own backyard, and wanting to take the car, he shouldn't be alone.

The extent of what this all meant—not only for her father, but for her mother, too—suddenly came crashing down on her. Life as her parents knew it was over.

Star was the best.

CHAPTER TWENTY-NINE

J ACKIE TOSSED THE TENNIS ball to Nikki, laughing when the collie overshot her attempted retrieval. It was her favorite time of day. Despite the slant of the evening rays, there was still a welcome warmth from the sun, especially following another day spent in stale air-conditioning. She wrestled the ball away from her dog and tossed it again. If Nikki had her way, they'd be out here until dark. Jackie could relate. Neither of them liked to be cooped up indoors on a beautiful late-summer day. Tomorrow's weather looked just as promising, and she'd taken the rest of the week off, leading up to Labor Day.

Her daughters were due to arrive midday. They would spend one last summer weekend with her before classes started up again. They hadn't made any big plans. Instead, they would enjoy sleeping in, lounging at the community pool if the weather was nice, and eating some of their favorite meals. All three of them had worked hard all summer. A few days of rest and relaxation was exactly what they needed.

Her ten days at home in July was the only other break she'd taken all summer. It had felt so good to reconnect with Kit, Annie, and Lynette. Lunch at Kit's grandmother's had also been enjoyable. The elderly woman's mind still seemed as sharp as ever to Jackie; however, she had noticed Hazel's shaky hands and hesitant steps. She didn't envy the challenges ahead for Kit and her aunt as they helped Hazel navigate the struggles of living alone late in life.

Besides, she had to deal with her own father's declining health.

She needed to make that call to Ron. She'd had the best of intentions, but a busy work schedule and her girls coming for a visit soon, kept giving her easy excuses to procrastinate.

Her life was becoming one long delay after another.

What was it Lynette had said about shedding her cocoon and spreading her wings?

Her cell phone vibrated in her pocket. She pulled it out and grimaced at a new text from her boss.

> I'm sorry, Jackie, but I need you to come in tomorrow. Something came up and I need to be out of the office. The new girl is still training. You can still have Friday off. Thanks.

She considered giving her phone a frustrated heave across the yard, but Nikki might mistake it for her ball and try to retrieve it.

How dare he? Her boss knew her girls were coming home. She had a sneaking suspicion the "something" that came up was a personal opportunity for him, and he wanted the day off instead of allowing Jackie to take it.

Nikki pranced impatiently around her, so she obliged by throwing the tennis ball yet again. She missed the enjoyment she used to feel after a long day at the office. There was no sense of accomplishment anymore.

That job had become her cocoon, and things were getting messy on the inside.

But the idea of slapping a resignation letter down on her boss's desk, while it would give her a momentary surge of satisfaction, would also mean the end of something she'd poured most of her life force into.

Her phone vibrated in her hand. This time it was Mack.

> Surprise! We're already on the road! See you in 3.
> LYFD

Her frustration melted away at seeing Mack's acronym for their life-long running joke: *Love, Your Favorite Daughter*. Unfortunately, neither would feel like the favorite when they arrived in three hours to a messy house and an empty refrigerator. At least the sheets on their beds were clean. She was too tired to run inside and whirl through the house, picking up and dusting. Aside from the lack of food, they wouldn't care.

Then the phone went off a third time.

> Please confirm you'll be in tomorrow.

She let her arm drop to her side. Nikki playfully nuzzled her hand with her sloppy ball, hard enough that the phone fell to the grass. She considered her dilemma as she pulled the ball from her dog's mouth again, tossing it for the umpteenth time across the yard and wiping the slime from her fingers. Nikki bounded off again. Bending over, she picked up her phone.

Nikki must have stepped on it in her excitement. The screen was shattered and black.

The phone was dead.

The land line rang inside her house.

She cringed. Now she'd need to buy a new phone. There was no way this one was salvageable. The least Nikki could have done was step on her phone *before* she read the texts from work.

She stared at the shattered phone, again picturing a cocoon, but this time the shell was cracking open.

She'd followed her company's procedures for taking paid time off, and she was technically already on PTO. She would ignore her boss's request to come back in. Kit was right. She'd allowed them to take advantage of her for far too long. Her daughters were already on their way, and there was no reason she should give up any of her precious time with them.

The damaged phone disappeared back into her pocket, she called Nikki over from where she was pawing under her favorite rose bush, and headed into the house to grab her keys. She'd ignore her compulsion to scrub the toilets before the girls arrived, but a quick trip to the grocery store would save her from having *hangry* kids on her hands.

Yes. She'd ignore Sam's request.

Something cold slapped against her shin. She lifted the corner of her beach towel and peeked down her leg to see a tube of sunscreen on her lounge chair.

"Can you do my back, Mom?" Hailey asked. "Mack refuses."

Tossing the towel to the side that she'd been using to protect her own face from the sun, Jackie swung her feet toward her daughter and sat up. "Where'd she go?"

"Swimming. I'm sure she's trying to catch his attention."

Jackie glanced toward the lifeguard station and understood which guy Hailey meant immediately. The young man was cute, and unlike her twin, Mackenzie didn't have a serious boyfriend at the moment. Squirting a big dollop of sunscreen into her palm, she got to work. "Look at this skin of yours. Not a sunspot or freckle to be found. I told you you'd thank me someday for always making you wear sunscreen."

"Yes, thank you, Mother, you were right again."

"Mock me if you must, but you don't want brown spots all over you like I have on my legs."

Hailey twisted so she could see. "Mom, those are barely noticeable."

She let the subject drop. Hailey was using sun protection, and even if her daughter wouldn't truly appreciate the habit until later in life, it was worth it. "I'm so glad you two could get away from your jobs before school starts up again. Are you excited to get back to your classes?"

Hailey shrugged. "Yeah, I'm ready to get back into a routine. My hours were so unpredictable this summer, it was hard to plan anything. I'm glad I won't be juggling all that anymore."

Jackie's hands stilled on her daughter's back. "What do you mean?"

Another shrug. "I quit. Yesterday was my last day."

"You *quit*? How are you going to pay rent? Do you have another job lined up yet?" Jackie sat back, concerned about the financial implications of her daughter's revelation.

"Chill, Mom. God, you are so dramatic."

Jackie shook her head as she screwed the lid back on the sunscreen. "No, I'm practical. I'm paying your tuition, but you handle your rent. That was our agreement."

Hailey sat back on her lounger, tilting her face to the sun. "I got my old job back at the school library. They told me in the spring that I could come back if I wanted to, and after working nights at the nursing home, I decided shelving books during daylight hours was a better deal."

Jackie jumped when a splash of icy pool water hit her legs. Mack blew her a kiss from the side of the pool, ducked back under the water, and swam away.

She settled on her lounge chair again with her towel back in place. Hailey's comment about her hours over the summer sunk in. "Hailey, how are you going to be a nurse if you don't want to work nights?"

The girl sighed. "I'm thinking about changing my major. Nursing isn't really for me. Bodily fluids are gross."

Never having been fond of bodily fluids either, Jackie couldn't argue the point, though Hailey's change of heart surprised her. "Are you sure?"

"No. But I doubt there's a sophomore at U-of-I that's sure. Or if they are, I bet they'll still have second thoughts before they graduate. Mom, how did you figure out what you wanted to do?"

Jackie opened her eyes under the towel, a kaleidoscope of colors meeting her gaze. "I was always interested in business. And that's such a broad category, it gave me lots of options."

"I hope I'm as lucky as you to find a career I love."

That reminded her of the texts from work that she'd ignored. Someone who loves their job wouldn't do that, would they?

It was then that she realized there were several important things she needed to discuss with her daughters. But she didn't want to have to do it twice. She held her towel out of the way again to check her watch. It was getting late.

"Why don't we head home and order pizza? Or whatever sounds good. I'm getting hungry, but I don't feel like cooking."

"I'm up for that. I'll see if I can get Mack out of the pool."

Jackie shrugged into her coverup before standing, preferring not to wander around in her swimming suit. She gathered their things and stuffed it all into the large beach bag she'd brought. Going to the pool with college-age girls meant hauling almost as much as when they were toddlers.

Her eyes caught on Hailey as she stood poolside, completely confident in her tiny white bikini.

"I remember when I could rock a bikini, too," she muttered, folding her towel.

"What?" Hailey asked, spinning around to face her. "Jeez, why are you in such a hurry?"

She was in a hurry because her bladder felt like it was about to burst, but she didn't have to announce that out loud. "Why don't I head home and get the food ordered? It looks like your sister is still busy distracting the lifeguard. Lucky for her, it's adult swim. When the little kids get back into the pool, convince her it's time to come home."

"Good plan." Hailey slipped into the water and swam over to her sister's side. She may not be in the market for a date, but Jackie suspected Hailey would enjoy ticking her sister off by butting in on her flirting session.

Jackie used to wish for a sister when she was a kid. Raising two girls of her own had helped her realize brothers are easier.

After sliding their leftover pizza slices into a baggie, Jackie poured three glasses of lemonade and took them out to her screened-in porch where she'd asked the girls to meet. They'd be home for two more days, but she wanted to give them time to digest the many things she felt compelled to talk to them about.

"You have us curious, Mom," Mack said, accepting one of the frosty glasses as she swayed on the porch swing next to her sister.

Hailey, engrossed in her phone, ignored them both, and Jackie gave one of the lemonades a shake, the sound of ice cubes against glass finally getting her attention.

It was still in the eighties outside, so she turned the ceiling fan on before sitting in the wicker rocker across from her daughters.

"Yeah, what's going on?" Hailey asked, sipping her lemonade. "Nothing's wrong, is it?"

Jackie set her lemonade on a nearby end table and rocked. It felt good to have her kids home. The house felt alive again. But she knew the feeling was only temporary. "I'm glad you're here. This is nice."

"Nice?" Mack echoed, her eyes narrowing. Never as good at wearing sunscreen as her sister, Mack's skin had the burnished bronze color Jackie used to sport in August, back when she was the same age as her daughters were now. "Something *is* wrong, isn't it?"

"Always my worrier," Jackie said, giving Mack what she hoped was a reassuring smile. But then she could have bitten her tongue over her words. That wasn't a label she wanted either of her girls to identify with.

"No. I don't want you to worry. But we need to catch up. The first thing I need to talk to you about is your grandfather."

"Why, did something happen to Grandpa?" Hailey asked, setting her phone aside—a sure sign Jackie finally had her full attention. "He's okay, isn't he?"

Was he? Jackie talked to him once every few days, and so far he seemed okay, but how long would that last? She updated them on the situation he was facing.

"Poor Grandpa," Mack said, pushing the swing higher with her bare foot.

Jackie nodded. "I know. I feel terrible for both Dad and Mom. It's a tough situation. And I need to give Ron a call, too, and update him."

"Good luck with that," Hailey said, shaking her head. Both girls were well aware of the painful rift in their mother's family.

Then Jackie remembered she had yet to tell them about Hoover. "On a happier note, you will never guess what your grandfather brought home."

Both girls shrugged, waiting.

"A dog! Your grandpa has a dog now. A spunky little thing named Hoover. And I'm afraid he might love her more than he loves me, his only daughter."

They met this announcement with shocked smiles. As if on cue, Nikki wandered into the room and plopped down in front of the swing. Hailey used her foot to pet the dog.

A phone vibrated. Hailey grabbed for hers. "Mom, do you mind if I go make a phone call?"

Jackie almost told her to go ahead, then paused. "Actually, I have a few other things we need to talk about. You're going to have to call him later."

"How do you know it's a *him* I need to call?"

"Oh, please," Mack said, the eye-roll telling Jackie she was right in her assumption the text had been from Hailey's boyfriend.

With a sigh, the girl sent off a quick text and set her phone aside again.

Jackie sipped her lemonade, set her glass back down, and took a deep breath. "I sold the house."

Silence.

"I hope you aren't mad."

More silence.

"I didn't think you'd mind, since you're both living full time in Iowa now."

"You're *moving*?" Mack finally said, her expression one of disbelief.

"Wait . . . are you moving in with Ben?" Hailey asked, a note of excitement creeping into her question.

This wasn't going the way Jackie had hoped. "No, I'm not moving in with Ben. Look, girls, I've told you many times, and you need to understand. Ben and I are not getting back together. Not now. Not ever. I'm sorry if it hurts you to hear that, but it isn't something I want to keep discussing. Ben has nothing to do with my moving."

"See, I told you," Mack said to Hailey. "It's not happening."

Hailey turned back to her mother, deflated. "If you aren't moving in with Ben, where are you going to go? Do you have to move back to Ruby Shores to help Grandma take care of Grandpa? What about your job?"

Jackie felt her frustration rise. Who was running this discussion?

Nikki got to her feet and whined. She stretched, then meandered over and dropped onto her back haunches next to Jackie's feet.

Jackie tried again, looking between her two daughters. "If you two would hush up and let me explain, this conversation doesn't have to take all night. Now, are you ready to listen?"

"Fine."

"Fine, go ahead. What are you waiting for?"

She cringed at the irritating word that used to be her ex's favorite. "I'm waiting for the two of you to quit interrupting. And if either of you say *fine* one more time, I'll ground you."

"We're too old to ground."

Feeling a bubble of laughter rising as she imagined what an outsider would think of the meanderings of this conversation, Jackie decided it was time to get straight to the point. "No, I don't have to move home. Mom has things under control there, at least for now. I'm moving because I thought I was going to get a promotion at work that would require me to relocate. I called to get a rough idea of what the house was worth, but ended up selling it to a motivated buyer. It all happened quick."

Hailey leaned forward on the swing. "Oh my gosh, Mom. Where are you moving to? I hope it's somewhere fun, and that you got a big raise, too, so you can fly us out to see you all the time."

Mack was looking back and forth between sister and mother, a more wary look on her face. "What happened with the promotion, Mom?"

She blurted out the whole ugly truth, including her dissatisfaction with her career trajectory. She hated to admit defeat to the two people who mattered the most to her, but she made herself do it. The only part she left out was her boss's request that she come in during their stay. If there were repercussions for ignoring the work texts, she wouldn't want them to feel any guilt over something she'd done.

Both girls climbed off the swing and hurried over to her, hugging her awkwardly since she was still sitting in the rocker, and Nikki insisted on sticking her body between them. She hadn't expected to get emotional, but their show of support brought tears to her eyes. She stood so the three of them could have a proper hug. Finally, Nikki barked. The dog got nervous around tears. All three of them were crying.

Jackie squeezed her daughters and pulled back, wiping at her eyes. "Why are you two crying? Are you that sad about the house?"

Mack shrugged. "Because you're hurting. And when you hurt, we hurt."

A smile tugged at her mouth. It was the same thing she'd been saying to the two of them since they were little. "I'll be fine. I promise. Go get us some more lemonade, will you? I'm going to let Nikki out, then we can talk some more."

"Can I go call quick?"

"No!" both Jackie and Mack yelled at the same time.

Mack smacked her sister on the shoulder. "We're having a moment here. Don't ruin it!"

"Fine!" Hailey shot back, and Jackie tried not to cringe.

Once outside with the dog, she took another deep breath, trying to bring her emotions back under control. She still wanted to talk with the girls about some ideas that had been rolling around in her brain, but they were still so preliminary she wasn't sure she dared. Then she remembered what Hailey said at the pool. It was okay for her to let her daughters know they may never feel like they have their careers totally figured out. Jackie used to think she had things figured out, but now she could see that wasn't true at all. She'd been settling, and that wasn't a way of living that she wanted to model for her daughters.

Once Nikki finished, she ushered the dog back into the porch. The girls were back on the swing, but they'd switched positions.

"Good thing the two of you aren't identical, or I may not have noticed the old switcheroo."

Hailey snickered. "I doubt even that would have tricked you, Mom. You always seem to be able to see right through anything we try to pull."

"True," Jackie said, hoping Hailey was right. It was a necessary skill for every mother to possess. "Now, where were we?"

"You're going to fill us in on your moving plans."

Leave it to Mack to get them back on track. "Right. But, here's the thing. I don't have any plans yet."

Hailey looked around the porch. "When do you have to be out?"

"In a month."

Both girls gawked.

"A *month*?"

"Mom, this is a big house. Full of lots of stuff. A month isn't long enough for you to find a new house."

Nikki leaned hard against her leg, as if offering her support against their annoyingly accurate observation regarding the very real time crunch.

"Believe me, girls, I'm aware. I've decided I'm not going to buy again right away."

They both nodded.

"That's probably smart," Mack said.

Jackie clasped her hands together, then leaned forward, elbows on her knees. "I need to purge some of this stuff. Wherever I ultimately end up living, it will be smaller than this space. I'll keep my favorite things, sell or donate the rest, and probably end up putting what I keep into storage. I need some flexibility right now."

"I suppose you have to think about your job, too. You don't want to have too long of a commute."

Thankful for the lead-in, Jackie smiled at Hailey. "I do have to think about work. And I have to decide if work needs to change, too."

It was Mack's turn to squirm. "That's an awful lot of change, all at once, Mom. Are you sure you're up for it?"

It was a fair question. But even though this was all new information for her daughters, she'd been chewing on these problems ever since she'd returned from Ruby Shores. "I am ready. I've recently realized that I've been settling in too many areas of my life. I thought I was getting too old to change. But I'm not. Heck, I'm not even fifty yet. You girls are doing great, and you're building lives of your own. Whatever I decide, you both will still play into it, because I know you have some challenging years ahead of you, too, as you fully transition into adulthood. I'm not abandoning you. But I think it's important for me to prove to you that change is a good thing. We all need to keep learning and growing."

Nikki gave a short bark, then lay at Jackie's feet, as if the entire conversation had worn her out, too.

Hailey's phone vibrated again.

She decided she'd dumped enough big life discussions on her twenty-year-old daughters for one day, and motioned to Mack to hand her sister the phone. She slapped her knees, then got to her feet. "Thanks for listening, ladies. That's enough for tonight. Think about everything I shared with you, and if you have any fabulous ideas for your old mother as to what she might want to try next, let me know. Because I do value your advice. Now, if you'll excuse me, I think a bubble bath is in my immediate future, followed by an early bedtime with a new book. Go, do your own thing, and we'll have more fun tomorrow."

Hailey got off the swing, phone in hand. "Thanks, Mom. You'll figure it out. You always do."

Mack patted the empty spot on the swing, and Nikki timed her jump perfectly, filling Hailey's seat. "She's right, Mom. If anybody can figure it out, you can."

"Keep the pep talks coming," Jackie said, heading toward the hallway to her bedroom. "Oh, by the way, we need to go to the phone store tomorrow. Nikki broke my phone."

As she shut the door behind her, she heard her daughter talking to the dog.

"How in the world did *you* break Mom's phone?"

CHAPTER THIRTY

J ACKIE USED HER BADGE to gain access to the elevators in her office building, the motions coming automatically. The drive in had been brutal, leaving her exhausted, and her work day hadn't even started.

It wasn't just her morning commute that was leaving her feeling depleted. Saying goodbye to her daughters on Monday afternoon had been hard. Aside from the serious discussion in the screened-in porch after pizza, the rest of their time at home turned out to be as relaxing as she'd hoped. They promised to race home and help her pack the weekend before the house sale was final. They'd had a challenging drive back with the holiday traffic, but they made it home safely, bracing for a busy week as they transitioned back into classes.

Calling Iowa City *home* for her daughters still caught in her throat.

Would that ever get easier?

Someone she knew from a different department noticed her step onto the elevator and pushed the button for her floor. She nodded her thanks, then tried to focus on the day ahead. Her calendar was full, given she'd been out Thursday and Friday. She'd ignored her boss's request to come in on Thursday. Was she walking into a mess? she wondered, fingering the new phone in her purse. Or would he accept her excuse and let it go?

Did she even care?

The doors opened and Jackie stepped into the hushed atmosphere where she'd spent the better part of the last decade. Before moving to this downtown office, her commute had been shorter, but she'd made the sacrifice because it meant more money and more responsibility. She'd come to hate that commute, especially during the brutal winters so common in Chicago.

Her office door was closed. She pushed the door open and stepped inside, hoisting her computer bag onto the desktop. She got signed on and dove in. She had an important meeting at ten that she still needed to prepare for so the information would be fresh in her brain.

The day flew by.

As she sent off yet another email, her eye snagged on the clock in the bottom corner of her monitor. How could it be a quarter after six already? She needed to get home. Nikki had access to the fenced-in backyard through the doggy door, but at this rate, Jackie wouldn't be home until seven. The dog would be starving. She was hungry, too. But since there was no one home to cook for with the girls back at school, she'd settle for leftovers.

She was stowing her computer in her bag, preparing to haul it home as she did every night for those times when work inevitably spilled over into her personal life, when a flash of color caught her eye. The sky had cleared following a midafternoon thunderstorm. Sunlight through her office window reflected off a glass prism on the corner of her desk. The prism was the top half of an award, not unlike the track trophies that used to line the shelf in her bedroom back home. She'd received it as top sales associate in the company a few years back.

The reflected light washed across her desk, the prism splitting it into a rainbow of colors.

It reminded her of the kaleidoscope she'd made at summer camp, and of her besties.

When Lynette urged them to bring more color back into their lives, Jackie was pretty sure this wasn't what her friend had in mind.

She turned at a knock on her office door.

"There you are, Jackie."

She had to bite back a frustrated groan at the sight of him. "Here I am, Sam. Right where I've been all day. And now I'm heading out. It's late. Did you need something?" She was fully aware that her less-than-friendly greeting held plenty of snark, but she couldn't muster up the ability to care. She was beat.

"Did you get my text last week? On Wednesday evening?"

She did her best to keep a neutral expression. "I must have missed it. I broke my phone on Wednesday, playing out in the back with my dog right after work. Was it important?"

Sam meandered into her office, though she hadn't invited him. "Yes, it was. I was actually hoping you could make it in on Thursday. But obviously that didn't happen."

He must have figured he could dish out a little snark, too.

She shook her head. "That wouldn't have worked anyhow. My daughters got in Wednesday evening, and we had a busy four and a half days. Is there something I can help you with tomorrow? Because I need to get going now."

Her directness seemed to throw him off. He let his eyes roam around her office. "No. It was a time-sensitive issue. I ended up having to handle it."

"I'm sure you did an amazing job, too, with whatever it was. Now, if there's nothing else . . . ?"

The words hung in the air, and she could see he was trying to decide how to respond.

When he remained silent, a slight flush to his cheeks, she looped her purse and bag over her shoulder. "Well, I'll bid you good evening then. I have to get home. See you tomorrow."

She wove her way around him, leaving him standing in her office. She suspected if she looked back, he may have been standing there, open-mouthed with surprise. He'd probably expected her to invite him to sit and vent his frustration over her failure to be at his beck and call. But she didn't miss a step.

Tomorrow was another day.

He'd either act like there was nothing wrong or take her to task. She really didn't care. He wouldn't even be here if she hadn't hired him in the first place.

She needed to get home. Nikki was waiting for her.

Nikki didn't meet her at the front door.

Jackie had a bad feeling in the pit of her stomach.

Where was her dog? Was she out back?

Then a terrifying thought occurred to her. The dog hated thunderstorms. A noisy one had rolled through a few hours ago. What if Nikki got caught outside in it? Lightning and thunder turned the animal into a mess of nerves. Jackie often wondered if something in Nikki's background contributed to the sheer terror that she always displayed during summer storms.

She kicked off her heels and dropped her purse and keys on the table in the entry, hurrying through the house and calling for the dog. She couldn't find her in the attached garage, either, which meant she must be in the backyard. Jackie exited the garage through the backdoor, still calling Nikki's name.

Something was wrong. Had she dug under the fence again?

There'd been one gut-wrenching weekend the previous summer when Nikki disappeared. Mack was home at the time and was the first to discover a mound of dirt alongside the fence. The hole dug beneath it didn't look big enough for a dog as large as Nikki to squeeze through, yet she was gone. The two of them wandered the streets for hours, well into the night, searching for the dog, knowing she had to be terrified and lost. They'd called the police and the local shelter just in case someone saw her. When Jackie eventually insisted they give up the search until morning, it had been one of the hardest things she ever had to do. But they couldn't keep yelling for the dog when people were trying to sleep.

Jackie still remembered the shrill ring of her telephone. The sun was only a smudge on the eastern horizon. It was an elderly man three blocks away. He'd found Nikki in his gardening shed, scratching and whining. It was a good thing she'd recently put updated tags with her phone number on the dog's collar.

Where could Nikki have disappeared to this time?

Rushing over to the same troublesome spot in the fence, her feet bare, Jackie prayed Nikki hadn't busted out again. Mud—or at least she hoped it was mud—squished through her toes, raising her anxiety even further. The storm must have dumped more rain out here than downtown.

She gave a sigh of relief when the ground near the section of fence Nikki escaped through before appeared undisturbed. It didn't take her long to check all around the fence. She couldn't spot any holes, but the dog wasn't in the backyard either.

Then she had another terrible thought. Had someone *stolen* her dog?

She snatched the buzzing cell phone from the inside pocket of her suit jacket. "Hailey, I can't find Nikki! It stormed today, and I was late getting home from work, thanks to my infuriating boss, and now she's gone!"

"Jeez, Mom. Hello to you, too. Did you check the basement?"

"The basement?" Jackie stopped pacing. "Why the basement?"

A staticky sigh. "Mom, you said it stormed. Did you get a lot of rain?"

Jackie hurried over to the glass rain gauge, attached to a butterfly lawn ornament on the edge of a neglected flower garden. "Oh, wow—almost two inches! We barely had a sprinkle downtown, as far as I could tell."

"Do you think it was enough to kick the sump pump on?"

There was standing water in a low spot in the yard. "Probably. Anytime water sits in the yard back here, that usually means lots of water around the foundation, too."

"I bet she's stuck down in the basement. It happens if she's home alone during the day and the sump pump kicks on. It makes a clunking noise, and Nikki always has to run downstairs to investigate. You maybe just never noticed her do it because you aren't home during the day. I found her down there at least twice. That door into the furnace room is easy for her to push open with her nose, but it's a pretty tight space. One time, Mack and I got home and couldn't find her anywhere. Then Mack heard her barking. She was stuck down there. I think she must knock the door closed with her butt. The next time when I couldn't find her, I knew right where to look."

Jackie prayed her daughter was right as she hurried back to the garage. She found a less-soaked patch of grass beside the house and used it to wipe the mud off her feet. "God, Hailey, I hope you're right. I don't know what I'd do if anything happened to Nikki."

She ran back through the house to the kitchen and then the door to the basement, glancing behind her to make sure she wasn't leaving muddy footprints. A frantic yet welcome yipping met her ears. "You were right! She's down there, I can hear her!" she cried into the phone as she hurried down the stairs. "I don't know why I didn't hear her when I first came in."

"If the air-conditioner was running, she may not have heard you. Oh, shoot. I'm going to have to call you back, Mom. I'm getting another call. I was just calling to say hello. Squeeze Nikki for me."

Jackie dropped the phone into her pocket and crossed the basement to the utility room. She bumped the dog with the door when she opened it, and while Nikki looked happy to see her, the way her ears drooped, she suspected the shut-in dog may have had an accident. A quick glance around the small room told her she was right. She could smell it, too.

"Come here, baby," she crooned, pulling the dog into her arms. "I bet you were so scared. I'm sorry I wasn't here. Don't feel bad. You couldn't help it."

Nikki got her spark back when she didn't receive a scolding. She burst through the door behind Jackie, ran around in circles a couple times, then sprinted up the stairs, leaving Jackie to clean up her mess. She couldn't even be mad at her dog. It wasn't the animal's fault she got stuck inside.

Wishing again that she didn't have such a long commute, she found a roll of paper towels on a nearby shelf she kept stacked with cleaning supplies. "I wish I had a job where I could take Nikki to work with me," she muttered, cleaning up the mess.

If she was going to be sending impossible wishes out to the universe, she might as well shoot for the moon.

"She already quit?" Jackie said, convinced she hadn't understood Sam correctly.

He called her into his office shortly after she'd arrived on Wednesday morning. She'd gotten in fifteen minutes late because more heavy rains were slowing traffic. She'd closed the basement door tight before she left so Nikki wouldn't get stuck down by the running sump pump again.

Her boss tossed a single sheet of paper her way, pointing at it. "I found that on my desk when I got in this morning. It's her two-week notice. We can't let her work it, of course, since she's going to another competitor."

Jackie snorted, not bothering to pick up the paper. "She hasn't even been here a month. I doubt she could have gleaned many corporate secrets. Did she say why she's leaving when she just started?"

"My phone rang at five after eight. It was her, calling from her desk. I went down and tried to talk some sense into her. Apparently the other company she was interviewing with came in with a much stronger offer and she won't have to relocate like she'd have had to do here after her training was done. The operating committee will not be happy with me over this."

Jackie noticed tiny beads of sweat on the younger man's upper lip, a sure sign he was plenty nervous over his poor hiring choice. Did this mean he would offer Jackie the position after all? Sam had made it sound like she was their second pick when he'd called her while she was back home.

If they offered it to her . . . did she even want it anymore?

The episode at home the previous night had left her shaken. Hailey had been a big help over the phone, but later, when Jackie tried to relax over a plate of warmed-up pasta and a glass of wine, a heavy wave of loneliness had settled over her.

The position she'd thought she wanted would mean even more hours, more travel, and a move that would take her farther from her daughters. It would be impossible for them to drive to see her for a long weekend. Even quick trips would require air travel.

"I'm sorry things didn't work out for you, Sam. You called me to your office. How do you think I can help?" she asked, prodding him a little to clarify his position.

He ran a hand along the side of his head, ruffling his hair. It was another nervous tic she'd noticed with him. "Look, Jackie, I suspect they're going to insist I post this position again."

It was turning out to be a morning of surprises. She'd been foolish to think *she* suddenly had a decision to make. Those pulling the strings around here had already decided for her.

She wasn't even in the running.

So much for being their second choice. That was just a lie meant to placate her, back when they thought they had a shiny new hire that would turn things around for all of them.

What a joke.

"I hope you'll be fine taking on some additional responsibilities, just until we get her replacement named. I know it's a lot to ask, especially since you initially expressed some interest in the position yourself."

Jackie smiled despite his ramblings. She couldn't help it. Her sudden happiness wasn't over the words he was stumbling over. He struggled with how to treat her. On the one hand, she knew he considered her a mentor of sorts, having hired him in the first place. On the other hand, he—or maybe others—no longer considered her a viable option for advancement. It should have hurt. But it was actually more of a revelation, and a welcome one at that.

He was probably looking at her now, seeing her as a dependable wealth of company knowledge, disappointed to be passed over—but if he handled her carefully, she'd save his ass.

She didn't need handling.

She needed a change.

He contributed to this mess, just like she had contributed to last night's mess when she'd unknowingly left the basement door open the morning before. And just like she'd had to do, he could clean it up.

She was going to have to find a new place to live. Suddenly, she knew she also wanted a new place to work. A place where they'd appreciate what she was able to bring to the table, and not take her for granted.

Maybe even a place where dogs were welcome.

As she stood to wish him good luck, she glanced behind Sam and through his office window. The morning sun was breaking through the dark rain clouds, and a graceful rainbow arced above the skyscrapers of downtown Chicago.

Instead she muttered, "That's more like it."

Lynette was talking about magical splashes of color and joy, like a rainbow. Would Jackie find a pot of gold at the end of the new, brighter path she intended to carve out for herself?

Sam wore a confused expression, but she chose not to enlighten or encourage him. She wasn't just walking out of his office. It was time for her to walk away from the career that no longer fulfilled her. It was the only way.

Chapter Thirty-One

J ACKIE PULLED INTO THE parking lot of the restaurant where she was meeting Kit. After weeks of packing up, she'd welcomed the distraction her friend's dinner invite promised. The house sale was going through, and she'd finally found a townhouse she could rent for six months instead of twelve. She had an appointment for the next morning to sign her new lease, which would start in three weeks.

Once inside, she found Kit seated at a table near a fireplace. September in Chicago ran both hot and cold, but this particular day held a chill, and the low-burning fireplace was a nice respite.

"I'm so glad you called," she said, giving Kit a quick hug. "My kitchen is packed away in boxes inside a storage unit."

Kit tore off a piece of bread from the basket that was already on their table and grinned. "That sounds like the perfect excuse to not cook. Good thing my conference brought me to town so I could invite you out for a decent meal. Were the girls upset with you for selling the house?"

Jackie shrugged out of her light jacket and sat across from Kit. "Not exactly upset, but it certainly surprised them. They came home to help pack last weekend. I wouldn't have finished it without them. The closing will happen at the end of this week. I'll stay in one of those extended-stay hotels until my lease starts."

A child at the table behind them let out a shriek. Jackie read the irritation on Kit's face, but it didn't bother her. She could empathize with the parents. Her twins had done their fair share of shrieking in restaurants when they were younger.

Kit turned her attention back to Jackie. "Is your new place closer to downtown? I know you've grown to hate that commute of yours. I don't know how you've done it this long. The traffic around here would kill me. It's even worse than Minneapolis!"

"I'm thinking it might kill me, too. No, the place I found isn't any closer to downtown. In fact, it's even farther out, but I had to find a place where Nikki would have plenty of room outside. It's a corner unit with a small yard and a park across the street. Plus, I didn't want to sign a full year lease."

"I'm sure you'll find something to buy again. Look closer to the office this time. There has to be something." Kit tapped a fingernail against her water glass as she thought. "But, Jackie, isn't your commute so much worse in the winter? It won't be too long before the snow is falling again."

Unable to keep her secret any longer, Jackie rested her arms on the table and leaned toward Kit. "It doesn't matter. I don't plan to drive downtown anymore, at least after mid-October. We rarely get snow before that."

"That's great news, Jackie! Are they moving you back out to one of their satellite offices? You seemed to like that before."

She took a sip of the wine Kit had ready and waiting for her. "No. I gave notice."

The bread in Kit's hand never made it to her mouth. "You *quit?*"

"I quit. You were right—they got too used to taking advantage of me. You won't believe this, but the woman they hired this summer for the job I applied for already gave her notice! And instead of giving me the job, they posted it again. That's when I knew it was time to move on."

Kit held up a palm and Jackie bumped it with her own. "About time! Hey, are you going to have any time off before you start your new job? If you are, come hang out with me in Minneapolis. I'm doing some remodeling, and you're good at that kind of thing. You could give me some pointers, and we'd play some, too. You could bring Nikki. Our association is pet-friendly."

Jackie laughed. "You have more faith in my ability to find another job than I do."

This gave Kit pause. "You don't have another job lined up yet?"

When she shook her head, Kit slapped the table. "Who are you and what did you do with my friend? Because my friend Jackie would *never* do that."

"I can be spontaneous," Jackie cried.

"Really? Since when?"

She shrugged, helping herself to a piece of bread. "I don't have to plan everything out. Adopting Nikki was completely spontaneous, and that was one of the best things I've ever done—aside from having my twins, of course."

"You haven't been spontaneous with your career, though. You've had a path mapped out at this company for nearly ten years."

"But I didn't know the road I picked would heave under the pressure of age discrimination."

It was Kit's turn to lean forward. "Do you think that's what happened? You aren't even old! You are more mobile than ever now."

"My gut tells me they aren't considering me for these positions anymore because they're worried that I can't keep up with the pace of technology changes. *I* know I can, but I'm tired of wasting my time trying to convince them of that. Is it age discrimination? I think so. Subtle, but still wrong. I'm going to find something new."

"Are you going to try to sue?"

The thought had crossed her mind, but the discrimination would be hard to prove, not to mention expensive and emotionally exhausting. "No. I'll let someone else fight that battle. I'm just going to go somewhere I'm appreciated and do work I enjoy. That's why I decided to rent instead of buy. I'm not even sure where we'll end up."

"We?"

"Me and Nikki," she clarified, pulling another grin out of Kit.

Their food arrived, and both fell quiet for a minute or two, lost in their thoughts.

Kit took a bite of her walleye and groaned in pleasure. "This is almost as good as the fish my grandpa used to prepare for us after one of his big fishing trips."

"The pasta is wonderful, too."

The silence resumed for another beat, and then Kit dropped her fork with a clatter. "You should move to Minneapolis!"

Jackie quit spinning the long noodle. "Why? My home is in Chicago."

"Is it?" Kit challenged, fully ignoring her food now. "Your daughters aren't here anymore. You quit your job and you don't have a new one lined up yet. You've made it clear you aren't getting back together with Ben. Your house sold, practically out from under you. Did you sign your new lease yet?"

Squirming, Jackie turned back to her noodle. "Tomorrow morning."

"Hear me out," Kit continued. "I know we don't talk as often as we should anymore, but anytime we talk about Chicago, I've just never gotten the sense that you love the city itself. You applied for that job a few months ago *knowing* that if you got it you'd have to move across the country within a year! The idea of a big move like that didn't seem to bother you. Chicago to Minneapolis is not nearly as drastic."

"Well . . ." she hedged, then took a big bite to give herself an excuse to think before saying anything more.

"Jackie, your folks are probably going to need some help in the coming year or two. How is your dad doing, by the way?"

Swallowing, Jackie took a sip of her wine before responding. "He had another incident last week. Mom insists she can handle it, but you're right. I am worried about him. And her, too."

"Ruby Shores is only a two-hour drive from Minneapolis. No planes required. And it's not that much farther for the girls. With your old house gone, they might not feel strong ties to Chicago either. They only lived there for . . . what . . . like, five years?"

Kit wasn't going to drop this.

"Why do you want me in Minneapolis so badly?"

"Because I miss you. Remember how fun it was when we lived in the same neighborhood as kids? And I worry about you. What kind of job do you want to find? Are you going to make a big career change, or just switch companies?"

Jackie had looked forward to this short reprieve from packing, but she was feeling anything but relaxed under Kit's interrogation. Her friend was asking tough questions, and she didn't have the answers. She'd try to deflect Kit's tenacity with an idea she'd been considering.

"I want a job where I can spend more time outdoors and Nikki can come with me. In fact, I'd love to find work with shelter animals. Senior animals would be even better. It's so hard to place older dogs and cats."

"Oh, seniors like us, you mean?" Kit said, and Jackie saw the teasing twinkle in her eye. "You don't want to pursue any legal recourse even though you suspect your career is being derailed because of your age. And I understand why you wouldn't want to take that battle on. But what you are describing would help animals facing age discrimination instead."

Laughing, Jackie rolled up another bite of her pasta. "I was kidding. That would be my *dream* work, but it isn't realistic. I work in marketing. I know nothing about helping animals."

But she'd planted a seed, and they continued to talk about the ways she might actually help the overabundance of abandoned senior dogs, even if it had to be in a volunteer capacity. They talked about that, but they also talked more about Minneapolis.

By the time they'd indulged their sweet tooths with a shared piece of cheesecake, Jackie had called to cancel her rental appointment for the next morning.

She hoped she wouldn't come to regret these rash decisions, and that she was right about her own spontaneity.

Kit was also able to convince Jackie to skip the extended-stay hotel and come straight to Minneapolis after closing on her house.

She popped her suitcase open and started transferring her clothes into the empty dresser drawers Kit insisted she use during her open-ended visit. Nikki wouldn't let her move more than two feet away, and she kept tripping over the big dog.

"You are *fine*. That cat is a third your size. She won't hurt you. Now, look out before I step on you."

Nikki's whine told Jackie that the dog wasn't convinced.

"You're just going to have to get used to her," she said, stowing her empty suitcase under the king-size bed. "This is home for now, but I promise you it won't be forever. I love Kit, but we are both used to having our own spaces."

A knock sounded on the open door to her temporary bedroom. Nikki rushed over to greet their hostess, her tail wagging so hard she'd have knocked the dreaded house cat sideways if it was close by.

Kit surveyed the room as she patted the dog on the head. "Getting settled?"

"I am. But are you sure I'm not imposing? Do you think Dean will mind? I see some of his clothes hanging in the back half of the closet."

Kit waved away her concern. "Of course he doesn't mind. He isn't even here very often."

"I'm surprised you two have never moved in together. You'd save so much money. And especially now that you're engaged. I don't want to stand in the way of that."

"You aren't," Kit assured her. "I own this place, and when his lease is up next summer, he'll probably move in. His apartment is so much closer to the airport, and he is always flying somewhere for work."

"Does that mean we should also start planning a wedding for next summer?"

Jackie had only been off work for two weeks, and the lack of structure was driving her crazy. The equity from her house was safely stowed in her checking account, and she'd built herself up enough of a financial buffer that she didn't have to find another job right away. But she wasn't used to having free time on her hands.

"We'll see. But first I want you to help me plan my kitchen remodel. I haven't had a functioning oven for six months, and I'm afraid the dishwasher is on its last leg."

Jackie dropped onto the bed and crossed her arms, studying Kit. "Why do I get the impression you still aren't overly eager to tie the knot with Dean, even though he finally got a ring on your finger?"

Kit sighed and turned away from the doorway, walking back down the hallway. "One step at a time, Jackie. If you're done unpacking, follow me. I want to show you what I'm thinking for the kitchen."

Kit had failed to mention she already had contractors lined up to start the kitchen remodel at the beginning of the month.

Jackie jerked awake to the scream of a power saw. She checked her phone screen, groaning when she saw she was due to meet Kit and Dean for dinner in an hour. They'd drive straight to the restaurant from work. Naptime was over.

Nikki stretched and cuddled into her side. Ever since the dog started going into work with her, she'd loved sharing an afternoon nap when they returned to Kit's.

"You're lucky Kit allows you up on her bed," Jackie said, pushing the dog away so she could sit up. She needed a shower.

She shuffled into the adjoining bathroom and groaned at the pile of soiled clothes next to the toilet. Laundry needed to be added to her to-do list when she got back. Her previous working wardrobe was useless in her new job at the shelter. She'd have to run out and pick up some more jeans and sweatshirts this weekend. The dogs loved her no matter what she wore, and since she seldom made it home without something unsavory soiling her clothes, she needed more wash-and-wear items in her closet.

"In *Kit's* closet," she corrected herself out loud, attempting to stretch the kinks out of her back while she waited for the shower to heat.

When she'd handed her resignation letter to Sam, fed up with no longer being valued at a place she'd poured so much of herself into, she'd done so without a Plan B. Yet, here she was, working a new job, in a new city, earning barely over minimum wage, with a whole new clientele.

And she'd never been happier.

What started out as little more than a shadow of an idea over dinner with Kit back in September had snowballed into a passionate pursuit.

Jackie wanted to create some kind of business that would help place dogs normally considered difficult to adopt out because of their age. She didn't yet know what it would look like, but two additional trips home to visit her parents had helped expand her vision. There was so much synergy between dogs and elderly people looking for companionship.

Hoover continued to brighten her father's days, despite his ever-declining mental state. The only hiccup was the dog's high energy. Hoover's vet guessed her to be about eight or nine years old, but she still had the spunk of a puppy. Since Glen's friend originally adopted her from a no-kill shelter, her exact age and background were a mystery. This was also the case with Nikki. Pets adopted from shelters often came with spotty background information.

Kit had been right that Jackie was usually more methodical about her career than she'd been over the past few months. Those tendencies were resurfacing again. She needed to learn more about how shelters operate, how animals come in, and how best to care for them. The final and perhaps most important step she needed to master was how to safely adopt them out to give them the best shot at a brighter future.

The first logical step was for Jackie to work in a shelter. It was the only way she'd learn quickly what it would take to bring her vision to fruition. The work was so much more physical than her old desk job, and her muscles screamed in protest after long days working with the dogs. But she was doing work that filled her up again—even on those days when her heart broke over the injustices some of the animals had clearly suffered.

She could make a difference with this work. Now she just had to figure out how to make a decent living with it, too.

CHAPTER THIRTY-TWO

NIKKI HURTLED UP THE steps to the front porch of Jackie's childhood home, thrilled to be free of the confines of her crate in the car's backseat. The drive had taken longer than the usual two hours thanks to the holiday traffic, and the poor dog had complained the whole way.

Even with the door closed, Jackie could already catch a whiff of roasting turkey on the frigid November air. It reminded her of the smell of the roast when she'd come here in July. So much had changed in the months since that visit. Back then, she'd been hoping she would land the promotion she'd convinced herself was the next best step in her career. When she didn't get it—and she learned her father was sick—advice from her girlfriends started a shuffle of her priorities that she never could have foreseen just days before, when the airplane tires had touched down on the tarmac on that hot July afternoon.

The front door opened before she could knock—Nikki had been making plenty of noise to announce their arrival. Her mother smiled and let the dog in, then glanced behind Jackie, as though checking if she was alone.

"The girls are only twenty minutes behind me," she told her mother, kissing her on the cheek as she entered the house. "You have flour on your nose."

Charlotte giggled, swiping at her face. "I'm sure I look a sight. It's been too long since I've been able to cook Thanksgiving dinner for all of you."

Jackie turned to face her mother as she kicked off her snow boots. "I told you we could go out if this is all too much for you."

"No, no, I'm excited to do it," Charlotte insisted. "You'll just have to cut me some slack if the cranberry ice doesn't properly set up. Your father doesn't care for it, so it's been years since I've attempted it."

"I'm sure it'll be amazing, Mom," Jackie said, hanging her winter jacket on the coat tree. "Now, put me to work before the girls get here so we can have fun once they arrive. Is Dad napping?"

Charlotte nodded, leading the way back to the kitchen. "He does best if he gets plenty of rest."

"That would explain why Hoover didn't meet us at the door." Jackie realized Nikki was probably already outside her father's bedroom, scratching at the door and whining for her miniature friend. The two dogs had hit it off when they met on Jackie's first trip home after relocating to Minneapolis, and it was comical the way the two pranced around the house together. "I better go make sure my dog isn't waking Dad up."

Charlotte checked the clock over the sink. "They'll be fine. Your father usually gets up about now, and he'll be glad to see her. I need you to check on the extra stuffing in the crock-pot, if you don't mind. I thought it smelled like it may be starting to burn."

Jackie laughed. "*That* I can handle. Just don't ask me to make the pies. That would be too much pressure."

"The pies are ready and waiting on the counter, dear," her mother assured her, heading to the sink. "I was just peeling the last of the potatoes when you got here."

Jackie laughed again when she peeked in at the potatoes in the pot. "I know the girls love your mashed potatoes, Mom, but you're making enough to feed an army."

Before Charlotte could respond, Jackie's phone rang from within the depths of her long sweater. She turned to leave the room to take the call, but her mother tapped her on the shoulder. "Check that stuffing."

Nodding, Jackie multitasked. She was relieved when she saw it was Kit on the phone, and not her daughters calling to say they were stuck in traffic—or worse. "Miss me already?"

Kit laughed on the other end. "Not hardly. My cat finally came out from under my bed now that Nikki's left."

"They don't fight that much anymore," Jackie insisted. "Besides, she gets a break every day when Nikki goes to work with me."

She lifted the lid off the crock-pot and inhaled the homey scent. Her mother was right, the stuffing was starting to burn, so she turned the heat way down and gave the contents a good stir, holding the phone between her ear and shoulder.

"Our dinner reservations are in forty-five minutes, and I'm sure you're busy, too, so I won't keep you. But I wanted to call with some exciting news."

"What could have happened in the three hours since I've been gone?" She heard a sneeze in the background. "And wish Dean a happy Thanksgiving for me. I'm sorry I missed him."

"I will," Kit said. "But I wanted to let you know that Lynette just called."

This was a surprise. She hadn't talked to Lynette since she dropped her off after visiting their old summer camp back in July. They often went months without talking, but she understood that the silences never mattered. The friendship between the four women would always be strong.

"Nice! Was she calling to wish you a happy holiday? Maybe she'll call me later."

"No, that wasn't why she called. Do you remember how she said Renee was running retreats in the winter out of that resort she inherited from her grandma?"

"I think it was actually an aunt that left her the resort, but sure, I remember."

"Oh, that's right," Kit said, excitement evident in her tone. "Whatever, that's beside the point. She was calling to tell us she signed us all up for one of Renee's retreats in early January."

Jackie put the cover back on the crock-pot and set the spoon beside it. "What? She signed us all up? As in you, me, and Annie?"

"Yep. And her, of course. Lynette didn't want to give any of us a chance to say no."

She leaned a hip against the counter, catching her mother's curious gaze. "What type of retreats are they?"

Kit snorted. "I guess I don't know exactly. But we have to go. Remember how we talked about it when we had lunch by the falls this summer? Lynette did say she'd set this up."

Jackie watched her mother drop one last hunk of potato into the pot, but as soon as she moved to pick up the heavy kettle Jackie called out, "Don't, Mom. I'll get it." Stepping back, her mother accepted her help. The last thing any of them needed was for Charlotte to injure her shoulder again after all the trouble it had given her the last year. "I'm not sure I can get time off work," Jackie told Kit as she grasped the big pot of potatoes. "I haven't been there very long."

"Jackie, this isn't like your old job. They are so lucky to have someone like you working at the shelter, and they'll do anything to keep you as long as possible. You can get time off."

She settled the pot on a burner and flipped the dial to high. "What if I'm in the middle of moving or something in January?" But even as she said these words, the notion of time away with her besties in January quickly grew in appeal.

The doorbell rang. She needed to go let her daughters in.

"I'm glad you called, Kit. Yes, that sounds like a lot of fun. And it will be great to catch up with Renee again. I'm in. Hopefully Annie can make it work, too. I don't think I'll have time to see her this weekend. But I have to go now, the girls just got here."

"Perfect," Kit said, and Dean sneezed again in the background. "I need to get Dean out of here, too. Hi to your whole family. See you Sunday night."

Jackie dropped her phone back into her pocket and followed her mother to the front door. She couldn't wait to see Mack and Hailey again. They'd been too busy for another visit since they'd driven back to Chicago to help her pack. They'd be starving after more than seven hours in the car.

Charlotte untied her apron and dropped it over a nearby chair. Jackie grinned as her mother patted at her hair. She was probably even more excited to see her granddaughters. They'd been apart for far longer.

But it wasn't Mack and Hailey standing on the porch when her mother swung the door open. It was her big brother, Ronnie, and he wasn't alone.

"You *came!*" Charlotte cried, falling into the surprised hug of her oldest child.

Jackie blinked twice, then met Ronnie's eyes over their mother's head.

Well, this explained the enormous pot of potatoes. But what would their father have to say about this expanded guest list?

A woman learns some things about her husband over the course of a fifty-five-year marriage, and Charlotte was no exception. Jackie had always marveled at the way her mother could handle her often difficult father. After Jackie had reached out to Ronnie to update him on their father's condition, Charlotte got to work. She'd always maintained a relationship of sorts with her son and his family, but it was strained given Glen's refusal to reconcile with his only son. Charlotte took a risk inviting Ronnie and his family, but she would referee any squabbles.

As Jackie passed the platter of dark turkey meat to her nephew, Theo, she gave him a wink, hoping it might help him feel more comfortable. There was a notable tension around the holiday table, but the fact all ten of them were there for the first time made the anxiety worth it. Still, even in the face of Glen's heartbreaking diagnosis, their deep, long rift couldn't easily be tossed aside.

"Congratulations, again, on your engagement, Piper," Jackie said, once her hands were free. "Tell me again what your wedding date is?"

"It's the second to last Saturday in June, the twenty-second. I'm so excited I can hardly stand it!" Ronnie's oldest daughter held up her left hand so the light could twinkle off her diamond.

Jackie loved the way her niece beamed. She couldn't help comparing her enthusiasm to Kit's excitement—or lack thereof—to discuss wedding plans. That was the difference between a bride of twenty-five and one of forty-eight. But Jackie suspected the vast range of excitement wasn't strictly age related.

"And I hope you'll come, Grandpa," the girl said, resting her fingers on the back of Glen's hand.

Piper had grabbed the seat next to Glen, clearly wanting to build a relationship with her estranged grandfather. Ronnie's two younger kids, Theo and Sage, appeared less excited by the prospect, despite their mother's subtle encouragement.

Jackie studied her sister-in-law. Nancy had only met Glen once, at her wedding to Ronnie. The tension around this afternoon's holiday table was nothing compared to the angst-filled hours of their long-ago wedding day.

When Glen failed to comment on Piper's plea, Ronnie cleared his throat and picked up his knife and fork. "Jackie, Mom tells me you're in the middle of a career change. I admit, I'm surprised. You didn't mention it when you called."

"That's probably because she was too busy telling you my personal business," their father chimed in, a sullen look on his face.

Charlotte dropped a helping of mashed potatoes on her husband's plate. "Glen, be nice."

Jackie almost laughed when her father rolled his eyes over the admonishment, but to her mother's credit, the man's shoulders relaxed.

She appreciated the conversation prompt her brother offered—talking about almost anything was better than a silent table. Even though she was excited about her new adventure, she still wasn't sure where it would lead her, though she didn't want to worry her daughters with her lack of clarity.

"I reached a point at work where I wasn't happy anymore, and I decided I didn't want to waste any more of my time doing unfulfilling work. You know what they say: life's too short."

"Isn't that the truth," Glen muttered.

Jackie was sorry she'd said it. Her father was facing the brutal reality of that old reminder. She tried to lighten the mood by sharing a fun, recent story from the shelter. An older black lab had mustered up the energy of a puppy when he met his new owner for the first time. The dog was at least thirteen, while the man had just turned ninety.

"Puts them at about the same age, if you consider dog years," her father pointed out, proving he was interested in what Jackie had to say about her new line of work.

"That it does, Dad. That old guy's face lit up the same way yours does when you pick up Hoover."

"Where is Hoover? And Nikki?" Ronnie's youngest asked.

"Grandma asked me to put them both down in the basement," Mack said, catching Jackie's eye.

Jackie could only hope Nikki would behave down there with the much smaller, much more anxious Hoover. She didn't want to have to clean up another accident. But it was good that they weren't both rummaging between all of their feet, searching for table scraps.

"Poor girl," Glen said, shaking his head.

Ronnie stared at his father for a minute, then sighed and looked back to Jackie. "Working in a shelter is a little different from the work you've done before."

"Is that your subtle way of asking me if I'm experiencing a midlife crisis? Because if that's what you're thinking, you aren't alone." She checked the expressions on the faces of her daughters.

Hailey shrugged. "Don't pull us into this, Mom. We have faith in you."

Glen set down his fork, and Jackie steeled herself for him to tell her how ridiculous she was being. She'd been waiting for it ever since she told him in a telephone conversation that she'd quit her job and was moving to Minneapolis to pursue something totally new. But it turned out he was still full of surprises.

"I think you're on to something, Jackie. Bringing Hoover home has really helped me get through some tough days. Tell Ronnie more about your ideas."

It wasn't exactly an olive branch between father and son, but it made Jackie feel a surge of hope that they could repair their relationship.

Better late than never.

Three months earlier, she'd worried they were destined for *never*. But the presence of Ronnie and his family at their holiday table was proof that it was never too late to at least try to repair life's most important relationships.

plans with friends

RETREAT AT
WHISPERING PINES

2019

EPILOGUE

Jackie never seemed to be able to sleep past 4:30 anymore. Her early mornings at the shelter—coupled with her fluctuating hormone levels—had shifted her sleeping patterns. She'd stayed in her assigned twin bed, listening to Annie's soft snoring from across the room, for as long as she could stand it. It felt like summer camp all over again.

When her back started to ache, she eased out of bed and padded softly up to the large, upstairs room in Renee's lodge. She hadn't tried to share a room with another female since college.

Someone had set out a table, and the hot carafe of coffee meant she wasn't the first one up, but no one else was around at the moment. She poured herself a cup, grabbed a yoga mat, and sat near the expansive windows that always offered an unobstructed view of the frozen lake beyond the glass. It was still dark out, but the sunrise would be magnificent, shining across the lake, if the clouds stayed away.

She was sad their retreat was almost over. It had been a magical few days of pampering, self-reflection, and reuniting with Renee and the rest of her dearest friends.

For Jackie, it felt like the official start of a whole new chapter in her life.

Six months earlier, she'd come home for her class reunion, not exactly unhappy, but certainly unsettled.

It could be her age. Her friends had recently reminded her during this retreat that she wasn't the only one feeling that way. Annie was worried about both her job and her marriage. Lynette was trying to act like her recent breakup with her unofficial boyfriend, Wyatt, didn't hurt, but her eyes told a different story. Kit still wasn't ready to plan her wedding.

The Kaleidoscope Girls weren't exactly thriving, though Jackie did feel she was making significant progress.

The early friendship the five had formed at summer camp blossomed again. Jackie was glad Lynette had kept in touch with Renee, their often forgotten fifth Kaleidoscope Girl—and the only one of them who seemed to have successfully found a new rhythm. She sensed a genuine opportunity to rebuild a stronger friendship with Renee.

As she pondered the potential gift of reviving old relationships, Jackie's thoughts naturally wandered to the long-standing rift between her father and brother. She felt as though there was hope and opportunity for them, too.

Footsteps on the wooden stairs told Jackie her alone time was at an end.

"Good morning," Renee said, balancing a tray of breakfast pastries on one palm and a large bowl of fruit in her other hand. "You're up early." Jackie started to move to help, but Renee shook her head. "No, don't get up. You look relaxed. And that's the best spot in the house, once the sun comes up."

Jackie smiled, relaxing. She appreciated Renee's respect for the peace of the early morning.

Once breakfast was laid out, Renee grabbed a mat of her own and joined her. "I'm so glad all of you could make it. You don't know how much it means to me that you all came here for one of our retreats. I hope it's been worth your time."

Jackie reached for Renee's hand. "Are you kidding? This has been amazing. You have a beautiful place here. And you're so smart to do these retreats when it's too cold to rent out your cabins. They aren't winterized, huh?"

Renee squeezed her hand. "Most aren't. The old duplex, back on the far edge of the property, is fine. That's where I lived when I first moved out here. My sister Jess did, too. The other cabins aren't too bad in the winter if the temperature is above zero and the wind isn't too strong. They all have fireplaces. We even used the smallest one for a bridal suite when Jess got married last month. But winters in Minnesota are too unpredictable. I even worry about a storm hitting during one of our retreats, but we've gotten lucky so far. The overnight guests stay here, in the bedrooms we added in the lodge, or in the duplex."

Jackie listened, intrigued. They'd wandered through the resort the previous day, and she'd tried to imagine what the property would look like during the summer. "Are you enjoying your new house?"

"Very much so," Renee said, grinning. "I love it out here. And it is even more special, now that Matt is here, too."

Jackie was inspired by Renee's story of how she and Matt met and married, along with the many other huge life changes the woman had gone through in the last few years. "It's funny . . . I was just thinking how, of the five of us, you are the only one of the Kaleidoscope Girls who has really found her place in the world right now. I feel like I'm getting closer again, after a tough couple of years . . . saying goodbye to first my girls and then a job I no longer liked . . . but I'm far from having everything figured out."

Renee leaned back on her elbows and crossed her ankles, looking up at the ceiling. "You give me way too much credit, Jackie. Most days, I'm still making it up as I go. This is all so different from what I'm used to. When I lost my job, just over three years ago now, I was terrified. I was a single mother to two teenagers, living in a city away from the rest of my family, who suddenly found herself unemployed."

"But look at you now," Jackie said, her eyes roaming around the large room that Renee used for many retreat-related activities. Beyond the closed door over Renee's shoulder sat a beautiful library, complete with its own fireplace and comfy chairs, where Jackie would happily wile away a winter day with a good book.

"I am thrilled with how far I've come, but we still have lots more dreams. If my Aunt Celia, the one who left me this resort, taught me anything, it's that we are never too old to start something new and to enjoy life. Even though we are pushing fifty, we're still just getting started. Celia stayed active into her early *nineties*."

Jackie grinned, wanting to believe the same thing.

"I am sorry you didn't get to meet Jess, though. I think the two of you would have lots in common."

Nodding, Jackie tried to remember what all Renee had told them about her extended family. "She's on her honeymoon, right?"

"She is. They are in Fiji. That's actually where I met Matt, and he still has a small house down there that he rents out. He had an opening, so Jess and her husband waited until now to go. I hope they are having fun."

"Fiji in January. It sounds fabulous to me," Jackie said, closing her eyes and trying to imagine the hot sun on her shoulders.

"Trust me, it *is* fabulous. We should all go there sometime. Together!"

More footsteps on the stairs signaled people were getting up and moving about. Their final sunrise yoga class would start soon.

"Where should we go?" Kit asked, plopping down on Jackie's mat and helping herself to a sip of her now-cold coffee.

"I think you two have been roommates for too long," Renee said, laughing.

"It won't be much longer," Jackie said. "I'm going to look for my own place as soon as we get back home."

Kit didn't look excited to hear that. "I heard something about Fiji. What were you talking about?"

"Jess, Renee's sister, is there now. On her honeymoon. Matt has a place down there," Jackie said, then an idea occurred to her. "You could see if Dean may want to go there on *your* honeymoon!"

Kit shrugged at the suggestion. "Or maybe the Kaleidoscope Girls could start up those annual trips we promised each other we'd do when we turned fifty."

"What promise was that?" Renee asked.

"Oh, that's right—you wouldn't have been there for that! It was at the end of our senior year. We talked about starting up an annual girls' trip once we all turned fifty, knowing we might not have time to do something like that until we were older. You know, jobs, kids, husbands . . . Not that all of us took that route, but who knew how life would turn out when we were graduating from high school?"

Renee sat up, smiling. "You're right, I missed that conversation. But I remember crashing your senior prom with you. That was so fun! We all had big dreams back then, didn't we?"

"We still do," Jackie said, surprising herself with the declaration. That kind of thought might not have even occurred to her six months earlier.

"I'd forgotten all about the annual girls' trip, Kit. But after spending this weekend with all of you again, plus all the fun we had at the reunion last summer, I'd be all for it. Where should we go first?"

More people were wandering in. Jackie, Kit, Annie, and Lynette weren't Renee's only retreat guests. Annie and Lynette joined them near the large windows.

Lynette yawned, keeping one eye on the sky as it lightened and the other on her friends. "You all look entirely too awake at this hour. What has you so excited?"

"I heard 'girls' trip,' " Annie said, taking a seat on her yoga mat. "It's about time! Where are we going? And when? I probably have to wait until after I get Relic graduated in early June."

Jackie motioned toward Kit as she got to her feet, cold coffee in her hand. "She was just reminding us about that promise we made each other back in high school."

"What promise? God, how can you all be so chipper?" Lynette asked, turning away from the morning shadows.

"To take an annual girls' trip when we turn fifty," Kit said, stretching out on Jackie's mat. "I know we aren't quite there yet, but maybe we should get a jump on it."

Lynette perked up, and a light that Jackie thought had been missing from Annie's eyes returned as the two began considering the possibilities.

"One of us should definitely be in charge of planning something," Renee said. "I mean, if you don't mind me jumping in on your fun."

"Mind? Are you kidding? You *are* one of the original Kaleidoscope Girls after all. We don't mind," Jackie assured her. "And since it was Kit with the excellent memory, I think she should plan our first official trip. We could take turns playing travel agent."

Lynette held up her right hand and grinned. "Technically, I think this retreat could count as the first trip. And since I arranged it all—with Renee's help, of course—I'm good for a few years before I have to plan another one."

"I don't care who plans it," Annie said, sitting cross-legged on Renee's mat and bending at the waist until her chest touched the wooden floor in front of her—a feat that had the rest of the women groaning. "I just know it's the best idea I've heard in a long time. We need something to look forward to. We've earned it!"

"I agree," Kit said. "I'll start researching places to go. Hey, where was that place in Mexico where the ranger told us the monarch butterflies migrate every year? Someplace like that would be a great idea."

Jackie smiled at the suggestion, squinting as the morning sun broke across the horizon. She wondered if any of the rest of her friends recognized the parallels between their current stage in life and that of the monarch butterflies. Each of them was in the messy middle of some large life transformations, but together, they all had the chance to learn how to soar again.

Author's Notes

I hope you enjoyed this first book in my new series. **Better with Friends** was so fun to write. I felt like I was on a trip down memory lane.

Growing up, I watched my mom nurture close relationships with women she'd known since grade school. They knew each other's history and their shared memories grew even more precious to them over the years.

Mom never stopped making friends. She made friends on the golf course, around the bridge table, with co-workers, and formed a special bond with many of the kids she supported through her job as a high school social worker.

I felt a twinge of jealousy, watching Mom spend even more time with her amazing friends after she retired. Meanwhile, I could feel myself drifting further apart from mine. Raising our young family and my busy corporate career left too little time for friendships.

I remember one particular morning as I helped Mom prepare an impromptu brunch. Her health was failing, but her support system was strong. As I arranged a dozen coffee cups on the countertop, she insisted that we'd need more. I looked at all of those cups in amazement, thinking I'd *never* have that many friends to invite over for coffee.

Mom was a very lucky woman!

If we're blessed with a long life, there will probably come a time when friends, both old and new, can once again play a more significant role in our own lives. Maybe we've outlived or outgrown a spouse. Kids we've raised are out on their own. But we'll always need our girlfriends.

The idea behind this series was born out of my memories of Mom and her friends. In these books, rich friendships will help a fabulous group of women navigate the under-explored season of midlife. I thought it would be fun to help celebrate these priceless friendships by throwing in some amazing trips. Because who doesn't love a girls' trip?!

I wanted the first book in this new series to take us back to the very foundation of the friendship between Jackie, Kit, Annie, Lynette, and Renee. It was so fun to imagine the five of them meeting at a summer camp in the early '80s. I enjoyed watching a couple of old movies, including "Little Darlings", to refresh my own memories of the '80s. Flashbacks of a long-ago softball game resurfaced, and I still remember the way our hair stood on end when lightning flashed nearby.

Then it was on to their high school years; a turbulent time for most everyone. I could feel the girls' anxiety during those last few months of their senior year: prom dates, graduation, and scary decisions about their next steps. Writing these chapters took me back to shopping for prom dresses with Mom, memories of a kind but painfully shy junior prom date, and that cute guy I went to my senior prom with that I married five years later (I celebrated our thirty-third wedding anniversary with my senior prom date this summer).

Kicking the book and series off with a trip home for a class reunion felt like the perfect way to tie it all together. Love them or hate them, reunions allow old friends to reconnect.

Each of these five friends will be the star of an upcoming book in The Kaleidoscope Girls series. Next up will be Kit in **Sunshine and Friends** (Book 2). After surviving a turbulent childhood, Kit will need the help of her friends to fight through old scars and new betrayals to uncover a better future. Can the warm beaches of Maui provide the perfect backdrop for Kit to begin her healing, or will the storms in her life continue to hold her captive?

Where we go to heal can have a significant impact on our personal journeys. If you've read my earlier series, Gift of Whispering Pines, I hope you were excited about the tie-ins I included in **Better with Friends**. Renee, the sometimes forgotten fifth Kaleidoscope Girl, kicks off the first book, **Whispering Pines**, in my earlier series. If you haven't yet read the books in that bestselling family drama, you don't want to miss them! I'll continue to weave Renee and Whispering Pines, her very special Minnesota lake resort, into this new friendship series.

You'll find more information on all my books and links to them on the biggest storefronts on my website. While you're there, be sure to sign up for my newsletter so you never miss the latest news, including release dates, glimpses into what goes into creating these books, and more. Thank you for coming on this writing journey with me. I love reading and writing alongside you!

www.kimberlydiedeauthor.com

THANK YOU!

Dear Reader,

I would like to thank you for taking the time to read **Better with Friends**. I am so grateful you selected it and I hope you enjoyed this first book in my Kaleidoscope Girls series.

If you don't mind taking a few more minutes with this book, I'd appreciate it if you would leave a review. Reviews are extremely helpful and much appreciated.

Next up in this fun series is **Sunshine and Friends (Book 2)**. A girls' trip to sunny Maui will give Kit a chance to seek advice from the women she trusts most in the world after she suffers a shocking betrayal. Pack your bags!

For links to all of my books and to sign up for my newsletter, please visit my website at www.kimberlydiedeauthor.com.

Wishing you my very best,
Kimberly

Sunshine and Friends - Book 2 Preview

Sunshine and friendship help chase away the shadows.

Packing is the last thing Kit Robinson needs to cross off the to-do list before her long-anticipated girls' trip. She can't wait to enjoy an icy cocktail under a hot Hawaiian sun with old friends where they'll toast the keeping of a thirty-year promise.

Kit's decision about the other big commitment she's been hedging on for far too long will have to wait.

But when a terrifying tornado sends Kit racing through a dark night, her time in the sun is in jeopardy. Surprises await her back home. Has Kit's estranged mother returned? If that dreadful woman is back, chaos isn't far behind. Kit's fiancé does his best to persuade her to stick with her original travel plans, but her grandmother needs her. Should she stay?

Then Kit stumbles across yet another secret and the wash of pain overshadows everything. How could the person she trusts more than anyone else in the world lie to her about something so important?

Overwhelmed, Kit needs to escape the lies. Her lifelong friends know how deep her scars run and they'll understand why these latest bombshells are rocking Kit's carefully orchestrated world.

Her friends will know what to do.

Escape to the lush vistas of Hawaii in Sunshine and Friends, book two of *The Kaleidoscope Girls* women's friendship series by Kimberly Diede. Life leaves scars. Will a wounded Kit retreat behind old walls, or can her best friends convince her that keeping an open heart is worth the risk?

Grab your copy of Sunshine and Friends today, because everyone deserves a trip to the tropics and a reminder of the power of forgiveness.

Reading Guide for Better with Friends

SPOILER ALERT

1) Importance of friends during different stages in our lives:

The author believes our friendships grow in importance as we age. Do you agree?

There are some special qualities to friendships that span a lifetime. When we form friendships as young kids or teenagers, our friends often get to know our families, too. They understand where we come from. We learn the value of respecting people's secrets. What are some other benefits of a long friendship?

2) How much impact do you believe "place" has on molding young people? The Kaleidoscope Girls spent their formative years in a small midwestern town where parents knew and supported each other. Some of them still have family living there, pulling them back from time to time in their adult lives. If you've moved away from the place you called home when you were a child, how do you feel when (if) you return now?

3) It was fun for the author to imagine how a twelve-year-old girl would feel at a rustic summer camp, away from family and everyday life. How terrifying would it feel to get your first period away from home? Would the fear be heightened because something as common and human as menstruation often feels like a taboo topic? Could you feel Jackie's misery when she realized what was happening? Do you think the way Kit

handled the situation, despite how antagonist Jackie was to her at first, helped cement their growing friendship?

4)   We are all told myths as children. Some stem from family history, religion, even local lore. The myth of Diamond Falls, passed on to the young campers by Wendy, their camp counselor, was fun for the author to craft. Will the Kaleidoscope Girls ever find genuine diamonds in the water near their old campground, or will life teach them that diamonds aren't really a girl's best friend after all? Do you have any myths unique to your childhood that have stayed with you?

5)   What are some of your favorite high school memories? If you went to prom, was it an anxiety-inducing experience? Jackie and her friends prom experience predated the more recent trend of fancy "promposals". Would you agree the pressures on today's kids are even higher than they were back then?

6)   Jackie spent most of her life trying to live up to her father's expectations. She wanted to fill the void created by the rift between her dad and her only brother. How do you think that impacted Jackie's relationship with her father? With her mother? With her brother?

7)   The rift between Jackie's father and brother had a tremendous impact on their family structure. Do you think her father regrets the way things played out? Thirty years later, he is a very sick man living under the shadow of a terrible diagnosis. Do you think it would be worth it for father and son to try to re-establish some kind of relationship now, or is it too late?

8)   The Kaleidoscope Girls are nearly fifty years old. What new challenges will they likely face with their aging parents? Some have empty nests at home, but are their caregiving days over?

9)   Jackie is sure that her age is impacting her ability to succeed in her corporate career. Instead of tolerating the ageism, she takes drastic measures in the hopes of building something more rewarding. Have you experienced ageism? Do you think it is a significant problem in our society today? What can we do to fight it?

10)   Reconnecting with old friends can be a challenge. Life commitments can make it difficult to stay in touch. If you think reconnecting is worth the effort, what things have you found that work well to keep friendships strong in a hyper-connected world that can sometimes lack depth in relationships?

11)   Fun traveling with friends:

Would you like to commit to an annual trip with old friends, like the Kaleidoscope Girls do in Better with Friends? If you've traveled with friends, either on a short weekend getaway or something more extensive, what are some of your favorite memories?

How important is the destination when you travel with friends? Some people love to keep busy while traveling, seeing as many sights and experiencing as much of the local flavor as possible. Others prefer plenty of rest and relaxation, talking with your fellow travelers. What's your style?

If you could travel anywhere in the world with any friends from your past, where would you go and who would you want beside you?

12) Symbolism played a big part in this story:

The metamorphosis of caterpillars into butterflies mirrored the changes the girls would go through, starting at that first summer camp and all the way through to the current day. A butterfly intrigues Jackie as she learns she didn't get the promotion she'd counted on. Kit will even build a career around butterflies. Do you agree that life is one long metamorphosis?

Artists can transform broken pieces of glass into something beautiful in a kaleidoscope. In what ways has life broken the Kaleidoscope Girls, and what have they done to build back something beautiful? Would you agree that changing the way we look at something can result in something beautiful, much like the shifting patterns we see when we twist a kaleidoscope?

13) What does the title "Better with Friends" mean to you? Do you agree friends can make our lives better? Has reading this book spurred you to reach out to anyone in your past to rekindle a dormant friendship?

ALSO BY KIMBERLY DIEDE

THE KALEIDOSCOPE GIRLS SERIES

BETTER WITH FRIENDS (BOOK 1)
SUNSHINE AND FRIENDS (BOOK 2)
FIVE GOLDEN FRIENDS (BOOK 3)
GIFT OF FRIENDS (BOOK 4)
LIFE WITH FRIENDS (BOOK 5)

GIFT OF WHISPERING PINES SERIES

WHISPERING PINES (BOOK 1)
TANGLED BEGINNINGS (BOOK 2)
REBUILDING HOME (BOOK 3)
CAPTURING WISHES (BOOK 4)
CHOOSING AGAIN (BOOK 5)
CELIA'S GIFTS (BOOK 6)
CELIA'S LEGACY (BOOK 7)

About the Author

Kimberly Diede writes contemporary novels that weave together family, friends, hope, and romance. She writes family sagas, suspense, and women's fiction that you'll find hard to put down. She truly believes we are never too old for second chances in life.

Kimberly enjoys spending the short months of her Midwest summers on the lakeshores of Minnesota and North Dakota. Nothing beats writing and hanging out with family and friends at their cabin. Her love of tradition and all things vintage comes through in her decorating and her stories.

Be sure to follow Kimberly on social media to catch glimpses of the junk she drags home to repurpose and to get updates on her latest books.

f facebook.com/KimberlyDiedeAuthor

⬡ instagram.com/kimberlydiedeauthor

𝓟 pinterest.com/kdiedeauthor

Made in the USA
Coppell, TX
06 December 2024

41845659R00236